Somewhere on the
Dark Side of the ID

by

V. Miles Capiston

DORRANCE
PUBLISHING CO
EST. 1920
PITTSBURGH, PENNSYLVANIA 15238

Dorrance Publishing Co
585 Alpha Drive
Suite 103
Pittsburgh, PA 15238
Visit our website at www.dorrancebookstore.com

ISBN: 978-1-4809-3618-8
eISBN: 978-1-4809-3595-2

Dedication

I want to dedicate this work to my wife, Sandra. She was very patient, and patient, and more patient while I worked to bring this story to life. Thank you, Sandra.

A few eons ago I knew a beautiful girl named Carolyn Okita. She once told me I should write a book. I didn't know that's what I wanted to do until I heard her say it. Thank you, Carolyn.

Who *the devil is this guy? He comes down here every day and sits there, facing me. He almost never looks at me. He looked at me twice in three weeks. Even then he looked me square in the eyes. That makes me think that he wants something from me. But what?*

I've never seen anyone act like that before. I wonder why he started coming here? Every man I see is looking at me or staring at my breasts.

When a guy looks at me, he looks at me from the neck down. Then he looks at my face.

When a man talks to me, sometimes he talks to my breasts. He will be looking at my breasts when he talks to me, seldom at my face! I wonder why I thought of that?

So why is this guy so different? When he looks at me, he looks me square in the eyes. Everyone else is looking at my breasts like there's something wrong with them. Why? Am I the only woman that wants to know why? It's so ridiculous! Men are so stupid!

For God's sake. Every girl's got two of them. They're just breasts!

The only one I want to look at me doesn't, and I don't even know his name!

I can't help thinking he wants something from me. What?

Why me? Oh, well. It is what it is.

These were the thoughts going through Joanna Kimble's mind as she sat at a table at a sidewalk cafe, near Waterfront Park.

She had returned three weeks ago from New Orleans, where she had gone to the Mardi Gras. She had an exciting time there. Now she was back home in Portland, Oregon. She was eating a hot cup of soup and a club sandwich on her lunch break. She liked sitting outside, where it was a cool sixty degrees. Eating the hot soup in the cool air seemed to stimulate her. She liked sitting at the sidewalk tables even when it rained, except when it was windy.

Sitting under the canvas awning, she liked looking at the rain. It was a pleasant experience that she looked forward to.

She liked looking at people in the rain. Some wearing rain coats, some wearing a hood or something on their heads.

Some, like herself, carried an umbrella whether it rained or not.

Today it was overcast, cool, and for some reason known only to God, it wasn't raining. The city never seems to sleep.

Even in the early hours of the morning when traffic is light, a crowd of people will suddenly burst out the door of an after-hours place.

There's always something happening somewhere in this city.

She loved the city, like most people that live there.

People were always going somewhere, doing something, or finding something to do.

Taxi-cabs, delivery trucks, city buses, streetcars, and an occasional police cruiser were constantly cruising by.

However, Joanna was looking for a face. The face of the man that had caught her interest three weeks earlier.

He had been coming to the cafe at lunch time ever since she had driven back from New Orleans. She guessed him to be nearly six feet tall.

He wore glasses that were rimless. Sometimes his glasses looked like they were almost invisible.

His eyes always looked like they were smiling. Even when he wasn't looking at her.

He was always well-dressed, wearing a form-fitting suit, and neat in his appearance. On days it rained, he wore a London Fog overcoat and black fedora hat.

The brim was turned down on one side of the wide brimmed hat he wore, the other side was curled up where he constantly grabbed the hat to put it on.

It was obvious, he had worn the hat for years. She liked looking at him, from the western boots on his feet to the hat on his head.

She only saw him about ten or twelve times. He almost never looked at her.

Today he wasn't there, and she missed him.

Men always looked at her. Most of them were intimidated by her.

It was rumored that she was making over two hundred thousand dollars a year. So, most men that knew her, or of her, felt she was above them.

As a result, most men looked at her from a distance, mostly at her breasts.

She was large breasted on her petite frame. So large were her breasts that she had difficulty buying a bra. She had her bras specially made.

She was five feet, one and a half inches tall, and she weighed 120 pounds in her bare feet.

Most of her female friends openly told her they envied her. They envied her slender figure with her large bust line, her nicely shaped bottom, and her exquisite face.

Everyone thought she was perfect. She didn't feel perfect. She didn't feel like she had any male friends at all.

Men were either coming on to her, would stare at her, or seemed hesitant to approach her.

Except one. This man never seemed to notice her. He started having lunch there about three weeks before.

He always sat alone, a few tables away. Twice he made eye contact with her. Each time he made eye contact with her, she felt drawn to him.

He didn't seem to know she existed.

But somehow Joanna knew that he wanted something from her. There was something about him that emitted strength, a compulsive power.

It was like all her senses were pulling her to him. She felt comfortable with that feeling. She liked being near him.

She knew when he was there. She could feel his presence. She didn't know why, but she could.

Once, when she was on her way to lunch, she found herself walking a little faster because she knew he was there. When she saw him, she slowed her pace.

She saw that he was reading a newspaper. She decided to sit at a table next to his thinking, *Maybe I can get him to talk to me.*

When he didn't, she ordered lunch, and tried to ignore him.

Both times when he made eye contact, something stirred within her and she felt drawn to him.

She could feel his strength whenever she was near him.

She had a feeling she was going to get to know him, and know him well. Call it intuition, or just a feeling, but that was one feeling she couldn't ignore.

She found herself looking forward to seeing him again.

Comfortable as she was in his presence, she wondered, *who is he? What does he do? Why doesn't he talk to me? How do I find out who he is?*

She was afraid speak to him. She didn't want him to think she was being forward, or anxious to meet him.

Joanna Kimble had an office at the Pacific Rim World Trade Center, working for a brokerage firm. She was well-respected there.

She had an uncanny ability to foresee the movement of the stock of the major corporations along the Pacific Rim.

She had a way of watching the market and the movement and momentum of their sales figures. She almost always predicted the movement of the market correctly.

What most people didn't know was because of this: she had a stock portfolio of her own valued at a little more than three million dollars.

If a major change or decision came out of a boardroom, she could figure out the reason for the decision more quickly than anyone else. Because of her abilities, her earnings were higher than most of the people that had an office there. For this she was envied by almost everyone, especially the men in her office building.

There was one man in her office building that had said more than once, "If I had her set of tits, I could open the right doors, too!" Gregory Dorn.

Joanna hated to be in the same office building with Gregory Dorn. His office was across the hall from hers.

If his office door was open, she would often hear him talking on the phone with someone, saying, "She has the nicest little ass, the nicest big tits, and the prettiest green eyes you'll ever see. Man, I mean quality. Someday I'm going to get the chance to nail her. And when I do, I'm going to find out her information sources. Believe me. I won't pass it up!"

When she heard him talking, she would get up and close the door thinking, *What information sources? That idiot couldn't analyze anything using logic if his life depended on it.*

She knew when he heard the door close, he would sit in his office grinning like a Cheshire cat.

She would sit in her office wondering, *how do I keep that creep away from me?"*

Joanna had finished her lunch, and was just sitting there, people watching, when she saw him again. The one that looked her in the eyes.

He was parking an expensive car, across the street from where she was sitting.

She sat there wondering how she could find a way to get to know who he is when three women and two guys from her office building came walking up to her table.

The guys were Don Leach and Gregory Dorn. They were all brokers including her friend Kathy Bates, along with Leigh Barns and Jamie Dodson.

Joanna looked up at them. "Hi, guys, what's happening?"

Gregory Dorn spoke first. "She already knows. She can tell us more about it than we can tell her."

Joanna was watching as the man had parked his car.

He was wearing his overcoat, but not his hat, as he was doing a dance of sorts.

He was casually stepping between the cars and trucks as he was jay walking across the cobblestones of the street.

There were no horns honking, as even the drivers of the cars were watching the way he was pointing his fingers and waving his arms half dancing, half strolling between the vehicles as he glided through three lanes of traffic.

She wanted to laugh.

Instead she turned and looked up at the guys and gals and asked, "What happened?"

Kathy Bates, looking at the next table said, "Keandra Group. They called a news conference and made a statement."

Joanna looked where Kathy was looking, and then at Kathy.

The man was sitting at the next table, ordering coffee. Once again she could feel the power of his strength.

She wanted to say, *hands off, I saw him first!*" But said, "What did they say?" Geoffrey Dorn said, "She can probably tell us more than we heard."

Joanna held up her hand to stop them. "Wait. You're talking about the Med Keandra Group?"

Gregory Dorn spoke again. "I'll bet ole "Frankenstein" himself knows you quite well."

"Shut up, Mr. Dorn! I'm trying to figure out what you guys are talking about!"

Jamie Dodson spoke up. "Why do they call him "Frankenstein" Keandra?"

"You're kidding. You really don't know?"

Jamie looked at Joanna quizzically and said, "No."

"He makes prosthesis. You know, prosthetics? Artificial arms and legs. They say he made a hand where the user can actually control the fingers. This guy literally replaces arms and legs. He makes ceramic knee, wrist, hip, and ankle joints that are superior to anything else being manufactured. He's also into pharmaceuticals. He owns hospitals! Good lord! He's the General Motors of the medical world. In fact, he owns the Keandra Coach Works, an ambulance manufacturing company. Not to mention, at one time he was thought to be the most brilliant surgeon in the world. I've also heard he is quite a character. Some people think he's a little loony. The word is he can be a cantankerous and a bullying old man. In fact, they say he talks to no one and has a relative doing all the dirty work for the companies. He also uses the relative as a go-between when communicating with the hierarchy of his companies. I wish I knew more about him. But that's all I hear."

Cautiously, Joanna looked at the man at the next table. She still felt that strange power that seemed to envelope her.

He was looking into his coffee cup, smiling.

What's he's thinking about that's amusing? she wondered.

"What did the Keandra Group say?" Joanna asked, while looking at Kathy Bates.

Kathy looked back at her. "They said they have discovered a woman with great capabilities, and they are grooming her to be the new CEO over the Med Keandra Corporations. She will take the helm of the Keandra Group in about two and a half to three years. That's all they said."

Joanna sat thinking for a moment and then said, ""Frankenstein" Keandra is very much like Howard Hughes was. Extremely hard working, and very much up on everything that's happening in his companies. Through his relative, he's in constant communication with his companies. It's hard to imagine that he is willing to turn the reins of his companies over to any one, unless something big and important is coming down.

"Whatever it is, I'm going to have a tough time finding it out. But I will find it out. I always do."

He has obviously chosen someone female to train for the job. These companies are so diversified and complex it will take two to three years for her to familiarize herself with what's happening in those corporations."

Joanna was having difficulty keeping her attention on the group. She wished she could find a reason to introduce herself to the man at the next table. *How can I meet this guy if people won't leave me alone?* she thought.

Gregory Dorn spoke up once again, "Why don't you level with us, Miss Kimble? I know you know more than you're willing to talk about. We have clients that are invested. We need to know what you know!" he said seriously.

"Everyone knows ole "Frankenstein" lives here locally. You just know too much not to have something going with him."

"Just what are you suggesting?" asked Joanna, getting up from her chair.

Gregory Dorn, looking down at her with his hands under her breasts, lifted them up and said, "Look, stupid! If I had these canons I could open a few doors myself!"

Panicky, Kathy Bates jumped back.

Joanna, without thinking, closed a small fist and slugged Gregory Dorn in his left eye as hard as she could.

Surprised, Dorn staggered back a few steps.

"Let me see you explain that eye to your clients," Joanna said angrily.

Joanna saw Dorn's fist coming straight toward her face when suddenly a hand was in front of the fist. The fist stopped just as suddenly.

Joanna looked up into the smiling face of the man that had been sitting at the next table.

Still holding Gregory Dorn's fist, he said, "I would wager a nickel that you didn't believe I would get here in time. You didn't believe I would, did you?"

She looked up at him in awe and thought, *He's looking at me! He's looking at me! Not my chest!*

Then she said, "You're not as tall as I thought you would be." She couldn't believe she just said that.

She looked at his face again. He was wearing glasses, and he was smiling.

His hair was parted an inch left of the middle with a wave on each side of the part and graying at the temples. His hair was fairly short. He was looking her right in the eyes.

Behind the smile she thought she could see pride on his face and wondered about it. Gregory Dorn, suddenly jerking his fist away said, "I'm going to whip your ass, little man!"

The man turned toward Dorn, smiled casually and said, "You've already made one mistake. Are you sure you want to make another?"

Gregory Dorn towered over the man by at least eight inches. He easily had sixty pounds on him.

Dorn went into a boxing stance.

Without hesitation, the man shoved his fingers straight into Dorn's solar plexus. Then it looked like he reached up and touched Dorn's Adam's apple.

Dorn was suddenly lying on the sidewalk, clutching his throat, kicking his feet. Joanna thought she heard the man quietly say, "Checkmate."

The man turned to Joanna. "I apologize most humbly. It appears I have stolen your thunder."

Surprised at his confidence, Joanna looked at him with her mouth hanging open when she heard him say, "You were correct when you said you would like to see him explain the swelling around his eye to his clients. That could be most embarrassing. Now that I've entered the picture, he will give me credit for the eye and that takes away most of the embarrassment. In any event, this day will be most memorable."

Joanna looked once more at the smiling man.

She looked at his glasses. They were rimless. The stems were so thin and light it looked like his glasses were just suspended on his face.

Again, she felt she could see pride behind the smile. "That's okay. Steal all the thunder you like. I don't have any use for it," said Joanna, wearing a smile of her own and thinking, *why am I talking like an idiot, and sounding like an idiot, and looking like a fool?*

She saw him looking down at her.

She watched him reach out and touched her under her chin, with his fingertips. "Look, I must go. You'll be alright. Sometime we will meet again. Until then."

Suddenly he laid a five-dollar bill on the table and was walking away from her, and soon was crossing the street, doing that little dance, all the while smiling as he stepped through traffic.

Joanna couldn't believe it. Awestruck, she watched him directing traffic.

Stopping one car, dance around the front of it, while waving the next car by.

All the while, people on the sidewalk watching him were whistling and applauding as he danced on the cobblestones of the street.

He was gone before she could even ask him his name.

Kathy suddenly spoke, "I don't believe it! Boy! It's unbelievable the way that man moved!" The very instant Dorn touched your boobs, that guy had murder in his eye. I had to leap out of his way. I mean, that guy was going for the throat until you socked Dorn. You might very well have saved Dorn's life when you socked him. Because when you socked Dorn, that man turned and looked at you with pure admiration."

Joanna, suddenly trembling, was looking at Kathy with a wondrous look, and said, "He was right. I didn't believe he would get there in time."

Then Joanna asked, "What are you talking about?"

Leigh Barns spoke up. "Kathy's right. He was ready to kill until you hit Dorn. After you hit Dorn, that guy looked at you with so much pride in his eyes, I think he would have kissed your butt! Wow! What a man! Why can't I find one like that? By the way, who is he?"

Don Leach spoke up, "I was watching, too. That man is dangerous! The way his face was twisted with hate. It would be best for you to stay away from him."

It was then that the police arrived on the scene.

Gregory Dorn was still on the sidewalk, sitting up.

Joanna watched as the police officer got out of the car. He had a smile on his face, but spoke in a serious manner.

Looking at Dorn he said, "I would like it very much if someone would tell me what's happening here."

Kathy said, "The man sitting on the sidewalk touched my friend here on her breasts."

The police officer looked at Dorn. "Would you stand up, please?" With some effort Dorn rose to his feet. "Would you show me some identification?" Dorn reached for his wallet. "Sexual assault can get you seven years in prison. Do you know that?"

Dorn looked at the police officer and said, "Look, when I touched her it wasn't a sexual thing. I was trying to make a point."

"It still comes out sexual assault. How did you get that shiner?"

Kathy said, "Joanna did it," motioning toward Joanna.

With a look of wonder on his face the officer asked, "You knocked him down?"

Joanna, looking at Dorn said, "No, a good Samaritan did."

"Where can I find this good Samaritan?"

Joanna looked at the officer, "He was driving away as you were driving up."

"I would like to talk with him."

So would I, thought Joanna.

Then she heard the officer ask, "Does anyone know his name?"

Wistfully Joanna said, "I wish I did. But no, I don't."

"Joanna, do you wish to press charges?"

Joanna looked at Gregory Dorn and paused. Then she said, "No. No, I don't."

"You are certain?"

"Yes, I'm certain."

The officer looked at Dorn, and handed him his identification. "If I were you, I would stay away from her. Way away."

Dorn looked at the officer, "I will. Thank you, sir." Dorn, with his head bowed, turned and slowly walked away.

The police officer looked at them all and said, "Have a nice day, people."

The officer turned and walked back to the police cruiser. He looked back at Joanna, then got in the police cruiser, wrote something down on a tablet, once more looked back at Joanna, and drove away.

Joanna Kimble looked at her associates. "Med Keandra Corporations is the only news?"

Don Leach responded, "Yes, but what do you think is going to happen?"

"I think the price of their stock is going to go down. But it won't stay down. The way "Frankenstein" Keandra runs those corporations, the price will go back up as sure as the price of gold. Tomorrow is the time to buy people! I'm going to look for the why. Why look for a new CEO when things are going so good? Why tell the world about it? New CEO or not, the Med Keandra Group is a big pile of blue chips!"

NEXT DAY

Joanna was sitting at her desk, staring at the two computer monitors and not seeing them, thinking about the day before and the events that took place.

Kathy Bates stood in the open doorway, smiling at her. "Okay, who is he, and what is his name?"

Quizzically Joanna looked back at her. "Who?"

"The guy that came to your rescue yesterday. I've been thinking about him all night. He knows you. I think he has known you for some time. So, who is he?"

"My soul mate," Joanna responded.

"What's his name?" Kathy asked.

"I don't know. I haven't met him yet."

Quizzically Kathy looked at her friend. with a frown on her face. "What is your definition of soul mate?"

Joanna looked up at the ceiling and said, "Personal hero, mentor, husband, father of my children. Someone who holds me when I break down and cry." She looked back at Kathy. "You don't really want to know all this."

"Oh, yes, I do," said Kathy, as she came into Joanna's office and sat on one of the chairs in front of her desk. Kathy leaned forward and asked, "What are you going to do now?"

"I'm going to take an early lunch and go down to the cafe and meet him."

"Are you sure he's there?" Kathy asked.

Joanna got up and got her coat. Just before she was going out the door she said, "Yup. If not, he soon will be."

Kathy sat in front of Joanna's desk, with a puzzled look on her face, as Joanna went out the door.

As Joanna walked down Second Avenue in the bright sunlight, she saw a car identical to the one the man was driving slowly going down the street ahead of her.

She was so focused on the car that she never even noticed that the sun was shining.

When she got to the cafe, she chose a table and had no sooner than sat down when she saw him crossing the street, doing that little dance he did the last time she saw him.

Holding up his hand to stop one car, waving another car to pass with his other hand, while bowing from the waist.

Then, pointing his finger at a car to stop, he would wink and appear to dance a jig or skip across the cobblestones in front of them.

Then, whirl around and point at them, while mouthing the words "thank you." The way he pointed at them was like he had known them forever.

The drivers of the cars looked at each other as if they had just seen God directing traffic. Joanna couldn't help herself, she laughed while watching him cross three lanes of traffic. When he got across the street, people on the sidewalk cheered and applauded him.

He walked casually to her table and said, "I would wager a nickel that you came here just to meet me."

Joanna looking up at him said, "You've got a whole drawer full of nickels, haven't you?"

"No. Actually I have a bottle full of nickels. What made you think of that?"

Joanna smiled a knowing smile. "I don't know, just something that came to mind." She could feel his strength again as she said, "My friend Kathy says you know me. Do you know me?"

Without hesitation, he said, "Yes, Joanna Kimble! I know you!" Joanna felt like he had just taken her breath away.

She thought, *My God! With the power of his strength he can control everyone! Should I be scared?* Then weakly she asked, "Where do you know me from?"

"I know you from nowhere," he said, smiling confidently.

She could see that he was enjoying himself. Joanna laughed a nervous laugh. Then cautiously asked, "Where, pray tell, is nowhere?"

"Do you really want to know?"

Still looking a little unnerved, Joanna said, "Sure. Why not?"

"Nowhere is a group of businesses. These businesses are owned by a very wealthy man. This very wealthy man keeps coming up with these programs or projects. Me, being a shirt-tail relative, it seems, I get stuck having to mobilize these programs, slash projects. To make a long story short, your name came up in one of these programs."

Joanna looking at him seriously asked, "Why me? What for? A job offer?"

He looked at her and smiled. "I don't know if I can say just yet. But I can say, I had to find two people. Surprisingly enough, one was easy to find. You! The other, not so easy."

The man, suddenly quiet, studied her face carefully. Then, almost in a whisper, said, "My, God! I've found her! I've found the other one! Ooh! Dammit!" Then he said, "I hope you don't mind if I get angry with myself." Quieter, almost like an after-thought, he said, "I am not prepared for this!"

He had a look of surprise on his face as he rose to his feet. She watched him looking at her carefully as he reached out and touched her face with his fingertips. Then softly he said, "I do apologize. I must go. You see, I am not prepared for this! I will see you again, as soon as I'm prepared. This is going to take some thought."

Joanna felt there was something wrong. Very wrong. She started to ask if there was something wrong when the waitress came to their table.

The man laid a hundred-dollar bill on the table and said, "Anything she would like for lunch, it's on me." Turning to Joanna he said, "Forgive me."

Concerned, Joanna stood up and started to ask, "Is something wrong?" Once again, the man was walking away from her.

Joanna looked dumb founded as she watched the man walk away from her. She wondered if she would ever see him again.

Once again she watched him do that little dance as he waded through traffic. Once again, people cheered and applauded him as they watched him dancing on the cobblestones of the street, as he glided through three lanes of traffic.

SEVEN WEEKS LATER

Joanna sat at the vanity in her bedroom, putting on her makeup. She was preparing to go to a party.

Several companies were celebrating a large merger. She was looking forward to meeting a lot of people she knew and hadn't seen in some time.

She was wearing a wrap-around gown with a Victorian neckline. The gown didn't show any cleavage; however, her breasts pushed out the front of the gown noticeably.

Looking at her breasts in the mirror she said, "Well, girls, as usual you're going to get more attention than I am tonight."

She thought about the man that looked at her so seriously. She wondered what he meant when he whispered, "My God, I've found her!" She had been thinking of him everyday.

She sometimes wondered if she would see him again. However, deep down, she had a feeling he was looking for her to come to him.

She actually felt lonely when she thought about him. Looking at herself in the mirror, she pictured his face as she talked to him. "Where did you go? Who are you that you can make me feel like this?"

She sat for a moment, deep in thought. Then she said, "I know you want something from me. I'll wait for you to tell me whatever it is, for as long as it takes."

She got up and put her coat on.

When she left the building, she got in a new Saab hatchback and started the engine.

The rain was pelting her car viciously as Joanna arrived at the Collier Suites Hotel in downtown Portland. She had the valet park her car.

As she went inside, she took off her coat. The place was almost uncomfortably warm.

Kathy Bates met her at the elevators. "Guess who's here?"

Joanna looked at her friend, "I'm almost afraid to ask. Who?"

"Your soul mate!" Kathy responded.

"Who?" Joanna asked again.

"Your soul mate! You know, your personal hero, husband, father of your children, and all those things I don't want to hear about. But, yes, I do!"

Anxiously Joanna asked, "What's his name?"

"I don't know. But he's speaking in there, and everyone is hanging on his every word."

As Joanna and Kathy entered the large banquet room, Joanna could see him smiling while standing at the podium speaking. "I have been speaking long enough." He leaned forward and smiled. "When I say that, it means you're tired of looking at me while listening to all of this drivel."

The whole room roared with laughter and applause.

Still smiling he said, "I want to add one more thing to this intellectual drivel before you all start yawning from boredom. I do know listening to this idiotic lexicon can be boring."

He paused while everyone laughed again. "Most mergers, in this day and age, fail. The reason they fail is because executives immediately start making changes in policy. Changes in policy must be made slowly so consumers don't get confused or frightened. That's when consumers leave, then other companies get their business. To keep this merger from failing, a lot of thought and research was done as to how fast, or slowly, to make changes in policy. Failing is not what this merger is all about. The importance of this merger is going to be felt immediately. Things are going to be so much easier, faster, you will wonder why it was so difficult to do the same tasks we were doing before this merger."

Then seriously he looked around the room into their faces. With his hands on the podium, he said, "So I say unto you, serve the food. Let's eat and fill our glasses with the spirits of our choice! And enjoy the warmth of each other's hearts! Let's celebrate our lives together, in the hope that the celebration never ends."

Immediately everyone stood and applauded. The standing ovation went on from the time he quit speaking until he found his place to sit.

As he made his way, at some he would point his finger in recognition. He smiled at them as though he had known each and every one of them forever. People were reaching out to touch him, pat him on the shoulder, or shake his hand.

Joanna turned to Kathy and said, "Boy, he's so popular! He could run for president! So why can't I find out his name?"

Joanna turned to a man standing near her and asked, "What's his name?"

The man looked at her and laughed boisterously.

It seems everyone knows him but me, she thought.

After everyone had been served and started eating, Kathy and Joanna were watching the man as he was eating.

Light seemed to trail along the top of his glasses as he talked to the man sitting next to him, when suddenly he turned toward Joanna and winked at her.

Kathy turned to Joanna and said, "I saw that! You didn't tell me that you've been working your wiles on him!"

"Kathy, will you do me a favor?"

"Sure, anything."

Wistfully, Joanna said, "Stop talking! I've got to figure out what to do next."

Servers were carrying trays with glasses of champagne all around the room. Without realizing it, Joanna had taken several glasses of the stuff, as she was visiting friends and colleagues. Joanna was starting to feel the effects of the champagne when she felt something bump her bottom. Turning around, she got dizzy.

Looking up she saw that she was looking into the face of the man she was most curious about. Slurring her words, she said, "It took you long enough to get here."

Looking into her eyes he said, "You can't always get away from people when you would like to."

She looked up at him. "I know about that. You don't have to tell me. Why don't you tell me what it is you want from me?"

"Let's go someplace quieter."

She looked up at him and felt dizzy. "Okay, let me get my coat."

After getting her coat, they walked toward the front doors of the hotel. Just as they went through the doors, she passed out.

With his left arm around her shoulders, and his right arm under her knees, he picked her up just as his car pulled up to the front of the building.

He whispered in her ear, "I'm surprised you made it this far."

One of the valets opened the passenger side door for him and he set her in the car. He reclined the seat a little, carefully laying her head on the headrest.

He tipped the valet and thanked him. Then he got in the car and drove away with Joanna Kimble into the pouring rain. The darkness, between the lights, seemingly glowed magically in the night. Quickly the car disappeared into the torrential downpour that mercilessly pelted the city.

⌒⌒

STRANGE SURROUNDINGS

Joanna awakened in a king-size bed. She was alone in the bed.

She didn't have to look or feel to know she didn't have any clothes on. *Who undressed me? I wonder where my clothes are?* She sat up and looked around the dimly lit room.

It was a very large room for a bedroom. There were two small chandeliers hanging from the ceiling—one on each side of the bed. They weren't turned on. There was a ceiling fan directly over the bed. It wasn't turning.

The furnishings were expensive. The room was furnished with lush carpets on the hardwood floor. The room was easily twice as large as the bedroom of her apartment.

She was surprised to see a bathroom sink with hot and cold running water installed in the L-shaped vanity.

There were three large dressers in the room. All three had large mirrors attached to them.

The doors to the walk-in closet were also full-length mirrors. The mirrors were reflecting the only light in the room.

A floor lamp in the corner was turned on low, near a closet. Other than the lamp, the room was fairly dark. There weren't any windows in the room. She had to go to the bathroom and wondered if there was anyone else around.

She saw a white terrycloth robe on the foot of the bed. She reached down, picked up the robe, and put it on.

Cautiously, she slipped out of the bed and walked across the room to the open door of a large bathroom. There was a full-length mirror on each side of the door of the bathroom.

There was a small light glowing in the bathroom. She looked around.

There were two of everything: two tubs, two toilets, two wash-basins, a bidet, and a large shower stall. One of the tubs was a Jacuzzi.

She saw herself in a full-length mirror on the inside of the door. *I look awful*, she thought.

When she came out of the bathroom, she decided to look around. She saw a mirrored door and slid it sideways to open it. When the door opened, lights came on inside.

It was a walk-in closet, full of clothes. Female clothes. She walked into the closet. Looking through the clothes, she decided that who-ever the clothes belonged to had good taste. She liked what she saw.

She looked at the bed. Looking at the pillows, even in the dark room, she could see that no one else had been in the bed with her.

As she was coming out of the bedroom, she saw a door to another room across the hall. She looked down the dark hall.

The hall was wide enough for two people to walk abreast of each other with room to spare.

On each side of the hall there were tiny little lights like stars on the floor. She marveled at the lights and thought, *What a neat idea.*

She looked back at the door. Opening the door, a small light came on.

She saw that this room was large, but smaller than the room she had been sleeping in. It was empty.

Following the lights down the dark hallway, she came to an-other closed door. Opening the door, a small light also came on in that room. She saw that this room was about the same size. It was also empty.

Across from this door was the open door of another large bath-room. There was also a small light on in this room. She noticed that there were no windows in any of the rooms.

From there she went into a very large dining room with a large kitchen to one side. There were windows in these rooms, up near the ceiling. The windows were horizontal, about two feet high and six feet long.

Looking to her left, there was a large living room, or party room, with a large fireplace in the middle of the room. The fireplace was about a foot above the floor, square and open on four sides, and built with decorative stone.

She went into the kitchen and looked around. All the appliances were stainless steel. She looked at the six-burner stove.

Opening the refrigerator door, she saw it had of all the normal stuff: eggs, milk, juice, bacon, as well as half a watermelon and other food stuffs. *It doesn't look like I'll go hungry,"* she thought. She liked the place. *This place is better than my place,"* she thought.

A doorbell sounded. She looked at the living room door. Going to the door, she tried to open it and found that she couldn't. It was locked.

Then she heard the door being unlocked. As the door opened, she knew without thinking who would be there.

The man she was most curious about was standing in the doorway, looking at her.

She pointed her finger at him and said, "Look, you! Tell me your name, or I'm going to sock you right in the eye!"

"Robb Michael," he said, holding his two index fingers up in the sign of a cross. "Please don't hit me. I've seen the damage you do when you sock somebody in the eye."

She looked back at him quizzically and asked, "Why do you have two first names?"

He held up his hands as though holding her away. "Look, of all of the things I've been accused of, I swear, I had nothing to do with that. My parents have to shoulder the blame for that one," he said smiling. "Everyone calls me Robb Michael, with two Bs."

She looked at him for a moment. "What have you been accused of?"

He cocked his head to one side and looked up at the ceiling then back at her. Then said, "You name it, I'm responsible for it. Everything from malpractice, to being irresponsible, to being reckless, to being amoral. I could go on and on, but it wouldn't help my case. I'm not so sure you want to hear about it anyway."

She stood looking at him, and thought, *this is really bizarre. He's talking to me like he has known me forever.*

She looked at him. Once again she felt drawn to him. She realized she wasn't wearing anything under the robe. Then she thought, *Oh, God! If he asks me to take off the robe, I'll probably do it!* Then she thought, *I'm afraid to ask who undressed me?* Pulling the robe tighter, she asked, "What case?"

"Well, I told you, the companies I'm associated with have these programs/projects. I'm in charge of some of these programs. And I'm way behind and can't possibly meet my deadlines. Therefore, I have taken a drastic measure."

Still feeling drawn to him, she took a step closer to him and asked, "What drastic measure?"

"I told you, your name came up as a candidate. But I don't have time to do this project in the right order. So, I've become a felon. I've captured you. In other words, I've kidnapped you."

Holding the robe tighter she thought, *this is getting more bizarre by the minute.*

"Damn you, Robb Michael! You can go to jail for that!" she said seriously.

She then wondered, *What's this going to cost me?*

She saw him smile at her.

"This program is important enough that I'm willing to go to jail."

As she looked at him, she could see that he was proud of her. "Okay, Robb Michael. Why me?"

He moved closer to her and said, "I like what I see when I look into your eyes."

Interrupting, she asked, "What do you see?"

He looked at her seriously. "I see intuition. I see self-assurance. I see pride, and I see someone that's able to meet a challenge." Then softer, "I see someone that's not afraid to stand up and fight!"

Joanna turned away from him and walked to the kitchen, and then turned back to him. "Are you saying that I'm your captive?"

Confidently, he said, "Yes, I am."

"Damn you, Robb Michael! You know? You're not as dumb as the rocks laying along the road, but you're gaining on them!"

She had no sooner than said it when she saw him smiling at her. She knew he was enjoying himself. He had crossed his arms. She could see the pride behind the smile. *He's looking at me,* she thought. *To him I'm not just a big pair of boobs!*

"Okay. What do you want me to do?" Then suddenly she said, "You know my car is still at the Collier Suites parking lot!"

"No, it's not. Your car is parked next to mine in my garage."

"Why did you bring my car here?"

"So you can drive it home."

Sternly she said, "Damn you, Robb Michael. I don't understand this." She thought, *this is getting really weird.*

"Why bother to kidnap me if you're just going to let me go? This isn't making any sense. I don't know what you're trying to do."

"I'm not just going to let you go. You have to negotiate your way out of here."

She looked at him and again thought, *this is really bizarre.*

Then he said, "The reason I brought you here is to force you to negotiate with me. If you want to get out of here, you'll negotiate with me."

She glared at him, "Well, you're going to lose. I'm pretty damn good at negotiating. I do it every day."

He smiled at her, "Good, I don't want you to lose. Look, I haven't got time to mobilize this program in the proper manner. That's why I captured you and brought you here. Tell me, are you hungry?"

"Starving!" she yelled back at him.

"Then let's eat," he said as he walked past her into the kitchen and opened the refrigerator door. Looking in he took out a carton of eggs and a package of bacon.

While Joanna watched, he turned on the stove and said, "Now I need to find some pots and pans."

She looked at him strangely and said, "You live here and you don't know where the cookware is?"

"No, I don't live here. You do. At least until you negotiate your way out of here."

Joanna crossed her arms under her breasts. "Try looking in the cupboards down next to the stove."

He opened a cupboard door and said, "A-ha! I knew you could tell me where they were hidden."

He took two frying pans out of the cupboard. Going back to the refrigerator, he opened the freezer door.

Looking through the frozen packages, he picked up a bag of tater-tots. Carrying the package back to the stove, he saw a breadbox on the counter.

"Check the breadbox. If there's any bread, make us some toast. I like mine toasted dark."

While making toast, Joanna watched as he was frying bacon and eggs and asked, "Do you cook for everyone?"

He looked back at her and smiled, and then said, "Oh, yeah, sometimes. I like preparing food for people. How do you like your eggs?"

Minutes later he deftly slid the eggs onto a plate with thick sliced bacon and tater-tots, along with the toast she had made.

After they had eaten, Robb Michael suggested a tour of the place.

First he guided her through a door in the kitchen, through a large laundry room with two, large, stainless steel sinks, and a washer and dryer.

Then through another door, there were three steps down. It was a large room. Looking around, she saw she was in a workout gym with concrete floor and walls.

The gym was complete with an elliptical, an exercycle, a treadmill, and other exercising equipment. On one end of the room was an indoor heated swimming pool, twenty by forty, under a huge skylight.

There was a fireplace built in the corner by the pool with patio furniture near by. She saw that there was a grid to cook on in the fireplace. There were recliners and a table and chairs. Also, another bathroom with a very large shower stall with four shower heads high overhead.

Looking around she saw there were some wooden benches here and there around the room. She saw the windows were two by four, laying horizontal about a foot below the ceiling.

The ceiling looked to be twelve feet high.

After showing her the place he asked, "Well, do you think you could handle living here?"

"I probably could. But it's not my intention to live here. Now, when do we begin these negotiations?" she asked.

He turned and looked at her. "Are you in a hurry?"

She looked back at him thoughtfully. She didn't answer.

Robb Michael started moving toward the door. "Let's take this conversation into the living room."

On the way, Robb Michael stopped in the kitchen and poured them both a glass of juice.

He carried them into the living room and set both glasses on the coffee table between two leather recliners. He sat in one of the recliners.

She sat on a couch across from him. She sat watching him as he picked up one of the glasses and sipped his juice.

Then he set the glass down and began to speak. "Joanna, over on the desk, you probably noticed there are three computer monitors. Inside the desk are two computers. Both are connected to the Internet. Turn the right one on and bring up the Internet, then I want you to check your bank account balance."

She got up and went to the desk.

After checking her bank balance, she came back to the couch and sat down. "How did you do that?" she asked.

She watched him smile at her and asked, "How did I do what?"

"My account has a hundred thousand dollars more than I've put in it."

She saw him fingering the breast pocket on the sport coat he was wearing.

He spoke again. "Joanna, go check your account balance again."

"I just checked it," she said.

"Check it again, please. Just for me." She sat, not moving, and looked at him. Once again he said, "Please." Once more she got up and slowly went to the desk.

When she came back, her face had paled.

She thought, *This is getting more bizarre all the time. Should I be scared?* Then she asked, "Who are you, and how can you do that?"

"I'm not anyone important. But the companies that I'm associated with are one of those huge conglomerates that sometimes manages to get things right. What did they do this time?" he asked.

"I've got an additional six hundred thousand dollars in my account. Who are you that you can you do that?"

He ignored her question.

She watched his face as he casually said, "A-ha. They got it right. Now, Joanna, you can take the one hundred thousand dollars and leave, right this minute. Or you can keep the seven hundred thousand dollars and live here, do research, and be an important part of this project."

"You said that I'm a candidate. What am I a candidate for?" she asked.

"I don't believe I can tell you at this time."

Under her breath she said, "Damn you, Robb Michael!" She paused, thinking to herself. Then she said, "You knew I wouldn't take the hundred thousand! Didn't you?"

He smiled at her. "I would have wagered a lot more than a nickel on it. Your curiosity as to what this is all about is working in my favor. So, do you accept this deal?"

Joanna looked as though she didn't believe what was happening to her and thought, *What the hell do I do now?* Then she said, "Okay, yes, I will accept."

She saw him studying her. She heard him say, "Now this deal is locked in. No changes can be made. I need you to sign this contract. Believe me when I say you are on your way to discovery."

He gave her a contract on a clipboard. He looked at her and said, "Read it. If you see anything you want to change, tell me, and we'll discuss it."

After she read the four-page contract, she signed it, thinking, *this contract is written about the same way I would have written it.*

Joanna got up and reached between the recliners and picked up a glass of juice, took a sip, then held the glass against her breast.

"If you can't tell me what I'm a candidate for, tell me what the other candidate is for."

She looked at him and saw he was looking her right in the eyes. "I don't know if I can tell you yet. The only thing I can tell you is that it is very important. Perhaps more important than the other thing, from my point of view. I can also tell you sex is involved. Lots of sex."

She interrupted. "I may have to take the lower figure after all. Who am I supposed to have sex with?"

"Me. No one else. Just me."

"Well, I think I can figure out why this project is more important to you."

"You might be wrong," he said softly. "It's an experiment in human endeavor."

Joanna drank the rest of the contents in the glass. Then she walked out into the kitchen, rinsed out the glass, and set it on the granite drain board.

Then, with her back to the counter, she leaned against it thinking, wondering what to do.

She saw Robb Michael come into the kitchen and stop about twenty feet away. Then she said, "I think I'll take the hundred thousand and go."

She stood watching him. He didn't come any closer.

Suddenly she heard him say, "That deal is already locked in. You have signed a contract. Remember? You are seven hundred thousand dollars richer. Now we're working on an entirely different deal. Before this is over, you will be substantially better off."

She started to speak when he held up his hand to stop her. "I knew you were the right candidate for the first position before I met you. When I was talking with you about it was when I realized you would be perfect for the other position, as well. I never gave it a thought you were suitable for the latter program until you had already been chosen for the first project. But the way you think, and your type of logic, made it clear. You are the best candidate for the other position, as well."

He continued, "However, I wasn't prepared to deal with you at the time. The reason I wasn't prepared was I expected the first candidate to be a man. However, the second candidate had to be a woman. I was taken by surprise when a woman was chosen for the first position. "Both of these positions are very important. Of all the programs and projects I have mobilized, I believe this is the first time I wasn't prepared. I'm a little embarrassed. For me, not being prepared is unheard of! I had to make preparations quickly!"

She looked at him and interrupted, "You say that the first position is usually held by a man?"

"Correct. When I realized you also had the right mentality for the second position, that was when I realized I wasn't prepared. That's the reason I left you that morning at the cafe. I had to make preparations quickly."

"What kind of preparations?" Joanna asked.

"Well, I had to put you in an environment that you could mobilize both programs. I believe it's going to be very difficult for you to handle both of these programs at the same time. I knew that you would need absolute privacy to do what I need you to do."

Robb Michael continued, "So I designed this compound. I got people mobilized to put it all together. This way it will be easier for you to make both programs come together. You will live here alone. I will not be here unless invited. I have a key to the place. But I will not use that key unless I believe there's an emergency. I want you to have as much privacy as possible, and I had to do it in such a manner that I wouldn't frighten you."

"Damn you, Robb Michael! You don't frighten me! You scare the living hell out of me!" She paused, then quieter she said, "But you don't frighten me."

She watched him looking at her, then heard him start to laugh. The laugh was a natural laugh, pleasant to listen to.

Once again she felt drawn to him.

Then he said, "Do you know what you just said?"

"Robb Michael! Whatever it was, it wasn't funny!" she retorted.

She watched while he laughed once again. Then she heard him say, "Yes, it was!" He laughed again, and said, "Tell me what you want to have so you can be the most important part of this project."

"What kind of a mentality do I have that makes me a candidate for this project?" she asked.

"You have a way of thinking, a certain kind of logic that makes you perfect for this project."

She looked at the floor and slowly walked toward the door to the workout gym. "What kind of logic do you have to have to have sex?"

"I told you, it's an experiment in human endeavor. Believe me, mentally you have got the qualifications for it," he assured her.

Going through the door she saw the room was dark. She looked back to see if he was following her.

He was still twenty to twenty-five feet behind her, strolling along at the same pace she was.

There was light coming from the ceiling. Looking up she saw moonlight shining through the large glass skylight over the pool.

Looking back at him, she saw he was reaching for a light switch. "Please, don't turn on the light. I want to be in the dark. I must have slept all day for it to be this dark already. It must be close to ten o'-clock. The sun sets late this time of the year."

She could feel him watching her as she walked along the edge of the pool.

Looking up through the skylight at the stars she asked, "Are you still waiting for an answer from me?"

"Yes, as soon as you can think of one. Don't be afraid to ask for anything, because this might well be a very difficult thing for you to do. If we can't reach an agreement, I will have to search for another candidate."

She looked up at the glass skylight once again. Suddenly she whirled and pointed at him. "Take me up into the stars!" she exclaimed. Then pointing upward, she said, "If you can take me up where I'm surrounded by the stars, no matter where I look even when I look down, I'll be your sex slave for as long as you live!"

She watched him turn and walk back toward the kitchen.

Still watching him, he turned and looked back to where she was standing in the dark. "Are you trying to ask the impossible?"

She looked at him, wondering if he could see where she was standing, and said, "Yes. For what you are asking, yes!"

She walked through the darkness, toward him. As she walked back into the kitchen, she thought she saw fear on his face and wondered if what she had said scared him.

Once again she felt drawn to him.

Then she remembered, before she even met him, she knew somehow it would come to this.

She wanted to hold him and let him know there some things you just don't ask someone to do!

When he said, "I will try to do as you ask, mainly because I don't have time to look for another candidate. Go get dressed. Don't wear a dress, wear pants and a blouse."

She looked bewildered, "Except for what I was wearing last night, I don't have anything to wear."

Speaking softly, he said, "Yes, you do. All the clothes in the closets are yours. I had people go to the places you buy clothes to find out what you like to wear and what sizes. I believe you will find everything you need in that room. Everything in there is new. Go get dressed."

As Joanna went down the dark hallway to the bedroom, she marveled once again at the little tiny lights along the edges of the floor.

As she went through the bedroom door, instinctively she reached for the light switch. The chandeliers lit the room like daylight.

She looked at the switch. Beside the switch there was a sliding switch to control the brightness of the chandeliers.

Searching through the closets, she found a pantsuit she liked and laid it on the bed. Looking through the dresser, she found panties and bras.

When she returned to the living room she didn't see Robb Michael anywhere. She started to see if he was in the gym when she heard the front door unlocking.

Turning she saw him. Robb Michael motioned for her to come out.

When she stepped through the door, she saw she was in another wide hallway that went two different directions.

He motioned her to the right and up some stairs to a deck about ten feet square, then through a door that led them outside. It was raining lightly.

His car was sitting there with the engine running. She looked up at him. "I thought you said that I would be driving my own car home."

"You're not going home yet. You live here now."

Then she remembered she had signed a contract to stay and live here, to do research. He held the door for her as she got in the car. Then went around the car and got in.

The wipers were on intermittent as he drove down a long paved driveway that seemed to go forever.

At the end of the driveway, he turned onto a paved, two-lane road. He drove carefully as he negotiated the curves of the winding road.

She looked over at him. "I like the clothes, especially the bra. I couldn't find one like this. I've had mine specially made. Where did you buy it?"

"They're made by a company called Trust Me. Those bras are not only fashionable, they have removable cups. I believe they're one of the best engineered support garments made. As big as you are, I thought you might like them."

"Robb Michael, where are we going?" she asked.

"Sit back and relax, we have plenty of time. It's a beautiful night. Enjoy the ride."

She looked out at the rain and the lights that made the rain soaked streets seem to glisten. He drove through the city and then out to Airport Way.

When he got to the airport, he turned into the National Guard gate and stopped at the guard shack. A guard came to the car. "Good evening, Robb Michael. How are you tonight?"

"I'm well, thank you. I've got a research flight this night. I believe they have the bird all ready for me."

The man, still standing in the rain said, "I heard you were coming in tonight. Tell me, does she have clearance?"

Robb Michael smiled at the man, "Yes, I cleared her about forty minutes ago."

The guard looked over at the taxiway. "It looks like they're waiting for you. But you can't lift off until I get conformation on her clearance. Have a nice flight."

"Thank you, I will," Robb Michael said.

Robb Michael drove the car over to a small building and parked. After getting out and ushering her into the building, he said, "You have to get into a flight suit. Come on, I'll show you how."

He looked at her in the light green pantsuit. She looked good wearing that color. "You'll have to strip down to your underwear to get the flight suit on," he told her.

Nervously, she undressed, and as she was putting on the flight suit she knew that her breasts were keeping the suit from closing.

Robb Michael came over to help her saying, "You're going to have to tuck them in. The suit is a must."

After suiting up, they got into a military vehicle and rode out to a plane with extremely long wings.

As they were exiting the vehicle, one of the guards came up to them and let them know her clearance had come through. It started to rain a little harder.

Robb Michael told a man to help her into the rear cockpit.

Joanna looked at the man and said, "I've never flown before."

The man looked back at her and said, "You've got nothing to worry about. Robb Michael is an Ace, one of the best pilots in the world—and I do mean the world. He's one of about four pilots that have landed one of these U2s on an aircraft carrier. With the wing span this baby's got, that's a near impossible task. He's also the only man I know of that out maneuvered a SAM with a U2."

"What's a SAM?" she asked.

"A SAM is a Surface to Air Missile. One of our enemies fired one at him, and he out maneuvered it till it ran out of fuel. It exploded harmlessly when it hit the ground. He's a strange one. He has a doctorate in surgical medicine, but he joined the Navy to be a combat pilot. He has shot down eleven enemy aircraft. It's rumored that he shot down a lot more, but they weren't confirmed."

"You mean he's a doctor?" asked Joanna.

"Yes, he is a doctor! I understand he is one of the best. He got picked by the CIA to fly one of these U2s off a carrier. They must have had a mission that wasn't close enough to a land base. The man's phenomenal. The way he flies is unbelievable, like that's what he was born to do. I don't know that I understand as much as I know about it. The government leases this U2 trainer to him for scientific experiments. Why, I don't know. I don't understand him, either. He excels at everything he does."

After he buckled her in, he showed her how to close the cockpit canopy.

She watched through the closed cockpit as the man and Robb Michael stood in the rain and talked for awhile.

The way Robb Michael stood there talking, it was like it wasn't raining at all. The rain didn't seem to bother him.

Robb Michael got into the cockpit in front of her. The plane's engine started with a low whine that became higher pitched as the engine accelerated. The plane taxied toward the end of the runway.

She heard air traffic control give him clearance to take off in the helmet she was wearing. Suddenly the plane was traveling down the runway. Water splashed up from the wheels as the plane accelerated.

It didn't seem to go very far at all when it lifted off. She not only felt the forward thrust, to her it felt like she was going up in an elevator. That's when she closed her eyes.

As the plane was gaining altitude she thought, *if he's a doctor, it could be that he wants me in a research project in sexual behavior. I wonder why he didn't say so?*

After about twenty minutes, the engines seemed to run quieter.

She heard Robb Michael's voice in her ears. "Joanna, open your eyes."

"How do you know my eyes are closed?" she asked.

"You are not saying anything. If you had your eyes open, you would be saying quite a lot."

Joanna opened her eyes. "Oh, my God! It's so beautiful! There's so many! How did you do this? How come there's so many? It's so beautiful! My God! You can't see this many stars on the ground. Where did they all come from?"

Everywhere she looked, she saw stars. Even when she looked down below the wings, she saw stars.

Sometimes when she looked down into the darkness, she thought she could see the curvature of the Earth.

Once again she heard Robb Michael's voice in her ears. "Joanna? Take a good look. I may never get to bring you up here again."

They flew around for over an hour when he said, "The reason you can't see this many stars when you're on the ground is because there's too much light on the ground."

After a long, quiet descent, the U2 flew over Mount St. Helens, Mount Adams, Mount Hood, and all along the snow-capped peaks of the Cascade mountain range, all the way down to Mt. Shasta near Redding, California.

They turned and slowly flew back to Portland and landed smoothly. They had no sooner landed when a truck came out on the runway.

Some men got out carrying some wheels and hooked them on the wings before Robb Michael taxied back to the hanger. It had stopped raining.

As she got out of the plane, she couldn't help herself. She looked up. She saw stars in the clear sky between the clouds.

After they got out of the plane, she looked at him. For some reason, she couldn't stop looking at him.

Back in the building, he helped her out of her flight suit and told her to get dressed.

Once they were outside, she heard him tell the man on the ground, "Log that flight as research, K U2 EXP-F, 1-P-R."

"Sure thing, Robb Michael. Everything will be taken care of." She saw Robb Michael turn to the man and shake hands with him.

Riding in the car on the way back, Joanna was thinking, *He took me up into the stars. He actually took me up into the stars! How could he have done that? I didn't believe he could do that. My God! I didn't believe anyone could do that! Now, I have to make good on the deal.*

Helplessly, she asked, "Is there anything you can't do?"

She waited for him to answer and then thought, *He doesn't want to talk to me.*

He didn't answer her for about five minutes. She watched him as he turned into the long driveway.

After he had driven about a quarter of a mile, he stopped the car and turned on the interior lights. She saw him looking at her. Searching her face, he looked into her eyes.

He reached out and touched her face with his fingertips, and calmly said, "I believe I can do anything, except save my own life."

What a strange thing to say," she thought.

Then she said, "When do you think you're going to die?"

He didn't answer.

He drove on up to the compound and switched off the engine.

As he got out of the car, he said, "I've heard it said that you begin to die the instant you are born."

He opened the doors for her as she walked back into the compound.

Joanna went straight into the bedroom and undressed. She wondered if she should wear a robe or go back to the living room, wearing nothing at all.

She decided to wear nothing and started walking down the hall toward the living room to let him know that she was ready for him.

Halfway there, she stopped and thought, *what am I thinking? I must be insane!* She went back for the robe, thinking, *I wonder what this is really all about. I'm not a prisoner. I feel I can leave anytime I would like. Why am I here? If I'm not careful, I can lose everything I've wanted since I first saw him. I'm going to stay and find out what this is really all about.*

She didn't really know what was expected of her, but decided she would do whatever he wanted.

When she entered the living room, she saw he was looking at his cell phone. When he looked at her, his eyes widened a little. "You've undressed."

"Well, dammit. You had to go and do the impossible." Softly she said, "So, I'm ready to do the possible."

She saw him looking at her quizzically. "I'm sorry? The impossible?"

Softly she said, "Yes, you took me up into the stars. I didn't think it was possible. It was so breathtaking. It made me feel so humble and small. How high were we?"

She saw him looking her in the eyes. "I can't tell you. What you want to know is classified. Even though I haven't been in the Navy for years, I'm still obligated to keep what's been classified secret, secret."

He continued, "All I can tell you is that we were over seventy thousand feet. That's twice as high as a commercial airliner flies. I don't know if you noticed, but when the engines were running very quietly up there, they were barely getting enough air to keep running. The air is very thin up there. We were on the inner edge of the atmosphere. That's another reason you can see more stars when you're up there."

She stood there looking at him, and then said, "When we were up there, you told me to take a good look, that you may not get to bring me up there again. Why not?"

She saw him smiling at her. "I had to get clearance to take you up there. To get you cleared, I told a half truth. I told them it was a research project, that you were an important part of the project. It wasn't all together a lie. You are involved in two very important projects. The deals I've made with you for these projects are to be kept between me and you. Our secret. If asked, you can tell anyone we have a deal. You can say anything you want to anyone, but not the content of the deals. If you tell anyone the content of our deals, the deals are off," he said.

"There are two computers in that desk over there. Both are on the Internet. They can be used at the same time. One of them is hooked up to two monitors. The computers are for you to do research and communicate with the outside world. I'm not going to give you a phone just yet. If you have a cell phone, you can use it, but you can use the computer to communicate with whomever you want. There is a web cam, microphone, and speakers on one of the computers. If something goes wrong with one or both the computers, let me know and it will be replaced immediately. You can research anything that interests you. I'm not going to tell you what to research. I was told you are more than qualified to do this. Part of the program is to see if you can figure out what needs to be researched without being told, and to see how far into the subject you will go without being instructed. If I told you why you were chosen for this program, and what this program is for, you would probably tell me to get someone else. Then run like hell." He smiled. "That's why I don't believe I should tell you more at this stage of the program."

She had stood in front of him while he had been speaking. She asked, "That's all you want me to do?"

"Yes, for now," he replied.

She watched him looking at her as she let the robe fall open and asked, "What about the other position? Are you ready for me to start that project?"

She knew she had surprised him.

He wasn't prepared for her because his eyes widened almost imperceptibly.

He stood up and took her by the lapels of her robe and pulled the robe together saying, "We have things to discuss first."

"Like what?"

"I told you when I brought you here the other night, I examined you."

"Yes, so?"

"I found something I didn't expect. Your hymen is intact."

She looked up at him and haltingly said, "You gave me a thorough examination?"

"Yes, I did!"

She glared at him, and thought, *well, he is a doctor.*" Then she asked, "We have to discuss that?"

"Yes, we do. You see, at your age, the hymen can become very tough. You're thirty years old. Most girls have had their hymen broken around age sixteen to nineteen. I recommend that you remove it surgically. It's your choice. If you decide to remove it naturally, it could be very painful."

She looked him straight in the eyes. "I want you to break through it," she said softly.

"Why me?" he asked.

"Because you can do anything except save your own life. So, if you break through it, maybe I can save your life. I trust you. Don't ask me why. Just trust me!"

He put his arms around her and pulled her close.

Cupping her head with his left hand, he pulled her face into his throat and whispered in her ear, "Okay, I will. I will trust you. But I wasn't planning to do anything this night."

With her face still buried in his throat, she said, "If you don't do it now, I may not have the courage to do it later."

He backed away from her. "That's the way you want it?"

"Yes."

"Okay, but first I want you to sign a medical release."

He pulled some papers out of his coat pocket and had her sign them.

MAKING GOOD ON THE DEAL

Together they went down the dark hallway following the tiny lights to the bedroom.

He went into the bathroom and brought back a bath towel. "Spread this under you. It will prevent a mess."

She took the towel over to the king-size bed and pulled the covers down toward the foot of the bed. After she laid out the towel, she went into the bathroom and turned on the reading light at one end of the bathtub. When she came out, she left the bathroom door open but turned off the lights in the bedroom.

Even then there was more light in the room than you would think because of all the mirrors.

She dropped the robe and climbed onto the bed where she watched him undress in near darkness. As she watched him climb over the end of the bed, she felt a little apprehensive.

When he reached her, he said, "Lie down. I want to look at your body." She felt tense, but she did as he had asked. He started touching her.

He ran his hands up from her waist to her breasts, then ran his hands over her breasts slowly tracing her areolas with his fingertips. With one hand, he started nicking her nipples gently with his fingertips. With his other hand, he started running his fingers from the inside of her knee up the inside of her thigh.

Suddenly she sat straight upright. Breathlessly, she said, "I thought you just wanted to look at me!"

He moved around behind her. Then he reached around her and cupped her breasts with his hands.

She saw that her breasts overflowed his hands. He was very gentle as he lifted them, holding her nipples between his forefingers and thumbs.

Almost whispering, he said, "I am looking at you. The light in here is so poor, I have to look at you by braille."

She sat quiet for a moment, then said, "By braille?" Suddenly she started to laugh.

Then he said, "It's not only more interesting this way. I can see you better."

Still laughing she held up her arms and softly said, "Look all you want."

He moved around to her side.

With his arm around her shoulders, he helped her lay down. Then he said, "I'm going to tell you a story. And I'm going to use your body as a map."

She looked up at him and said, "Okay."

"There was this man and woman. There were two mountains between where they lived." He placed his finger near her armpit and said, "The man lived here."

Placing his other finger near her other armpit he said, "The woman lived here."

Leaving his hands where they were, he said, "The woman called the man and said, 'Meet me down at the delta.' The man said, 'Okay', so they both started walking."

Then moving his fingers, one around her breast and the fingers of his other hand over her other breast, he nicked the nipple.

As he nicked her nipple he said, "The woman was in a bigger hurry, so she went over the mountain, and stumbled on something."

Still moving, his fingers slowly passed down her naval.

He stopped moving when he arrived at her pubic area and said, "The man turned to the woman and said, 'You know? Those two idiots on the bed should meet here at the delta, too.'

What do you think, Joanna?"

Joanna looked at him and softly said, "I'm ready."

She watched him position himself over her. She felt him entering her and suddenly it hurt.

He stopped and said, "Your hymen stopped me. Are you sure you want to do this?"

"Yes, I can't think of anyone I would rather have do it than you."

"Foolish girl. Didn't your mother warn you about guys like me? Now I'm going to push in. This is going to hurt. Are you ready?"

"Yes."

She had no sooner than answered him when she felt him plunge into her.

She screamed and then said, "Oh—God!—Damn!—That hurt!"

She felt the tears running down her face as she looked up at him through teary eyes. His eyes looked wet.

"You were right," she said, "that hurt!"

Softly, almost in a whisper he said, "Yes! It did!"

When he pulled out of her she yelped again.

As he got out of bed, he said, "Don't move until I clean you up."

He reached back and threw the bottom half of the towel over her like a diaper. Then he went into the bathroom. He wasn't there very long.

When he came out, he put his trousers on and left the room. A minute later, he returned. He went to the bed and threw the towel back. She looked at the clock. It was three o clock in the morning.

She felt a pin prick. "Did you just give me a shot?"

He smiled down at her. In a voice that was almost a whisper he said, "Yes, I did. Goodnight, Joanna."

THE FOLLOWING DAY

When Joanna woke up she found herself alone once again in the king-size bed. She reached down for the towel. It wasn't there.

She lay there, thinking, *what am I doing here? He said it himself. 'If I knew what this is all about, I would run like hell!' So why am I running to him instead of away from him? Well, I'm still curious to know what this is all about. For what they're paying me, I think I'm going to stick around and find out.*"

She looked at the bedside clock to see what time it was.

She couldn't see the clock. There was a note folded over it. She picked it up and read it.

"Joanna, change the tampon as needed until there are no traces of blood on it. Then discontinue use. You shouldn't need them more than a day. Tampons are by the sink in the bathroom."

She looked at the clock. It was nearly three o'clock in the afternoon.

She got up and looked at the bed. There was no mess or traces of a mess. *Thank God he's a doctor,"* she thought.

Joanna showered, then wearing nothing but her robe, she sat at the computer desk.

The desk was huge. She opened a door on the left side of the desk. There were two computers in there. She turned on the left one. Two of the monitors on the desk lit up. *Good,* she thought. *Just like the computer at the office.*

She turned on the computer on the right. It was the one she had used before. The monitor on the right lit up.

She saw it was the one with the web cam, headphones, and microphone.

There was a keyboard and mouse on the desk and another keyboard and mouse on a shelf that slid out two inches below the other keyboard.

On the upper keyboard, she brought up the Internet and then the market read outs.

On the lower keyboard, she brought up the Internet, then sent Kathy Bates an email. 'You may have to close my office for me. I'm being held captive and can't come in.'

Then she started doing market searches. After a while she checked her email.

The first was from Kathy Bates. 'Who's holding you captive? And where?'

Quickly she sent another email. 'My soul mate. And I don't know where! Don't send a rescue team anytime soon!'

Then she read the rest of her emails. By the time she was finished, she had another email from Kathy, which read: 'See what happens when you use your wiles on really good-looking, intelligent men! Don't expect me to feel sorry for you! You deserve everything that's happening to you.'

Joanna traded emails back and forth for the rest of the day.

Late into the evening, she decided Robb Michael wasn't coming, so she went to bed early. She was lying in bed with the lights off, wondering what was going to happen next, when she sensed him come into the room.

She knew it was him. She couldn't hear or see him, but she knew he was there. She felt him get on the bed. Then heard him say, "Are you still awake?"

"You weren't here today. I missed you," Joanna said.

"I was near. I thought that you might want to be alone, after last night."

Casually she said, "I don't know. Maybe. Anyway, I kept myself entertained."

She felt him lie down on the blankets beside her. Then out of the dark she heard him say, "If I owe you an apology for anything, consider it given. Hurting you wasn't in the plan."

Now isn't that strange, she thought. *I never even thought about last night until he just mentioned it.*

Then she said, "Last night didn't work too well, did it?"

"No, not too well," he replied.

She felt him cross his legs and she asked, "Have you had a lot of experience with women?"

"Oh, yes. A lot more than I probably should have."

"How come? Why have you had more than anyone else?"

He lay quiet for a moment and then said, "When you're the shirt-tail relative and share the same last name as a very wealthy man, well, things come a lot easier. Most of my adult life I've been in bed with a different woman almost every night. There's the possibility that I will again. When it comes to women, we men are strange that way."

She was silent for a moment and then said, "I'm not sure that's what I wanted to hear."

With that she turned over with her back to him.

She felt him turn toward her and put his arm around her waist. "I've never lied to you and I never will. I told you there are those that say I'm immoral, careless, spoiled, reckless, and selfish. I don't live in a black and white world. Whatever the truth is, that's what I am. Ever since I can remember, I've lived my life somewhere between black and white. I shall always live my life somewhere between the dark side and the light side of the ID. I'm not going to apologize for being what I am. They say everything in my life came too easy. Well, it did. I'm not going to apologize for that, either."

They lay quiet for a while.

Then sleepily she said, "You're the only man I've ever met that everyone applauds when you jaywalk across the street."

With that Joanna Kimble snuggled up to him and fell asleep.

NEXT MORNING

When Joanna awoke, she found herself facing him with her face buried in his throat.

He still had his arm around her waist and the other arm around her shoulders. She was partially uncovered with one breast fully exposed. She felt so comfortable that she didn't want to move.

As she was lying there, she reminded herself, thinking, *he's telling me if I knew what this was all about, I would run like hell. So why am I still clinging to him instead of running away from him? Just stupid, I guess.*

She had to go to the bathroom. She rolled out of his arms and slid out of bed.

Padding toward the bathroom with her bare feet, she heard him say, "I was beginning to think that you were going to sleep all day."

She looked at him. He hadn't undressed. He had slept on top of the covers. He was wearing a blue suit, but he had kicked his boots off. They were lying on the end of the bed.

He still had his eyes closed while lying on the bed.

When she came out of the bathroom, she saw he was looking at her. She felt she should cover her nakedness, but she didn't.

Then he said, "If you put some clothes on, I'll take you out for breakfast."

Relieved, she smiled to herself because she saw he was looking at her face while he went out of the compound.

She dressed in brown pants and a pink blouse. When he came back, he was wearing dark blue slacks and a pink shirt with a light blue windbreaker. They noticed that they were both wearing pink. They laughed about it.

He took her to a place called The Chauncey's Pub for breakfast. It was a lively place, and it seemed that everyone there knew him. He introduced her to them all.

She ordered the breakfast special. When it came, she couldn't believe her eyes. The platter was almost overflowing. The chicken fried steak was easily five inches wide and ten inches long, covered with country gravy with sausage bits in it. There was a pile of hash browns so big, she knew she couldn't eat them all, let alone the three eggs and toast that came with it.

While she was looking at the plater full of food, Robb Michael started laughing. She looked up at him and said, "Is this for real?"

The waitress said, "Robb Michael, tell her she has to eat the whole thing."

It was delicious. Even so, she ate less than half of the steak, only one egg, and a small portion of the potatoes.

When Robb Michael paid the bill, the waitress put the rest in a take home box and gave it to her, saying, "Take this with you. Now, I put a plastic knife and fork in there so when you get up to the freeway entrance, there will be a man standing there with a sign saying he's homeless and hungry. You can give this to him. Now don't even think about it. We get rid of all our garbage that way. That's why we don't have a garbage can."

Joanna looked shocked. "Is she serious?"

Robb Michael smiling shook his head negatively, and said, "Come along, time to go. There's places I want to take you."

Joanna sat watching him as he drove towards the freeway.

As they were turning onto the ramp she said, "Stop by the panhandler."

He was holding a sign that said 'Homeless, hungry. Please help. God bless.' She saw Robb Michael watching her as he stopped the car.

Joanna powered the window down and called the man over and said, "Here's a nice breakfast for you."

Bewildered the man looked at her and then hesitantly said, "Uh, okay."

As they drove away, Robb Michael said, "That was a very noble thing to do. If you keep feeding the world's hungry, you might even be canonized."

Then smiling he said, "Did you notice the new Nike shoes and how clean his old clothes were? I wonder how he manages to keep that pathetic look on his face."

Joanna looked back at him, smiled, and said, "If you had his pouch and midriff bulge, you would look pathetic, too."

They both laughed as he turned onto Highway 213.

THE NORTH FORK SANTIAM

After having driven through the countryside for an hour and a half, Joanna decided they were either going somewhere, or they were taking the long way back to the compound.

When they drove into a small town called Mill City, he pulled over and parked the car.

He pointed out a nice looking house a couple blocks away, down by the river.

"I own that place. I was born and raised in that house there by the river. I used to go fishing in that river every morning before school. Every morning I ate trout and eggs for breakfast. I still fish that river. I pulled a stint in the Navy. I've sailed all over the world, but that river was, and is, the most important waterway in my life. This is the North Fork Santiam River.

If I wasn't fishing after school, I was swimming in a tributary called the little North Fork Santiam. I want to take you there."

She looked at him. He gave her a strange look, then said, "We drove past it getting here." Joanna watched him as he drove slowly through town.

He stopped and bought four blankets and half a dozen bath towels at one store, and then stopped at a small market.

As they went into the market, he asked, "If you were going to have a picnic, what would you prepare?"

"Chicken, potato salad, I don't know. Are we going to have a picnic?" He looked at her questioningly. "Yeah, I think so."

He bought deep fried chicken, potato salad, macaroni salad, cheese crackers, root beer, and a smoked ring sausage, a salt and pepper shaker, a jar of jalapeño peppers, two cans of Pork and Beans, and some brown mustard.

He drove for about twenty minutes to a pleasant, wooded area with lots of trees and underbrush.

After stopping the car, he got out, got the blankets, and then started walking toward the river.

Joanna, carrying the food, found herself following him as he walked down to the river's edge.

He took two of the blankets and spread them out about ten feet from the water, one on top of the other. He motioned for her to sit on the blankets.

Then he asked, "Do you want to swim first or eat?"

"I didn't bring a swim suit," she replied.

"You don't need one. Your panties and bra will work."

She looked at him. "What are you going to wear?"

"My shorts, they look more like a bathing suit than underwear.

She watched him as he sat in a lounging position on the blankets. He was looking up at her as she set the food down on one corner of the blankets.

Then she sat on the blankets herself. She looked at him thoughtfully. "Why have you brought me here?"

"I wanted you to see from where I came. I grew up in this area. My father was a doctor here. He made house calls to all the surrounding towns in this area. We lived in Mill City, but my father practiced medicine here and Gates, Mahama, Lions, and even Detroit up past the two dams on the north fork of the Santiam River."

Joanna watched him as he spoke.

"Somehow my father managed to secure a full boat scholarship into Harvard Medical School for me. My first year at Harvard, I was younger than most. I fell in with a bunch of business investors. I learned from them. I started investing. I was under age so I had to hire an agent to make my business transactions for me. I managed to earn enough from my investments that I could have paid my own way through the next six years of school."

He was silent for a moment. Then he reached into the bag of food and withdrew a chicken leg and a container of macaroni salad. She watched him as he opened the jar of peppers and stabbed a plastic fork into the contents.

"Aren't those peppers too hot to eat?" she asked.

He took a bite out of the pepper, and then the chicken leg. He chewed and swallowed before he began to speak again. "No, they're not bad. Do you know how to tell if peppers are too hot to eat?"

She looked at him and shook her head and said, "No."

He smiled at her and said, "You stab a fork into the peppers and pull one out of the jar. If the tines of the fork start to melt, it goes without saying, the peppers are too hot to eat."

She laughed and said, "Shut up and finish telling me about your father."

He opened a can of Pork and Beans, looked at her, and said, "My father was very disappointed in me. He told me several times that he sent me to school to become a doctor, not an investor."

He was silent for a moment. "I can't remember the number of times he let me know that I was a disappointment. I may have been playing the market, but I finished school at the top of my class. He was a man with old-fashioned beliefs. He couldn't understand why I would be paying more attention to the stock market than to medicine. I didn't know I was. Even in med school, I was doing research on genetic disorders along with medical studies. When I finished med school, I was set financially, so I joined the Navy.

"After six years, I got out. I built the Holly Street Clinic in Portland, up on a 102nd and Holly. The clinic is actually a small hospital. Then my father couldn't understand why I rented all the offices to other doctors. In the whole of my life, I have only practiced on special cases, pioneering new surgical procedures."

She watched him as he prepared the ring sausage. He cut the sausage into two-inch pieces. Then he made a shallow cut lengthwise and peeled the transparent skin off the meat.

He told her to hold the sausage between her thumb and index fingers, while holding a bottle of root beer in her left hand, and the cheese crackers in her right hand. That way she could choose which to take a bite of or drink without setting anything down.

When she started eating, she looked at the way he had showed her how to hold everything. Then she raised her eye brows, smiled, and began to eat. While they ate lunch, they talked about everything and anything, working their way into each other's minds.

They went swimming. The water was cold.

While swimming, they swam down to a bridge that made a *lapity lapity lap* sound every time a car or truck went across it.

She watched him as they swam under the bridge. She heard him say, "One time I threw my best friend off this bridge. After I threw him in, I had to jump in to rescue him. Because he screamed all the way down, I didn't know if he could swim. It turned out that Eli Nelson—that's his name—could swim better than me. Strange thing, it made him madder than hell when I threw him in. Whenever I mention it to this day, the way Papa Eli reacts—Papa Eli is what I call him—I can't help but believe he's still mad at me."

She looked at him seriously, "Did you push him?"

He laughed at her question. "No, I picked him up and tossed him over the rail. When he screamed all the way down to the water, it surprised me because Eli Nelson is the most fearless man I've ever met. To this day, he's not afraid to mix it up with two or more in a fight.

There were several times I've had to watch his back when he was fighting. I love the guy, and I'm not afraid to say so. Ever since junior high school, he's been one of my closest friends."

Quietly they swam back to where the blankets were spread out. As she come out of the water, she suddenly felt cold. She watched him spread the other two blankets on top of the first two blankets. Through his wet underwear, she could see his thick member.

She heard him say, "Get under the blankets and take off your wet things so you can get warm."

She did as he asked.

Then he got under the blanket and removed his wet clothes. While they were warming themselves under the blankets, they talked for quite a while about childhood experiences and the growing pains that seem to detour the best made plans at those ages.

She felt warmth from his body heat and snuggled closer to him, saying, "Why are you so much warmer than me?"

She felt him wrap his arms around her, and then he rolled her over on top of him. "I just know how to get warm, especially when there's a girl nearby."

She felt his manhood stiffen and thought, *He wants to do it again.* She was looking into his eyes when she opened herself to him. He rolled her onto her back and then slowly entered her.

Then he started making long, slow movements. She clung to him as he continued to make the slow movements.

Then she thought, *this is what I was made for. But am I sure I should be doing this?*

She saw his hand come up. Using the back of his hand, he brushed the auburn hair away from a green eye.

Suddenly she felt dizzy, and knew that she was having an orgasm. She felt weak. She could no longer cling to him and relaxed her arms.

He never stopped. He continued the long, slow movements for a long while.

Suddenly she felt it building up inside her once again, as the dizzy spell seemed to envelope her.

She felt him push farther into her, then felt his warmth fill her. They laid there for a long moment, not speaking.

Suddenly she asked, "Are we going to be alright?"

"We must," he replied. Then quieter, he spoke again. "We must." She felt him cling to her.

He held her for several minutes, whispering near her ear. He was whispering so quietly she couldn't hear what he said.

He pulled out of her and rolled off her.

With one hand between her legs, she got out from under the blankets and walked out into the river.

She looked back at him. He was leaning on one elbow, watching her.

It was the first time she had seen him look at her, all of her, as she washed herself in the little North Fork Santiam River.

MILL CITY

As they were driving, she asked if he would stop at the house he grew up in. He turned the car around and drove back toward Mill City. When they arrived, he unlocked the door and showed her in.

She looked around the place curiously. Wandering through the house, she marveled at the simplicity of the place.

When they entered the bedroom, he came up behind her and put his arms around her and cupped her breasts with his hands, and said, "You want to try out the bed?"

She looked back at him and said, "I'm your sex slave, remember?"

After they made love, she felt him get up. She watched him get dressed and walk out of the room.

She felt so comfortable that she lay there and dozed for another half hour before she got up and went looking for him.

She found him sitting on the river bank, fishing. "Are you catching anything?"

He turned and looked at her, "They're hitting pretty good. I got five. I'll stop and clean them, and take them home for breakfast."

BACK AT THE COMPOUND

They returned to the compound at about eight-thirty in the evening and snacked on some of the food left over from the picnic.

Robb Michael sliced the ring sausage while Joanna opened a box of cheese crackers and the potato salad.

While they were eating, Robb Michael opened the jar of peppers and two cans of root beer to wash it down.

After they had eaten, she got up and put the leftovers and chicken in the refrigerator. They sat quietly at the kitchen table for a while. She turned to him and said, "You can stay the night again, if you like."

After making love, he fell asleep. She got up and turned on a computer, then she sent Kathy Bates an email. 'You may have to help me. I've fallen in love with my soul mate. I don't know if I'm supposed to.'

After sending the email, she thought about the house on the edge of the river. Robb Michael had made love to her there for over an hour. The way he made love to her, she felt that something was driving him. Then she did research for an hour before returning to bed.

When she climbed into bed, he reached for her and pulled her close. She started to say something, then she realized he was still asleep. She fell asleep in the comfort his arms.

NEXT MORNING

When she awakened, she knew she was still lying in his arms. She felt so comfortable she wanted to stay there.

She looked into his face. His eyes were closed, but she knew he was awake. "Are you going to make love to me? Or are you just going to lay there and think about it?"

He rolled her over on top of her. "I've thought about it long enough."

After they made love, they washed each other under the four-head shower stall in the exercise gym. The shower heads were almost three feet higher than her head.

With the water plastering them from four sides, she looked up at him. He was looking back at her. She knew she must look awful. Her reddish-brown hair was plastered to her head.

Suddenly he cupped her head with his hands and kissed her passionately as the water assaulted them mercilessly.

After they showered, he picked her up and carried her over and threw her into the deep end of the pool.

She came back up, spluttering. "Damn you, Robb Michael!" she yelped. "I wasn't expecting that!"

"Too bad," he said as he dove in and pulled her over to the pool's edge.

They frolicked in the water for over an hour. When they decided to get out, he went over to a nearby towel closet and took out a couple towels. First, he roughly toweled her off, and then dried himself.

Once again he picked her up. "Am I going back in the water?"

"No, not this time," he said as he carried her through the kitchen and back down the dark hallway to the bedroom.

He placed her on the bed. As he climbed in after her, he said, "We need a little more exercise."

After they made love, she asked, "Is it okay if we fall in love?"

"This is an experiment in human endeavor. I don't know the answer to your question. Anything you want to do, I suppose, I don't know. It might not be a good idea, but I must make note of it."

She got out of bed and went into the bathroom. When she returned, she saw he had fallen asleep.

She got back in bed and snuggled up to him. *I don't know if I should fall in love. God! I think I already have!* she thought. *I wonder if he was serious about what he said.*

Once again he reached for her in his sleep, and once again, Joanna Kimble fell asleep in the comfort of his arms.

MORNING SEX

When she awoke, she was alone in the bed. She got up and, without dressing, walked down the dark hall toward the kitchen. There she saw him with his back to her, sitting at the kitchen table reading a newspaper.

Suddenly he said, "*Momma Mia* is playing at the Auditorium. Would you like to go?"

She thought for a moment and then said, "How did you know I was behind you?"

"I don't know. I just knew."

She walked up behind him, put her arms around his neck, and said, "I'd love to go. What time does it start?"

He turned to face her, found himself facing a pair of bare breasts, and said, "It starts at seven, so we should leave here at five so we can get parked, and seated, before the show starts." Then he said, "Are you ready for more?"

She pulled his face into her breasts and said, "Remember the deal? It was forever, remember?"

With that they followed the tiny, little lights of the dark hallway to the bedroom once again.

After they made love, he got up and went into the kitchen.

He prepared trout and eggs with hash browns for breakfast. She had never had trout and eggs for breakfast before. She loved it.

AFTER THE SHOW

As they were coming out of the theater, everyone around them was commenting on what a great show it was.

It seemed everywhere they went almost everyone there knew Robb Michael. Everyone seemed to gather around him, wanting attention. It seemed to Joanna that Robb Michael took the time to greet every one of them.

As she watched him, he suddenly turned to her and said, "I'm sorry, Joanna, I seem to be popular all of a sudden. Please have patience with me just a little bit longer. I see a man that owes me some nickels."

Joanna followed him as he walked over to a man standing in a group, talking. As they approached the group, Robb Michael said, "I see James Reader."

A man turned and said, "Well, I'll be damned! How the hell are ya, Robb Michael?"

Before Robb Michael could answer the man, he turned to the group and said, "Everyone, I want you to meet Robb Michael, the best client I've ever had."

After greetings all around, James Reader said, "One thing you never want to do is wager against this man. He always wins."

He then spotted Joanna and said, "My God, Robb Michael! This one is gorgeous! Where did you find her?"

Robb Michael never answered him. Instead, he turned to Joanna, closed one eye in a long wink, and quietly said, "I'll wager a nickel I can make this man pay me in nickels. Do we have a wager?"

She looked at him with disbelief on her face. Meekly she said, "No."

Robb Michael turned back to James Reader and said, "Speaking of wagers, I believe you owe me seven nickels."

"By God, I believe you're right. Here, I'll pay you right now."

With that, James Reader reached in his pocket and pulled out some change. He handed Robb Michael a dime and a quarter, and said, "There, we're even."

Robb Michael looked at the coins and said, "Ah, no! This is thirty-five cents. What you owe me is seven nickels."

The man looked at him and said, "Robb Michael, seven nickels is thirty-five cents."

Robb Michael looked at the man and said, "James, the wagers were for a nickel. Therefore, I feel I should be paid in nickels."

Joanna felt her face flush. She knew Robb Michael was controlling the situation. She started to laugh uncontrollably. Tears started streaming down her face as James Reader took the coins out of Robb Michael's hand. Still laughing, Joanna sat down on the sidewalk to keep from falling down.

Watching through teary eyes, she saw James Reader reach into his pocket and pull out his change. He handed Robb Michael a nickel, then turned to the group and asked if anyone could change a quarter for some nickels. A woman in the group took the quarter and gave him three nickels and a dime, which he promptly gave the nickels to Robb Michael.

Concerned, James asked, "Is she alright?"

Robb Michael looked down at her straight faced and said, "Oh, yes. I'm sure she is." Then held out his hand for more nickels. James then asked if anyone could change a dime for two nickels. Another man took the dime and gave him two nickels, which again James gave to Robb Michael.

Reaching in his pocket and pulling out more change, he looked at it and asked if anyone had a nickel for five pennies. A man walking by gave him a nickel and told him to keep his pennies.

James thanked the man and gave the nickel to Robb Michael. In the meantime, Joanna stopped laughing and was wiping her eyes with a tissue. A man reached for her to help her up when Robb Michael, shaking his finger at him, said, "Don't touch her. She's not through laughing yet."

Turning to James Reader, he said, "James, I have a great deal of admiration for you. It isn't everyone that can rally his friends and get money from them, and a total stranger to pay his gambling debts. You'll always be in good stead with me."

Suddenly Joanna started laughing all over again.

With that Robb Michael reached down, picked her up, slung her over his shoulder, her breasts almost coming out of the top of the gown she was wearing, and carried her toward the parking garage. She was still laughing when the valet brought his car around.

He set her down and was opening a door for her when a woman came running up to them, and tearfully said, "Doctor, I want to thank you. Thank you so very much. I don't know how I can ever repay you."

Robb Michael looked at the woman with a gentle smile on his face. "It's alright, Mrs. Anderson. The fact everything turned out well is all the thanks I need."

The woman, with tears streaming down her face, looked at Joanna. "Your husband saved my son's life! And he never charged us anything! He wouldn't let us pay!"

Embarrassed, she hastily walked away. Joanna solemnly watched him as he watched the woman walk away. Quietly he got in behind the wheel of the car.

After they had driven for awhile, she asked, "Is there anything you won't do?"

After a long pause, he said, "Silly girl, you shouldn't ask questions about things you already know the answer to."

"Will you take me home and make love to me?"

Another long pause, "Silly girl, what did I just say?"

Joanna smiled and thought, *Good God! I've never seen anyone so confident in my life!*

LATER THAT NIGHT

After they made love, she got up and went to the bathroom. When she returned, she lay down beside him.

Quiet for a moment, she said, "That guy, James Reader. He said something that hit a nerve. He asked you, 'Where did you find this one?' That bothered me."

She paused and then asked, "Does everybody know you've had a different woman in your bed every day?"

"I'm afraid so. My reputation extends all the way back to my days at Harvard. I've had a strong sex drive since I was very young. Today they say people that have a strong sex drive are sex addicts. Male or female, they say we're sex addicts. I've never felt like an addict. But when I'm in the mood, I want sex. I'm just in the mood more often than other people."

"What's the most times you've had sex in one day?" Joanna asked.

"I don't know. I've never kept track."

A long pause, and then, "How many girls have you been in bed with at one time?"

"Five. I was invited to a party by the patient of a colleague. When I got to where the party was, I discovered the party was me and five girls. Later one of them told me they had gotten together and planned it."

Quizzically she said, "You had sex with each of them?"

"Yes. We were playing sex games well into the daylight hours of the following morning. During the night, I saw those girls do things I didn't know they would do to each other, not to mention what they were doing to me to keep me going."

Interested she asked, "Like what?"

He thought for a moment and said, "Use your imagination."

"I'd rather you tell me," she said, smiling.

"Well, I can honestly say I had a pussy eating contest with two of them."

Joanna felt her face flush and said, "Why?"

"Because I wanted to win. I thought I did, but they said I lost. They said, 'Whoever takes the longest to get their girl off is the winner.'"

Joanna was quiet for a moment, and then said, "How many girls have you had sex with?"

It was his turn to be quiet for a moment.

"Possibly as many as a hundred a year."

Then she asked, "Are you going to keep having sex with other women?"

"Would it bother you if I do?"

She thought for a moment, and said, "Me first!"

Changing the subject, he asked, "How many times did we make love today?"

"Five."

Seriously, he asked, "Am I too much for you?"

"No. Sometimes when we're involved in a marathon of sex, my insides ache, my breasts ache from being sucked on, and my jaws ache from sucking on you. Sometimes when you suck on me orally for a long period of time, and get me off repeatedly, I can feel sensations in my clitoris every time I take a step. Even then I can't help but feel I've never felt better in my life."

As he listened to her, he interrupted, "Are you ready to go again?"

"Sure!" she answered, "Anytime! I just found out I'm a sex addict!

SIX WEEKS LATER

Joanna was pacing the floor, waiting for Robb Michael to arrive. She went back to her computer. Scrolling up and down, she studied the figures she had been researching. She sensed him rather than heard him when he came in.

Without looking at him, she said, "I've noticed that you seem to have connections with darn near everyone. Do you have any connections with anyone in the Med Keandra Group?"

"Yes, as a matter of fact, I do. I thought you knew I do. Why do you ask?"

"Because they should be warned. They've got an embezzler that's siphoning off millions."

"How did you come to that conclusion?" Robb Michael asked.

"If you look here at their profit margin, against the dividends paid to each shareholder, it doesn't match. The dividends paid comes to less than the profit margin, less net of operating costs. I don't know how much less. It's not a lot per individual shareholder, but it's still quite a lot over all. Whoever is doing this is getting fat city."

She turned to look at him.

The instant she saw his face, she saw pride. She could tell. He was really proud of her.

She asked, "What did I do?"

"Nothing much. It may well be that you've saved that company millions of dollars. I'll get in touch with someone I know and see if there's something to it."

Joanna was getting dressed. Robb Michael had told her they were going out for dinner. He knew she liked Chez Henri's, famous for their crawfish, so he took her there. They had crab cocktails, then had their fill on steak, shrimp, and crab legs. After dinner and drinks, they went back to the compound. They went for a dip in the pool.

After frolicking in the pool for more than two hours, they showered. He picked her up and carried her into the bedroom, and there he made love to her for more than an hour. They had slept for about three hours when she felt a buzzing. She felt around and found his phone vibrating under her on the bed.

Opening the phone, she heard a female voice say, "Doctor! You are needed at the hospital!" She woke him up and told him. Silently he got up and dressed. Just as silently he left. Joanna lay in her bed, wide awake. She felt lonely.

She wasn't wearing anything. Silently she threw the covers back and got out of bed. Without dressing she went out to the living room and sat at her computer. She still felt lonely. For a few hours, she busied herself doing research. When she couldn't stand it anymore, she laid on the couch and went to sleep.

Suddenly she awoke to find him looking down at her. He reached down and took her by the hand and pulled her to her feet.

She looked at him. He looked tired. His eyes were bloodshot, and he needed a shave. He put his arms around her and held her. They stood in the middle of the room while he held her, not saying anything. She still wasn't wearing anything.

Hand in hand he led her into the bedroom. Once there, he went into the bathroom, showered and shaved. When he came out, he said, "This night I would not like to live over," then climbed into bed and drew her to him. Exhausted, he fell asleep.

The way he was holding her, she felt comfortable and didn't want to move. She wasn't lonely anymore. She knew it had been a bad day.

Remembering the woman at the parking garage, she wondered if he had saved another life.

NEXT MORNING
Joanna awoke to find him talking on his cell phone. From what she was hearing, she guessed him to be checking on a patient's condition. She got up and went into the bathroom. When she came out, he had put on his trousers. He looked to be in deep thought. She went over to him. He reached for her and pulled her close.

He sat down on the bed and then buried his face between her breasts. In a near whisper, she heard him say, "Her vital signs aren't good. I wonder why she is still alive?" All the while he was clinging to her tightly.

Then she heard him say, "Joanna, I have a bed at the hospital. But last night, tired as I was, I couldn't stay there. I had to come here. Stay close to me, Joanna. I need you to stay close to me!"

She heard his phone vibrate on the night stand. "Robb Michael, your phone's ringing."

She saw him reach for his phone next to his glasses. When he answered, he said, "Yes? Yes, Mr. Kahn. I think I'm going to lose this one. It's tearing me apart. What I saw in that baby was horrific. No, her vital signs aren't anywhere near what they should be. They're a long way from being good. I don't know if I can face her parents when she goes. Yes, Mr. Kahn, she's standing right here."

"Joanna, Mr. Kahn would like to talk to you."

Taking the phone, Joanna said, "Hello?"

"Joanna, I don't know if you remember me. My name is Douglas Kahn. I am Robb Michael's friend and attorney. It's very important that you listen to me and do as I say. You must get him away from there. Take him somewhere. Anywhere. Somewhere he can be away from his thoughts. He did a rough surgery last night. There's a good chance the patient won't make it. I know this man well. He got too close to this one. If this little girl dies, it might push him over the edge. You've got to get him away. Think of someplace and take him there. Can you do that?"

Joanna looked at Robb Michael and suddenly felt confident. "Yes, I can do that."

"Good! Take him now!" With that she heard the phone go dead.

"Who is Douglas Kahn?"

"He is my lawyer, and possibly the best friend I have," he answered.

"If he's your friend, why do you call him mister?" she asked.

He studied her face for a moment, and then said, "Because he holds a very important position with the companies. As such, he is entitled to be addressed formally, especially when other people are near."

"Am I supposed to do as he says?"

He looked like he was trying to gather his thoughts, and then said, "I think you should. He's the reason you're here. He's the one that came up with your name as a candidate. Why? What did he tell you to do?"

Softly, she said, "He told me to have you take me to the little North Fork Santiam River and fuck you until you can't stand up, several times today."

He turned and looked at her. "He actually said that?"

She looked back at him and said, "Pretty much. Come on, let's get dressed and get out of here."

THE LITTLE NORTH FORK SANTIAM

Joanna drove on their way down to Mill City. She had never driven his car before. As she drove, she heard him call the hospital four times before they got to Mill City.

If he's still calling, the girl hasn't died yet, she thought.

As before, they stopped at a store and bought cheese crackers, a smoked ring sausage, root beer, and deep fried chicken. This time he didn't buy any hot peppers.

Joanna couldn't remember how to get to the swimming spot on the river, so she told Robb Michael to drive.

After they arrived, Robb Michael parked the car up near the road.

He then watched incredulously while she stood between the car and the road and pulled off her clothes.

After she had removed all her clothes, she held out her arms and said, "I'm ready! Why aren't you?"

She saw him watching her breasts sway as she reached in the car and brought out a plastic bag. A little above a whisper she heard him say, "Thank God for gravity."

She put her hand in the bag and brought out a bathing suit. First, she slipped the bottoms on. Then she took a top that looked big enough, but when she put it on, it was obvious that it wasn't near big enough.

Her breasts overflowed the cups. With that, and breasts jiggling, she started marching down the road, toward the bridge.

Robb Michael slipped off his clothes down to his shorts and went striding after her.

When he caught up with her, she was standing in the middle of the bridge, looking down at the river. Without looking at him she asked, "How far is it down to the water?"

"Twenty to thirty feet, maybe a little farther, I don't know."

She heard a car coming. When she turned to look at the car, Robb Michael picked her up and tossed her over the railing.

On the way down she yelled, "Damn you, Robb Michael!"

She hit the water like a canon ball and was plunging down toward the bottom of the river with her arms over her head. Her top slipped off.

She heard a noise and looked up to see Robb Michael swimming down toward her. She felt him grab her by the wrist as she was going down and start dragging her upward.

She never touched the bottom. She started kicking her feet on the way up to the surface. When they reached the surface, she had her arms around his neck.

She was about to say something when she heard a female voice up above them say, "Are you alright down there?"

Joanna looked up at two women looking over the railing and said, "I don't know yet. I just got here."

The woman yelled back down to her, "We thought we saw a murder-suicide."

Robb Michael started laughing. She turned to him and said, "I knew you would think that was funny."

"It was!" he laughed.

They started swimming for the beach at the river's edge.

As they got there, she was walking out of the water when she noticed the top of her bathing suit was gone.

She never covered herself. She just started walking up toward the road, where the car was parked.

As they got in the car, Robb Michael looked at her and said, "You know, your tits are hanging out."

"Really? I didn't think you would notice."

He started the car and drove it down into the parking area, near the river's edge.

When they got out, she watched as he opened the trunk and got the blankets and towels. He carried them down near the waters edge while she brought the food.

After he had the blankets spread out, he got under them and asked, "Are you going to get under the blankets with me?"

Without saying anything, she got under the blankets and pulled them over her head.

Then she lay her head on his belly and took him into her mouth, thinking, *thank you, Mr. Douglas Kahn, for making me prove my worth!*

ON THE WAY HOME

After making love, they decided to leave. They never ate the lunch they bought. Along the way, she heard him call and check on the girl at least four times.

As they neared Portland, he told her to drop him off at the Keandra Surgical Hospital.

Joanna nodded her head and said, "Is that little girl going to make it?"

"The life force in that baby is very strong. It refuses to leave her body. Her vital signs haven't changed in eight hours. She should have died six or seven hours ago."

"What was wrong with her?"

"That baby's body was full of tumors.

She had over twenty tumors in her stomach and her intestinal track, plus three more on one of her kidneys. I started cutting them out. I removed one of her kidneys. The more I cut, the more I found. With all the cutting I had to do, she shouldn't have survived it. They just told me that her parents are still at hospital."

She looked at him. "Are you going to be alright?"

"Joanna, I'm scared! I'm always scared when I do one of these surgeries. I've never lost a patient! Every time I do one of these surgeries, I feel the patient's going to die before I even start."

Joanna dropped him off at the hospital entrance. She then drove to the parking lot and parked the car.

When she entered the hospital, she went straight to the intensive care unit.

As she got there, she saw Robb Michael talking to a young couple in the waiting room.

Robb Michael turned and looked at her, then excused himself. He came over to her and said, "Please, stay with me. Once again I had to tell these people that their baby may not make it."

She caressed him sympathetically. She felt his arms go around her. This was the first time she saw him when he wasn't confident.

While he held her, an attractive nurse came up to them and said, "Doctor, your patient is awake."

He looked toward the nurse and said, "Thank you." Then he let go of Joanna.

As he went into intensive care, the attractive nurse gave Joanna a cool look of appraisal, then she followed Robb Michael. As Joanna watched her following him, she knew she had just seen someone that had been in Robb Michael's bed.

On the way to the compound, she asked, "Is the little girl going to be alright?"

"I don't know. I'm just now finding reason to hope. I don't know why she's still alive."

He didn't look at her while he drove.

When he drove to the door of the compound, he stopped the car, then asked, "Is it okay if I stay with you? I don't want to be alone."

She opened her door.

As she got out of the car, she said, "I'm here forever, remember?"

Then she thought about the day, and every bizarre thing he had done since she met him. She thought about the night he kidnapped her, the picnic by the river, and making love in the little house by the river.

Then she thought about how he picked her up and threw her off the bridge. *The more he does, the more I love him*, she thought.

Almost absently pointing at a garage door. He said, "Your car is behind that door. The code to open the door is five, one, seven."

Then she thought, *I'm not going anywhere.*

When Joanna awoke the next morning, she was alone in the king-sized bed. As she started to crawl out of bed, she noticed a note folded over the clock.

She picked it up and read, 'Gone to hospital. Baby's going to live. When the baby awoke up this morning, she said she's hungry. That's a plus! See you later. Thank you for being there.'

LATER THAT DAY

Joanna was working at her computer when Robb Michael came into the compound, carrying a vase of flowers.

He came over and set the vase on one end of her desk. She turned and looked at him, "What are the flowers for?"

"You, my way of saying thank you for staying with me when I needed you.

"I allowed myself to become too stressed out on this case. You stayed with me, helped me through it. Thank you."

She looked at him and smiled. "I believe I told you, I'm here forever, remember?"

Joanna leaned back in her desk chair and said, "Can I ask you about something?"

"Yes. Anything you would like to know."

She looked at him seriously. "That attractive nurse that was up at intensive care. Was she one of those that shared your bed?"

"She is one I like more than most. Her name is Julie Lane. Yes, I took her out a few times. She's a strange one. She has never asked me for anything, but she always seems to be there for me, yet she seems to be distant.

"I took her to see *Miss Saigon*. The play was a tear jerker. I think that you would like it too. Why do you ask?"

Joanna paused for a moment and then said, "The way she looked at me. It was as though she was wondering what I had that she didn't. I think she wanted more with you."

"Possibly she did, but I didn't feel I could give her more. Let me tell you something, Joanna. Years ago, when I was just getting started with this organization, I met a very attractive woman. I started taking her out, and I was getting pretty serious about her.

"Then one day I happened to overhear her talking to another woman. She was telling this other woman how she was going to be set for life because my last name is the same as my shirt-tail relative. After that, I would ask a different woman out every night because I couldn't be sure what their motives were.

"Once in a while, if I liked the girl, I would take her out a few times. I took Julie out several times. I may take her out again.

"One day you may have to live the same way. That worked out fairly well for me. I was always so busy, I never had time for a quality relationship anyhow."

Joanna looked at him seriously. "Did you ever feel you missed out on something? Just because you never got to know anyone better?"

He sat on the edge of her desk and closed his eyes, with his head bowed. "I realize it now that I've gotten to know you. However, some of those relationships were disastrous. I wouldn't want anymore with them.

"Even so, now I wish I would have shared more with some of them. At the time, I didn't know what I was missing, so it didn't matter.

"Since I've come to know you, I've learned so much, I sometimes wish I could have met you ten years sooner."

Joanna looked up at him and thought, *I have the same wish, my darling.* Then she thought, *I wonder if I didn't agree to the second program if he would have asked Julie Lane.*

But she said, "If you're hungry, I can fix us something to eat."

He opened his eyes and smiled at her. "Thank you. I would like that."

THREE DAYS LATER

Joanna, as usual, was wearing only a robe while she was working at her desk. She looked down and smiled. She sensed him coming up behind her. Patiently she waited for him to say something or touch her.

Robb Michael came up behind her, reached into her robe and started caressing her breasts. While doing that, he said, "Why don't we go into the bedroom and make love on the floor? When we're done, we can make up a lunch and go have a picnic. I know where there is a beautiful house where we can sit on their lawn and eat our lunch. Now, if you don't wear any underwear, we can make love on their lawn when we finish our lunch.

"You know the blankets are still in the car, so the only things missing are the sandwiches and the cheese crackers and the smoked ring sausage.

"What do you say?"

She smiled. "Ask me after we get finished on the floor."

Joanna made up a lunch, and they got in the car and drove down the long driveway to the road. But this time he turned the opposite way than usual.

They stopped at a supermarket and bought a couple hundred dollars' worth of groceries.

Then Robb Michael drove around the hilly area until they came to a large house on a hill. It was a bright, sunlit day, and the sunlight seemed to hit the house just right.

Joanna looked at the house and sighed. "You can buy me a house just like this one. With the snow roof, it looks like a chalet. My God! It's gorgeous! Do you suppose they would sell it?"

"I imagine they would if you offered enough money."

She looked around at the surroundings around the place. The driveway was wider than a two-lane road. There was a turn-around in front of the house.

Across the driveway from the house was a paved parking lot that looked like it had space enough to park forty cars.

The way the place was designed you couldn't see the parking lot from the street.

There was a hedge growing on the street side of the parking lot with tall trees all over the property.

She turned toward Robb Michael. "You know, I've got an idea. Let's ask your shirt-tail relative to buy it for us."

"We best not. Right now he's not too happy with me. He believes that I'm treating you terribly. He thinks I'm not paying enough attention to you. He could go on and on about it until you are tired of listening about it."

Joanna looked at him incredulously. "No! You have never treated me badly. I'll tell him that! I've never been happier in my life than I have been with you, and I'll tell him that, too!"

Robb Michael reached over and touched her face with his fingers. "Let's get the lunch you made and eat."

Joanna smiled. "Do we have to eat all of that food you bought?"

"Whatever we don't eat we'll take home." Then smiling, he said, "We'll have leftovers for months, or until the rest of the food is gone."

Robb Michael spread out a blanket, while Joanna laid out the food.

After they had eaten, Robb Michael said, "Joanna, take off your clothes." Joanna looked around and then said, "Right here?"

"Yes, right here."

As she removed her clothes, he also undressed.

Then he laid her down, and while nuzzling her ear, he entered her.

He made love to her with slow movements while whispering in her ear.

"I want the cantankerous old goat to see that I'm treating you right."

"Do you think that he can see us?"

"I think so. This is his place. He lives in that house!"

Suddenly, she said, "Oh, God! I'm having an orgasm!" She cried, "If you're telling me the truth, I'm going to kill you!"

ONE MONTH LATER

Joanna sat at her computer desk, trying to research, but couldn't bring herself to pay attention to what she was doing.

She was waiting for Robb Michael. He hadn't been there all day. Sometimes it was like that. He wouldn't show up until late. When she heard him come in, it was almost eight o'clock.

He came over and sat on the edge of the desk as she leaned back in her desk chair and looked up at him.

He looked at her and smiled. "Sorry. It seems I'm leaving you alone more and more. Do you need anything?"

She looked at him seriously. "Yes."

"What do you need?"

She looked at him, watching for his reaction. "You once told me that you could save anyone's life but your own. Well, I need you to save mine. I'm going to have a baby, and I'm Catholic!

"Well, you know the rest of that story. With this situation, I'm not supposed to be not married. So, save my life. Can you do that?"

He smiled as if smiling to himself, and said, "Believe it or not, I can do that."

"Well, now I'm curious. How?"

"Well, I'm hungry enough I could eat you, or we could go out and eat. Then I can get on the phone and make arrangements to save your life.

"Now, I must do this delicately, or I'm going to have the whole medical world mad at me. And if they don't get mad at me, the Catholic world most certainly will. Trust me! I can do this!

"Believe in me! I can save you! The church may hate me forever if I don't do this right. Oh, hell, they're going to hate me forever anyhow."

She interrupted, "If you aren't going to tell me, tell me what we're going to eat! I'm starving!"

He frowned at her. "If we hurry, we can make it to Chez Henri's before they close."

She jumped up, smiling. "Okay! I'm ready!"

He smiled at her. "No, you're not! Not unless you want to wear that robe!"

She looked down at herself. "Give me one minute, and I'll be ready."

THREE DAYS LATER
ROBB MICHAEL BUYS HER A NEW NIGHTGOWN

It was after six o'clock when Robb Michael appeared.

Joanna was sitting at her desk, wearing nothing but a robe, when suddenly she felt his presence.

She was startled when she looked up and saw Robb Michael standing in front of her wearing nothing but a pink satin robe, belted at the waist with a purple belt, and a bright green satin tie tied loosely around his neck, with blue bunny slippers on his feet.

She started to laugh. Robb Michael, smiling, asked, "Why do you laugh at what I'm wearing?"

She laughed even harder. "Because what you're wearing matches the smile on your face." Then she laughed again.

Robb Michael, still smiling, handed her a purple shopping bag. "I want you to put this on."

She took the bag and took out the contents. There were a pair of slippers that looked like a pair of white rabbits, and a nightgown.

She gave him a quizzical look, and then slipped the robe off. She put the nightgown on. She could tell the gown was very expensive. It was white and went clear to the floor. It had a Victorian neckline, but was backless all the way down to her bottom. It had a little bit of a train, about two feet long, that dragged on the floor. It was sheer. You could see the dark outline of her areolas and the dark pubic area through the material.

He told her she had to wear the bunny slippers, too. Hearing that, she burst out laughing.

She looked at his bunny slippers, and laughed again. She put on the white bunny slippers. "Why are we wearing slippers?"

"We must wear slippers. We can't go outside bare-footed."

Almost panicky, she said, "We're going out?"

"Oh, yes. We must hurry or we'll be late. Now pick up your train. We must not let it drag on the ground."

Joanna picked up the train and started to follow him out the door. Then she stopped. "I have to be careful how I walk. I'm jiggling all over the place. Are you sure about this?"

"Certainly. Now go get in the car."

He held the car door for her as she got in.

As they were going down the long, narrow drive, she asked, "Where are we going?" "Milwaukie."

"What's in Milwaukie?"

"A big little to-do."

"And we have to be dressed like this?"

"Yes."

She looked over at him curiously. "What kind of a to-do is this?"

He kept his eyes on the road as he spoke. "It's kind of a ceremonial thing. Believe it or not, it was planned years ago."

"Were we invited years ago?"

"Ah…no. We were invited a day before yesterday." Twenty minutes later, they drove into Milwaukie.

Robb Michael drove through the middle of town and into the parking lot of a church, parking the car beside a new black Cadillac.

She looked around and asked, "We're getting out here?"

"Yes."

Almost panicky she said, "Dressed like this?"

"Yes. It's all been arranged."

She sat in the car for a moment, thinking, *this is going to be another one of those bizarre moments. I hope I survive this!*

A tall man, impeccably dressed in a black suit, got out of the black Cadillac.

She looked up at him, thinking that she knew him from somewhere.

Then he spoke, "Miss Kimble, how nice to see you again."

From behind her, she heard Robb Michael's voice. "Mr. Kahn, I'm so very happy to see you. Did you find everything?"

"Yes. I found all of the people and brought everything."

Turning to Joanna, Mr. Kahn said, "Let's go in."

Joanna was looking around in the bright sunlight. She looked up at the sharp sphere of the church and all the surroundings.

Robb Michael took her by the arm and led her around the building and into the church.

As they went through the door of the church, Kathy Bates came running up to her and threw her arms around her.

Surprised, Joanna hugged her back, saying, "Hi! Did you get invited to this shindig, too?"

Kathy stepped back and looked at her quizzically.

"Ah. Yeah. I was told that you needed a bridesmaid!"

Joanna gave her a vague look.

"A brides…"

Suddenly her eyes were wet, and she choked a little.

With tears streaming down her face, Joanna turned to look at Robb Michael.

He had something of a small smile on his face. "I would wager a nickel that you didn't actually believe I would save your life. You didn't believe I would, did you?"

Slowly she walked over to him.

Putting her arms around him, with her face against his throat, she started crying, thinking *I knew that he would do something. But not this!*

Teary eyed, she turned to look at Kathy, "Yes, I want you to be my bridesmaid."

Then she heard Robb Michael say, "Mr. Kahn, do you have a small box for me?"

Douglas Kahn reached in his suit coat pocket and his hand came out with a small box.

Robb Michael said, "Mr. Kahn, would you open it, please?" Douglas Kahn opened the box, and Robb Michael reached in the box and extracted an engagement ring.

The ring was a three-eights of an inch wide. It had half-carat diamonds all the way around it and a two-carat diamond placed on top, boxed in an odd stager with four, one-caret diamonds.

As Robb Michael was placing the ring on her finger, he said, "This ring asks a question. What do you think?"

Sheepishly, unbelievingly, she asked, "Are you really going to marry me?"

He had a small smile on his face again. "Silly girl. Didn't your mother ever tell you not to ask questions you already know the answer to?"

Without thinking she looked up at him and sheepishly said, "No."

"Well, I'm going to give your mother the opportunity to tell you. She's standing right behind you, along with your father. You didn't know that, did you?"

Joanna suddenly threw her arms and hands over her breasts. "With me dressed like this?"

Joanna turned to face her mother as she heard her mother's voice, saying, "He's right, you know. You shouldn't ask questions about something you already know the answer to."

As she was hugging her mother, her father said, "Don't worry about how you are dressed. Your future husband already told us how you would be dressed. He also told us to invite anyone that we thought might be interested, so we invited your sister. Phyllis and Eric should be here any minute."

They all moved into the church's interior. The pews were wood benches. They walked down the aisle, between the benches, and toward the center of the church, where they met the priest quietly listening to all their banter about their lives.

When Kathy asked, "Why do you want to marry this guy?"

Before Joanna could answer, she heard her older sister's voice, "Yeah Jo, why do you want to marry this guy?"

Joanna looked around at Robb Michael, Mr. Kahn, her parents, and then the priest. They all were looking at her, waiting for an answer.

Suddenly, slowly, she said, "Well, Phyl, he's the most exciting personality I've ever met! I mean ever!"

Phyllis asked, "What's the most exciting thing he has ever done with you?"

"Well, for one, he sprung this wedding on me. I didn't even know I was getting married until I got here!"

They all laughed.

Then Kathy asked, "What other exciting thing has he done?"

She saw Robb Michael was looking at her, smiling like a cat that got the cream. Joanna stood a little straighter, pushing her bust out a little farther.

Then she said, "Well, about six or seven weeks ago, he threw me off a bridge into the Little North Fork Santiam River.

Astonished, everyone was looking at her when suddenly the priest blurted out, "Damn you, Robb Michael! Why do you do that?"

Suddenly all eyes were on the priest.

Robb Michael started laughing as the priest suddenly blurted, "He threw me off the same bridge! He's always been smaller than me, but he's strong as a bear! He picked me up like I didn't weigh anything, and threw me off that same bridge!"

Kathy went over to Robb Michael, who was still laughing, and seriously said, "This isn't funny! You threw a priest off a bridge? How could you?"

Robb Michael, still laughing a little, said, "He wasn't a priest at the time. He was my best friend. We grew up together. He's still one of my closest friends. Besides, it seemed like the thing to do at the time.

"I give him the chance to get even once in a while. I even let him pick up the tab at lunch today."

Astonished, Joanna turned and faced the priest. "You're Papa Eli!"

She took his hand in hers. "He told me all about you. He told me that you never forgave him for throwing you off the bridge. Why not?"

Eli hesitated, then said, "I have vertigo! When I looked down from that bridge, the water looked like it was a thousand feet down. I thought I was going to die before I even hit the water."

Robb Michael stopped laughing. "If I would have known that you had vertigo, I would never have thrown you off that bridge. Why didn't you tell me?"

"Doc, don't ask questions. You're not my confessor. Joanna, do you really want to marry this bum?"

She looked Eli right in the eye. "Oh, yes, just as soon as I can."

Then the priest looked at her. "I know what he did while you and he were down at the river," he said accusingly.

Joanna cautiously looked at him as he spoke.

"He stopped at that little store, bought a smoked ring sausage, cheese crackers, root beer, and a jar of brown mustard, and then fed it to you, didn't he?"

Meekly she said, "Yes. He bought a jar of peppers, too, but I didn't eat any of those. How did you know?"

The priest blurted, "He always does that! I'm surprised he didn't buy a can of Pork and Beans."

She looked back at the priest and said, "He did. I didn't eat any of those, either."

Robb Michael interrupted, "Come on now, Papa. You didn't expect me to let her go hungry, did you?"

The priest, smiling, said, "You know, Doc, maybe we better get you two married before this turns into a brawl!"

Robb Michael was smiling, laughing to himself, as everyone lined up as per the priest's direction.

The priest then asked, "Is there a ring bearer?"

Douglas Kahn stepped forward.

Robb Michael, speaking softly, said, "Douglas, you have been my best man for nearly twenty years. It would please me very much for you to be my best man once again. Here. This day."

Douglas Kahn, with moist eyes said, "I would be honored."

He paused, and then said, "Robb Michael, of all of the things I have done for you, in all of the years I have been with you, I believe the best thing I have ever done was bring you and Joanna together."

He then stepped up beside Robb Michael as Kathy stepped up next to Joanna.

Father Eli Nelson raised his hands and motioned for all to stand. "My dear friends." Then more softly, "My dear, close friends."

You have come together, in this church, so that the Lord may seal and strengthen your love in the presence of the church's priest and this community. Almost in a whisper, he said, "My God, I love this."

Then he said, "Christ abundantly blesses this love." Still speaking softly, he said, "He has already consecrated you in baptism, and now He enriches and strengthens you by a special sacrament so you may assume the duties of marriage in mutual and lasting fidelity.

"And so in the presence of the church, and all here, I ask you to state your intentions.

"Robb Michael, and Joanna Kimble, have you come here freely and without reservation, to give yourselves to each other in marriage?"

Robb Michael and Joanna looked at each other.

Then in unison they both said, "Yes."

The priest motioned for all to sit down. Then he said, "Who gives this woman to this man?"

Joanna's father stood up and said, "Joanna's mother and I."

Joanna's sister also stood up and said, "Me, too! And about time!" Then they sat back down.

"Robb Michael, do you take Joanna to be your wife? Do you promise to be true to her in good times and in bad, in sickness and in heath, to love her and honor her for all of the days of your life?"

Joanna saw him look at her.

Once again she could see pride in his eyes. And then heard him say, "Yes."

Then the priest said, "Joanna, do you take Robb Michael to be your husband? Do you promise to be true to him in good times and in bad? In sickness and in health, to love him and honor him for all of the days of your life?"

Joanna found herself studying his face. Then she said, "Yes, I do."

Then Father Eli Nelson said, "You have declared your consent before the church, and all that are here. If there's a ring, place it on her finger now."

Douglas Kahn gave the ring to Robb Michael, to which Robb Michael placed the ring on Joanna's finger.

The priest then said, "This never-ending circle symbolizes your never-ending love for each other. May the Lord, in His goodness, strengthen your consent and fill you both with His blessings."

Then holding his arms out, he said, "In celebration, all stand with me."

Everyone stood up. Then speaking loudly, Father Eli said, "What God has joined, men must never divide. Amen! You are now husband and wife!"

Smiling, Father Eli said, "Doc, I want you to know the reason I didn't ask anyone if they had any reason for this wedding not to continue. It was because I wanted to make sure that I could put you in a trap you can never escape from."

Softly Robb Michael smiled and said, "Okay, Father! But don't think you'll ever be forgiven! God forgives, but I have to think about it a lot!"

Then turning to Joanna, he said, "Even when we were in junior high school, I called him Father or Papa, and he called me Doc. That's how much we knew about each other."

"Damn it, Doc! If you don't shut up and kiss that girl, I'm going to!"

Robb Michael turned and looked the priest in the eyes. "Papa! I would never try to stop you! But me first, alright?"

With that Robb Michael kissed her. She hoped the kiss would never end.

While Robb Michael was kissing her, the priest said, "I've known Robb Michael most of my life. And I can tell you all, this marriage will last till the day he dies. When he decides to do something, it's forever!"

After everyone was through hugging and kissing each other, Joanna saw Robb Michael, still wearing his shiny pink satin robe, bright green tie, and blue bunny slippers, walk out the door of the church as she was hugging Father Eli.

Joanna was showing everyone her wedding band. It was white gold and looked to be a three-eighths of an inch wide with quarter carat diamonds staggered around the edges and a gold band around the center.

She was wondering what the plan was going to be when Robb Michael came up behind her and spoke quietly in her ear.

She looked down and smiled as she listened to him. "Well, my darling wife. I believe I've captured you once again.

"By the way, if it's a girl, I want to name her Michael Jo. I've wanted a girl named Michael Jo ever since I met you."

Still smiling, he said, "Now, I've brought you that white wrap-around dress you like. After you put it on, I'll take you and all these people to Chez Henri's and feed you all, unless you have a better place in mind."

She turned and faced him.

She was surprised to see he had dressed in a formal black suit.

Then she took the clothes from him.

In a low voice, she said, "You know, I like Chez Henri's."

Then, breasts jiggling, she walked toward the ladies' room.

DINNER AT JAKE'S

Joanna sat and listened as everyone was talking when she heard her sister, who was sitting next to her, ask Father Eli, "Why did you allow Joanna and Robb to be practically naked at the ceremony?"

"Robb Michael. Nobody calls Robb Michael, Robb. Everyone has called him Robb Michael since I've known him. Ever since I can remember, his parents even called him Robb Michael. In answer to your question, "We were in junior high school when I told Doc I was going to study for the priesthood when I got out of school. I knew he was already studying medicine. Believe it or not, Robb Michael was studying medicine when he was in sixth grade. A year later, I told him I was going to be a priest.

"He told me that he and his bride would stand naked at his wedding. He made me promise to marry them. I'm glad no one asked that question during the ceremony."

Father Eli laughed a little, and then said, "Because Robb Michael would have stripped off the robe and stood there wearing nothing more than his best smile, the tie, and the bunny slippers."

Suddenly Joanna found herself saying, "I would have taken off the gown if he asked me to."

Saying that, she remembered the first day in the compound when she was wearing only a robe. She remembered thinking, *I would take off the robe if he asked me to.*

Father Eli interrupted. "You all noticed that I'm bigger than Robb Michael. But Robb Michael projects an image of being much bigger than he is. Nobody knows why.

"There have been a lot of people that believed he's bigger than me until they see us standing together. He is the only man I've ever met that is completely boundless, absolutely limitless."

"I agree with you, Joanna. He is a very exciting personality. I, too, have seen him do extraordinary things, and for that reason, I would have let them stand naked at your wedding."

Douglas Kahn suddenly said, "Here! Here! I agree! Robb Michael is the most exciting personality I've ever met! Since I started working with him, I have seen him do some of the most extraordinary things I've ever been witness to, especially in the operating room! Joanna, I couldn't agree with you more."

Father Eli continued speaking. "Robb Michael once told me that everyone should be naked when they're married, and when they die, because they're naked when they're born."

Phyllis looked at Joanna's rings. "My God, Jo! I think you've got a million dollars on your finger!"

Joanna looked at Robb Michael questioningly.

Robb Michael leaned over toward her and whispered in her ear. "I put the rings on the expense account."

She looked at him, wide-eyed, and quietly said, "My God, Robb Michael! Who are you that you can do that?"

He smiled at her, "I'm the shirt-tail relative of a well-known name. Because of that I get perks. If you don't know who I am, look at your marriage license and find out who you are."

Joanna looked at the marriage license she had been holding in her hand.

Phyllis looked over at the license and jokingly said, "Who the hell is Keandra?"

Joanna sat there, wide-eyed, while Robb Michael looked over at Phyllis and said, "You pronounced it wrong. It's not Keen. It's Key-ann. It's pronounced Key-ann-dra."

Phyllis suddenly, wide-eyed, said, "Oh! I've heard that name!"

"Of course you have," said Robb Michael nonchalantly. "It's a fine Irish name. Depending on where you are, when you speak it."

Joanna, still wide-eyed, turned and looked at him. "Like in 'Frankenstein' Keandra? That's why you have two first names."

"There you go, talking about that cantankerous old man again."

As they were leaving, hugging and kissing everyone, the valet brought Robb Michael's car around.

Robb Michael held the door for her as she got in the car. While leaning on the door, he asked, "Where would you like to go on your honeymoon?"

Sitting in the car, she looked up at him, and asked, "Anywhere?"

"Yes, anywhere."

"I want to go to Paris, France, and make love in the dark, under the bridges as the boats and barges are going by."

"What! You don't want to make love in the old man's front yard anymore?"

"Yes! Yes, I do! On the way back to the compound, stop at the old man's house. I do want to make love in his front yard!"

"Would you like me to knock on his front door first?"

She looked at him with half a smile and a stern look on her face. "Get in the car! I'll decide that when we get there."

THE FRONT YARD IN THE MOONLIGHT

When Robb Michael drove into the driveway, he drove half way up to the house before he stopped the car and turned off the lights.

She watched him as he opened the trunk and took out the blankets.

She stripped off her clothes and stood naked in the middle of the yard with her arms folded under her breasts.

The night air felt warm as she looked up at the house. There was a light in what she thought might be the front room.

Then she turned to see Robb Michael looking at her in the bright moonlight.

She lowered her arms and went over to the blankets and laid down.

She watched him as he came over and joined her on the blankets.

As they were making love, she found herself clinging to him.

When it was over, she laid there with her eyes closed and her arms out from her sides, one hand on the grass, damp from the evening dew. Quietly, she said, "I'm cold."

She felt him get up.

A moment later, she felt a blanket fall over her. And then another one.

She felt him get under the blankets with her. She clung to him once again.

As usual, when she clung to him, she fell asleep in his arms.

THE NEXT MORNING

When she awoke, she found herself in a tangle of arms and legs.

As she was untangling herself from him, he woke up. Lazily, he said, "What are we doing?"

"The sun's coming up," she said as she sat up on the blanket. "Maybe we should get up and get out of here before someone comes along and wants to know what we're doing here."

She watched him as he was looking at her breasts, and asked, "Is something wrong?"

He reached up and lifted her breasts one at a time and gently squeezed her nipples.

A dark yellow fluid seeped out. Then he said, "No, everything's normal. Your breasts are bigger and heavier because they are filling with a fluid called colostrum.

That's what's seeping out of your nipples. Your nipples are swollen and darker in color. That's also normal. Do you still want to go back to the compound?"

"Yes. It's cold, and I need a shower."

He reached up and lifted one of her breasts again and said, "Okay, I'll take you back to the compound if you spend the rest of the day in bed with me and let me suck on them all day."

Sitting there, thinking with the back of her hand pressed to her mouth, she saw him look at her thoughtfully.

She looked down at him. He was leaning on one elbow, looking up at her.

Taking her hand away from her mouth and reaching down she took a hold of his swollen member. She said, "Okay, you've got a deal on condition that I can suck on this cock as long as I want."

BACK AT THE COMPOUND

After they got back to the compound, they took a hot shower under the four-head shower in the workout gym.

While they toweled each other off, they fondled and sucked on each other.

After they headed toward the bedroom. Along the way, smiling, she said, "We can make this longer than all day if you like.

"I'm here forever, remember?"

He stopped her in the dark hallway and pulled her close.

He reached up and cupped her head with his hands. Very slowly, gently, he kissed her mouth.

They took short naps between the love games they played all day. They woke up about ten in the evening.

She watched him walk out of the bedroom without clothes on.

A few minutes later, she watched him come back with his arms full of food. He set everything down on the floor at the foot of the bed.

She climbed down to the foot of the bed with her face leaning into her hands and watched him as he spread out a large beach towel on the floor.

Then he set a box of cheese crackers, a smoked ring sausage, a squeeze bottle of brown mustard, two bottles of root beer, and two large brandy snifters on the center of the towel.

Curiously she watched as he dumped the cheese crackers in the middle of the towel, then watched as he cut the ring sausage into two inch lengths and peeled the transparent cover off the pieces, handing her a piece.

She slid down off the bed and sat on the floor by the towel as he handed her the mustard. She put some mustard on her sausage and said, "What? No chicken?"

He opened a bottle of root beer and poured the root beer into a large brandy snifter saying, "Don't tell Eli about the chicken. He might think something's wrong, or that I'm changing the menu to something kosher."

He handed her a brandy snifter full of root beer.

She laughed while grabbing a hand full of cheese crackers and said, "Something kosher?" Then they laughed some more.

While they both sat on the bedroom floor having a picnic and wearing nothing more than their birthday suits, she studied him. "Don't you drink anything besides soda pop?"

He thought for a moment, "Yeah. Water."

Still studying him, she asked, "You don't drink any hard liquor at all?"

Without hesitation, he said, "No. I almost never drink anything alcoholic. Don't get me wrong, I like to drink, but with my practice I can't be drinking. I have a specialized practice. At this moment I don't have a single patient, but the phone can ring and it could be ether Mr. Kahn or the hospital telling me I have a patient that needs immediate surgery. I have to go and I must not be drinking."

"You don't have any patients at all?"

"No. Remember that little girl I performed surgery on a little while back? Her doctor called me and told me she needed surgery. He didn't even know what was wrong with her. He wanted me to open her up and explore her body for damage.

"So I opened her up to have a look. When I saw all those tumors, my heart sank. I just knew she was dead. But I had to start cutting anyway. I can't think of a single reason why she survived.

"But the minute her vital signs were normal she was no longer my patient. She went back to the care of her doctor, but she can become my patient again. I may have to open her up again to make sure I got them all."

Joanna looked at him with a look of disbelief. "My God! How do you handle the pressure?"

"I've got twenty-six corporations I'm looking after. That pretty well keeps my mind off my problems."

She paused thoughtfully and then said, "Now that my name is Keandra, whatever became of the embezzler? Did they catch him? If so, how?"

"Catching them wasn't hard. I called Mr. Kahn. Mr. Kahn called security.

"The investigators at security are pretty good. Mr. Kahn had them find you for me.

"By the way, there were three of them. They had almost seven million dollars stashed away, most of which we recovered. Now if you are done eating, get back in bed, and I'll tell you a bedtime story."

She cocked her head to one side and looked into his face. "Is this going to be a fairy tale?"

"No. There's no fairies in this tale."

She paused for another long moment. "When the old man dies are you going to inherit the companies?"

"No, but you will. So will the baby you are carrying in your body."

"Why won't you inherit them?"

"Well, let's just say that the old man and I had a falling out."

"What was the argument about?"

Robb Michael laughed a little. "He doesn't believe I'm treating you right. He thinks you might leave before we're done with these programs."

She suddenly asked, "Does he know I'm pregnant?"

"I think so. He knows we were married, so I believe he knows."

Joanna sat eating the cheese crackers and smoked sausage. She took a long drink of root beer. As she set the snifter down, she suddenly had a look of comprehension on her face. "That's what this program is all about, isn't it? He wanted me to have this baby right from the beginning, didn't he?"

Robb Michael smiled once again. "Yes, he did want you to have this baby. Does it surprise you?"

She looked at him thoughtfully. Then as though she was talking to herself, she said, "I should have thought of that a long time ago. I was so focused on the sexual aspect and what it was all about, I never even gave it a thought about becoming pregnant."

Then she said, "Look! You tell him this is my baby! And I'm going to raise it all by myself! Never mind! I'll tell him! I'll not have any interference from him or anyone else!"

Robb Michael asked, "Does that include me?"

"Of course not! It's your baby, too. But I want to raise this baby to be strong-minded and healthy. Not a spoiled pansy who's afraid to go outside in the rain! What can you tell me about him?"

Robb Michael smiled and said, "I'm starting to believe he's in love with you. That's why he doesn't think I'm treating you right. He's a little jealous and maybe a little over protective.

"As for how you want to raise your baby, I think I can get the old man to go along with that.

"I think he figured it out some time ago. You can be tough. If he hasn't figured it out, go sock him in the eye. He'll figure it out."

Smiling a knowing smile, she burst out laughing.

Then he said, "You know, I'm glad you wanted to get married. That solved a lot of possible legal problems in the future."

"What kind of legal problems?"

He smiled once again. "You know, one day you'll get a long note from that cantankerous old galoot, explaining everything. From him you'll find out more than you want to know."

TWO MONTHS LATER

Joanna was sitting at the kitchen table, wearing nothing but her robe, drinking coffee and remembering some of the embarrassing moments of her honeymoon.

The first night they were in Paris, Robb Michael took her to one of the bridges. It was dark, and they were making love.

Her dress was open all the way down the front.

Her whole body was fully exposed, and she was having an orgasm when suddenly a floating restaurant that was passing by turned their spotlight on her.

In the spotlight, her orgasm seemed to go on forever.

She started to get hysterical. She wanted to start screaming, but instead she started laughing hysterically.

Tears were streaming down her face.

Meanwhile, the boat stopped, all the while keeping her in the spotlight.

Robb Michael was on his knees in front of her.

The men on the boat started singing. All the while, she couldn't stop laughing.

Rob Michael later told her they were singing the French national anthem.

Joanna couldn't help but laugh a little, and blush, while she sat there thinking about it.

As she was thinking about it, she remembered Robb Michael looking at her with a concerned look.

She wondered why.

After the spotlight incident, Robb Michael took her to Italy, Germany, Great Britain, and then Greece.

It never failed to surprise her that everywhere he took her they encountered people that knew him.

In England, one man Robb Michael introduced her to asked Robb Michael, "Why do American men have this fetish with big bosoms?"

Robb Michael replied, "It wasn't her bosoms that drew my interest. I was more interested in her thinking logic."

The man gave him a disbelieving look and said, "A woman with thinking logic? Really?"

Then she started thinking about the trip over. They had taken a corporate plane.

Robb Michael made her take the controls of the plane for awhile.

It was different than she thought it would be. The plane was smooth and easy to control. She told Robb Michael she wanted to learn how to fly.

He told her she was probably the only civilian that flew a jet the first time she was at the controls.

Then he told her he had planned all along to teach her how to fly.

LATER THAT SAME AFTERNOON

Joanna was sitting at her desk when she sensed him.

She sat there looking down, and smiled while she waited for him to touch her.

Robb Michael came up behind her and wrapped his arms around her while reaching inside her robe and cupping her breasts with his hands.

Then quietly he said, "I would get myself a cup of coffee, but my hands are full."

She said, "I'll get you one," and started to get up.

He stopped her, saying, "Sit still, I'll get it in a minute. Right now I'm playing, and when I'm done playing, I want to examine you."

"Examine me? Is that all?"

"Well, I might have to do some extracurricular surgery," he said while nuzzling her ear with his lips.

"Really?" she asked, "Will it hurt?"

"No. I will administer an anesthetic to the area. The injection will be absolutely painless."

She smiled shyly. "Well, if you don't do it right, you'll have to do it again and again until you get it right. Understand?"

"I'm a doctor. I believe I can get it right the first time. Then I'll still do it again. That's why doctors practice, and practice, and keep practicing."

After they made love, he gave her a thorough examination.

While examining her, he put the stethoscope in her ears, placing the end of it on the inside of her left breast.

"What do you hear?"

"I hear my heart beat."

He then placed the end of it low on her belly. "What do you hear?"

She smiled, "I hear the baby's heart beat. It's beating much too fast, isn't it?"

"No. Keep listening. Listen closely. Now tell me what do you hear?"

She listened intently.

Then excitedly, she said, "I hear two heart beats!"

"Yes. You are hearing two heart beats. I'll wager a nickel they're both boys."

"How can you tell?"

"Because I would like at least one of them to be a girl. You better start thinking of a couple of names if you want to be able to tell them apart."

Joanna studied him for a moment and then asked, "How old are you?"

"Why do you want to know?"

"I'm wondering how old you are going to be when the babies are legal age."

He gave her a strange look. Then, "On August 19th, I was fifty-six."

Joanna couldn't help but feel amazed and then said, "I would never have believed you are twenty-five years older than me. You don't look or act like you're any older than I am."

"Have I deceived you?"

"No. I think I might have deceived myself."

"Does it bother you I'm that much older than you?"

She smiled and then said, "No. Maybe it's better you're that much older than me. However, sometimes I've felt like I'm older than you."

She saw him smile.

"Really? Am I that much of an adolescent?"

"Oh, yeah. Sometimes I think you can't keep your hands off me. Other times I'm certain of it."

She saw his face change. "Does it bother you?" he asked.

She smiled a secretive smile, "Oh, yeah! Don't stop. I like it when you touch me! I like sleeping with you. You're a good bed partner.

"Sometimes you reach for me in your sleep. Sometimes you don't. Either way, I'm comfortable sleeping with you. Whether I wake up in your arms, or on the other side of the bed, I'm comfortable. Don't stop.

"By the way, how many children do you want?"

She watched him as he seemed to be in deep thought.

Then slowly he said, "How many are you willing to have for me?"

Without hesitation, she said, "You name the figure."

She watched him.

His face changed a little bit. Then he answered, "Six. If one of them is a girl, I want her name to be Michael Jo."

"Michael Jo?"

"Yes, I believe I once told you I wanted a girl, and I want to name her Michael Jo."

She remembered he had once mentioned it. Then he said, "Well, we'll keep trying until we get her. Okay?"

He was quiet for a moment. And then with a doubtful look on his face, he smiled and quietly said, "Of course, we...will... keep trying."

Hearing the way he said it, she couldn't help but think something was wrong.

She swept the thought from her mind and then said, "We can't keep trying until after I have these two. But keep trying, you probably will."

Then she laughed.

A MONTH LATER

Joanna had just stepped out of the pool and was about to step into the shower when Robb Michael came into the workout gym.

"Are you going to join me in the shower?" she asked.

"No, go ahead and shower. Then I want to show you something."

After she showered and was drying off, he grabbed a towel and helped her dry off and started speaking. "You know, I had this compound built specifically for you to implement two projects at the same time.

"I knew trying to raise a baby and mobilize another project at the same time would be difficult at the very least. So far, you've done a very good job putting it together."

He picked up another towel and roughly helped her dry her hair while he was talking.

"I told you I would never lie to you. I have not. However, I have been deceptive. That normally wouldn't matter, but something happened that makes it matter."

She looked at him questioningly.

"We got married," he said. "That makes it wrong to deceive you any longer."

He put the towel down and handed her a terrycloth robe. "You better put this on. I want you to take a walk with me."

With her hair still damp and stringy, she put the robe on and belted it as he led her through the compound.

He led her out the front door into the hallway. Instead of turning right and going up the stairs, he turned left.

He led her about twenty feet down a dark hallway and opened a door to the right. They stepped into a dimly lit room.

Joanna had no sooner stepped into the room when she stopped.

She looked around, trying to take it all in. She was standing on a large dance floor at least thirty by thirty feet square.

The room was huge with a ten-foot ceiling. Hanging from the ceiling was a large, mirrored, disco-ball.

The ball was slowly turning, casting different colored lights in all different directions in the huge room.

In front of her, about twenty feet from the dance floor, was a bar.

She walked across the dance floor to the well-lit bar and looked around. The bar was U-shaped, ten by twenty by ten. In front of the bar were cushy bar stools.

Behind the bar were mirrored shelves. The shelves were stair stepped from the floor up, holding just about any kind and brand of liquor you could name.

Above the bar were racks holding drinking glasses of every kind and description.

There were tables and chairs on a lush, carpeted floor with exotic lighting everywhere. Joanna turned and looked at him. "Is this a nightclub?"

He smiled. "No, this is the party room in the basement of my house."

She looked at him wondrously. "This is your house?"

"Yes. The time has come to tell you where you are. The times I wasn't with you, I was never more than two or three doors away.

"The times I was away on business, Mr. Kahn or someone was here. You were never alone. That's why I told you to wear a robe. Mr. Kahn has a key to the place and comes and goes as he feels it's necessary. He has a desk near mine in my office. Come, let me show you the rest of the house."

She followed him up the stairs that came out where the dining room met the living room.

The dining room was a large room with two large mahogany tables, each with sixteen swivel rocker armchairs around it.

On one side of the room was a china closet with so many place settings in it, Joanna couldn't guess the number.

Robb Michael told her to look around the house any time she liked.

She looked at the polished hard wood floor and said, "Just looking at this place I would guess that you have some rather large dinner parties here."

He smiled a small smile. "Yes. As a matter of fact, I was about to suggest having your parents and the rest of your relatives over for Thanksgiving dinner.

Also, I want you to invite any friends you would like to have come. After all, it's your home, too. By the way, I don't know if I told you, I have no family. I'm the last in my bloodline."

She looked at him wide-eyed and said, "Let me see the kitchen first."

He smiled at her and said, "You didn't catch what I said." Then he said, "Yes, by all means, go look at the kitchen."

She walked through a large doorway into a very large kitchen. All the appliances were stainless steel. There was an eight-burner stove with two large ovens and a griddle between the burners.

Next to the stove sitting, on the floor, there was a five-gallon water bottle. The water bottle was almost full of nickels. The refrigerator was the largest she had ever seen.

Looking around she said, "This looks more like the kitchen of a restaurant."

She heard him start laughing.

"That's true, but if you look in the refrigerator, you'll find a good supply of smoked ring sausage, and the cupboards are well stocked with cheese crackers, so we won't go hungry.

"But seriously, you won't be cooking any large meals in here unless you want to. When I'm having a large dinner party, I have one or two chefs from the hospital's kitchen come in and cook.

"I pay them double their normal wage, and on holidays a lot more. Don't think you are going to be overdoing yourself. Come, let's look through the rest of the house."

She looked back at the water bottle and said, "Do I get to spend all of those nickels?"

"Those nickels are all my winnings. They're not to be spent. They're there to remind me I'm not to wager unless I'm certain I'm going to win."

She went out of the kitchen, through the dining room, and into the living room.

Looking around she saw that there were ten-foot ceilings and lush carpets on the hardwood floors, with plush furnishings.

Looking across the room, she saw another doorway. She walked across the room and looked in the doorway. It was a library.

My God! she thought. *This place is a palace!*

This room was smaller, thirty-five by forty-five. The shelves were crowded with books. "Have you read them all?" she asked.

He smiled a small smile while nodding his head. Quietly he said, "Quite a few of the volumes are medical. Some are case histories. Some are surgical procedures that haven't yet been approved by the AMA.

"Some are just books that have been written by some of us that are full of ourselves."

From there he took her into his office. She looked around the place carefully. He sat at his desk and called her over.

Then he showed her a button under his desk. "This is the way into the vault."

When he pushed the button, the wall behind his desk started sliding sideways to reveal another room with a huge vault door.

Astonished, she asked, "Is this a bank?"

"No. This vault is a library of records for all of the corporations we control."

He opened the vault and took her inside and showed her around. There were shelves similar to the shelves in the library with ladders on rollers so you could climb up and retrieve the binders the shelves held.

Behind the shelves, out of sight of the vault door, was the biggest safe she had ever seen.

"What's in the safe?" she asked quietly.

Just as quietly, he answered, "I believe, perhaps, a little more than a billion dollars."

"Oh, of course," she answered flippantly.

From there she went back into the living room and looked around. It was a large room. There were several large easy chairs and cushy couches with hardwood floors and attractive carpets around all the furniture.

There was a huge fireplace on an inside wall that was made with decorative stone.

There was another fireplace in the center of the large room.

There were very large windows on one wall.

She walked over to one window and looked out on to the front yard. It was then she realized where she was.

She was looking out at the lawn they had been making love on.

She turned around slowly. "I thought you told me that 'Frankenstein' Keandra lived here."

She watched his smiling face as he said, "No. I jokingly said a cantankerous old man lived here."

She laughed a little and then said. "Yeah, I believe you deceived me a little."

He interrupted saying, "'Frankenstein' Keandra lives across town. Come along, I want to show you our other bedroom."

He took her by the arm and led here into a bedroom that was larger than the master bedroom in the compound.

Suddenly she felt him lift her up like she weighed nothing and placed her on the king-sized bed. "I have wanted to put you in this bed since before I met you."

After they made love, she sat up in bed, looking around. The place was neat as a pin.

As she looked around, she said, "I have always heard single men are sloppy house keepers. Looks like you keep this place clean and neat."

She watched him as he got out of bed. He took her by the arm and led her into an adjoining bathroom. The bathroom was huge.

Like the bathroom in the compound, it had two of everything.

Two wash basins, two toilets, a bidet, and two tubs. One of the tubs was a Jacuzzi. There was also a four-head shower stall.

As they were showering, he said, "There's another house on the property. The place is about three thousand square feet. That house was on the property when I bought the place. I had this house built. There's twenty-eight thousand square feet of floor space in this house, not counting the compound. There are nineteen bedrooms and twenty-four baths.

"In the little house, there's a young Japanese couple living there, Mr. and Mrs. Numura. "She's the one that keeps this place clean and neat. He keeps the landscape manicured. "Sometimes I have them in for dinner."

She saw a hair dryer, picked it up and dried her hair.

They were both naked as they stood in the bathroom, talking.

Suddenly she asked, "Robb Michael? What do you want me to do?"

"I want you to do what you want to do. I want you to continue your work on the programs. I also want you to go to school. I want you to learn how to fly. But other than that, do what you want.

"The only reason I showed you the place is that I just wanted to get honest with you.

"You once told me you wanted this house. Well it's yours. If you like, I'll have Mr. Kahn transfer the deed into your name."

Joanna looked at him and thought. *My God! Is he in love with me? I hope!*

She watched him dress and then she picked up her robe and put it on.

Then he said, "Now, tell me. What do you want to do? Live here? Or would it be better for you if we live in the compound?"

She thought a moment. "The compound.

"With Mr. Kahn and others coming in I wouldn't be able to concentrate. So yeah, the compound would be better.

"Besides I would be wandering around the house exploring."

She saw him smile as he said, "You'll be exploring anyway.

"Tell me, do Eric and Phyllis have children?"

"Yes, two girls and a boy. Ten, eleven, and thirteen. One girl's older and one girl's younger than the boy."

"Why weren't they at the wedding?"

"Because they were told we were half-naked."

Robb Michael smiled and said, "You tell them on Thanksgiving we will be wearing clothes, so bring the whole family."

As they came out of the bathroom, the phone in the house started ringing.

Robb Michael went to the phone and answered it, said a few words, and hung up the phone.

"That was Mr. Kahn. I have to go to the hospital."

Joanna looked at him anxiously. "Can I go?"

"Yes, if you get dressed quickly. I may be there for a while, maybe hours."

She headed back to the compound while he went out to start the car.

THE HOSPITAL

Mr. Kahn met them as they entered the hospital.

"You have a young boy, sixteen years old. He was playing football and collapsed. His heart doesn't want to keep beating. Something's wrong in there. He's out and in. They've got him on life support. They can't do anything with him. He's already been prepped."

Robb Michael didn't say anything. He headed for the elevator.

Mr. Kahn turned to Joanna. "Come with me, Joanna. Would you like a cup of coffee?" "Yes, I would. Where do we wait?"

As they were on the way to the cafeteria, he said, "We'll get a pot of coffee in the cafeteria, and then we'll go up to the theater."

She looked at him incredulously. "The theater?"

"Yes, we can watch the surgery from there."

In the theater, she saw a big, glass dome. Looking down through the glass she could see everything.

The doctors, nurses, and all the support people.

As they stood there watching, she asked, "How did you meet Robb Michael?"

Without looking at her he said, "He saved my life."

Once again she looked at him incredulously. "He saved your life?"

"Yes. I have a genetic disorder. I was told there was no help for it. I had a hole in my heart and a bad valve. At that time, they didn't have any answers. They didn't know what to do or how to do it.

"As they were telling me this, a young doctor that looked like he should still be in high school, spoke up and said, 'I would wager a nickel I can fix you up, but I wonder who I would pay the nickel to if I fail.'

"Then he said, 'I wouldn't worry about it though. If you want to worry about something, think about the million dollars I'm going to charge you along with the nickel when I win.'

"After hearing him talk, I could see my doctor was so angry at him. He wanted to kill him.

"I found out later the young doctor was almost thirty years old, but I swear he looked to weigh about a hundred and twenty-five pounds and sixteen, maybe seventeen, years old.

"After the doctors left my room, I heard my doctor cursing loudly at him in the hall. After the cursing stopped, I heard the young doctor say, 'I'll wager a nickel, you're wrong.'

"Then my doctor yelled, 'You're wagering more than a God-damned nickel!'

"That young doctor came back into my room. He told me he had been studying genetic disorders like mine even while he was in medical school.

"He said that he thought of a way to make corrections, but hadn't tried it yet.

"Then he told me that just because I haven't stopped breathing doesn't mean that I'm not already dead.

"He said, and I quote, 'Yes Mr. Kahn, you are already dead. However, they will not bury you until you stop breathing. Imagine that. Now if you sign this medical release, I will take you downstairs and bring you back to life.'

"I didn't feel I had any choice, so I signed the release.

"A nurse there told him he had the bed side manner of a monster. He replied, 'Yes, I do! Now take him downstairs and prep him. We must not waste any more time.'

"The last thing I heard him say before they put me out was, 'I hope you have someone that will pay me a nickel when you awaken.'

"When I woke up, he was sitting beside the bed.

"The first thing I heard him say was, 'Mr. Kahn, I believe you owe me a nickel. I'll give you a few days to pay up.'"

Joanna thought, *I bet Robb Michael is Dr. 'Frankenstein'. I'm going to try something.*

"I hear that they call him Dr. 'Frankenstein' because he makes artificial body parts."

Douglas Kahn was suddenly wide-eyed. "No! That's not why they call him Dr. 'Frankenstein'."

Joanna, startled, looked at Douglas Kahn and said, "It's not?"

"No! Heavens no! They call him Dr. 'Frankenstein' because he brings people back to life!

"When I awoke after surgery, we were talking a little while when the nurse that said he had the bedside manner of a monster came in."

"The instant she came through the door Robb Michael started waving his arms and strutting around the room very dramatically shouting, 'IT'S ALIVE! IT'S ALIVE! IT LIVES! IT BREATHES! IT'S ALIVE!'

"Then he told the nurse, being as how he never wagered a nickel with her, she owed him a dinner date instead.

"I distinctly remember, he told her he would pick her up at seven.

"He called all of the nurses and orderlies in to the room and told them they were not to help me get up or down. They were only there for me to take their hands, or arms, to pull myself up. They were not to pull on me unless I asked them to."

"If they helped pull me up, there would be damage to what he had done in my chest. Basically, I was to do everything myself, because if it hurts, I would stop by myself. They were there only to keep me from falling. Even from falling back onto the bed.

"He has given those instructions to the nurses and orderlies for every patient he has had.

"A couple of days later he came in and laid a slip of paper on my chest. When I read the paper, I was astonished. It was a right-to-lien notice.

"You see, in Oregon, if you're going to lien a property or a business, you have to serve a right-to-lien notice within twelve days after the work was done. Then you have thirty days in which to file a lien in court.

"So I asked him if he expected me to pay him within a month. He said, 'No, only a nickel.'

"He said he was being sued and he would trade my services for the million dollars I owed him.

"Well, I won the suit easily. He hired me to represent him full-time. I had him investigated. I was shocked to find out that not only was he thirty years old, he was also a hero.

"He was a Navy fighter pilot. He flew a U2 for the CIA on some dangerous missions. I don't believe there's anything in this world that he's afraid of.

"I heard later he made my other doctor pay him a nickel. I heard my doctor threw the nickel at him. I love that confidence that he is. He is so certain he can do anything. He'll do it just to prove he can.

"To him, everything in life is just a game. Even when he's at war, it's just a game. Every time he wins at whatever he's doing, he says, 'Checkmate.'

"He goes anywhere he wants without fear. You know, he was accepted at Harvard when he was only thirteen years old.

"He has no boundaries that govern his life like other men. He goes where he wants, when he wants.

"You already know he does anything he wants, and absolutely everyone likes him.

"The day I hooked up with him was the beginning of a beautiful friendship. I've been with him ever since. I will be with him for as long as he wants me. He has always paid me more than I could have made in private practice.

"I've never heard of him charging anyone for his services. He has always worked his medical practice, no charge.

"Both of my sons, Richard and David, were born with the same heart defect. Dr. 'Frankenstein' Keandra corrected them both.

"By the way, I've paid him a nickel several times in my life. I've never been able to win when wagering against him."

Joanna had been listening when she interrupted. "What was he being sued for?" "Malpractice. A man he operated on after me was in recovery the same time I was."

"The man's wife heard Robb Michael had operated on him when there was no possible way to save him.

"She was suing because she believed Robb Michael was just prolonging her husband's pain and suffering.

"When we got to court, she still believed her husband was dying.

"When I put Robb Michael on the stand, he told the court her husband was cured, and would need no farther medical attention for the condition he was suffering from.

"She didn't believe him, so the court ordered her husband to undergo a thorough examination. When the man was given a clean bill of health, the court ordered her the pay Dr. Keandra's bill, and threw the case out.

"Like me, that man is still alive today.

"Robb Michael made out a bill, and while handing it to the judge, he said, 'My standard fee.'

"I had watched him make out the bill."

Douglas Kahn handed Joanna a slip of paper with the amount of the bill on it, '$0,000,000.00',

"I've kept this piece of paper ever since that day in court. Robb Michael has a way of twisting words."

Joanna looked at him and smiled. "I know about that!"

Douglas Kahn continued speaking. "After the trial, things were quiet around here for a while, then Robb Michael did another impossible surgery.

"Almost every doctor in the hospital signed a petition to have Robb Michael barred from this hospital.

"They didn't know he owns the hospital.

"When they noticed Dr. Keandra's last name was the same as the hospital, they wondered about the connection.

"That's when Robb Michael started telling people he was a shirttail relative of the hospital's owner.

"Robb Michael didn't want people avoiding him like he had seen other people avoid their employers.

"Robb Michael only does a surgery once in a while, but has always been successful.

"He pioneered new types of surgeries, everything from new joints to lower intestinal disorders.

"It wasn't long before the other doctors started referring their patients to Dr. Keandra.

"Robb Michael knew he looked too young to be the boss, so when anyone asked him if he was related to the owner of the companies he owns, he started telling everybody he was just a shirt-tail relative.

"When he would visit one of the businesses, they would come up to him and ask him to pass a message to the owner, something they felt the owner should know. When they found out the owner was appreciative of them, they looked forward to seeing Robb Michael.

"He became very popular with everyone working for him."

They watched for a while as Robb Michael was operating.

Then suddenly, Robb Michael stopped moving. He just stood there staring into space. His eyes looked watery behind his glasses.

Joanna, watching, said, "Something's wrong, Mr. Kahn. What's he doing?"

Douglas Kahn watched for a moment and said, "Once in a while he stops like that. One time I asked him why.

"He told me sometimes he doesn't know what else to do, so he prays.

"You have probably noticed when you listen to him talk, he's very simplistic. His whole life is.

"When he goes out to eat with friends, or clients, he'll order exotic meals.

"But when he's by himself, or with close friends, he'll eat a simple hot dog, or a piece of ring sausage and crackers and wash it down with a bottle of root beer or cream soda. For being one of the wealthiest men in the world, he sure doesn't let it show.

"Sometimes I need to get with him on some legal matters. If I can't find him, I drive down to Mill City. There he'll be, sitting on the bank of the Santiam River, fishing.

"When he notices that I've found him, he'll stop fishing.

"Then he'll take the fish he caught into that little house there on the river bank, clean and cook them.

"Then we feast on them, and he'll eat Pork and Beans cold, while still in the can. I swear, when I watch him eat those Pork and Beans, he looks like he was savoring every spoonful, as though he was eating a rare delicacy. His life is so simple compared to most people."

Douglas Kahn turned to face her. "I sincerely hope the two of you can live the dream. I hope his simple life style isn't too much for you."

ON THE WAY HOME

They had been at the hospital for over nine hours.

Robb Michael handed her the keys to his car as they came out of the hospital and said, "You drive. I'm tired."

She smiled at him. "I got a history lesson last night."

Robb Michael reclined the seat a little when they got in the car and laid his head back on the headrest.

"If you've been talking to Mr. Kahn, then you got a long history lesson. He's good at that, bless his heart. He doesn't have a lot of people to tell the history to, for security reasons, so when he can talk to someone, he'll talk their ear off."

As Joanna drove out of the hospital parking area she said, "Well, Dr. 'Frankenstein', you've done it again."

Robb Michael smiled and said, "Who are you talking to?"

"I'm talking to you, Dr. 'Frankenstein'."

"I'm not Dr. 'Frankenstein'," he retorted. "Dr. 'Frankenstein' lives back there in that hospital."

"I hear that he makes artificial body parts and puts people together that are half artificial. Then he makes them go out and live like other people.

"They can't understand why he doesn't just go out at night and dig up dead bodies and get body parts and transplant them.

"Me, I don't get involved with that kind of stuff. I'm Dr. Robb Michael Keandra. I live across town in a big house on a hill, with a pregnant wife."

Joanna laughed a little, then drove without speaking for a moment, then softly said, "Oh, yes, with a pregnant wife."

Joanna Keandra was silent as she drove the rest of the way home. Her husband had fallen asleep.

THANKSGIVING

Robb Michael told her, "This day promises to be a great day."

He had brought in a chef from the hospital to prepare the feast while he was setting the table and getting the dining room prepared.

Joanna was watching him out of the corner of her eye while she was showing her family, and Kathy, through the house.

Joanna was used to being in the house by now, so she strolled through the place like it was nothing special.

She took them down to the party room in the basement.

Going behind the bar she said, "Name your poison and I'll fix it for you." Her father and brother-in-law had a Scotch neat.

She opened bottles of root beer for her nieces and nephew.

While she was fixing drinks for her mother and sister, Kathy said, "You know, I could get used to living in a place like this."

Joanna noticed her sister was watching her. "Is something wrong, Phyl?"

Phyllis was quiet for a moment, then, "Jo, you've got a million dollars on your finger, two thousand dollars' worth of opals on your ears, a two hundred-thousand-dollar diamond pendent hanging around your neck, you're living in a thirty-five-million-dollar house, and you act like none of it matters."

Joanna fired right back at her. "It doesn't matter, Phyl. I had money before I married Robb Michael. The reason I'm wearing this stuff, and living in this house, is because the man I love wants me to!

"If Robb Michael wants me to wear a gunny sack and live in a mud hut on an island off the coast of Columbia, I will do it!"

Kathy spoke up, "Why would you?"

They all looked at Joanna quizzically. "Because Robb Michael looked at me."

"He didn't stare at me. He didn't stare at my tits. He didn't talk to my tits. He talked to me! He didn't come on to me. He never once asked me, 'What's your sign?' or 'What's your fetish?' He never said anything suggestive. In fact, I had to come on to him.

"That's why I will do anything he says, anywhere he says, anytime he says. I think I was in love with him before I even met him."

She stopped talking when she saw Robb Michael coming down the stairs.

Robb Michael casually approached them and said, "The dinner table is loaded with food. Now, if we don't go up there and eat some of it, the table might collapse."

Joanna led the way as they all migrated toward the stairs.

THE TABLE

Joanna looked at the table. It had so much food on it that it looked like it might collapse.

There were large silver trays with a carved roast turkey and a baron of beef, bowls of dressing and mashed potatoes, and bowls with gravy, peas, corn, and everything you would have on your table, and more.

There were pies placed here and there around the massive table, along with small cakes. It was a feast fit for a king.

After they were all seated, Phyllis's oldest girl asked, "Who's going to say grace?"

"I am," said Joanna. They all bowed their heads. "We all have a great deal to be thankful for. I'm thankful for all of you being here. We all have more than most. Eric and Phyl for their children. All of us for our parents.

"And me, I'm most thankful of all because something greater than all of us brought Robb Michael and me together. That's all that needs to be said. Amen."

Robb Michael pushed a serving cart with the large silver tray with carved turkey around the table, stopping at every place setting so those sitting there could serve themselves.

When he stopped at Eric and Phyllis's son, he gave the boy the wishbone. Then he said, "With all the pretty girls in this world, you may need this one day."

The boy looked back at him and said, "With my two sisters, I need it now."

The room roared with laughter, after which Robb Michael set the tray in the center of the table and sat down at the head of the table.

As Robb Michael began serving himself, Joanna's father asked Joanna, "How did you and Robb Michael meet?"

Kathy interrupted, "That was classic! A guy named Gregory Dorn grabbed Joanna's breasts. Robb Michael was sitting at the next table at this sidewalk cafe.

"Suddenly, I saw Robb Michael jump up and start to rush Mr. Dorn. By the look on Robb Michael's face, I thought Robb Michael was going to kill him!

"Then Joanna socked Mr. Dorn in the eye. Mr. Dorn was taking a swing at Joanna, and Robb Michael caught his fist with his hand! Yeah! It was classic!"

Roger Kimble, with a look of surprise on his face, said, "That must have been exciting!" Joanna smiled and said, "It was. But not as exciting as being kidnapped by Robb Michael."

Joanna's mother suddenly said, "He kidnapped you?"

"Yeah, about seven or eight weeks after the incident with Mr. Dorn. I went to a merger celebration. Robb Michael was speaking there. I got a little tipsy and passed out. Robb Michael brought me here.

"He had a compound built on the back of the house before he kidnapped me. He put me there and told me I couldn't leave until I negotiated my way out." Joanna smiled. "Instead of negotiating my way out, I negotiated my way in."

Anyone looking at Joanna would have known she was enjoying herself telling about it. After dinner Roger Kimble asked, "Why did you kidnap her?"

Robb Michael looked at her father and then said, "I was in trouble. I needed her help with something. I was falling behind on a program I was working on. It was the only way I could think to get her attention. I told her the only way I would let her leave was to talk to me."

Roger Kimble looked at him with a stern look on his face and asked, "Can I see this compound you kept my daughter in?"

Robb Michael looked at him and asked, "Do you really want to see that dungeon?"

Joanna's father glared at him. "I certainly do!"

"Okay, follow me." Joanna followed Robb Michael down through the party room.

Looking back, she saw that everyone else was following too.

When they entered the compound, everyone was surprised. The place was very much like the house.

There were hardwood floors with lush carpets in front of the furnishings. Everyone was oohing and aahing as they looked around the place.

Joanna's father started down the hall saying, "Are these lights on the floor the only lights in this place?"

Joanna laughed, "No, there's a wall switch at each end of the hall.

"I didn't know about the light switches until after I had been living here for a few weeks. I never turn the lights on."

Joanna followed him down the hall to the master bedroom. As they were entering, he said, "Oh, I see. There's a light inside the light switches."

Joanna turned on the chandeliers.

Roger Kimble suddenly said, "My God! How big is this place?"

Robb Michael said, "Seventy-eight hundred square feet."

Amazed, Roger Kimble said, "I like this place better than my condominium.

"How long did he keep you here?"

She smiled. "I'm still here. I like it here better than the house. Sometimes there's so much activity in the house that I can't keep my mind on my work, so I stay and work here. Robb Michael comes home here from the house at night."

Kathy asked, "Why do you work at all?"

Joanna looked at Kathy and smiled. "I made a couple deals with him. I'm also going to school. I'm learning how to fly.

"One of those deals was to be here forever with him. Being how I'm here forever, I have to prove my worth. You know how it is."

Roger Kimble gave her an astonished look. "You are learning how to fly? Why?"

"Oh, yeah. Anything for my master. I soloed a month ago. Now, I'm flying jets."

From the bedroom, Joanna led them all, with astonished looks on their faces, through the compound to the workout gym."

Kathy asked, "Do you swim in the pool?"

"Yes, every day. After I was more than three months along, Robb Michael told me to swim every day."

Kathy perked up. "You're going to have a baby?"

Joanna looked down and smiled while holding up two fingers.

Kathy's eyes widened, then looked excitedly at Robb Michael saying, "Really? Twins?"

Robb Michael looked at Kathy with an innocent look on his face and said, very seriously, "Don't look at me. All I did was have sex with her."

Then Robb Michael pointed at Joanna accusingly, "She's the one that got pregnant!"

The compound roared with laughter.

Roger Kimble turned to his daughter. "I've been told that he's rich and you don't even care."

"That's right," said Joanna. "If he was poor and wanted me to live in a mud hut with him, I'd be willing to support him."

Robb Michael looked around at everyone and said, "If I would have known that years ago, I wouldn't have worked so hard to make money."

Once again the compound roared with laughter.

As everyone was leaving, Joanna's father stood in front of her. "You know? For years I wondered if you were ever going to find someone.

"Well, now that you've found someone, I want you to know I don't understand your relationship with Robb Michael. The way you and he were married. The way the two of you live. What you are doing is alien to me, but if you are happy with it, so am I."

With that, he kissed his daughter, shook hands with Robb Michael, and asked, "Why did you build the compound when you had this house to keep her in?"

Robb Michael looked at him and seriously said, "For what I've got her doing, she must have absolute privacy."

Kathy Bates came over and hugged Robb Michael and spoke quietly in his ear. "Take good care of my friend, Jo.

"She's very much in love with you."

Watching Kathy, Joanna thought to herself, *I couldn't have said it better myself. She forgot to tell him, I'm going to spend the rest of my life with him.*

TWO WEEKS LATER

Joanna had been watching Robb Michael as he prepared the smoked ring sausage and crackers, with slices of Colby-jack cheese, for the picnic by the fireplace.

Neither of them was wearing anything.

Suddenly she said, "What's the matter? You tired of eating turkey?"

He laughed. "You're damn right. We sent half of the leftovers home with your relatives, and we still had more than we could eat.

"The rest of that turkey went in the garbage today. The way I feel at this moment, I would rather eat you ten times a day than ever eat turkey again."

She couldn't help smiling. "What are we going to have to drink at this picnic?"

"Well, we could have root beer, cola, maybe cream soda. I really like cream soda…

"Then there's the wine I've got stashed behind the bar in the party room. Or I can just sit here and drink you in."

Joanna looked down at her breasts, smiling, and said, "You really like them, don't you?" He never answered.

Joanna never felt happier in her life. She got up and went to the party room for the wine.

She had opened the wine at the bar and brought back two wine glasses, which she filled after she sat down in front of the fire.

Handing him a glass of the dark red merlot, she asked, "Are you sure you can drink this?"

"I think I can risk it. I never was much of a wine drinker."

With her glass raised, she said, "Here's to Christmas at my folks' place. We don't have to cook."

"Oh. We're doing Christmas at your folks' place? I wonder if your mother will make me set the table and serve the food?"

"I don't know, she might."

She saw him looking at her breasts, and once again said, "You like them. Don't you?"

"Yes, I do. As your pregnancy matures, they are constantly changing. They're nice to look at. I like looking at all of you. I know it's what you've got between your ears that makes everything work. I like that more. I can't help but admire you for your capabilities."

They ate and drank their wine as they lay naked by the fireplace.

Joanna noticed that he only drank half of the dark red merlot in his glass.

THREE WEEKS LATER

Joanna was preparing lunch when Robb Michael came into the compound.

She looked at him and said, "I'm fixing lunch. I had a feeling you would show up. I always do, you know. I can really tell when you are near. Sit down and eat."

She watched him as he pulled up a chair and sat down.

Then she asked, as she placed a bowl of soup and a tuna fish sandwich in front of him, "What have you been doing today?"

"I went to town and bought a new Ford 4x4 truck."

She looked at him. "Are you going to haul something?"

He smiled. "Yeah, well, golly. I thought I would haul you out to Damascus and cut down a Christmas tree and haul it home."

Joanna perked up. "Okay, when do we go?"

After they finished lunch, they got in the new truck and drove out to a tree farm near the small community of Damascus.

Robb Michael told her, "Go find a tree that you like and stand next to it until they come and cut it down for you. If you don't stand next to it, someone else might, then they'll get the tree."

Joanna started looking through the trees slowly, looking for that perfect tree.

Suddenly she asked, "How big a tree should I get?"

She saw him look at her and say, "How big do you want?"

"Boy! You're a big help!"

She looked through the trees for twenty minutes. She found one about seven feet high.

She was practically dancing when a man with a small chain saw came over, and cut it down for her. The man loaded it in the back of the truck for them.

On the way back to the compound, they stopped at a few stores and bought decorations for the tree.

The stores were crowded with shoppers. Joanna squeezed between the shoppers gathering up Christmas decorations, sometimes looking back to see if Robb Michael was still behind her.

She hadn't lost him. She saw him looking at people, watching them as they sorted through different items.

As they would put something back, someone else would pick it up.

Joanna was happier than she had ever been before in her life. She loved being with him. She felt special being with him in public.

She wanted it to go on forever.

CHRISTMAS

Joanna loaded all the Christmas presents into her Saab hatchback. To her surprise, the car started right up after sitting in the garage for seven months.

The last time she looked, Robb Michael was doing paperwork in the library.

It was cold and frosty outside as she let the car warm up.

Robb Michael came into the garage and got in the car with her. "So we're taking this car today?"

Joanna smiled. "Yeah, this car knows the way. It's been there before."

"Really? I didn't know this car got around that much."

"You'll never find out," she said as she backed out of the garage.

"Really?" he asked.

"Really, I don't tell everything," she said.

Joanna drove to the east side of Gresham, a city that borders the east side of Portland.

Once they arrived, they braved an icy cold east wind that was biting their ears as they carried presents to the open door of Joanna's parents' place.

Joanna's father greeted them as they came through the door.

Both Joanna and Robb Michael, their arms full of presents, carried them straight over to the Christmas tree and put them down.

Eric and his children were sitting on the couch, watching television. Joanna's mother and sister were in the kitchen preparing Christmas dinner. Robb Michael followed Joanna out to the kitchen.

"Is there something I can do to help?" Joanna asked.

Her mother said, "Your father is going to carve the turkey, but there's a ham that needs to be sliced."

Joanna went to a drawer and took out a large butcher knife.

Robb Michael reached over and took the knife out of her hand. "You better let me slice the ham. I have more surgical skill than you do."

Joanna's father turned and asked, "Do you have to have surgical skill to carve a turkey?"

Robb Michael smiled at him. "I hesitate to answer out of fear that it might create a scheduling problem."

Everyone smiled as they continued to prepare the food.

After they had eaten, everyone migrated toward the tree.

They all drank hot toddies of cider mixed with cinnamon and orange juice, and they snacked on brownies while Joanna's nieces and nephew passed out presents.

In the late afternoon, the party slowly came to an end as they ate pie and ice cream. Joanna hugged and kissed everyone in her family as they were preparing to leave.

As they were driving home, Robb Michael said, "It might be a late night. Eli Nelson is coming over after ten o'clock mass at the church, so if you want to take a nap before he gets here, it might be a good idea.

"Sometimes Eli and I bring in the early daylight. We usually go out partying, but tonight we are staying in."

Joanna felt good. She smiled at the prospect of having Eli over. Tonight promised to be interesting.

Robb Michael and Joanna arrived home a little after six in the evening. They made love and then took a nap until nine-thirty.

THE CHRISTMAS PARTY

Eli arrived at eleven in the evening.

Joanna met him at the front door and was surprised to see that Eli had a woman with him, as well as two bottles of wine.

As they came in, Eli said, "Joanna, this is Emily Van Hatten."

She was an attractive woman with reddish blonde hair. Joanna looked at her and the way she was dressed, a simple skirt and white blouse.

She was a little taller than Joanna. Joanna noticed the woman had a nice figure. She looked to be about forty to forty-five years old.

Eli was wearing slacks and a blue shirt. Both were wearing coats that were open in the front as he introduced them.

"Emily, this is Joanna Keandra, my close friend's wife."

The two women shook hands in that uncomfortable way that women do, then Joanna led them through the house to the compound.

When they entered the compound, Robb Michael was in the kitchen putting several kinds of crackers, snacks and three ring sausages on a big plater.

Joanna took their coats and put them on the couch.

Robb Michael looked at Eli and the two wine bottles he was carrying and said, "I see you brought a lady with you. Are we going to ply her with the wine?"

Then he said, "Joanna, bring glasses for the wine." He picked up the tray of food and headed toward the workout gym.

Once they were in the gym, smiling, Robb Michael carried the tray over to the patio table and set it down in the center of the table.

Eli picked up a corkscrew and pulled the cork out of one of the bottles of wine.

The workout gym was dimly lit and there was a fire in the fireplace, extra wood was stacked nearby. They all sat at the table.

Robb Michael took the bottle of wine from Eli and began pouring the wine. Eli picked up a paring knife and began slicing the sausage into two inch lengths.

Both Joanna and Emily watched, fascinated, while Eli made a shallow cut lengthwise on the pieces of sausage, and began peeling the transparent covering off the sausages.

Joanna said, "I'll bet I can tell you who taught you how to do that."

Eli started laughing, "Joanna, you haven't been married no time at all, and you've already got Robb Michael figured out."

Robb Michael put some of the sausages on the grill in the fireplace.

They were all smiling when Joanna said, "Emily, in a minute one of these guys will teach you how to eat."

Emily looked around the table. "They are going to teach me how to eat?"

"Oh, yes!" Joanna retorted. "They've got this eating down to a fine science."

Eli interrupted, "You guys be nice. Emily didn't have any place to go tonight, so I told her I would be on my best behaver if she came along to this shindig with me."

Robb Michael smiled and said, "Why did you tell her a thing like that? You're no fun at all."

Then he poured everyone another glass of wine. Robb Michael put a glass in Emily's left hand, then he picked up a piece of sausage and placed it between her forefinger and thumb.

With her hand wrapped around the glass, he said, "Emily, with your right hand, pick up some crackers, then turn your left hand and take a bite of sausage, take a bite of cracker, chew a few times, and then wash it down with the wine."

While Robb Michael was showing Emily how to do it, Joanna was already doing it and took a bite of her sausage at the same time. Soon after they were all doing it.

After taking a bite of the sausage, Emily said, "My good Lord. This is really good, better than I thought it would be!"

Robb Michael smiled, saying, "It's a little decadent. But decadence is allowed in this place and time."

Emily looked at Robb Michael and said, "Did you say decadence is allowed?"

They all laughed.

Emily was on her third glass of wine. It seemed like someone re-filled her glass every time she set it down.

She turned to Eli and said, "Father Eli, I know you warned me about this guy, but I'm starting to think the warning wasn't strong enough."

Eli responded with, "Emily, I told you when we are here you must not call me Father. We won't discuss religion, and Robb Michael won't discuss business. We don't talk about our work here."

She looked back at him and asked, "Why not?"

Robb Michael interrupted, "Because Eli and I have our own religion.

"And now that you are here, you must be baptized in that religion, or you will never understand life the way we do."

With that, Robb Michael got up and went around the table. He picked Emily up and carried her over to the pool.

She was wide-eyed and looked panicky as he stepped onto the steps at the shallow end of the pool with her still in his arms.

When he was waist deep in the pool, Robb Michael took his left arm out from under her and sprinkled water on her face, saying, "I now baptize you into the unholy order of stupid idiots.

"This entitles you to do idiotic things and have idiotic thoughts and ideas. Then, of course, you must plan on doing those idiotic things. You should fit right in.

"After all, you have to be a little stupid and an idiot to get in-volved with people like Eli and me!" All the while Eli was laughing. Joanna couldn't believe what she was seeing.

As Joanna saw Robb Michael carry Emily, looking wide-eyed and somewhat bewildered and panicky, over to the edge of the pool and set her on the deck. She found herself saying, "You are so lucky, Emily.

"You have gotten yourself baptized into something I have yet to be baptized into."

Meanwhile, Robb Michael climbed out of the pool and suddenly swooped up Joanna and carried her over to the pool.

He stepped back into the pool and also sprinkled water in her face, saying, "I would have baptized you a long time ago, but Eli wasn't here to watch.

"Smart as you are, you can still be pretty stupid. After all, you married me, didn't you? Someday you'll figure out what I just said, but in the meanwhile, I'll still love you."

As he placed her on the deck, next to Emily who was still sitting wide-eyed on the deck, he said, "Now show me how smart you girls are, and go get some towels and get dry."

All the while, Eli was roaring so hard with laughter that he had tears in his eyes.

Joanna led Emily over to the towel closet, near the shower stall, and got them each a couple of towels and a couple white terry cloth robes.

Then they stepped into the huge four-head shower stall. There they took off their wet things and dried themselves off.

The two women looked at each other. Emily was looking intently at her.

Joanna asked, "Is something wrong?"

Emily said, "No. From the size of your boobs and the swelling of your midriff, I would say that you are going to have a baby."

Joanna smiled. "My boobs were nearly this big before I got pregnant."

Joanna looked at Emily from her reddish blonde hair, all the way down to her dark reddish pubic area, and thought, *She's at least four inches taller than I am, and big, too. At least a double D.*

Then she said, "There are towels and robes in this closet.

"Grab whatever you need, and come with me to the laundry room. We can get our clothes dried."

As they were coming from the laundry room, Joanna thought, *I like her. I like her a lot. I'd bet that she has a lot of friends.*

Back at the table, Joanna saw that Robb Michael was still wearing his wet clothes. Both men stood up as the girls sat down.

Robb Michael reached over and picked up his glass and held it up. "I wish to propose a toast."

Everyone picked up their wine glass and looked to Robb Michael expectantly.

"Here's to the unholy order of stupid idiots and to everybody in it." Making a funny face, he said, "Boy! Aren't we lucky?"

Everyone drank.

Suddenly Eli started laughing again. The longer he laughed, the harder he laughed.

Everyone watched as Eli laughed. Robb Michael asked, "What's so funny?"

Eli pointed at Robb Michael, "You! You baptizing Emily!"

Eli said between his sobs of laughter. "You baptized Emily!" Eli couldn't stop laughing. "Emily's a nun!" he said between his sobs of laughter.

Robb Michael looked dumbfounded while Eli once more roared with laughter. Then Joanna started laughing.

As the laughter started dying down, Robb Michael looked at Eli and said, "When you say none, do you mean doesn't get none, doesn't want none, isn't going to look for none, kind of none?"

Eli looked at Robb Michael. "My friend. She's not only a nun, she's a mother superior." Joanna laughed once again.

Robb Michael looked at Emily standing in front of him wearing nothing but a small smile and a terry cloth robe.

He said, "Emily, you are the only one here that's entitled to wear the title of superior sister. So, I say unto you, if there's an apology in order for anything that's happening here this night, consider it given. Other than that, the party must go on."

With that Robb Michael started striding toward the laundry room, saying, "I'm going to get out of these wet clothes."

As they all watched him go, Eli, suddenly serious said, "You know, Joanna, I'm concerned for Robb Michael.

"I've known him for most of my life, and I've never seen him pray."

Joanna interrupted. "I have," she said casually.

Eli was startled. "You have?"

Joanna looked at him evenly. "Yes. Just the other day, I saw him praying over a young boy that was on his operating table.

"You know, Eli, you and I, and possibly Mr. Kahn, know Robb Michael Keandra better than anyone else.

"We know he is so talented, so totally different than anyone else in this world.

"We know what very few people know. We know anyone that meets him knows he's special.

"But they don't know how special, because they don't get to spend enough time with him to find out.

"Most people that meet him see someone that's kind of nerdy. But they don't know what is really behind that posture.

"He knows how to make things happen that nobody else can, but I know him better than you and Douglas Kahn.

"Douglas Kahn told me the reason they call him Dr. 'Frankenstein' is because he brings people back to life.

"It's true, I've seen him do it."

Emily interrupted, "Oh! He's that Dr. Keandra! Well, that explains a lot."

Joanna continued speaking, "One night, when I was drunk, Robb Michael kidnapped me and brought me here."

Eli interrupted, "Robb Michael kidnapped you?

Joanna continued talking. "When I woke up the next morning, he told me he wasn't going to let me leave until I negotiated my way out of here. Instead of negotiating my way out, I negotiated my way in."

Joanna saw that Emily and Eli were looking at her with a concerned look on their faces. "Don't look at me that way. Robb Michael used to eat lunch at the same place I did.

"Before I even met him, I knew he was someone truly different. During the whole ordeal, I wasn't frightened.

"I felt I could leave at any time.

"The reason I didn't leave was because I was curious to know just what he is all about. I still am.

"I'm going to stay here for the rest of my life, just so I can be near him."

Joanna saw Robb Michael come into the workout gym.

Eli looked at her, comprehension showing on his face. "Yes, I agree. His greatness really shines through."

Emily suddenly spoke. "Personally, I think he's kind of loony."

Joanna smiled. "Everyone does when they first meet him."

Eli, deep in thought, quietly said, "Joanna, what you've told me makes me extremely happy. I'm so elated at what you've told me. I'm going to throw Emily in the pool to celebrate." With that, Eli picked up an unsuspecting Emily and threw her in the deep end of the pool.

When Emily hit the water, she had her arms in the air. The terrycloth robe slipped right over her arms.

Joanna heard Robb Michael before she saw him as he ran across the floor and dove head first into the pool.

Robb Michael went in deep and brought Emily back to the surface.

As he swam toward the shallow end of the pool, she was coughing and choking.

When he reached the shallow end, he carried Emily out of the pool and laid her face down on the deck.

Then he slipped his left arm between her legs and lifted her a little while using his right hand to push firmly on her back. "Come on, Emily, cough it all up."

She coughed up about a cup of water.

Robb Michael kept pushing intermittently on her back, saying, "Come on, Emily.

"I want you to cough up some more. I've heard of people drowning on a tablespoon of water, so cough up some more for me."

Joanna and Eli watched uncomprehending as Emily coughed and sputtered.

Joanna and Eli watched as he turned her over, then picked up her nude form and carried her over to the bench by the shower stall.

They followed him over to where he had laid her face down, still coughing and spitting.

"Come on, Emily, cough up the rest of it." Robb Michael got a bath towel and laid it over her. Joanna, get another robe. One for me, too."

Eli, watching, asked, "What just happened?"

Robb Michael smiled and said, "Eli, before you throw someone in the pool, you're supposed to ask them if they know how to swim."

Eli and Joanna looked at each other, then at him. Eli, concerned, said, "I assumed she knew how to swim. How did you know she couldn't?"

"When I baptized her, she was panicky, frozen with fear. She couldn't even speak. She clung to me so tight I had to get her out of the water quickly.

"Fear can be a good thing. But nobody should be that scared. That's why I apologized to her."

Joanna brought a couple robes over. One was white the other was pink. Robb Michael chose the pink one, and hung it on a nearby exercycle.

Then he walked over to the pool, fished out the other robe, carried it over and threw it on the floor of the shower stall.

Joanna asked, "Why did you take the pink robe?"

"Because I like being noticed. When someone like me wears pink, everyone notices. You did when I was wearing my wedding robe."

While everyone laughed, Eli went over to Emily, who was coughing while she laughed and seriously said, "I'm so sorry, Emily.

"How stupid of me. I don't know what to say." Robb Michael looked around and laughed.

"Don't even think about it, Eli. I did the same thing when I threw you in the river the first time. I never even thought to ask you if you knew how to swim.

"When you screamed all the way down, I dove in after you, thinking you didn't know how to swim.

"After that I never would jump in to save you.

"That's why we all belong to the Unholy Order of Stupid Idiots.

"Superior sister, you are still alive, and we all intend to keep you that way."

Everyone went back to the table by the pool.

"Emily, would you like something to eat or drink?" asked Robb Michael as he sat down at the table.

Joanna saw her looking at him, like she couldn't stop looking at him.

After a pause, Emily said, "Yes, I would like another piece of that sausage and another glass of wine."

Joanna watched as Robb Michael cut the sausage and put some of the short pieces on the grill in the fireplace, then he stabbed a hot piece with a fork and grabbed an open can of Pork and Beans, put a spoon in it, and gave it to Emily.

Eli poured the wine.

Then Emily said, "Robb Michael, I see you don't drink much. You haven't drunk even a half a glass of wine. Why not?"

Joanna interrupted. "Dr. Robb Michael is on call at the hospital. If they call, he has to go."

They ate and drank while talking until three o'clock in the morning.

The party came to a slow end. Joanna took Emily back to the laundry room to change her clothes.

They all said their farewells and goodbyes as they walked toward the front door. Joanna saw Emily hug Robb Michael and kiss him on the cheek.

Emily said something to Robb Michael. Joanna didn't hear it while Eli hugged her, and said, "Goodnight, Joanna. It was a wonderful night."

Joanna then hugged Emily and said, "I hope you're okay with the way the night turned out."

"The night turned out great. I don't think I'll ever drink water again."

They all laughed as she continued, "I want you to know you're right about Robb Michael. There's a lot more to him than you notice at first glance.

"Do you believe this? I just hugged a man wearing nothing but a pink robe."

As Eli and Emily opened the door to leave, everyone raved at the same time. "It's snowing!"

Happily, they all made comments about the snow.

Joanna watched as Eli and Emily got into Eli's Buick. She noticed Emily was looking back through the falling snow at them as they drove away.

After Eli and Emily had gone, they went down to the party room. Robb Michael went behind the bar. "Would you like a night cap this early in the morning?"

She saw him pour himself a shot of bourbon. "Yes, pour me one, too." She watched him pour her a shot.

Then asked, "What did Emily say when she kissed you good night?"

"She just thanked me for saving her life."

"After you pulled her out of the pool, she was looking at you all night."

He looked at her seriously. "That had to be a very traumatic experience. It might be a good idea to invite her over to play in the pool. Then, maybe, she will overcome her fear of water."

Joanna looked at him over the rim of the shot glass, and asked, "Is it okay to get personal?"

"Sure, what do you want to know?"

She paused for a moment and then asked, "If Emily wasn't a nun, would you fuck her?"

"Yes. Whether she's a nun or not has nothing to do with it. She's a beautiful woman. I would take her to bed without even thinking about it. Would it bother you if I did?"

Joanna watched him as he downed the shot of whiskey, and then downed her own.

She thought about Julie Lane, the nurse up on ICU, and the other women she had seen that she knew had been in his bed.

As she thought about them, she realized that she liked them. Everyone of them.

Then thinking about each one of them again for a moment, she said, "Probably not. I like Emily. She not a dumbbell. She's down to earth, and you can tell she's a hard worker. She actually has calluses on her hands. Pour me another, please."

He smiled and poured her another shot. "I noticed."

Then Joanna said, "You know, Eli was asking about you tonight."

He turned to her with a serious look on his face. "About what?"

"Whether or not you pray. I told him that I've seen you pray over a patient on your operating table."

Robb Michael started laughing. Once again it was a natural laugh, not forced.

When he stopped laughing he said, "Would you like to hear my prayer?"

She looked at him and smiled, "Sure, why not."

He looked at her and said, "GOD!—DAMN IT!—I'VE JUST KILLED THE DAMN PATIENT! WHAT IN THE HELL DO I DO NOW?"

"I don't always say the same prayer, but it always goes something like that."

She gave him a weird look. "Why would you say a prayer like that?"

"Because I figure I've just killed the patient, or I'm going to kill him, trying to save his life.

Now don't ask me to explain that last statement, because I can't. What do you say we dance?"

They danced to Christmas carols, along with everything else.

After dancing, she went over and downed her shot of whiskey, and asked, "You wanna fuck?"

"Silly girl! I love it when you talk dirty. You know, you are asking silly questions again."

GOING ON A TRIP
Joanna awoke at about eight.

She saw that Robb Michael was still sleeping.

She got out of bed and went to the bathroom.

She sent Kathy an email: "Last night we danced to Christmas carols. Believe that? What we did to those Christmas carols was absolutely sinful, but you don't want to hear about all that."

In her mind, she could hear Kathy's voice, 'Yes I do!'

When she came back, she looked at Robb Michael, still sleeping, and crawled back in bed with him.

She no sooner than pulled the covers over herself when Robb Michael reached for her in his sleep.

He pulled her over to him with one arm around her waist, the other around her neck, with one hand cupping her breast.

She waited for him to start making love to her. When he didn't, she knew he was still asleep.

Once again, she snuggled up a little closer, and fell asleep in the comfort of his arms.

At eleven-thirty in the morning, she awoke to the vibrations of his cell phone on the night stand.

She shook Robb Michael to wake him.

Waking up, he asked, "What's happening?"

"Your phone's ringing."

Answering his phone, Robb Michael said again, "What's happening?"

Robb Michael laid there, massaging her breasts and listening to his phone.

Suddenly she heard him say. "Alright. Yes. I'll come right up there." With that he hung up the phone.

He lay there quietly while massaging, fondling, and stroking her. Then he said, "We better get dressed. We have to go to Seattle."

As they were dressing, Joanna asked, "What's happening in Seattle?"

"The workforce at one of my manufacturing plants is rebelling against the supervision.

"They've shut down all of the machines in the plant. I don't understand it. The union's not involved.

"The union told them to go back to work, and they told the union they weren't going back to work until they talk to me, so I'm going to go up and let them talk.

"Mr. Kahn is going to meet us at the airport. We'll take the corporate jet."

They arrived at the plant at two in the afternoon. It was cold. There was about two inches of snow on the ground.

When they got out of the car, Joanna looked around at the surroundings.

The place was massive.

There were hundreds of men, possibly more than a thousand.

Some were sitting with their backs to the wall of the building.

Others were in groups, standing around talking, yet others appeared to be loitering.

When they saw Robb Michael get out of the car, they all but mobbed him. All of them were yelling, "We gotta talk to you!"

Some were saying other things about machines screwing.

Joanna didn't understand.

Robb Michael held up his hands to quiet them. They all pretty much quieted down.

Robb Michael loudly said, "Why don't you all go back to work? You all know me well enough to know I'll come around and visit with you all. Leastwise, I always have.

One of the men said, "This is important enough to wait on! We have important stuff to tell old man Keandra!"

Robb Michael smiled, then said, "If you have something to tell that cantankerous old goat, don't tell me." Pointing at Joanna he said, "Tell her.

"She's my wife, Mrs. Robb Michael. Old man Keandra will listen to her before he'll listen to me. All you've got to do is look at her to know why."

A lot of the men laughed.

Robb Michael said, "Look. I have to go inside and talk to supervision."

As Robb Michael walked away, two or three groups of men gathered around Joanna. Douglas Kahn stayed behind with Joanna.

Joanna turned to face some of the men asking, "What's so important?"

One of the men said, "Look, there's some graft or something going on!

"The company's buying some new automatic screw machines. They're the wrong ones. This company always bought Index machines.

"Now they're trying to bring in some off-brand. Word has it that the guys in the office are getting a kickback for pushing this sale through.

"I know guys that work for other companies that have those machines. They tell me those machines always come out of adjustment.

"We hear that they're buying a hundred and twenty-two of those machines.

"The Index automatic screw machines are far superior. Tell the old man that, will ya?"

Joanna looked at them in disbelief. Then she said, "Yes. I'm going to see the old man as soon as I get back to Portland. I'll be sure he gets your message."

With that, the men turned and started walking back into the building. Joanna followed them inside.

She stopped just inside the door.

Suddenly she heard the whine of the machines as they were starting up, one after another.

Joanna turned and focused on Douglas Kahn. "Mr. Kahn, I'm not sure what just happened. But whatever it was, it was important enough for these men to shut this entire plant down.

"I think I better meet with that cantankerous old goat and keep him informed," she said smiling. As they were walking toward the office door, Robb Michael came walking out.

He had a look of wonder on his face. "How did you get them to go back to work?"

She looked up at him and smiled. "I didn't tell them to go back to work. I just promised them I would meet with that cantankerous old goat as soon as I got back to Portland."

Robb Michael stopped walking.

She saw he was looking at her.

Once again, she saw pride in his eyes.

Then he smiled and said, "This day is the greatest day of my life. Come on, I always walk through and greet the workers whenever I come and visit any of the plants."

On the way back to Portland, Joanna told Robb Michael what the men had told her.

Douglas Kahn told Robb Michael he was on it.

TWO WEEKS LATER

Joanna was downtown Portland doing some shopping when she saw Emily standing on a corner, waiting at a crosswalk.

Joanna walked up to her and said, "Remember me?"

"Of course, I do. How are you?"

"I'm good. Do you have time for coffee?"

Emily looked at Joanna and said, "I'll make time. How's Robb Michael?"

As they crossed the street, Joanna said, "He's fine. Right now, he's out of town."

Joanna led Emily into a coffee house on S.W. Broadway.

They both ordered a coffee and a small cake, then they sat at a table.

Joanna said, "Speaking of Robb Michael, he suggested that I invite you over during the day, when you can, so we can get in the pool.

"He says you should wade around in the pool, and maybe learn how to swim. He said it's important that you overcome your fear of water."

Emily looked thoughtful, then said, "When would be a good time?"

"Anytime. Right now, if you like," Joanna replied, "Do you have a car?"

"No, I ride the bus and the light-rail. I'll need a ride back when we're through," she replied.

"Not a problem," Joanna said. "I have my own car."

As they finished their coffee, Joanna asked, "What time do you have to be back?"

Emily smiled, "I don't. I have all day to myself."

GETTING IN THE POOL

As soon as they arrived at the compound, Joanna showed Emily through the place.

As Emily looked through the compound, she asked, "How long did Robb Michael keep you here before he married you?"

Joanna beamed a bright smile. "Three months and five days. I liked this place better than my apartment. Which I still have, by the way."

"Why do you still have an apartment?"

"The lease runs out next month.

"I told Robb Michael that I wanted to keep it so we would have someplace to stay in town. He told me he owns a small townhouse in the west hills. So, I'm going to let the apartment go."

Joanna led her into the workout gym.

When they were at the pool's edge, Joanna said, "You can take off your clothes and leave them on the table."

Emily looked at her wide-eyed. "You don't wear a swim suit?"

"No, there's no need. We're always here alone. We never wear anything."

"What if someone comes in?"

"Nobody ever comes in to this part of the house except me and Robb Michael. I always keep the door to the compound locked. Besides me, Robb Michael is the only one with a key."

Joanna smiled at her and said, "You don't have anything to worry about. Robb Michael has seen you naked anyhow."

It was Emily's turn to smile. Smiling sheepishly, she said, "You're right about that."

Looking at Joanna's breasts, she said, "I'll bet those get a lot of attention from guys."

"Yeah, they get more attention than I do."

Emily looked at her seriously, "You may not believe this, but when I'm wearing a habit, men look at them as though they can see right through it. A habit makes you as close to being unseen as possible, but not to men."

Joanna went over to a cupboard, reached in and brought out a life preserver and said, "Put this on. Robb Michael had it specially made for you. The night he pulled you out of the water, he sat down and drew it up on paper. Then he had one of the companies he owns make it for him."

Joanna helped her into it.

It was a simple floating device that fit on her shoulders, with straps that went under her arms, and then buckled in the front.

It wasn't a vest. It was more like the shoulder pads that football players wear, with pads under her arms that went to her waist where it buckled.

When it was on her, it didn't cover her breasts.

After they got it on, Joanna said, "Let's go test it.

"Robb Michael says it will keep the wearer's head above water and allow the wearer to swim while wearing it."

Joanna led Emily down the steps at the shallow end of the pool.

They walked, hand in hand, toward the deep end of the pool.

Joanna said, "Now hold my hand, and we'll walk only far enough the water is over your breasts—or tits, as Robb Michael calls them.

"Then I want you to lift your legs to see if you float. If you don't float, stand up again."

"Please don't let go of my hand," said Emily, as she did what she was told.

The water came about half way between her lower lip and the bottom of her chin when she started to float.

Joanna said, "Now use your arms to pull yourself through the water to see if you can swim. Kick your feet."

Emily started paddling her way back toward the shallow end of the pool.

Then, she stood up and said, "I'm not sure I like this. I keep getting my face wet."

"We all do. That's the way it is when you're swimming."

The girls frolicked in the water for over two hours before they got out.

As Joanna was taking her home, she said, "I really enjoyed today. We can do it more often, if you like."

Emily smiled a small smile. "I don't have a lot of free time. I do volunteer work at the hospital, plus scheduling other work at the church.

"But I would like to come. I think I learned a little about swimming.

"I would like to do more, but I don't want to interfere with you and Robb Michael's home life."

"Anymore it seems that Robb Michael is away doing business during the day. But, he's always home at night.

"Why don't I give you a key to the compound door? Then you can come and go when it's convenient for you."

"Thank you, I would like that."

"Always wear your life preserver," said Joanna quietly.

"Oh, I will. You can rely on that.

"I learned a little about how to control myself in the water today. I don't want to be in the pool alone. I'm not confident at all."

ONE MONTH LATER

Joanna was swimming in the pool when she heard the doorbell.

She never bothered to answer because she knew it would be Emily. Emily had been there almost every day in the last month.

After the doorbell rang three times, she saw Emily come in the workout gym door.

"You didn't answer the door," said Emily, as she walked across the floor to the pool.

"No need, I knew you had a key," said Joanna.

Casually, Emily removed her clothes and put on her life preserver. As Emily was getting in the pool, Joanna was getting out, saying, "I'll go make us some tea."

Emily looked at Joanna as she came back to the pool.

As Emily got out of the pool, she said, "Good Lord, Jo. You're getting a good-sized bump in front."

"Yes, and Robb Michael says swimming is the best exercise. It doesn't wreck your knees or hips," Joanna said as she set the tray on the table.

Emily looked at Joanna, then seriously said, "You were right about Robb Michael. There's a lot more to him than meets the eye.

"You can't believe how I felt when I was on the bottom of the pool, sucking in water. I looked up, and there he was, coming down for me.

"It's unbelievable how strong he is. He pulled me up out of the water faster than I went down under."

"I know," said Joanna, "he did the same thing to me when he threw me off the bridge.

"I was still on my way down when he grabbed my arm and started me on my way back up."

The two of them sat, talked, and sipped tea for half an hour before going back in the water.

TWO MONTHS LATER
JOANNA GOES ON A TRIP

Robb Michael was busy making breakfast for them as Joanna managed to drag herself to the kitchen table.

"Robb Michael, why do you always get up so early?"

"Work, work, work," said Robb Michael as he slid some eggs on to some hash brown potatoes already on her plate.

"Why do you always have to go on these trips?"

"I don't have to. You can go in my place. You've been at the Seattle plant."

Joanna perked up. "You mean it?"

"Sure. They know you, so why don't you go and play CEO for a day? They're only having a production meeting today.

"Then you can go and greet the workforce, smile a lot and let them tell you everything that's wrong with the place.

"Listen to them carefully. Sometimes they're right.

"Then you get to come back here and let the old man know everything that's wrong in this world, according to them.

"In the meantime, I'll go back to bed while you take care of business."

Joanna hesitated.

"Really?"

"Sure, why not?

"You can handle it, and it will give you something to do besides hang around town all day."

Joanna looked at him. Excitedly, she said, "Okay, what's the procedure?"

"There isn't one. You just take this briefcase, and while you are in transit, study the journal that's inside. You'll figure it out."

She looked at the briefcase. "What's the combination?"

He smiled at her. "What's our wedding date?"

She smiled back at him. "August twenty-second?"

"That's the combination. Eight, two, two. If you forget that, I'll boot you right in the butt."

LATER THAT NIGHT

At eight in the evening, it was cold and there was about six inches of snow on the ground that wasn't there when she left that morning.

When Joanna walked into the compound, she felt good about herself.

She had taken care of business. It was a lot easier than she thought it would be, and she didn't want it to end.

On the way to Seattle, she read the journal.

During the meeting, she wrote in the journal the same way Robb Michael had.

On the way back, she flew the plane. She was happy about everything that day.

Robb Michael's style of keeping circumstances, happenings, and facts recorded in his journal gave her a head start at the meeting.

She could tell, they were impressed with the way she chaired the meeting.

When she arrived home, she saw that Robb Michael was sitting at the table, drinking a cup of coffee.

"You're drinking coffee this late in the day?" she asked, as she set the briefcase down on the table.

"Yeah, well, I had a tiring day. Something unexpected came up that I had to take care of."

"Oh really? Like what?"

She watched Robb Michael's smiling face as he said, "For one thing, it snowed. I hear they got damn near two feet in east county."

Then he said, "Oh, no, you don't. You came in here smiling like the cat that got the cream. You go first. How did it go today?"

"Great! When do I get to go again?"

"Day after tomorrow, if you want. We've got a chip plant in Boise.

"Mr. Kahn tells me you were a sensation today. He seems to think that you're the man for the job in Boise, too."

Joanna was practically dancing. "Yes! Yes! I'll go."

She saw he was looking at her and said, "What?"

"Remember, you're pregnant. If you start getting tired, you let me take over. I don't think I can handle it if you lose those babies."

"I'm okay. Really, I am. I really am. You know? When I was talking to some of the guys in the plant, they shut their machine down.

"Some of the others told me they couldn't shut their machines down because the temperature of the machine will change and the tolerances will change.

"These guys are really serious about their work. Yeah! I want to go." With that she sat down and started telling him about her day.

TWO MONTHS LATER

Joanna was tired.

She had gotten up early to see Robb Michael off to work. She felt like she was carrying a large watermelon in her belly. Robb Michael told her that she couldn't go to work for him anymore until after she had the babies.

Thinking to herself, *after I have the babies I will be too busy to go. Oh, well, it was fun while it lasted.*

It seemed to her the babies were kicking her on the inside like they were trying to kick their way out.

Then she thought, *My God! I hope they're not fighting in there!*

She wanted to have those babies as soon as she could so she could get her life back to normal, whatever normal is, or will be. She was wondering if she still knew when the phone rang.

When she picked up the receiver, she heard Douglas Kahn's voice come out of the phone. "Joanna, I'm upstairs in the house.

"The priest that married you is here. Would you like me to send him down?"

"Yes, Mr. Kahn, he knows the way. Mr. Kahn, you would make a good butler. Did you know that?"

He laughed, "Yes, your husband tells me that all the time."

Then she laughed, saying, "Maybe we should hire one. I'll talk to him about it. In the meanwhile, send Eli on down."

Joanna met Eli at the door with a cup of coffee in her hand.

As he came through the door, she said, "There's another cup of coffee on the table."

Eli smiled and said, "Thank you, Joanna, that's just what I need right now.

"Tell me, have you seen that husband of yours lately?"

"Isn't he upstairs?"

"I didn't see him. Mr. Kahn says he's taking care of business."

Joanna looked at Eli quizzically. "That's strange. Usually, where you see Mr. Kahn, you see Robb Michael. I wonder where he's at?

"Robb Michael has Mr. Kahn with him all the time to solve legalities as they go when they're doing business.

"In fact, Robb Michael sends Mr. Kahn with me when I'm doing business."

Astonished Eli asked, "He has you doing business?"

"Sure, all the time. I've done things for him in Seattle, Boise, Sacramento, Los Angeles, even in Reno, and Waco, Texas."

Eli stared at nothing for a moment. "Now that's strange.

"I didn't think that he would trust anyone but himself to make decisions when it comes to business.

"Tell me, how much do you know about Robb Michael?"

"Not a lot. I'm learning more about him all the time. You know, I can tell when he is near. I can feel it. Why do you ask?"

"Because I believe there are things you should know about Robb Michael."

"Like what?"

"Let me start at the beginning. When we were kids in school, they gave everyone an IQ test. Robb Michael tested higher than anyone that's ever been tested in the state of Oregon.

"His test scores were so high they couldn't believe what they were seeing, so they tested him again.

"The results were the same. His parents requested the school not to tell anyone how high it was.

"Everybody had heard it was high, but nobody knows how high except the government. The government wanted to put him in special schools, but his parents refused.

"When word got around that he had a high IQ, the other kids in school got the word around that Robb Michael was smarter than anyone else.

"Robb Michael was just a skinny little kid, smaller than everyone else in the school.

"Bullies were picking on him all the time, wanting him to prove he was smarter than they were. Sometimes they would beat up on him.

"His father was a doctor. Robb Michael began reading his father's medical books at an early age.

"It was no time at all before Robb Michael learned how to hurt someone just by touching them in the right spot."

Joanna interrupted, "Yes, I saw him do that. A guy I worked with touched me, and Robb Michael jabbed him in the stomach, then touched his throat.

"Suddenly, Mr. Dorn was on the ground, choking and trying to catch his breath."

"Yes, suddenly the bullies aren't bullies anymore," said Eli. "They learned to leave him alone. He knew how to hurt them and they knew it.

"They were right. He was smarter than they were, but they couldn't see it.

"Then, just because I sat next to him and talked to him a lot, they started picking on me. Robb Michael put a stop to that real fast.

"Then people started calling him a skinny little nerd.

"Not to his face, but to each other. Robb Michael hated it, so he started working out to build up his physique.

"He didn't seem to get any bigger, but it wasn't long before he was as strong, or stronger, than anyone in school.

"At about that time, everyone noticed he was doing things nobody else could do. For him, it was always success.

"He is the only man I have ever met that will walk without fear anywhere he wants to go. He has never failed at anything. Never ever! If he plans to do something, he will do it.

"He was accepted by Harvard at thirteen, while I had another five years of school to go. He excelled there too. However, he always kept in touch with me.

"That's the way he is. He won't stop trying until he is successful.

"Christmas, when I told you I have never seen him pray, I was shocked when you told me that you had, because most of the people I have met with a high IQ don't believe in God at all.

"With their thinking ability, the idea of God is beyond their thinking capability.

"I have read Einstein believed there is a God, but most of the high IQ people I've met do not believe in God at all."

Joanna looked thoughtful, and then said, "Mr. Kahn told me when Robb Michael is in surgery and doesn't know what to do next, he prays.

"Tell me, Eli, have you seen or heard from Emily? I haven't seen her in over a month."

Eli looked stricken. "She has broken her vows and has left the church. I don't understand why. She has always excelled.

"Then suddenly, she's gone. I wish I could talk to her, get her to come back."

Joanna had a look of wonder on her face. "That's why I haven't heard from her. It must be something she doesn't want people she knows to ask or know about."

Eli and Joanna talked throughout the afternoon.

MAY EIGHTH

At 7:50 AM, Joanna delivered twin boys, Robert Michael Keandra and Roger Scott Keandra.

Although giving birth was an ordeal, Joanna was all smiles. She was glad it was over.

She had a baby in each arm as Robb Michael came into her room.

Joanna looked at him and said, "Do you like what you see?"

She watched him as he opened the front of her nightgown, exposing her breasts. "There is no way you or anyone else could know how much I like what I see," he said softly.

As he spoke, she was looking at her puffy, swollen nipples.

Then he picked one baby and put him to her breast. Then he picked up the other baby and put him on the other breast.

He looked at her and smiled. "I'm looking at a picture that will be in my mind till the day I die."

He saw that she was uncomfortable, so he picked up one baby and held it while she held the other one.

She asked, "Well, what do you want to do now?"

Robb Michael smiled at her. "You know. Time to start thinking about Michael Jo and how soon we can get her here."

She laughed a little, then she said, "You are in too big of a hurry, but we'll work on it as soon as I can."

MAY FIFTEENTH

Joanna had been fascinated with Robb Michael and the babies since she brought them home from the hospital.

Except for the four to five hours during the day that he was taking care of business, Robb Michael had been changing their diapers, bathing them, and holding them ever since they were born.

Watching him, she said, "Why haven't you been feeding them? You're doing everything else."

Robb Michael had a trace of a smile on his face. "You've got me at a disadvantage.

My tits aren't big enough.

"But don't you worry. As big as your tits are, none of us are going to go hungry."

She smiled back at him. "I noticed that you're getting your share. Is there a reason that you're doing that? I've never heard of a man nursing before."

"I'm sure that there's a lot of men that do." Then he said, "Yes, as a matter of fact there is.

"I'm checking my vitals before and after to see what the difference is.

"Your milk is full of antibodies, and God knows what else. You've got more milk than you need to feed the boys.

"I had a special breast pump made. I want you to pump your breasts after you feed the boys. As big as you are, you don't want to be stretched out of shape by letting them get too big."

She looked at the pump. It was a glass case about two feet square, and eight inches wide.

Inside the case she could see a motor and a mechanical mechanism with two pistons that moved back and forth, with some plastic hoses, and suction cups for her nipples.

"Feed the boys whenever your breasts start getting bigger, and then pump them again."

She looked at him seriously. "Are your vital signs different?"

"Yes. My white cell count is quite a lot higher. Why? Does it bother you that I'm drinking your milk?"

"No, it feels good. If you like, I can put some in a glass for you."

Robb Michael smiled at her once more. "No, I don't want you to do that. It's better if I suck it out of you."

"Really? Why?"

"Well, to start with, I enjoy sucking on you. I always have.

"If you put your milk in a glass, the temperature difference of the glass will kill the antibodies. You would have to keep the glass exactly the same temperature as your body to protect the antibodies. Understand?"

Once again she asked, "How long do you want me to nurse the boys? Five or six months?"

"No. You should nurse the boys until they push you away.

"There are studies that show the longer you nurse a baby, the higher the baby's IQ will be, so nurse them till they push you away.

"It wouldn't hurt anything if you nursed them for a few years.

"Expose yourself to them in their early years. If they come and suck, let them. They will know when to stop.

"You know, it's strange, people will feed their children milk from an animal, but not milk from their own species.

"In Japan, a woman nurses a child on average four years.

"Here in the States, some women don't nurse at all. I've had some women tell me, 'No kid is going to suck on me!'

"Some women never learn what they're supposed to be. The one's that do nurse, do so only a few months, some for up to a year.

"When a child becomes a toddler, it becomes more difficult for a woman to nurse a child and take care of her household duties at the same time.

"They should all nurse until the child pushes them away. Some babies push away early. The milk from a woman is far superior for a baby than milk from any animal.

"The milk from an animal is just food because the DNA doesn't match.

"Your milk is full of other things that are important for a baby because the DNA matches."

She smiled. "Do you want me to feed you before I pump them?"

"Only when I'm here. If I'm not here, pump them immediately after you've fed the boys. If there's anything you need, tell me now because I have to go and do a few errands."

She smiled and shook her head no. Then she said, "Do you want me to feed you before you go?"

With a small smile on his face, he said, "Ask a dying man if he wants to live."

She got up, stood before him and opened the front of her gown. While she caressed him, Robb Michael began sucking on her breast.

JOANNA FLYS THE U2

Late in the evening, Robb Michael told Joanna to leave the boys with Mrs. Numura, the grounds keeper's wife.

He told her he had something he wanted her to do. They got in his car and he drove to the airport.

It was raining pretty hard as they drove through the darkness. When they got to the National Guard gate, Robb Michael turned in.

After getting cleared, he drove over to the same building that he had taken her before.

While they were suiting up, she wondered why they were doing it.

When they were suited up, they got in a military van and rode out to the U2.

It was still raining steadily when they arrived on the tarmac.

Standing next to the plane, Robb Michael said, "You get in the front cockpit. I'll be in the rear."

After she boarded the plane, Robb Michael checked her out on the controls, then got in the rear cockpit.

Through her helmet, she heard him say, "Remember where your wing tips are and taxi out to the end of the runway.

"Now you have little wheels under the wings, so be careful.

"The wings can be damaged."

As she taxied out to the end of the runway, she felt uncomfortable.

The plane seemed to handle okay, but the wing span made her uneasy as she maneuvered the plane.

She had more than fifty hours flying time in jets, so she wasn't nervous at all, except about the wing span.

The rain didn't let up.

Robb Michael communicated with the tower as she maneuvered into position at the end of the runway.

In her helmet she heard the tower give them clearance to take off.

As she pushed the throttle forward, she heard Robb Michael's voice in her helmet. "This bird wants to fly all by itself.

"As you're going down the runway, it will lift off all by itself. When you lift off, the wheels under the wings will fall off.

"Just control it as you go. You can gain altitude as fast or slow as you want."

The plane quickly went splashing down the runway, and then she felt it start to lift off.

Gently she pulled back on the stick, and instantly retracted the landing gear.

She felt the same feeling she did the last time she flew in this plane.

She not only felt the forward thrust, she also felt like she was going up in an elevator.

As they rose above the clouds, she heard him say, "If your wiper is on, turn it off."

She turned off the wiper.

After she got up to fifty thousand feet, she heard Robb Michael say, "Keep climbing until I tell you to level off.

"I'll control the throttle for you."

Then she heard the engine running more quietly.

Robb Michael said, "Level off now."

Wow! What a rush! she thought.

Once again she heard Robb Michael's voice in her ears. "One year ago today, I brought you up to the stars.

"This year, I thought I would let you bring me up here and show me all of the stars I might have missed that night.

"That's why I have you sitting in the front cockpit.

"On a standard U2, the cockpit I'm sitting in doesn't exist. This cockpit is for training purposes.

"In the standard U2, you are sitting in the pilot's seat."

She looked up through the bubble at the stars, and once again wondered how they got there.

She looked at the altimeter and couldn't believe what she was looking at.

She flew around at that altitude for about ten minutes before starting to descend.

As she descended, she turned north and went joy riding over the northern Cascades. Then she asked, "When you were flying over enemy territory, what was it like?"

There was a long pause, then she heard his voice in her ears.

"Most of the time it was boring, but there were times I was challenged. During those times, I had to play some pretty dangerous games."

Suddenly, her mind was full of questions.

But she never asked them.

Two hours later she set the plane down on the runway.

Some men drove to the runway and put some wheels on the wings to hold them up, then she taxied back to the hanger.

Once they were back in their street clothes, he let her drive home. On the way, she took the back way in to the compound.

She stopped the car halfway up the long driveway and said, "I want you to know, before long I'll be able to do anything.

"Maybe even save your life."

Feeling proud, she smiled as she drove the rest of the way up to the compound.

When they went to bed that night, they never made love.

She just snuggled up and laid in his arms, wondering what it must feel like flying over enemy territory in a U2.

TWO WEEKS LATER

Joanna started interviewing people to be a nanny for the boys. While she was interviewing possible nannies, Robb Michael had told her he was going to buy some more cars, so he wasn't there when she was hiring a nanny.

The nanny would have to be willing to live in, willing to travel, and not afraid to fly. She was instructed to call Joanna 'Mrs. Robb Michael' as everyone else she did business with.

It was something that worked.

Joanna didn't want anything to change in her business relationships with the people she did business with.

The nanny she hired was a fair-looking, single woman named Janice Lyman.

She was large-busted and maybe twenty pounds overweight. She was well-dressed.

The room they gave her was in the main house. It was a large room with a large private bath and a refrigerator, plus a microwave.

She could use the kitchen to cook if she wanted.

The nanny was surprised to see that Joanna took care of the babies herself whenever she could, even when they had flown to some distant city.

Joanna nursed the babies and changed them herself, except when she was in a meeting with people and couldn't.

Joanna almost never left the babies at home. She took them with her most of the time.

When Robb Michael kept the babies home with him, he had Joanna store her milk in baby bottles in the refrigerator.

The nanny was surprised to see he was just like Joanna. He took care of the babies himself.

He changed them, fed them, and gave them a bath when needed.

When he saw her watching him while he fed them a bottle of milk, he told the nanny his tits weren't big enough to nurse them.

Janice told Joanna that she was married to some kind of a loon.

Joanna, with a perturbed smile on her face, said, "I know."

SIX WEEKS LATER

Joanna didn't see much of Robb Michael. He seemed to be busy at something.

He would come home late in the evening and make love to her, and then hold her till she fell asleep in his arms.

She liked it when he did this.

She knew he was ether taking care of business or had been at the hospital doing an emergency surgery.

Sometimes, when he came home to the compound, it seemed like he was totally exhausted. But he made love to her anyway. She knew he was trying to get her pregnant.

She always kept herself ready for him.

Sometimes she would wake up and find him gone, then come home in the morning, fix her breakfast, and go back to bed.

Then sleep for hours.

FOUR MONTHS LATER

Joanna was surprised.

Sometimes, it seemed, Robb Michael was taking care of the boys more than she was so she could take care of business for the companies.

Now, it seemed, she flew the plane herself with the pilot as a copilot.

Most times, Joanna would take the boys and the nanny with her.

Often she would be gone most of the day.

Sometimes she would take care of business with a conference call, other times via a computer link up.

Of course, now the boys were crawling all over the place.

It seemed that the nanny had her hands full with them, no matter where they went, but the nanny didn't care.

After she had gotten her first paycheck, and saw how much she was being paid, she decided she could put up with a lot more than she was.

Joanna was already making plans for Thanksgiving. It was less than a month away.

Robb Michael told her that he would be gone most of Thanksgiving. They should have a late dinner.

He had already made arrangements for one of the chefs at the hospital to come and prepare the dinner.

THANKSGIVING

This time they had Thanksgiving in the compound. Joanna liked it better. She could keep track of the kids and her babies better.

While she, her parents, and her sister Phyllis were visiting, Eric was watching their children while they played in the pool.

Robb Michael arrived home just as dinner was being served. Janice helped in the kitchen and attended the babies.

Once again Eric and Phyllis's oldest girl asked, "Who's going to say grace?"

Robb Michael said, "I am."

Even Joanna had a surprised look on her face.

Robb Michael bowed his head and said, "Lord, we aren't going to ask for anything. We already have all we need and more.

"We all have each other. We are already truly blessed. Amen."

With that, Robb Michael got up and personally held the serving tray with the turkey and a pork roast on it for Janice to serve herself.

Then he said, "Thank you for all you've done."

Joanna turned and said, "That goes from me, as well. Thank you, Janice, for all of your help."

Janice looked toward them with moist eyes and said, "The truth of your prayer just hit home." Then he went around the table holding the platter for them all.

When he got to Eric and Phyllis' youngest girl, he said, "This year the wish bone is all yours." The girl was all smiles as she served herself the wish bone and a drum stick.

Phyllis looked at her daughter and said, "Jean, you know that you can't eat all of that. Why did you take it?"

Robb Michael replied, "Because she wanted it. On days, like this day, it's okay to take a little extra, because no one is going to go hungry."

Robb Michael turned to the older girl. "Dani, would you like the other drumstick?"

The girl looked at her mother. Phyllis looked at her and nodded.

The girl smiled, took the drumstick and said, "Uncle Robb Michael, would you teach me how to do business?

"I want to learn business, so I can live like you and Aunt Joanna do."

Phyllis looked at her daughter and calmly said, "Dani, you're not old enough to get involved with things of that nature.

"Now, I don't want to hear another word about it. You and I will have a discussion when we get home."

Robb Michael looked at all his guests and said, "Very good. Now, after we eat, I want you to take all the leftovers home with you, otherwise I'll be eating leftovers for a month."

Robb Michael and the girl looked at each other and smiled. She saw him nod his head at her.

The nod was almost imperceptible, but she saw it and wondered, while he said, "I would like to keep some of the dressing and turkey gravy.

"I've discovered I like it with eggs in the morning."

CHRISTMAS

Joanna awoke at seven in the morning. Both the babies were crying.

Robb Michael was gone.

As she got herself out of bed, she wondered where he was.

After she got them cleaned up and bathed, she took them to her bed and nursed them both at the same time. Then she started pumping herself.

She watched the pistons of the pump silently slide back and forth as she planned her day. Everyone was supposed to be at her parents' place again this year.

After she pumped herself, she put the babies down for a nap and gathered everything together for the trip to her parents' place.

Dinner was scheduled to be at four in the afternoon.

Robb Michael appeared at two in the afternoon. As he entered the room, he asked, "Have you eaten lunch yet?"

"Not even breakfast. Are you fixing?"

He smiled at her. "Anything for a starving girl."

With that he went into the kitchen and got a pot, filled it half full of water and put it on the stove.

Joanna looked in on him as he was preparing the food.

"Not too much. We're eating dinner at four," she said casually. He prepared poached eggs on toast.

After they had eaten, she got up and stood before him, opened her robe and said, "I'm going to feed all of my boys. Would you like dessert now, or after your two sons?"

"Now, of course."

As he started sucking on her breast, she asked, "Who were you with this morning?

"Is she anyone I know?"

He stopped sucking for an instant. "Yes." And then started sucking again.

"Is she pretty?"

He stopped sucking for another instant. "Of course." And started sucking again.

"Who is she?"

He stopped again. And said, "Gentlemen don't speak of such things.

"Besides, if I told you, it wouldn't satisfy your curiosity, and my two sons might never get their fair share.

"I never want to do that."

He seemed happier than she had seen him in awhile.

Once again he started sucking on her breast. She laughed a little as she wrapped her arms around his neck and held him close.

As they arrived at Joanna's folks' place, Dani rushed out to help them carry the gifts into the house.

Everything went pretty much as the year before, but Joanna noticed Dani was hanging around Robb Michael a lot.

NEW YEAR'S EVE

Joanna wondered what Robb Michael had planned for the night as she dressed for the occasion.

He had been gone all day, but had come home in a joyous mood.

All Robb Michael told her was they were going to pick up Papa Eli and bring in the new year somewhere at a Mexican restaurant.

Robb Michael had a limousine pick them up, then they went to Milwaukie and picked up Eli.

They arrived at the Mamacita's at about nine in the evening, the place was packed. People were lined up to get in.

They were about to leave and go somewhere else when they were told there was seating in the bar, so into the bar they went.

After they were seated, they sat and talked while waiting for the waiter. After a while, a waiter came to take their order.

They all ordered large portions and a pitcher of margaritas.

There were three men sitting in the next booth. The men were loud and boisterous.

They were making so much noise that they were distracting everyone in the bar.

Joanna started to say something and was drowned out by the boisterous trio.

Eli turned to the trio of men and asked them to tone it down a bit.

One of the men jumped up and asked Eli if he wanted to make something of it. Without blinking, Eli stood up and slapped him a good sound slap.

The sound of the slap on the face sounded like a gun shot. Watching it all, Robb Michael started laughing silently to himself.

Another one of the men stood up and yelled, "Hey dumb fuck! You think you can mix it up with a longshoreman and get away with it?"

Eli answered him with a solid punch in the mouth.

The third man started to get up and Robb Michael, laughing, stood up and waved his finger in front of the man's face and said, "If you don't sit down, you're going to have more trouble than you want."

The man looked bewildered at Robb Michael and blinked.

The other two men were looking at each other and looked like they were ready to jump on Eli when a Mexican waiter came up to Eli and asked, "Are you all right, Father?"

"Yes, I'm fine," Eli said cheerfully.

The men stood looking at the waiter when one of them asked, "He's your father?"

The waiter turned toward the men and said, "Yes. He's the priest at my church."

The men looked back and forth at each other.

Then Eli said, "I am going to assume that you gentlemen arrived here by car. I want you to use the front of that car as an altar.

"Now, you gentlemen go out in the parking lot, kneel before the front of that car, and say twenty Hail Mary's.

"Then ask the Holy Mother for forgiveness for behaving in an uncivilized matter. Go along with you now."

One of the men said, "I don't know how. I'm not Catholic."

Another stood slowly shaking his head negatively.

The third man said, "Come on, I'll show you how." With that they went out the door.

Eli reached over, picked up his glass and drank down the contents. Setting the glass down he said, "Joanna, pour us another margarita."

Robb Michael started to laugh again and said, "Eli, I think you were a little rough on that bunch.

"I think they would rather you hit them again than have to say all those Hail Mary's."

As Joanna poured the drinks she knew this was going to be another one of those nights.

A MONTH LATER

Joanna was getting the boys dressed when Robb Michael came into the compound.

He hadn't been there for a few days.

She looked up at him and said, "Hello, stranger. Did you get sidetracked? I haven't seen you in a while."

He smiled at her and said, "As a matter of fact I did. Come outside. I want to show you something."

They each picked up a baby and went out to the driveway. It was cold, but the sun was shining.

There was a new Chrysler Limousine sitting there.

Robb Michael asked, "Do you like that?"

She looked at the car, while walking around it slowly. "Yes, I love it.

"It's so different. Where did you get it?"

"I bought nine Chryslers and had them stretched at the Keandra Coach Works where we make the ambulances.

"I drove this one up from California last night. Coming over the pass, I got to drive it in snow. The day before there was so much snow I couldn't get over the pass.

"It's not as long as most of the stretch limos. Therefore, it's easier to drive around town.

"I'm going to keep this one here and place the others at some of the companies that have a lot of traffic with dignitaries and the like.

"I think the design of this car makes a more attractive limo than the other high-class vehicles. I'm going to have more of them made and put them on the market. What do you think?"

She smiled at him. "Let's take it for a ride."

Robb Michael opened one of the back doors. "Give me that baby," he said as he got in the back of the limousine.

As she gave him the boy she was carrying, he said, "Let's see how good of a chauffeur you are."

"Okay, where are we going?"

"How do I know? You're driving. Now close the door and drive."

After closing the door, she walked around the car and got in behind the wheel. It was warm and comfortable in there.

She turned to say something but there was a window about a foot behind her seat.

Suddenly she heard his voice come through the radio speakers. Sounding very much like a snob, he said, "Don't look back. Just drive."

Feigning anger she glared at him and said, "What?"

Still sounding like a snob out of the speakers she heard, "I didn't say talk. I said drive." She started the engine and drove out the back way, down the long, narrow drive.

When she got to the end of the driveway, she turned left and headed toward city center.

She drove around for over an hour. She marveled at how well the car handled, considering how long it was.

When she drove back to the compound, she stopped the car and looked to the back seat.

Robb Michael had a baby sitting on each side of him.

Both babies were asleep. So was Robb Michael.

She sat there looking at them and thought, *And me, without a camera.*

Quietly she got out of the car and went into the compound and got a camera.

VALENTINE'S DAY

Robb Michael had been gone the last two days.

It was late in the afternoon when he returned to the compound.

He took her to Chez Henri's for dinner, after which they went to Nick's Comedy Club. She loved it there.

Then he brought her home to the party room. They played music and danced most of the night.

Janice was watching the babies.

At about two-thirty in the morning, Robb Michael turned to Joanna, and said, "It's time to close the bar."

She looked up at him and said, "Really?"

"Really," he replied. "In this state, bars are supposed to be closed at 2:30 AM, and not serve booze again until 7:00 AM"

She looked up at him and asked, "What do we do till seven?"

He pulled her close and in a low voice said, "You know."

Smiling, she asked, "I know?"

"Yes, silly girl, you know.

"You know we should get very serious about making a baby. Don't you know?

"Somebody has to populate the Earth, why not us? Sometimes I feel that we're not doing our share."

Joanna went in and checked on the boys before going where he was waiting for her.

THE FIFTEENTH OF MARCH

Joanna had just bathed her sons when Robb Michael came in and helped her towel them off, then they carried them to the kitchen.

Robb Michael said, "You go ahead and nurse them, and I'll fix breakfast."

"Where have you been this morning?" she asked.

"I hired a chauffeur for the Chrysler this morning."

She looked at him. "What's his name?"

"I don't know, I haven't met him yet."

She gave him a curious look. "You're kidding, I hope."

"No. I haven't met him yet.

"He's the grounds keeper, Mr. Numura's, brother.

"It seems he's a race driver. He was racing in Europe and got bumped off the track. I'm under the impression he has been in the hospital for some time.

"Mr. Numura asked me if his brother could come and stay with them after he gets out of the hospital.

"I told him he could if he would be willing to be our chauffeur while he is here. I had Mr. Kahn check him out.

"It seems that Mr. Numura's brother has won more than his share of races. He is well known in racing circles all over the world."

TWO WEEKS LATER

It was late in the afternoon, and Joanna had just nursed the boys and was pumping herself when Robb Michael came in.

She saw him watching her as she pumped her breasts.

The nipple suction cups seemed to be jumping in unison, with the two pistons connected to a wheel in between them moving back and forth in the glass case of the breast pump. Clear tubes, white with her milk, went from suction cups on her breasts to two baby bottles. From there, two clear tubes with nothing in them went to the breast pump.

"You need any help with that?" he asked, smiling.

"Only if you have a better breast pump."

"I do. Allow me demonstrate it for you," said Robb Michael, sounding like a salesman.

With that he removed the cone shaped suction cups from her nipples and led her over to a chair.

When he sat down, he pulled her over and sat her on his lap.

She put her arms around his neck as he began sucking on her breasts.

After about twenty minutes, he stopped and said, "We better stop for now. I have a man waiting for us upstairs in the driveway."

"Why's he waiting for us?"

"He's going to give you a demonstration ride in the Chrysler.

"Come on, let's not make him wait any longer. It's pretty cold out there."

"Why did you keep him waiting at all?"

He looked at her and smiled. "Because he's on the payroll, for one. And for two, I had something better to do."

A little embarrassed, she said, "You did have something better to do, didn't you?"

Then she laughed.

After she had dressed, she followed Robb Michael out to the driveway.

There she saw the hood was up on the car and a man looking at the engine of the car.

By his posture, she could tell he knew what he was looking at.

He was wearing black slacks, a white sweater vest, and white blazer. He wasn't wearing a hat.

When he looked up and noticed them, he slowly lowered the hood and pushed it down until it latched.

He walked back and opened the door for them. Joanna and Robb Michael got into the car. Joanna watched as the man got in the driver's seat, started the car and drove out the back way. The car went smoothly down the long, narrow drive.

When they got to the road, he turned left toward Portland. He drove the car expertly through the curves in the road. It was a smooth and comfortable ride.

When they got to Highway 26, the driver turned toward the coast.

Joanna felt the car suddenly surge forward as he throttled up going down the on ramp. Joanna leaned forward so she could see the speedometer.

She gave Robb Michael a wild-eyed look. "We're going a hundred miles an hour! Shouldn't we tell him to slow down?"

Robb Michael casually sat back on the seat. "No. I told him to take us to a coffee shop as quickly as he could, so he is going to be driving fast.

"I want you to keep your wits about you and watch how he does it.

"Look and see how close he follows other cars and how he maneuvers around them. Now, sit back and relax as best you can."

She saw that they were approaching slower traffic.

Instantly she felt the car slow down, following the car in front of him at a safe distance. The car in front of them slowly passed the car in the right lane and then pulled over into the right lane in front of it.

Instantly the Chrysler leaped forward, passing both cars as it sped down the highway.

As they were approaching the Vernonia turnoff, they were approaching another slower car, but this time they didn't slow down.

The driver kept right on going.

Joanna braced herself for the impact when suddenly the limousine went off the highway onto the long slow curve of the highway to Vernonia, a small community west of Portland.

The car didn't slow down until they approached the first curve.

The car sped up for some of the curves and slowed down for others.

Joanna finally figured out the driver had absolute control of the car.

When they arrived in Vernonia, the car went slowly toward the center of town.

He parked the car in front of a coffee shop called the Logger's Rest.

The driver got out and held the door for them as they exited the car. Robb Michael told the driver to come inside the coffee shop with them.

Once inside, they all ordered coffee and a snack cake.

The place was rustic-looking place with a wood stove in both the bar and the cafe section.

They sat near one of the stoves. It was glowing a dull red as it radiated heat, warming the area around them.

Robb Michael looked at Joanna and said, "Mr. Numura and I have been driving all over the countryside this morning.

"In fact, we were here at this coffee shop earlier this morning, that's how he knew how to get here." He looked around and said, "I like this place. Let's come here more often.

"I was having him demonstrate his driving skills for you.

"When I'm not here, I want to make sure you have someone that can get you to where you're going."

Joanna didn't quite know what to say. "Well, okay, if you think it's necessary."

Robb Michael looked at her and said, "Trust me. I believe it's necessary."

With that, Robb Michael focused his attention on the driver. "Mr. Numura, I'm going to give you a hiring fee."

He reached in his coat pocket and took out a billfold, extracted fifteen one hundred dollar bills, laid them on the table, and said, "I will pay you this much every week. You work for me until you decide to leave us. Is that satisfactory?"

The driver looked at him and said, "More than satisfactory.

"When do you want me to start?"

Robb Michael slipped a Visa card out of his billfold, told him to sign it under his name, and then told him to sign his own name when he uses it and gave it to him. Then he said, "You started this morning when you started the car."

Then Robb Michael gave him a key ring. "These are the keys to all of the vehicles in the garage, except Joanna's Saab.

"She will give you a key to her Saab if she wants you to have it.

"There's a Lincoln MKZ in the garage you might want to use to explore the city and surrounding area.

"Or, if you wish, use the Chrysler. I don't care which car you use. You are to take care of, and service them, as they need it. They are all at your disposal.

"You can drive any one of them as you feel the need. There is a Ford pickup that your brother uses. You need to take care of it, too.

"I do not want you to wear a uniform. Dressing the way you are now is satisfactory.

"Perhaps you should wear a hat, a driver's cap, a cloth one in nice weather, perhaps a leather one in bad weather.

"Now, we won't need you a lot for awhile.

"I want you to drive all over this area and around the city till you get to know how to take us everywhere we like to go.

"Joanna will give you a list of places we go so you will have time to learn this city."

As they were returning to the house, the man drove with the flow of traffic. It was a comfortable ride.

MAY EIGHTH

Today was the twins' birthday.

Joanna went down and bought a large birthday cake. Later in the afternoon, they had a birthday party.

She cut the cake in half and placed half in front of each boy. The boys made a big mess playing in the cake.

Robb Michael was having the time of his life watching them. She wondered who was having more fun—the boys or Robb Michael.

After she cleaned them up, Robb Michael took them outside and let them play on the front lawn.

He played with them for some time.

All the while, Joanna sat on a blanket watching them.

MAY SEVENTEENTH

Joanna was nursing the boys when she heard Robb Michael come into the compound. He was dressed in a dark blue suit. She liked looking at him when he dressed like that.

"What have you been doing with yourself?" she asked.

"I brought 130 new cars. I'm having them stretched down at the Coach Works.

"By the way, I have plans for you tomorrow night. You might want to fit that in your plans."

THE EIGHTEENTH OF MAY

As usual it was raining on this date.

Robb Michael had Mr. Numura drive them out to the airport in the Chrysler.

Janice was watching the boys.

When they arrived, it was raining even harder.

The guard at the gate asked, "Are you guys sure you want to go up tonight?"

Robb Michael leaned toward the open window and said, "It's not raining up there."

Robb Michael instructed Mr. Numura how to get to the building where they had to suit up.

After they suited up, a military vehicle took them out to the U2.

Once again, Joanna occupied the rear cockpit.

They sat in the plane with the engine running for about ten minutes before they got clearance to take off.

The U2 went splashing down the runway.

Before they were a fourth of the way down the runway, Robb Michael lifted off and took it up fast.

They were above the clouds fast.

Joanna said, "Were you in a hurry to get up here?"

"Oh yeah, I wanted to be sure it wasn't raining up here. If it was, I didn't want to miss it."

He took the U2 up to maximum altitude and leveled off.

Then he said, "You take the stick."

She took the stick and asked, "Where am I going?"

"I don't know, you've got the stick."

She turned north and descended to forty thousand feet.

Then flew over Mount Rainier and tuned south.

She flew down over the Sierra Nevada's to Mount Whitney, the two highest points in the continental United States, then back home to Portland.

When they got out of their flight suits, they found Mr. Numura asleep in the front seat of the car.

They had been gone almost five and a half hours.

NEAR THE END OF MAY
Joanna was nursing the babies when she heard Robb Michael come into the compound.

He had been gone for three days.

She wanted to ask him where he had been.

She believed he would have told her if he wanted her to know.

"Hello, stranger, have you been on safari?"

He watched as his sons were sucking on her breasts. "As a matter of fact, I have.

I captured a couple more limousines. I drove the Lincoln home. Mr. Numura is bringing the other one home as we speak.

I'm going to hire another driver. I'm also having two more houses built for the drivers to live in.

The other driver will be driving visitors and business people around town to wherever they have to go to get things done."

When Joanna was through nursing, they each carried a baby out to the driveway.

It was the color of Bing cherries. "Wow! That's kind of different."

"You like it?" She walked around the car.

"Oh, yeah. I love the color.

"Is this one mine?"

"If you want it. I don't care.

"Either way you will be riding in it. I figured we would be using them both."

About that time, Mr. Numura drove up the driveway in another limousine.

This one was darker.

She looked it over as it come up and stopped behind the Lincoln. "What do you call that color?" she asked.

"Marine Cordovan.

"I'm having all of the limousines that are used for business painted that color. Except the Chrysler. It will remain black.

"It will be the car I use if I need it. You get the Lincoln. The Lincoln won't be used for business, except by you.

"The Buick will be used for guests that need to be driven around town."

As they were returning to the compound, she heard him tell Mr. Numura to keep all cars parked in the garage, except the ones being used.

THE FIRST OF JUNE

Joanna and Robb Michael each picked up a baby and headed to the shower.

Joanna had said she wanted to bathe the boys when Robb Michael suggested they take them in the shower with them.

Robb Michael turned the water onto half speed, and only lukewarm. When they stepped into the shower, both boys started crying.

Joanna sat on the floor with them and started soaping them up to sooth them.

One of them started nursing. Robb Michael pushed the baby away from her breast and started nursing himself.

Squealing, the boy started pushing at Robb Michael's face. Robb Michael allowed the boy to push him away.

Then the boy started nursing again.

Then the other baby started nursing and Robb Michael started doing the same thing to him. First he would push one baby away from the breast, and then the other.

The babies were squealing and pushing Robb Michael away from the breast, and then he would push the other one away from the breast.

Joanna started laughing as she watched the three of them fighting over who would get to suck on her breasts.

Robb Michael played that game for awhile. Then he got up and turned off the water. Joanna was still laughing while Robb Michael helped her up and started toweling her off.

After he toweled her off, she got on her knees and called the babies over so she could towel them off.

That's when they both noticed it, both babies walked to her.

As they watched the boys take their first steps, Robb Michael said, "Joanna, they're growing up."

"Yes," she replied, "They are, aren't they?"

Then both were toweling them off.

Robb Michael asked, "What are your plans for this day?"

"I get to play bridesmaid for Kathy. She's getting married this afternoon."

Robb Michael looked at her and asked, "Do I get to go?"

"Yes, but you can't be a bridesmaid."

"Well, I certainly don't want to have anything to do with the groom."

THE FOURTH OF JULY

Joanna was watching as Robb Michael was playing with their sons on the lawn of the front yard.

Robb Michael and the boys were walking around barefooted in the grass, while she was preparing food on the blanket she had spread out for a picnic.

She had made sandwiches and had prepared a ring sausage, cheese crackers, and had non-spill cups with root beer in them for the boys.

Robb Michael came over and sat on the blanket and the boys, who seemed to follow him everywhere he went, followed him over and sat down, too.

She looked at him.

His eyes looked moist behind his glasses.

She felt there was something wrong, but then she dismissed it from her mind as she watched Robb Michael giving the boys cheese crackers and sausage to eat.

After they had eaten, Robb Michael reached over and unbuttoned her blouse, exposing her breasts.

When he started sucking, the boys came over and started sucking, too, playing that same game of pushing each other away from her breasts and taking turns sucking on them.

After a while, Robb Michael stopped playing the game and just sat and watched through moist eyes as the boys nursed their mother.

Once again, Joanna had that feeling something was wrong.

Again, she dismissed it from her mind as Robb Michael said, "You know. You make beautiful babies."

"Are they just as beautiful when you make them one at a time?"

She looked at him and said, "I don't know. So far I've only made them in pairs."

THEIR SECOND ANNIVERSARY
Robb Michael had told her he didn't want to go anywhere, he only wanted to stay home and celebrate together.

They had a catered dinner in the party room.

After the caterer left, Robb Michael went over to the jukebox and punched in some music.

Then he poured them a drink while she sat on one side of the bar.

He was on the other side, playing bartender.

She noticed he had more than one drink as they talked for quite awhile, then he asked her to dance.

As they were dancing, he said, "Yesterday, when I was at the hospital, I let it be known I'm working with my last patient.

"There is something more I have to take care of that will take a few days, but I don't believe it will be fruitful.

"This day I retired from medicine."

She looked up at him and asked, "What are you going to do now?"

"Become a full-time baby maker."

He took off her clothes and carried her over to a couch, then removed his own clothing.

She reached over and took hold of his member, and asked, "What do you want me to do with this?"

"I don't know, you've got the stick! What do you want to do with it?"

After they made love, he asked, "Do you want to get bombed?"

"Do you?"

"Yeah, I think I do."

"I don't know if my liver will stand it, but I'm willing to gamble."

He poured them another drink as they sat naked at the bar.

A MONTH LATER

Joanna noticed that Robb Michael may have retired from medicine, but not from business.

He was gone about half the time.

She never knew what he was doing, but he seemed happier.

Their sex life seemed to pick up. She knew he was serious about getting her pregnant again. After making love one night, she watched him as he got out of bed.

As he got up, she saw him flinch.

"Oh!" he said as he stood up.

He stood still for a moment, holding his back. "Are you alright?" she asked, watching him.

"Oh, yeah. Just a growing pain," said Robb Michael as he continued into the bathroom.

When he came out, she asked, "What's a growing pain?"

"That's a pain that keeps growing," he said, smiling.

"How long does it keep growing?" she asked as she watched him climb back into bed.

He wrapped his arms around her and said, "A growing pain is like love, it keeps growing until it kills you.

"Come on, let's get busy doing something constructive."

"Is trying to kill each other constructive?" she asked.

THEIR THIRD THANKSGIVING

This year Robb Michael had insisted that Eli come to Thanksgiving dinner.

As usual, Robb Michael had a chef come in and cook the meal. There was a ham, roast beef, and turkey with dressing, plus barbecued baby back ribs and candied yams, and you know all the rest.

They all gathered around the fireplace and drank hot toddies Robb Michael had made and talked about the early snow storm that was invading the landscape.

Robb Michael assured them that there was room for all if they had to stay overnight.

Kathy and her husband were still honeymooning and were snuggled together on a love seat.

Robb Michael told everyone that the meal was going to be served in the party room this year.

One of the tables from the dining room had been moved down to the party room. There were two serving carts holding food.

Robb Michael pushed the cart with the turkey around the table so everyone could serve themselves.

When he got to Eric and Phyllis' oldest girl, he gave her the wish bone and said, "Dani, be careful what you wish for. It might come true."

The girl looked at him and said, "Thank you.

"I hope you don't mind, but I'm going to say grace this year."

"Good, it's about time we stole some of Eli's thunder," said Robb Michael. "That also means I won't have to struggle stealing Eli's thunder while making up things to say."

Dani and Robb Michael smiled at each other as Robb Michael said, "Your turn to struggle."

Eli interrupted, saying, "Steal away. I've had a monopoly on prayer for years."

The girl bowed her head and said, "Dear God, Robb Michael is right. We have so much that we have no need to ask for more.

"Thank you for having Robb Michael and aunt Joanna inviting us all here for this feast. Amen."

Phyllis looked at her daughter and said, "Dani, that isn't how you were taught to pray. I think you should add a bit more to your prayer."

Eli interrupted once again.

"When we're in this house, we have always done things a little differently. That was a good prayer, Dani."

Thanksgiving was celebrated not much different than it was celebrated anywhere else.

Everyone had eaten more than their fill, then had dessert.

I SHALL ALWAYS LOVE YOU

Joanna looked at Robb Michael.

He had dressed in a business suit.

She still liked looking at him when he dressed like that.

That's the way he was always dressed before she met him, or when he was going on business.

She watched him as he walked around their bedroom, gathering his things and his London Fog overcoat.

He seemed to be moving more slowly, almost hesitantly.

When he spoke, his voice was a little rasping, sometimes with a crackling sound in his throat when he breathed.

She went over to him and asked, "Are you alright? Maybe you should see a doctor."

"I'm going to see a lot of them when I get to the hospital."

She smiled at him. "I think you should consult with one."

He gave her a lazy smile. "Why would I consult with a bunch of quacks that have to have a machine tell them what's wrong?"

She wrapped her arms around his neck and said, "You don't look well. Do you have to go?"

Softly he said, "Sweetheart, there's one time in a man's life when he has an appointment he must keep.

"That means no cancellations.

"There's no getting out of it.

"I'm on my way to my appointment."

Then softly he said, "I must go, but I want you to know I shall always love you."

He looked at her with a small smile and then softly said, "Goodbye, my sweet captive."

He kissed her gently and then turned toward the door.

Joanna watched him as he walked toward the door.

She wished she could say something that would make him stay.

When he reached the door, he looked back at her.

The way he looked at her, she knew he didn't want to go.

She started to take a step toward him as he turned and went through the door.

THE FOLLOWING MORNING

Joanna had just finished pumping herself after she nursed the boys and was preparing to give them a bath.

Robb Michael didn't come home the night before. She was wondering where he had gone.

It was eight o'clock in the morning when she heard the door bell chime on the front door of the compound.

She hadn't heard that door bell since the first days that she lived there.

When she opened the door, she was surprised to see Douglas Kahn standing there.

She knew instantly there was something terribly wrong when she looked at him. He looked terrible.

She could tell by looking at him that he had been up all night. His hair wasn't combed, and his eyes were red as if he had been crying.

She looked carefully at his face and said, "Come in and sit, Douglas. Can I get you something to drink? Coffee? Or something stronger?"

Douglas Kahn looked like he was about to start crying. As he sat on the couch, he said, "I would like some brandy, if you have it."

She went to a cabinet and took out a bottle of cognac and poured about three fingers in a water glass.

She handed him the glass while still holding the bottle.

Douglas Kahn drank it down.

She poured another three fingers in the glass.

Clutching the bottle to her chest, she sat down across from him.

Watching his face, she asked, "What's wrong, Douglas?"

Douglas Kahn started to answer, but started crying. He wept openly and sobbed loudly.

His heart-breaking sobs poured out of him as though he would never stop.

Then suddenly he stopped, and said, "Today is December twelfth. At long last he's gone, Joanna."

Joanna looked at him questioningly. "Who's gone?"

Seriously he looked at her through moist eyes and exclaimed, "Robb Michael!"

Joanna froze in her chair and stared at him.

"Goddammit, Douglas Kahn! What the hell are you talking about?"

Comprehension began to show on his face.

Then quietly he spoke, plainly and clearly. "My God! He didn't tell you! I'm sorry, I thought you knew."

As he was speaking, Joanna glared at him intently and said, "Tell me what?"

His voice quavering, he said, "Robb Michael knew he was dying, Joanna.

"Before he even met you, he knew he was dying.

"When he discovered he was dying, he had all of his people looking for someone to take his place."

As Douglas Kahn was speaking, she could feel the hair on the back of her neck stand up. "We found you and had you investigated.

"He was so certain of you and your qualifications that he had it put in his will that you were to be the CEO over the Med Keandra Group.

"He did this, Joanna—

"Before he even met you, he did this. That's how certain he was of you."

He looked her square in the eyes and said, "Joanna?"

"Dr. Robb Michael Keandra passed away this morning at 6:17 AM."

Joanna felt as though someone had just ripped her heart out and threw it into oblivion.

She began to tremble. Her breathing became very heavy as she sat quietly trying to take it all in.

She wanted to scream, "No!"

She wanted to scream loud enough for the whole world to hear.

She opened her mouth to scream, but she couldn't find the voice to do so.

She choked as tears streamed down her face. She started to tremble even more.

Her voice, taut and quavering, quietly she said, "Please, go on, Mr. Kahn."

Joanna sat in a daze as she listened to him.

"When I picked him up last night, he told me he would be gone soon.

"I asked him what he wanted to do.

"He told me he had some business to take care of before he went to the hospital.

"He had me take him several places last night.

"He told me he didn't want me to tell anyone where he had been this night. You know how he talks.

"Sometimes, when he told me where he wanted to go, he would fall asleep momentarily, then awaken, fully alert. At four-thirty this morning, he told me he wanted me to take him to the Holly Clinic.

"That's where he is now.

"After we got there, he thanked me for being there for him. Then told me he wanted me to go home.

"He told me he wouldn't be needing my services any longer. I told him I should stay. The way he was walking, I was afraid he would fall. He got a little angry.

"He said, 'Douglas, for the last two years and eleven months, I believed I was dying before my time. I was mistaken. My time is now. Douglas, you have been my best man for nearly twenty years. I'm going in there to die! I don't need a best man to die! Dying is a private thing. I want to be alone when I die!'

"I watched him turn and slowly walk into the clinic.

"After he went in, I sat in the car for over an hour. I didn't know what else to do.

"I didn't want to leave. The thought of leaving him was unbearable.

"Joanna, he saved my life!

"He saved the lives of both of my sons. He saved the lives of countless others. He was always there for whomever needed him.

"If I would have left him, I could never have forgiven myself, so I went into the clinic and inquired about him.

"The nurse on duty told me he told her he was going to lie down for a cat nap, and he didn't want to be disturbed.

"The way he was walking, she assumed, he had been drinking.

"Quietly, I said, 'No, he hasn't been drinking. I've been with him all night.'

"I stood there for a while and then told her I would appreciate it if she would go in and check on him.

"She looked at me for a moment, and then said, 'Okay, if you're that concerned, I'll go check on him.'

"I watched her as she walked rapidly down the hall.

"About halfway down the hall she opened a door and went in.

"She was in there for a long moment. When she came out, she was walking slowly as she came back to me.

"She looked at me and said, 'You knew, didn't you?'

"I didn't answer. I waited for her to tell me.

"Suddenly she told me just as she went in, he choked a little. Then his whole body relaxed. His head turned a little toward her. She said she looked at the clock. It was 6:17. She knew he was gone. He's lying in there, under a sheet. She said he's naked and thought we should dress him before rigor sets in. She and I went in and dressed him.

"Then I came here to inform you. I didn't know you hadn't been informed of his impending death."

Once again Douglas Kahn started crying.

Joanna watched him as she sat in a daze, tears flowing down her face.

Suddenly she said, "What did he tell you to do, Mr. Kahn?"

Suddenly Douglas Kahn, speaking in a shaky voice, was all business. "He told me funeral arrangements were already made.

"He didn't want me to give you his will for at least a month after the funeral, but I can tell you he left you in charge of the Med Keandra Group.

"The Med Keandra Group has assets of seventeen trillion dollars, give or take a couple hundred million.

"He could tell you to the exact penny of how much he had."

Suddenly astonished, Joanna was visibly shaken and shuttered.

Wide-eyed, Joanna interrupted, "Did you say trillion?"

"Yes, this isn't something that's publicly disclosed.

"The Wall Street mongrels, as Robb Michael called them, are saying the group has assets of four to five trillion. We nether confirm or deny.

"The Keandra Foundation alone has assets of more than five trillion.

"He made me promise to stay with you, the same as I stayed with him, to help you with any legalities that you might get tangled up in."

Joanna looked at her sons, remembering how proud Robb Michael was when they took their first steps.

He seemed to be walking on air that day.

Still astonished, she turned back to Douglas Kahn. "Mr. Kahn, I don't know if I even know how much seventeen trillion dollars is!"

Douglas Kahn smiled for the first time that day. "As I said, he did.

"And he was certain you could control it.

"He was proud of you before he even met you. In fact, he was wondering how to meet you without scaring you off.

"He would go down to that open-air cafe and sit, just so he could watch and be near you.

"He would talk to me about how best to meet you. He didn't want to meet you on a professional level, or on a business matter.

"He wanted to meet you socially, in a more personal manner. He was hoping to marry you, but in his mind, he only wanted to have a business arrangement with you. I don't know how he planned to do that.

"At the same time, he was surprised at himself when he fell in love with you."

Douglas Kahn started speaking softly, more slowly. "Still he would have married you even if he hadn't fallen in love with you.

"He wanted to be certain you would inherit and be in control.

"It's hard for someone to contest a will when a spouse is there to take over. With the money that's involved here, we may still have some problems.

"That's why he felt it was absolutely imperative that he marry you. He wasn't certain if you were in love with him.

"I, too, was surprised when he told me that he had fallen in love with you. You see, I have seen him with several women in the last twenty years, possibly numbering more than a thousand.

"Some he genuinely cared about. He even provided for some of them in his will.

"He was so proud of you, even after the marriage.

"You never even slowed down on the two programs you had agreed to.

"You know how he was, business always comes first.

"He made certain that any deal that he negotiated had to come around right for him.

"To my knowledge, he has never failed in business, or his private life, except for the fight for his life, he was the winner!

"Sometimes, I believe he actually won that fight, too, the way he controlled life till his end.

"He always won! He never lost! Ever!"

Douglas Kahn looked at her. "My God! I loved that confidence that he was!"

ONE DAY LATER

Joanna was in Robb Michaels' office, looking through various documents and papers.

She didn't know what else to do with herself.

She hadn't slept well the night before.

She had gone down to the Holly Clinic to look at Robb Michael's body. She had to be given a sedative before she left.

She was up and down with her sons most of the night.

She wanted to go back to bed, but knew she wouldn't be able to sleep if she did, so she came up to the office to keep herself busy.

There was a newspaper laying on the desk. The headline read: "DR. ROBB MICHAEL 'FRANKINSTIEN' KEANDRA DEAD! At fifty-eight!"

Douglas Kahn came in and handed her a letter, saying, "Believe it or not, this came in the mail this morning."

Joanna looked at the letter and was surprised to see it was addressed to her. She looked at the return address. It was from Robb Michael. Her hands shook a little as she held the letter in her hands. Hesitantly she picked up a letter opener, opened the letter, and then unfolded the page inside.

My Dear Sweet Captive:

By now you know what I meant when I told you if you knew what this was all about, you would run like hell.

I tried to have you prepared before I had to leave you.

I'm certain you will do well at the tasks I've set before you.

In another few weeks, Mr. Kahn will give you my last will and testament.

I know you are still not sure of what to expect.

For now, I want you to more or less go with the flow.

No matter what anyone says, there is nothing at all that's all that important.

There are a few of the corporations' presidents that will be panicky and try to have you thinking there are certain things that are so important they must be done before this day comes to an end.

You will know who they are when they start calling the office in a panic.

Just because I'm not here anymore, they'll be panicky and feel they should be doing something, anything.

Calm them down as best you can.

Let them know nothing is going to change, that we are alright.

These people are the best. They're knowledgeable, competent people, but some people are insecure and don't handle death well.

Comfort them.

Let them know things are going to be alright.

I love you, and I have faith in you.

I have come to know you well enough to know you will handle it well.

Under the left computer, in your desk, you will find an envelope.

It's very important you find it.

Remember when the announcement was made that the Keandra Group was grooming a woman to be the CEO of the Med Keandra Group?

You are that woman, Joanna. I'm certain that we chose well.

Let my sons know I love them.

Save this letter.

Some day I want all my offspring to read it and everything else I've written.

Mr. Kahn will tell you when.

I'm trying to make sure I get everything done before I go.

Whatever I don't get done before I'm gone will be lost to the ages and will no longer matter.

I shall always love you.

Robb Michael

P.S.: I would wager a nickel Michael Jo is snuggling comfortably inside your body. Like the boys, she will soon let you know she's here. I wanted to be here when she arrives, but you know what they say: 'Best laid plans.'

If only it were true, she thought.

After she read the letter, tears flowed down her face as she folded it and put it back in the envelope.

She slid it into her blouse, against her breast.

Douglas Kahn watching her, nodded understandingly.

Suddenly she said, "Mr. Kahn, in the postscript, Robb Michael said that he would wager a nickel that I'm pregnant with a baby girl."

Douglas Kahn gave her a look of surprise.

Then he said, "As long as I have known Robb Michael, he may have lost a wager, but I have never heard of him losing a wager.

"So I say unto you, congratulations, Joanna.

"From past experiences with Robb Michael, I would wager that you are pregnant, and it's going to be a girl."

Tears welled up in his eyes and then said, "It's gone."

Joanna looked at him quizzically.

He looked back at her and said, "It's gone. That confidence that he was."

THE FUNERAL
ONE WEEK LATER
Joanna had the babies washed and fed.

She had the nanny watching the babies as they all boarded the black Chrysler limousine.

When she entered the church, she noticed most of the people in there were women.

The service was short and simple, as he had requested.

Joanna was shocked to see how many people were at the cemetery as they followed the hearse carrying Robb Michael's remains to the gravesite.

There must have been thousands of people standing all around the cemetery.

As she got out of the limousine, everybody in her path parted to make way for her.

All the way to the gravesite she heard people in a low voice saying, "It's Mrs. Robb Michael," and then more of the crowd would part, making a path for her.

As she approached the gravesite, she saw Eli Nelson standing near the headstone to give the graveside service.

She was surprised because a different priest had given the memorial service at the church.

After the casket was placed over the grave, Father Eli Nelson stood, looking down at it. Speaking loudly, he said, "I am at this moment the angriest man I hope you will ever see. "For God to take this man away from us, it makes me damned angry!

"I have known this man all of my life!

"As a child, he walked the world completely without fear!

"He fought in combat without fear!

"There were no limits in this man's life!

"He was my closest friend.

"In our youth, we played together. We swam together. And all our lives, we partied together.

"I can't tell you about him because you already know what he was!

"You are all going to miss him, but none of you more than me.

"Wherever you are, Robb Michael, you will always be in our hearts."

With that the casket started lowering itself into the grave.

Eli, with tears streaming down his face, and his head bowed, turned and walked away.

After the gravesite service was over, Joanna and Janice, with Robb Michael's sons, got in the limousine and started back to the compound.

She remembered him saying that of all the limos that he looked at, the Chrysler 300, with the angular windows, was the most attractive.

Then she wondered why she even thought of that.

Along the way, she heard Douglas Kahn's voice in her mind. *He knew he was dying. Before he even met you, he knew he was dying.*

His voice had been haunting her ever since Robb Michael passed away.

Then she thought, *if that's true, then everything he did with me was deliberate and planned.*

She thought, *His obsession with sex with me.*

His drinking my milk.

His checking his vital signs every time he did.

It was like he was forcing himself to do everything he did.

Her loins ached for him as she thought about him.

Thank God I was ready for him, she thought. *Ever since the night he took me up into the stars, I was ready for him.*

If I had known he was dying, I would have found a way to do more.

But what more could I have done?

Oh, God! I hope he did everything he wanted to do.

I loved it when he was sucking my breasts before and after my giving birth.

I loved sucking on him! Oh, God!

Even while thinking of him, I want to feed him from my breasts!

I want him inside of me!

I ache for him

LATER THAT AFTERNOON

Joanna felt restless.

She paced the compound without purpose.

Janice was watching her sons.

Joanna went into the exercise gym and got on a exercycle and peddled furiously.

After about five minutes, she stepped off the machine and went into the living room. Janice was sitting on a couch. The babies were down for a nap.

Joanna paced the floor then asked, "Janice, will you watch the babies for awhile? I've got to go somewhere."

Understanding, Janice nodded her head affirmatively.

Joanna went out and got in her Saab and drove across town to Mount Scott.

As she approached the gravesite, she noticed there were several women near the grave. Joanna parked her car and watched them for a moment.

She saw, when they looked at each other, that they saw themselves in each other's eyes. Joanna got out of her car and started walking toward them.

As she approached them, she heard one of them say, "Oh, God! It's his wife!"

Instantly they all turned to walk away.

Joanna found herself saying, "Stop. Please, don't go. He would want you to stay."

They all turned to face her. Then she said, "I want you all to know something.

"Almost three years ago, Robb Michael made me a couple of business arrangements. He wanted me to have his children for him.

"I had two sons for him." Quietly, she said, "He wanted a girl.

"And he wanted to train me to take over the companies after he passed away.

"You see, he knew he was dying before I even met him.

"After I agreed to the terms of the agreements, I fell in love with him, and he married me.

"Now I know you all have fallen in love with him too, or you wouldn't be here.

"In our late-night parties, Robb Michael told me about all of you.

"I didn't know about which of you he told me about in particular, but I know he cared about most of you.

"I was told that he has some of you listed in his will.

"Mr. Kahn will be getting in touch with those of you Robb Michael felt special about.

"He was so special to so many, so many of you were special to him.

"You are all welcome to come here whenever you wish.

"I'm certain that's what he would have wanted. If that's what he wanted, then that's what I want.

"You see, I loved him for what he was. He was a man without boundaries.

"His relationships with women were the same to him as his relationships in business, boundless, without limits.

"He wanted us all so much, he created a good, healthy atmosphere with whomever he was sexually involved with."

With that she walked over to the grave, stood quietly for a moment, and then said, "Damn you, Robb Michael!

"You shared your whole history with me. But you didn't tell me when you were going to go!

"I wish you had told me!"

It was then she discovered she could cry. Her sobs racked her whole body as they burst out of her.

Then she collapsed on Robb Michaels grave as she cried, screaming hysterically.

The others gathered around her and helped her to her feet, then walked her to her car.

As she regained her composure, a new Chrysler minivan drove up and stopped a couple of hundred feet away.

Joanna couldn't help but notice, it was classy. It was glossy burgundy in color.

With a special grill, chrome running boards, tinted windows all around with bullseye fog lights and high-speed road lights, it was a special ordered car.

Joanna thanked the women for their help and concern, then she said, "I must leave now, but you stay as long as you like.

"Tell the woman in that minivan she can stay, too." With that she got in her car and started the engine.

As she was driving away, she drove slowly past the minivan.

The woman in the van was reaching into the back seat for something as Joanna drove by. Joanna couldn't help but think the woman in the van was extra special to Robb Michael. Like the classy Chrysler 300 limos that Robb Michael had made, that minivan was something Robb Michael would buy.

Then she put it out of her mind as she drove back to the compound to be with her sons.

When Joanna arrived at the compound, she went straight to her bedroom. She took out Robb Michael's stethoscope and laid it on the bed.

Then she took off her clothes and laid on the bed. Putting the stethoscope on, she listened to her heart.

She placed the stethoscope on her abdomen. At first she didn't hear anything.

Then she heard it, a heart beat. It was beating faster than hers.

She was silent for a moment then cried, "Damn you, Robb Michael. Why didn't you tell me?"

THREE DAYS LATER

Joanna was in Robb Michael's office when she heard the doorbell.

When she opened the door, she was surprised to see her sister, Phyllis, standing there.

"Come in, Phyl," she said and then asked, "what brings you out here?"

Her sister stood and looked at her for a moment.

Then she stammered, "It's Dani!

"She's got money, Jo! Lots of money! Hundreds of thousands of dollars!

"She got it from Robb Michael!

"I don't know what to do. All she will say is she made a deal with him."

Joanna looked at her sister and asked, "You asked her, and all she will say is she made a deal?"

"Yes, and I don't know what to do."

"Knowing Robb Michael, I don't know if there's anything you can do," said Joanna.

"When Robb Michael made a deal, he told whomever he made the deal with never to tell anyone what the deal was, or he would cancel the deal. So, take my word for it, Dani will never tell.

"Although I don't mind telling you, I'll be wondering about this for a long time."

"Have you taken her to a doctor to see if she's intact?" Phyllis and Joanna looked at each other.

"I'm afraid to. I'm afraid of what I'll find." Phyllis started to cry.

Joanna held her and said, "Robb Michael's dead, Phyl.

"We may never find out unless she decides to tell us.

"But I wouldn't hold your breath, because that's the way people are with him.

"Even now that he's dead, I wouldn't count on her ever telling you. How did you find out?"

"I heard her crying and went into her room.

"She was crying because Robb Michael died.

"She had her computer turned on. I looked at the monitor. It had financial readouts on it.

"Her total at the bottom of the page was $740,000."

Phyllis looked at Joanna and asked, "What am I going to do?"

"Don't do anything. Just go home and wait. It'll be alright."

After Phyllis left, Joanna had to admit she was wondering, too.

THE WILL
SIX WEEKS LATER

Joanna was sitting at Robb Michael's desk when Douglas Kahn came in and sat at his desk.

He had an oversized travel bag with him that he had pulled into the office and stood up near his desk.

Joanna looked at the travel bag and said, "Are you going somewhere?"

He smiled at her "No. What you are looking at is Robb Michael's last will and testament."

Joanna looked at the bag and asked, "What's in it?"

"Envelopes, hundreds of them, and I must deliver each one of them to the person designated.

"I'm going to be busy."

He got up and unzipped a flap on the front of the bag.

He reached into the flap and pulled out a large manila envelope with *Joanna* written on it and handed it to her. "This is the first one.

"This is the original will."

After handing it to her, he said, "There are two certified copies. One copy is being kept at the Foundation. That copy is sealed, never to be opened except if there's a court case concerning the will. All of them have been signed, and witnessed.

"The other's in my desk, at my home office. You can read the will whenever you like. "Basically, it says you inherit everything accept the Foundation. The Foundation will stand alone.

"You will see I have been appointed CEO of the Foundation, but you have a Chair on the Board.

"You'll find it says that I must appoint my successor immediately, in case of my sudden death. I appointed my son, Richard Kahn, and I have it in my will.

"Both of my sons have had a Chair on the Board of the Foundation for the last four years.

"My son, David, will also be your counselor when I'm not available. You'll find him very capable. David is due here at any moment."

Douglas Kahn paused for a long moment, and then said, "Joanna, I miss him. I miss him terribly.

"Every time I come into this office, I find myself looking for Robb Michael, hoping to see that look of anticipation he always had when he was working on something.

"What a joy it was working with him."

Joanna nodded understandingly, and then said, "I miss him, too, and so does everyone I talk to.

"Most of the time I understand, but sometimes I wonder if I'm not performing well enough at the corporate offices, and that's the reason they're missing him.

"The one thing I don't want is for those chairmen and supervisors to lose confidence in me."

Douglas Kahn interrupted, "Nonsense.

"Robb Michael purposely had you taking care of business for over a year before he died.

"He did this so everyone would know you are capable, and you are!

"So never believe you are not capable.

"Even Robb Michael asked me if people were questioning his abilities. It's always good to question yourself, but don't let it show too much.

"It's always good to let people know you don't have all the answers, but don't overdo it."

With that Douglas Kahn took hold of the travel bag, and retreated to the door, saying, "My turn to play postman."

Less than a minute after Douglas Kahn had left, Joanna started crying.

Her sobs spilling out of her long and hard, sometimes hysterically.

THE SAFE

After regaining her composure, Joanna started reading the will.

After she skimmed through the will, on the last page there was a handwritten sticky note: *'Joanna, under the left computer, in your desk, is an envelope. The combination of my safe in the vault is in this envelope.'*

She had forgotten about the envelope Robb Michael had told about in the letter. She decided she would read the will more thoroughly later.

She went into the compound and looked under her computer where she found the envelope.

On the envelope, it was written, *'Joanna, this is the combination to my safe in the vault. Keep this somewhere safe. This box is one of a kind. When I had this box special made, they didn't want to do it. They tried to have me have another vault inside this vault. Not even Mr. Kahn has the combination to this box.'*

She went back up to the office.

She pushed the button that slid the sliding wall to the right, then went into the vault room. Inside the vault it looked like a library.

There were shelves that went all the way to the ceiling with ladders that were on rollers that traveled along the shelves.

On the shelves were the journals containing the records of all the companies. She walked through the aisles of the shelves.

Around the end of the aisles, out of site of the vault door and past a steel desk with a computer monitor and a lamp on it, was a large safe.

The safe was at least fifteen feet long, ten feet deep and looked to be eight feet high. It took her three tries before she got it open.

When she opened the door, she got the shock of her life.

The safe was full of money, large bundles of money.

On top of the money was a briefcase.

She reached up and took the briefcase down.

On the briefcase, there was a sticky note: '*Joanna, you already know the combination.*'

She rolled the tumblers to eight-two-two. The case opened.

There was a slip of paper on top of the contents.

THE NOTE

Joanna, in answer to your question, there's a million dollars in each bundle. Behind and under the money, there are two thousand gold bars. Each bar weighs thirty-two troy ounces. At last count, there is fifty-one bundles of money. You can start selling the gold. When I purchased the gold, it was listed at $240 an ounce. As I write this note, it's now at $1,855 an ounce. Sell all you can. Sell it slow. You don't want to flood the market and have the price fall.

JOANNA

My God! She quickly calculated, and then thought, *There's $1,213,200,000 in this safe!*

Looking back at the note, she thought, *I wonder if Douglas Kahn knows how much the Keandra fortune is really worth?*

Looking at all the money made her dizzy.

She thought, *My God! This is incredible!*

Once again, in a daze, looking at the pile of bundles of money, she thought, *Good God is this even possible?*

Good Lord! I thought he was kidding when he said there was a little over a billion in this safe." Then she looked back at the note.

THE NOTE

You want the price to stay up. Now, the market will make a correction and fall. When the price goes down, stop selling, except to special costumers, until the price starts back up. In this case is a journal, a record of everything I've done since I discovered I am dying. Take your time reading it. You've only got the rest of your life. In thirteen years, Mr. Kahn will call you and all the children together to have you read this and one other journal to them. The reason is to let the children know, at an early age, it's okay to do whatever you will, as long as you control what you do responsibly. We have more than most people in this world; therefore, we will do more than most people in this world. To be accepted, we must never flaunt what we do. It's important to be responsible for everything we do. A lot of what I've done in my life is unacceptable for society, but the fact I've controlled it responsibly, society allowed it.

Robb Michael

Joanna placed the note back in the briefcase.

She closed the case and locked it.

Then she locked the safe door and spun the dial. She closed the door of the vault and locked it, spun the dial.

She slid the wall closed behind his desk and headed for the compound.

Once there, she went in her bedroom, opened the case, took out the journal, and laid down on the bed. Then she started reading.

THE JOURNAL

As I write this, I will be trying to see if I can find a way to deal with a problem in which there is no solution.

It's useless, of course.

However, I've begun this journal to make a record of my life for anyone that reads it.

I want anyone that reads this to know what I am. They may not like what I am, but this is what I am, and what I'm doing with the last days of my life.

One thing that's obvious is the fact that literally everything in my life came easy.

It's as though I have the Midas touch.

Everything I touch seems to turn to gold.

I felt that the glory would go on forever. Let me define glory.

You may think there's glory in sports and the game.

I'm certain you've heard there's glory in business and in war.

If you believe any of that bullshit, you're kidding yourself!

There is only glory in winning and success!

This morning I discovered I'm no longer winning.

Fact is, I am going to die.

In little more than two years, I will no longer be.

Therefore, no more chance for glory.

For the first time in my life, I'm losing.

After looking at the x-rays, my colleagues informed me there is no way I can save this patient, that I should inform the patient so that he can get his affairs in order.

Small as that growth is, it's obvious it's not something that can be dealt with. He will not be here much longer than two years.

They don't know I'm the patient. After all the things I've done, I've come to the conclusion I'm capable of saving anyone's life but my own. Believe that?

Me! Dr. Robb Michael Keandra is dying! Me! I am the patient! In a couple years, I will be nothing more than a memory!

Perhaps not even that.

There's a growth on my liver! It's inoperable!

This thing is going to spread and take in all my vital organs.

What will I do?

Nothing, God damn it! There's nothing I can do about it! Damn it! I can't even get a transplant with this damned thing!

Therefore, any successes I may achieve now will be out of necessity, not the joy of winning.

The realization that I'm coming to an end is overwhelming.

I must calculate how long I have and what I can get done, if anything. I don't know for certain, but I believe I have about two and a half years.

I am not prepared to die!

You know, reading back on this can be very discomforting. It pisses me off! I am so damned angry!

I'm not sure what I should do, but I'm starting to feel desperate. I don't feel I have time to think. It's nearly impossible to think when you feel desperation. But think, I must.

I must leave desperation behind. Also, I must not tell anyone about this. If anyone finds out that I'm dying, they'll be pitying me. Pity is something I won't stand for, so I will not say anything about this.

If I don't do the right thing, a lot of people are going to be out of a job, possibly some will be destitute.

With 77,000 people working for me, I must do something. But what?

My God! With all that I have, I still have nothing in my life. I don't even have a bloodline.

I'm the last living member of my family. Do I have time to start a bloodline?

My God! I do hope so!

I must!

Since writing that last line, I have come to the conclusion, I must find a new CEO to guide the corporations after I'm gone.

I could sell everything off, but then the corporations would slowly fade away, one by one, until there's nothing.

When someone takes over a company, the first thing they want to do is make changes. That isn't what I built these companies for.

People don't know how to work with something that's already working, so they feel they absolutely must change things for the better.

But it never seems to get better, so the company slowly fades away, and nobody understands why.

If I were to sell out, to whom do I leave the money? The Foundation? That may well be the best solution.

However, I believe, with all the women I've played around with, it should be pretty easy to find a woman willing to be the mother of my child, providing the price is right.

But how to guarantee the companies will still be there when the child is old enough to take control?

I must find a woman that is intelligent enough to see to a proper education for the child.

I also must find someone bright enough to be the CEO over the presidents of the companies.

I'm not sure how to do this.

I must find these two people as soon as possible.

I will enlist the help of Mr. Kahn. I have always trusted Mr. Kahn's judgment. He has proven consistently that he is competent and capable.

Mr. Kahn has a desk in my office. I have kept my office in my house.

I designed this magnificent house. Most of my work gets done here.

Quite often Mr. Kahn and I will sit and discuss strategies.

It seems this house is always full of business people. The parking lot near the house always has several cars parked in it.

However, since I've discovered this thing growing within me, there is less and less being done here. I must remedy that.

To completely surrender to this thing is not satisfactory. I'm not sure that I want to do business here anymore.

ELEVEN AM, MARCH NINE
Mr. Kahn never fails to surprise me.

Three days ago, when I told him I would be dead in about two and a half to three years, he was very calm and sympathetic.

He asked me what I wanted him to do.

When I told him I wanted him to find me a man to become my new CEO, he was surprised to see I was thinking that way.

He told me, when most people are told they're going to die, they give up on everything.

He said, when he was told that he was dying, he not only gave up on everything, he resigned himself to it.

When I told him I wanted him to find a woman for me to start a bloodline with, I thought he was going to fall out of his chair.

Honestly, it staggered him.

After explaining I wanted children to inherit the Group when they grow up, he looked at me in a way, I believe he was questioning my sanity.

He wondered if the Group was even going to exist when they were old enough to inherit. I told him I plan to make certain it does.

We discussed the kind of woman I would need.

He pointed out she would have to be someone that would raise a child in the proper manner, and make sure the child was properly educated.

Then he asked me how many children I wanted.

I told him I always planned to have six.

Once again he almost fell out of his chair.

After much discussion, Mr. Kahn told me he would do his best to bring these things about. I now believe if I hadn't discovered that I'm coming to an end, I may not have ever thought to have children.

Mr. Kahn surprised me. He found a candidate for a CEO within two days. He says he has never met her, but has been told by several people in the industry that she is a power house thinker and highly respected in the business community.

She is, in fact, capable.

She pulls down over two hundred thousand a year as a stock broker.

She is also financially independent. There are those that believe she's a financial genius, worth a few million.

I told Mr. Kahn I would rather he find a man for the job.

Mr. Kahn informs me this woman is very well-suited for the job.

I want to get a good look at her before I meet her, possibly observe her for a week or two.

When I meet her, I want to meet with her socially, not professionally.

The reason for this is a little difficult to explain. You see, running these corporations is more like a hobby to me.

My expertise is in medicine. I managed to find good people to run these corporations for me.

Except for quarterly meetings, and other small business dealings, that leaves me free to practice medicine.

It just happens I know how to run a company. Whomever I choose to run these companies must know that.

Sometimes it is a problem for a woman to take over.

In my experience, women of this type are of strong character, and therein lies the problem.

They're a little pushy, forceful, coercive, and built like a linebacker. I've found them to be more aggressive than men.

I want to see her, before I meet her, so I can work out some kind of strategy on how to approach her.

She may not be someone I like, but like her or not, she may very well be capable.

I would like that.

I never gave it a thought he would discover a woman for the job.

Her name is Joanna Kimble, leastwise, that's what he told me.

He said she can be found at a sidewalk café, near the water front park, every day at lunch time.

She always sits alone, so she should be easy to find.

Mr. Kahn said, if necessary, he could find a reason for us to visit her offices.

After giving it some thought, I decided I would rather meet with her socially, someplace public, like a bar or cafe.

She has an office at the Pacific Rim World Trade Center, a short distance away from where she has lunch.

I'm going to see if I can get close enough to talk to her without arousing her suspicions.

Somehow, the name Joanna, in itself, makes me a little nervous.

TWO PM, MARCH NINE

This day I drove downtown to get a good look at Miss Joanna Kimble.

The woman I saw must have been the wrong woman.

The woman I saw is not what I would call a linebacker. This one looked more like she would be soft and gentle, not the least bit the coercive type.

Most likely I saw the wrong woman because this one is small, maybe five or five-two.

She has auburn hair and very pretty green eyes. Even though she was wearing an overcoat, you could tell she is very large busted.

She didn't look to weigh more than 110 pounds, but she looks to be carrying twenty pounds of tit.

She was the only one sitting alone, maybe she was the right one after all.

With the information at hand, it's hard to tell. I'm going to have Mr. Kahn look into Miss Joanna Kimble's past.

I want a few candid photos of her. I must make certain who I'm looking for.

I would still rather he find a male candidate, although I must say, this one is nice to look at.

I just spoke with Mr. Kahn. He told me that we already looked into Joanna Kimble's past. I should have known.

He also brought up an interesting thought.

Any male we might find that's suitable is probably already a CEO of his own company.

I told him to keep looking. It would please me to have more than one candidate.

I also told him that maybe one of our own people is suitable. I told him to start checking them out.

As long as Mr. Kahn has been with me, he has made me believe that he knows what I want.

TWO PM, MARCH TEN

Mr. Kahn called and told me, he had a friend introduce him to Miss Kimble.

He was pleasantly surprised. She was much more than he expected.

He told me when I meet Miss Kimble I would know I would have to look no further.

He seems pretty certain Miss Kimble is the logical choice. He said I would figure it out.

I'm still trying to figure out what he meant by that.

Sometimes he will say something like that, just to see if I'm paying attention to what's going on around me. A sparring game we seem to play.

MARCH TEN

This morning, Mr. Kahn delivered photographs of Miss Joanna Kimble.

Shock of all shocks! I was looking at the right woman after all! This woman is beautiful!

I must find a reason to talk to her. I need to find out for myself how much business sense she has.

I want to watch her for a while.

Why I pictured her built like a linebacker, I'll never know. I do want to get involved with her.

I want to know how she thinks. I must be careful. I must not scare her off.

My investigators informed me that she seems to have more business sense than most young business people.

She is extremely bright and well thought of, but a little reclusive. She is very much a loner.

Mr. Kahn says, for that reason in itself, I should get on with her very well. Like me, she likes to eat lunch by herself and lives alone.

The one thing I don't want to do is frighten her.

My God! With what I've got in mind, how do I keep from frightening her?

Now the task changes.

I must look for a woman that's not only willing to have my offspring, but capable of raising the child in the proper manner.

The child must have the proper education and early childhood training.

Where can such a woman be found? The world is full of them, and I haven't got a clue where to look.

I do hope I'm not embarrassing Mr. Kahn.

He never seems to question anything I ask him to do.

JOANNA

Joanna stopped reading for a moment, digesting what she had read.

Then she thought, *My darling, you have never ever frightened me, and Douglas Kahn is the most loyal of friends.*

There should be more people like Douglas Kahn in this world.

Suddenly she felt tired.

She put the journal down and decided to sleep for awhile. Reading the journal was hitting too close to home just now.

NIGHT OF THE SAME DAY

Joanna had slept for a few hours when she was awakened by Janice.

The babies were hungry.

She got up, put on a robe, and then told Janice to bring them to her.

She nursed them at the same time.

It was a pleasant feeling as the boys, sitting on her legs each holding a breast in their hands, were sucking on her.

After nursing her babies, she pumped herself.

She watched the machine Robb Michael had made for her as though she was in a trance, watching the pistons in the glass case moved back and forth.

She always liked the feeling it gave her as it did its job.

After she was done, she took her sons into the shower with her.

After she soaped them up, the boys frolicked under the downpour of the shower as they were being rinsed off.

After she put them in bed, she went back to her bed and laid down, then picked up the journal.

THE JOURNAL
TWO PM, MARCH TEN

I went down to the cafe to have lunch.

This day is a nice day.

I sat and observed Miss Kimble for over an hour. You can tell she really enjoys sitting in the fresh air. She takes a long lunch, and she takes her time while eating.

She is very meticulous in her speech and demeanor. She never speaks to anyone unless they speak to her.

She's not a messy eater. She cleans up after herself as she eats. She neatly places her dishes and leftovers near the edge of the table.

I find her to be very interesting.

When I look at her, I can't help but fantasize about her. She's drop dead gorgeous.

She has a magnificent pair of tits that are hard not to look at.

I usually don't find women with extra large breasts attractive, but small as she is, her large breasts seem to enhance her figure.

Much as I would like to take her to my bed, that could be a terrible mistake. It could very well make her unapproachable.

I'm going to make it a habit to have lunch there every day. If I observe her for a while, eventually I'll find a way to approach her.

I'm grateful that the food is very good there.

MARCH ELEVEN

This day I went down to lunch, rain showers interrupted most of the day. I wore my hat and overcoat.

I noticed the rain didn't seem to bother Miss Kimble much.

She sat watching people and traffic while she was eating, her umbrella hanging on the edge of her table.

Sometimes a car would splash water on the deck near where she was sitting.

For the most, part she ignored it.

I tried not to watch her too closely. Not looking at her is most difficult.

The one thing I don't want to do is make her think I'm some kind of a lecher.

It might be that's exactly what I am, a lecher, lusting after her.

I made eye contact with her this day.

When she looked at me, I couldn't help feeling she knew that I'm going to be involved with her. She looked at me with cool appraisal, like she knew something I didn't.

I couldn't help wondering if she knew that I'm going to be a large part of her life.

I can't help but think she likes my hat and the western shoes I wear. I noticed she looks at me and my clothes.

I wear a suit almost every day. Other times, I wear a sport-coat and slacks. I see her looking at me and the way I'm dressed.

That could be a plus.

I don't wear the hat every day, mostly when it rains or when I want to keep the sun off my head.

Maybe I should buy a new one. This one is getting a little saggy. I think not.

This one is comfortable to wear.

I don't usually have a problem getting involved with women.

However, every woman I've ever been involved with has been a temporary involvement.

My involvement with miss Kimble has to be permanent, that means no coming on to her.

I must be very careful in my dealings with her.

I need her, and I know it.

MARCH TWELVE
I arrived at the cafe a little early.

There were only a few people there, and I sat at a table near where Miss Kimble sits.

I got bored waiting, so I purchased a newspaper to read while I waited for her.

I read through most of the paper and was folding it up when I saw Miss Kimble striding toward the cafe.

She walked with an air of confidence and purpose as she was striding toward the cafe.

When she saw me, she slowed her walk.

That tells me that she has noticed me. I quit looking at her.

Out of the corner of my eye, I watched her casually walk to a table next to mine and sit down.

For the most part, I pretend not to have noticed her. I pretended to read my newspaper.

I could smell her perfume.

I had to suppress a sudden urge to reach for her. I wondered if she knew it.

Under the brim of my hat, I watched as she ordered a club sandwich and a cup of soup.

Several times I noticed her looking at me, and wondered if I should speak to her, then decided against it.

I didn't want her to think I was trying to pick up on her, which, of course, is exactly what I'd like to do. It's not that easy.

I don't dare risk scaring her off.

I've never had to be this careful about meeting a woman before. I'm not certain how to do it.

It's an absolute joy watching her.

She's a marvelous dresser.

The clothes she wears are very Victorian, yet somehow, still very provocative.

Her clothes show off her figure tastefully. This day she's wearing a tight turtleneck sweater, and slacks. The sweater was white. The slacks were black.

A memorable sight.

NINE AM, MARCH THIRTY

I've been watching Miss Joanna Kimble pretty closely for the last two weeks.

Twice I've made eye contact with her.

I told Mr. Kahn I love watching her.

Mr. Kahn tells me I can be arrested.

He says watching her, as closely as I have, is called stalking. He says there's a law against it.

Imagine that! Like I even care.

What I must do is more important than thinking about legalities.

Besides, I like stalking Miss Kimble. It's a most enjoyable experience. I can't help wondering if she knows that I'm stalking her.

This morning I had Mr. Kahn call a news conference and make an announcement.

I want to be near Miss Kimble when she hears about it. Hopefully she'll make the right statement. If she doesn't, I'll be wasting my time with her.

My investigators are keeping me informed as to her whereabouts, at any given moment.

THREE PM, MARCH THIRTY

This day was nearly disastrous!

After the announcement was made, I was late getting to the cafe.

After I got there, things appeared to be working fine.

I couldn't help but smile.

She was telling her associates my life history, pretty accurately until some stupid son of a bitch groped Miss Kimble.

His name is Dorn! He groped Miss Kimble right out in public.

I completely lost it.

I was on my way to kill the bastard when Miss Kimble slugged him in the eye.

In the whole of my life, I don't believe I was as proud of anyone as I was of her at that moment.

In that instant, I knew she's the one for the job!

She not only said all the right things, she let it be known she's a fighter.

I like that! I really like that!

It was obvious she had already researched the Keandra Group.

I like that, too.

I believe I handled it well enough. I wanted to stay and talk to her.

However, I knew the police would soon be on the scene. As I was leaving, I turned to look at her. I was so awed by her I couldn't help reaching out and touching her face, then I left.

The one thing I don't need right now is to be involved with the police.

But I can thank Mr. Dorn for one thing, he gave me a legitimate reason to meet with Miss Joanna Kimble.

With that stupid act, he could have brought down all that I'm trying to do. I still think I'd like to kill him.

It's strange, when I was in combat, I wasn't trying to kill anyone.

It was more like playing a game of chess.

I was more interested in out maneuvering the enemy to save my own life than ending the game.

In fact, when I ended the game, under my breath, I would say checkmate. I still do.

After putting that rotten bastard down, I found myself saying it.

Oh, well, enough about killing.

After seeing Miss Kimble and listening to her talk to her colleagues, I'm certain she's perfect for the job.

I'm going to instruct Mr. Kahn to put her in my will, leaving her in control of everything as quickly as he can.

Mr. Kahn is to be executor of the will and the Foundation.

She will be executor and CEO of the corporations and all I leave her.

There are things I must do more quickly than I am. If I'm going to make this thing come together, I'm going to have to move more quickly.

I must find a woman to start a bloodline with. How in the hell am I going to do this?

I can't imagine myself saying, "Hey lady. I'm going to die soon, and I want ya ta have my kids so ya can raise them after I'm gone."

Oh, yeah! This is going to be a piece of cake!

JOANNA

Once again Joanna stopped reading and thought, *it would have been a piece of cake.*

But you would never have done that.

You were too worried about personal appearances to have done something like that.

I would have done it. But you would have been uncomfortable with the whole situation.

You would have felt that you were losing control.

You were right not to tell anyone you didn't have long to live.

Joanna thought about it a while longer.

Then once again she began to read.

THE JOURNAL
TWO PM, MARCH THIRTY-ONE

My God! This day I discovered something I should have noticed yesterday.

The person to be my replacement is the same person I want to be the mother of my children. I must stop focusing on her tits.

I wonder if Mr. Kahn noticed it. I'd wager he did, and that's why he's sparring with me on this thing.

If this woman knows what's in line for a child, when the child grows up, you can bet she will see to it that the child will get the proper education needed to deal with that future.

Why I didn't see it sooner, I'll never know. I don't have time to do what I have to do. To top it all off, I not only made a mess of everything, I made a complete ass of myself this day.

I've been so secluded in my desperation; I never saw the obvious.

I've never felt so embarrassed in my life. I must stop and think.

This is the first the time in my life I wasn't prepared to mobilize a project.

Once I decide what to do, the most important thing is not to frighten Miss Kimble, if I haven't already.

But at the same time, I must put her in a position where she has to negotiate with me.

I must figure out how to do this. Nothing seems to come easy with this project.

I must keep trying.

So far, everything I try to do, seemingly has a disastrous turn to it.

After I get my shit together, I'll figure out how to negotiate with her.

I'd wager more than a nickel that she's going to be the next CEO of the Med Keandra Group.

With the resources I've got, she doesn't have a prayer of getting away.

JOANNA

Joanna stopped reading and thought, *Damn you, Robb Michael.*

I'm sure you know that there's a law against entrapment. Oh, well, I was never frightened. I was never, ever frightened.

I wondered sometimes about his logic.

When he talked, I sometimes felt I had to help him along.

Remembering those days, Joanna couldn't help but smile.

THE JOURNAL
THREE-TEN AM, APRIL ONE

I've been awake all night.

I don't know how to get things done in the time I have left.

I have decided to kidnap Miss Kimble, and keep her in a place suitable where she will have to negotiate with me.

I'm going to have one of the companies build a compound to keep her in.

To do what I want her to do, she will need complete privacy, so I will have to take great care when designing the compound. How in the hell am I going to make this come around?

I DON'T KNOW and I don't know WHO TO GO TO FOR HELP!

However, it's obvious that Miss Kimble is very capable, but it seems I'm not! I'm starting to believe I'm the April fool!

I must make certain Mr. Kahn has changed my will in her favor. I'm certain she's perfect for both positions.

Now, I must prepare a plan for negotiations, then possibly I might actually get some sleep.

TWO PM, MAY SEVENTEEN

This day my contractor informed me that the compound is complete.

I went down and inspected the place to make sure it was furnished the way I had instructed.

They have done a fantastic job.

Now, all I have to do is move Miss Joanna Kimble in, and I must do so in such a manner that she knows she is safe and has a lot of say in the events of her life.

If this doesn't work, I don't know what I'll do.

I've never felt so desperate, or so alone, in my life!

Tonight, I am supposed to give a speech at the Collier Suites Hotel.

Good God! I don't even know what the hell to say! Oh, well, I'll wing it when I get there.

I think I'm better at winging it than most.

It seems that for the first time in my life I have to run to keep up.

I find this to be unbelievable.

Me, I'm the dunce!

MAY EIGHTEEN

Well, last night I did it.

I've kidnapped Miss Joanna Kimble. She's down in the compound now.

I captured her at the Collier Suites Hotel.

What a welcome surprise to see her walk into that banquet room while I was giving a speech, making a complete fool of myself.

I had to ignore her most of the evening.

Finally, when I could get close to her, she was a little bit under the influence.

She wanted to talk.

There was no way we could have come together with any kind of discussion, so I gave her a shot that put her out.

I took her to the compound where I gave her a complete physical.

I was shocked to find her hymen is still intact.

She seems to be in perfect health.

When I checked on her at noon, she was still sleeping, her vital signs are good.

The drug I gave her is working longer than normal. It might be because she had been drinking.

If so, that would explain why she's still out cold.

It's almost eight-thirty in the evening. I believe it's time to go down and awaken her.

MAY NINETEEN

I negotiated with Joanna last night.

She scared the hell out of me.

It was easy enough to get her to agree to the research project, but she wasn't all that interested in talking to me about the second project.

She told me I had to take her up into the stars before she would agree to sign a contract with me on the second project, then she would become my sex slave for as long as I live.

When she said that, I felt like she hit me with a sledge hammer.

When a woman like her says something like that, it makes you want to live forever.

If she would have asked for three hundred million dollars, I would have agreed to it.

She's going to get it all anyway.

But, she wanted me to take her up into the stars, that means I had to get clearance to take her up in the U2. I didn't know if I could, but I had to try.

I was really surprised when they cleared her in less than a minute. However, when we arrived at the airport, clearance hadn't come through yet.

Just as I thought they had changed their mind, clearance came through.

I took Joanna up in the U2, and gained a sex slave…for not long enough.

For some reason, it brought back memories of the missions I've flown.

I thought about the times they came up to get me.

Twice I had to outmaneuver surface-to-air missiles.

Once I had to take on a MiG-21 that fired a couple of air-to-air missiles at me.

That one scared me.

Too late, I saw him coming.

He was coming up fast. He knew he couldn't come up as high as I was, so he fired two missiles at me on his way up.

I turned and dove straight at him.

His missiles went over me. As I went over him, I dropped a couple of flares.

His missiles turned and came after me.

The MiG-21 also turned to come after me.

When the missiles sensed the heat from the flares, they turned.

I remember quietly saying "checkmate" as they flew up his tail pipe.

As I think about dying, I think I would rather have died that day than the way I'm going to.

As I took Miss Kimble up in the U2, I was expecting her to be frightened.

I don't think she was frightened so much as she was apprehensive. It was more like she didn't know what to do.

On the way back to the compound, she asked me if there was anything I couldn't do.

To a point, I stayed honest with her. I told her I believed I could do anything except save my own life.

She asked me when I thought I was going to die. I didn't give her an honest answer. I told her I had heard you begin to die the minute you're born.

The truth is, I believe you begin to die after you stop growing into adulthood.

If you think about it, it's all downhill from there.

Later we had a serious discussion about how to begin her sex life.

That also had a disastrous turn to it.

Last night I did the one thing I never wanted to do! I hurt her! She wanted me to break her hymen.

When I broke though, I felt a pain like I've never felt before. It felt like I had ripped my foreskin off!

If it hurt me like that, her pain may have been excruciating.

I immediately put her to sleep and removed the rest of her hymen surgically.

Now I'm afraid that she might leave.

I don't want to lose her. I want more than anything for her to stay.

I'm not sure how to bring up the subject.

I will say this though, when I was speaking to her earlier in the evening, I told her I had kidnapped her.

She didn't show any fear, or if she was afraid, she was very good at not letting it show. She was calm, very calm.

I can't help but smile a little.

She very calmly let me know I'm the smartest rock laying on the road.

I think she wants me to know, before this is over, I'll be the dumbest rock laying on the road.

I'm starting to agree with her.

I've got to say it. I'm so proud of this girl I'm about to burst. She's not afraid to talk to me. She will even talk back to me.

I really don't know what to do next.

The only thing I can think to do is to go down and stay quiet, let her bring up the subject.

As I write this, it's late into the evening.

I have intentionally stayed away from her.

I plan to not bring the subject up. I lounged around, impatiently, in my living room all day.

I plan to let her tell me if she wants to continue without any coercing on my part.

As of right now, I will never lock her door again.

If she stays, I want to take her down to the Little North Fork Santiam River.

There are things I want her to know. I will be more comfortable taking her there to talk to her.

I want her to see that maybe, just maybe, I'm a normal human being after all. Or am I? I know people that will never believe it.

Miss Kimble isn't the only one I've heard say I'm a little loony.

I remember when I was in junior high school, a lot of people started calling me a skinny little nerd.

I had to struggle to outrun that image.

I worked out to build my upper body strength. After I built myself up physically, I still didn't look any more muscular than anyone else.

I looked the same as anyone else. But somehow, I seemed to be as strong, or stronger, than anyone else.

The one thing I don't need is for Joanna to picture me as nerdy, or some kind of a loon. I want to take her places and do things.

Of all the women I've been with in my life, I've never wanted any of them to think of me as some kind of a cracked nut.

I'm not sure exactly where else to take her.

I can't help myself. It's late, but I've got to go down and make sure she is alright.

MAY TWENTY

I slept on top of the blankets with Miss Kimble all night.

When we got up, I had to go up and change my clothes.

Then I took her to breakfast at the pub. I knew she would like the place.

After that, I took her to Mill City and, from there, to the Little North Fork Santiam River.

The water was colder than hell, but we made a day of it.

We swam and talked about our childhoods, then we made love at the river's edge.

I feel more for this woman than I have ever felt for any other woman I've ever been involved with.

I don't know if it's a good idea to fall in love with her. I'm starting to question myself.

Falling in love is not part of the deal I made with her. It might make her run from me.

I have to be very careful.

She is such an incredible thinker.

I must make sure she doesn't ever want to run from me. Running from me isn't acceptable.

If she wants to leave, I won't stop her, but still, she's the one to be CEO, no matter what.

I've made certain that she inherits. I'm not sure I'm doing the right thing at all.

She has the most analytic mind I've ever encountered.

She's beautiful, but it's not helping. I can't help but admire her body and fantasize about her.

I just know I have to have her incredible thinking powers to take over after I'm gone.

What I must have is for her to honor the deals she agreed to.

I don't believe she knows how important research is to success. I owe my success to research.

As she is researching, it will come to her.

That's when she will know what I need from her, however, it doesn't justify holding her prisoner.

MAY TWENTY-EIGHT

This day I'm the happiest man living.

For the last week, I've been walking on eggs making sure she knows she's safe. Joanna acts like nothing bad ever happened.

I can't help it. I'm falling in love with her. I've said it before, I must be very careful. I could lose her.

I took her to see *Mamma Mia*. Loved the play. Might go see it again. I happened to see James Reader there.

Made him squirm a little looking for nickels. So much fun.

Made love to Joanna five times trying to get her pregnant. As much as I enjoy making love to her, I don't seem to be succeeding.

I'm starting to get concerned.

It might be I'm over doing it. That may be the reason she's not getting pregnant.

She seems game to climb in the sack anytime I ask her.

The smell of her perfume mixing with her natural body odor drives me to do more.

The question: Am I asking too much?

Damn it! I don't know!

I'm getting overanxious.

Now that I take time to think, I realize I'm expecting her to get pregnant too soon.

JUNE THIRTY

This day I went down to the Holly Clinic for a sperm count, and to keep my DNA on file.

Someday it might be necessary to have that file.

I never thought about it before, but with all the women I've had in my bed, to my knowledge, none of them have become pregnant.

Now I'm wondering why. Can it be they were all on birth control?

I'm waiting anxiously for the results. If I test negative, I'm already dead.

I just haven't laid down yet.

SEVEN PM, JUNE THIRTY

Great news! I tested positive! I have a good sperm count.

Now that I know, maybe I'll have better luck.

I think I'll ask her if she would like to go down to the Little North Fork Santiam River for a swim.

I like it there. I like it there a lot, I always have.

The morrow seems to hold promise.

As usual, I feel I'm the luckiest man alive.

Oh, yes. The morrow holds great promise.

JULY TWELVE

My God! This girl is really good. Through her research, she figured out we have an embezzler.

I'll have Mr. Kahn get the investigators on it and ferret him out.

I'm beginning to think Miss Kimble can do a better job controlling these companies than I can.

I'm not one bit sorry for any decisions I've made about her. She's even better than I was led to believe.

I'm absolutely certain my group of corporations will be in good hands when I'm gone.

P.S.: She is not yet pregnant!

Last night she reminded me I had sex with her five times yesterday.

I'm still trying too hard? Possibly, but I can't help it.

If I could've, I would have done five times more.

JULY THIRTEEN

Had to go to the hospital last night to work on a kid.

I swear to God! When I opened that kid up, I was so frightened at what I saw I wanted to close her up.

Tumors, dozens of them!

But I stayed with her and started cutting.

Why she's still alive, I'll never know!

To get them all, it seemed like I was cutting her life away. I had to cut away so much!

I can't get that baby out of my mind!

No six-year-old baby should have anything like what I saw inside of her!

I know she's going to die. I feel so helpless.

Damn it! I can't do anything but wait for the call.

I told her parents there's very little hope of survival. Seeing their faces, I don't want to face them again.

Joanna is waiting for me in the car.

For some reason, Mr. Kahn told her to take me to Mill City. I'll finish this when I get back.

ELEVEN PM, JULY THIRTEEN

This night the baby woke up! That baby has to have the strongest life force I have ever witnessed.

Her vital signs are closer to normal than I can believe. It seems I've lucked out again.

If ever there is a time to thank God, now is it!

However, I must start to think about my practice.

I have been criticized by my colleagues, and others, for most of my life for the way I've lived.

My practice has always been selective. If I'm not pioneering new surgical procedures for knee or other joints, I'm trying to develop surgical procedures for people that are terminal.

The only patients I take are those that are terminal, or those that have severe joint damage. People that know there is no hope for them.

I've trained several doctors on how to do joint replacement.

I've never wanted to be a practicing physician.

But when someone is dying, such as myself, I would try to save them. I've had extraordinary luck doing this.

I expect every patient I operate on to die. Somehow, when I'm cutting, it comes to me on how to save them.

If someone came to me with the same condition I've got, I would try to save them with surgery.

But, like every case I've worked on, I would be expecting the patient not to survive.

Now with my condition starting to worsen, I must start considering when to stop practicing.

I must get back down to the compound and focus once more on Joanna and what I'm trying to achieve.

Besides getting her pregnant, I want her to know what I am.

I want her to tell my children what I am.

JULY FOURTEEN

It seems the baby is going to live! Don't ask me why.

I must find a way to thank Joanna for staying with me.

Usually Mr. Kahn is there when I get stressed, but Joanna was better for me.

Last night, when I thanked her for staying with me, she reminded me she's here forever.

I haven't yet discovered how to tell her: I'm not!

The other day when she went with me down to the Little North Fork Santiam, I picked her up and threw her off the bridge into the river.

Feigning anger, she yelled all the way down.

I knew she could swim, but I jumped over the railing anyway. I wanted to be with her. I wanted to feel her body against mine.

It seems that I scared the hell out of a couple of old ladies. They thought I was killing her.

When we swam over to the beach, we laid out the blankets.

After we got under the blankets, she decided to eat my cock. I fed it to her as slowly as I knew how.

She handled it better than I thought she would. It seems that all I want to do is fuck her!

I wish I could do more to make her life better! I think more than flowers are in order.

Last night she asked me about Julie Lane, the nurse at ICU.

I told her the reason I don't date any one woman steadily. Joanna's intelligent enough. I think she will know she can't trust anyone where money is concerned.

As strong as her sex drive is, she will have to constantly be on guard against gold diggers, especially those that will undermine what she is trying to achieve.

There are those that are always wanting to know: Why do you want to build that? Why do you want to bring that together?

Why do what you're doing? Don't you have enough money?

The only thing they understand is what they want. They'll never truly understand the glory of success.

She may have to take several lovers in her life, if only for self preservation.

I'm hoping that she will be getting pregnant soon. I may still be trying too hard. I still want to get her to marry me.

As independent as she is, I don't know how to do that, either.

JOANNA

Joanna read the last paragraph three times.

Then she thought, *all he would have to do was ask. I would have married him. All that I wanted him to do was fuck me!*

If I had known what a pleasure sex was before I met Robb Michael, I would have been having sex way before I was.

But then, maybe my children wouldn't have been his. Good God, I don't want to think about that!

If Robb Michael were here right now, that's still what I'd want him to do!

Then she thought about the rest of what he had written.

I think I would have married him that first night, if he had asked me.

He's right! When there's big money involved I'm going to have to be careful!

Especially after seeing what's in that safe! It may well come to going on the prowl for sex!

Then she read on.

THE JOURNAL
JULY SEVENTEEN

This day I took Joanna to the front yard of my house and had a picnic.

Joanna was enthralled. She wants my shirt-tail relative to buy the place for her.

I'm starting to believe she likes my taste in architecture. I loved building this house.

Having that big basement party room, with ten-foot ceilings throughout the house, was one of my better ideas.

The walk-in vault is mainly for keeping records. I am putting a sticky note on this page:

'Not even Mr. Kahn knows that the walk-in vault has a basement, too. I have another big vault down under this one. The combination is the same as my big safe in the vault upstairs.'

I loved living in this house until I moved Joanna into the compound. Now I think I like living in the compound with Joanna.

Good God! I believe I'm falling in love with her! That's not part of the plan!

It was wonderful making love to her on my front yard. I want to do it again and again.

When I took her back to the compound, I drove all the way around the hill.

I didn't want her to know the compound is connected to the back of my house.

Don't ask me why. Just stupid, I guess.

I could have just driven her up the driveway, to the back of my house, to the compound.

Yeah. I'm just being stupid.

AUGUST NINETEEN

Last night Joanna made me the happiest man in the world.

It seems, after much effort, we are going to have a baby!

Thank God! It's about time!

I've always wanted to have six!

I was an only child. I don't want any of my children to have to grow up that way.

This one may have to do.

However, if I can find a way to have six, I'll do it!

Now, I must make plans for a wedding. It's seems Joanna doesn't like the idea of being pregnant and not married!

This is more than I could hope for.

I wanted to find a way to marry her ever since I moved her into the compound.

This solves a lot of possible legal problems in the future. I've been wondering for weeks how to ask her to marry me.

When she told me she's pregnant, again I wondered how to ask her.

I decided not to ask her. I'll get the license and get everything certified. Then take her to the church. Mr. Kahn is taking care of everything.

On top of it all, I'm another year older today. What a birthday present! No time for celebrating.

I just remembered a promise to one of my closest friends. I must do my best to keep that promise.

The question is: How do I keep my promise for me and my bride to be naked at the wedding ceremony?

I'll figure out something. I always do.

AUGUST TWENTY-THREE

Last night I married Joanna. Oh, so much fun.

I met Joanna's mother, father, her sister Phyllis, and her husband Eric.

You could tell that they're related. The genetics are obvious.

Both Joanna's mother and sister are packing around more tit than necessary for two.

I couldn't help it. I found myself harassing Eli.

After all these years, Eli let it be known he has vertigo when he looks down.

I wish I had known this years ago. Because I didn't, I've done a lot of things wrong.

We joked about things we did as kids. My Lord, the memories!

Joanna is so beautiful! I couldn't keep my eyes off her. I couldn't help myself.

After the ceremony I told her, "I've captured you again."

Now that I think about it, I'm the one that got captured! She captured me a couple days after I met her and I wasn't even aware of it.

Well, now I've got everything I want to have, except the six children. When I've gone, Joanna will be in charge of all businesses.

There is no doubt in my mind she will raise this child to the best of her ability.

I don't know what to name it. If it's a girl, I would like to name it the same way my parents named me.

My father's name was Robert and my mother's name was Michael. My mother wanted to name me after him and her.

My father didn't want me named Robert, so I went through life being called Robb Michael.

Because of this, I would like to name my daughter 'Michael Jo', after me and Joanna.

After sitting here and giving it some thought, I've decided to let Joanna name it if it's a boy.

I don't even care what she names it, as long as the last name is Keandra. Right now, I believe I can sit here and make plans. That, in itself, is kind of silly.

I'm not going to be here!

Any plan I make, most probably, wouldn't be workable at that time anyway. It seems society changes a little with each generation.

Joanna and I need to talk about this a lot, if only for something to do.

As we were leaving Chez Henri's, I asked her where she would like to go on our honeymoon. I believe we are going to Paris, France.

She wants to make love under the bridges, like she has seen in the movies. If that's what she wants, that's what we will do.

I think I'll take a corporate jet. We'll have more privacy, but it seems there's a lot of commotion when I land someplace in my private jet.

For some reason, she was shocked to find out her new last name is Keandra.

After all the research she had done on the Keandra Group, I thought she knew. With her analytic mind, I thought she would have figured it out some time ago.

I wonder if she thought her last name was going to be Michael?

Oh, God! Heaven forbid.

Now she wants to meet 'Frankenstein' Keandra, whoever he is. I don't think I've ever heard of him. LOL

Now that we are married, Joanna, I know you will be reading this. So, if you see your name 'Joanna' on these pages, don't pay it any mind. It's nothing but a bunch of drivel anyway, and not even intelligent drivel.

The reason I started this journal was to give you, or anyone else, some kind of reason as to why I'm living the way I am. I know you think everything I do with you is bizarre.

It may well be bizarre, but it's the only way I can get you to do what I need you to do, without letting you know that I dying.

Finding you was the most important, and wonderful thing, that could ever happen to me. I'm in love with you, Joanna.

I'm afraid to say it to you, because love wasn't included in the deal I made with you. Divorce is something you can do at any time.

If you divorce me, it could ruin all my plans. The one thing I don't want is to give you a reason to leave me.

Last night you finally figured out the reason for all the sex. It was so you would get pregnant.

I was really impressed with you last night. You let it be known that no one was going to raise your baby but you.

I want you to know I wouldn't have it any other way. As long as I'm here, I will make suggestions along the way, but how you decide to educate the child will be completely up to you.

There are some people I have provided for when I'm gone. Other than that, you will be the sole owner of all I possess.

I don't have to tell you, this baby you and I created is going to inherit a rather large estate when you're gone.

I know you will have this child prepared.

JOANNA

Joanna read this page of the journal three more times, and then thought, *Damn you, Robb Michael. I know you told me our babies were going to inherit. But I never gave it any real thought until just this moment. As for your bizarre behavior, you couldn't have done it better. I loved it!*

OH, GOD! He knew! He knew I would have married him and had his children. That's the reason for the bizarre behavior! He didn't want to tell me that he was dying!

With a frown on her face, she got up and went into the house and into the office where she pushed the button that slid the wall to one side, revealing the vault room.

After opening the vault, she stepped inside and carefully looked around. The place was like a library with shelves and aisles, and with journals and ledgers neatly placed on them.

There were sliding ladders on each of the aisles so you could climb up to the higher shelves and move up and down the aisles.

She walked around the place carefully, looking for the basement door. Everywhere she looked, she saw no door.

Carefully she surveyed the room. The room was about forty by forty.

There were four aisles about twenty-five feet long that went all the way to the ceiling.

Out of sight of the vault door, next to the big safe, there was a steel desk with a mahogany top that overlapped the desk and a desk chair.

The big safe couldn't be seen from the door either.

She sat in the desk chair and looked around the room wondering where Robb Michael would hide a door to the basement.

There was a desk lamp and computer monitor on the desk. She reached over and turned the lamp on.

She opened a door on the desk and saw a computer sitting in there. She wondered where the keyboard was, as there was nothing on the desk except the lamp and the computer monitor.

She tried to move the lamp, but it was fixed to the desk. So was the computer monitor. It couldn't be moved.

She opened the top drawer in the center of the desk. There was the keyboard.

She pulled the drawer out farther, and there were compartments with pens and paper clips and other accessories.

She turned on the computer. As the computer came on, the monitor asked for a password.

Without thinking, she put in the password to her computers in the compound. Surprise, surprise, the password cleared the way.

She noticed an icon that read 'Joanna.' She clicked on it. A page came up.

It read, "Joanna, close the keyboard drawer and push."

As she closed the drawer, she noticed that it sprung back a little. It didn't close tight. The drawer was recessed under the desk top, but, she could feel the drawer spring back out about a quarter of an inch when she tried to close it. It was a strong spring.

When she tried to push it closed, it would come back out.

She pushed in the drawer harder, about a half inch. Suddenly the desk silently started to rise, straight up.

She pushed herself back, away from the desk, as it rose silently into the air.

The desk, mounted on a scissor lift, raised until the bottom of the desk was about six feet off the floor.

She looked down the stairs that were under the desk.

It was dark. Cautiously, she started down the steps. After she went down six steps, she saw a light switch.

Switching it on, she saw the whole room below her light up. When she got to the bottom of the stairs, she looked around the room.

This room looked to be a lot larger than the vault upstairs, at least three or four times as large.

It had another stairway of about four steps at the opposite end of the room.

She figured out her bearings and came to the conclusion that this room extended under the vault room, Robb Michael's office, and extended under the library.

Which, she thought, meant there was another way into the vault.

As she surveyed the room, she saw it wasn't that different than the room upstairs.

There were four aisles of shelving. These aisles of shelves were twice as long and held bundles of money.

"I know," she said out loud, "there's a million dollars in each bundle."

She didn't bother to count the bundles, but thought, *My God, Robb Michael. You're a hoarder. You have hoarded money to no end.*"

Suddenly, she felt tired. She wanted to lay down and sleep. Joanna went over to the safe door.

This door was a vault door. It was embedded into a concrete wall.

She tried the combination. The door unlocked on the first try. She had a feeling what she would find when she opened the door.

When she opened the door, she stood looking at the contents in a daze.

She thought, *My God! Am I really seeing this?* The vault didn't have what she expected.

The vault inside was about thirty by sixty feet, and was mostly full of gold, platinum, and silver bullion.

She was too tired to deal with it.

She started to close the door when she saw a slip of paper taped to the inside of the door. She took the slip of paper down and started to read it:

My dear sweet captive,

> *If you are reading this, it means you have found the entrance under the desk. I know what you are thinking. I'm hoarding my wealth. Perhaps, but I have other reasons. The reason the money is here is because of an unstable market. There is nothing in the market right now worth risking our money on. So, I advise you to store the money until the market is more stable. You'll figure it out. You have a real talent for reading the movement of the market. The bullion can be sold anytime you can find a buyer. The bundles of money on the shelves is from bullion sales. The gold was purchased at $244 an ounce. As I write this, gold is $1,855 dollars an ounce.*

At this price, sell the gold. In a market that is making rapid changes, this money can all be lost. I wouldn't gamble with it. Remember, as the economy gets better, the price of gold always goes down. I trust you will do well. The prices I paid for the gold, silver, and platinum are listed in the ledger. Read the ledger, over on the shelf, and check the contents of the computer in the desk upstairs.

Robb Michael

Joanna smiled a sleepy smile and thought, *I know you would only wager a nickel.*

She pulled the door closed and locked it, then she spun the dial. She went up the stairs and looked at the desk that was still six feet up in the air.

She saw a button and a note taped to the bottom of the desk. The note said, *'Joanna, there's a switch over the keyboard that turns off these buttons so that nobody can accidentally find their way into the lower portion of the vault like you did.'*

She pushed the button and watched the desk silently, slowly descend to the floor.

Opening the drawer to the keyboard, she felt around above the keyboard.

She found nothing. Then reaching farther back, she found it. She flipped the switch and closed the drawer, then she pushed hard on the drawer to see if the desk would rise.

Seeing that it didn't, she closed and locked the vault, then spun the dial.

She walked through the vault room and pushed the button that slid the wall shut.

She went back to the compound and checked on her sons. Exhausted, she slipped off her clothes and went to bed.

THE NEXT MORNING

Joanna awoke early, nursed her sons, and then took them into the shower stall and turned on the water.

The boys jumped around and stomped their feet and squealed frantically as the lukewarm water plastered them mercilessly.

She knelt before them and soaped them up while they danced around under the raining water.

On her knees, she hugged them while she let the raining water wash the soap off them. While hugging them, one, or both, would start nursing.

Watching them, emotionally she said, "Your father liked sucking on them, too."

After getting them dressed, she fixed them scrambled eggs and served them with a small glass of juice for breakfast.

She had Janice watch them while she went back to her room and pumped herself, afterwards she went back in the house to do an inventory on the vault.

Joanna went into the office and slid the sliding wall to one side, then she walked inside the vault room.

The vault room was about ten feet deep and thirty-five feet wide.

To the right of the vault door were shelves and cabinets containing office supplies. She opened a door to one of the cabinets and took out a legal tablet and a ball point pen. She opened the vault.

Going inside, she went around the shelving, straight to the desk, opened the middle drawer and flipped the switch that turned on the buttons.

She pushed hard on the center drawer. Instantly the desk started to rise.

Going down the stairs, she flipped the light switch on as she went. She went straight to the shelves.

Like the shelves upstairs in the vault, they went all the way to the ceiling. She guessed ten feet high.

There were sliding ladders on all the shelves.

She went up the first ladder and started counting the bundles as she rolled along on the ladder, logging the figures on the tablet.

After an hour and forty minutes, she finished counting the bundles, then she went straight to the vault door and opened it.

She looked at the room behind the vault door.

Just looking at the mounds of bullion stopped her in her tracks.

Good God! she thought. *Robb Michael, you've got more reserves here than they have in the Federal Reserve Bank downtown.*

She slowly surveyed the room. There were mounds of bullion everywhere in the vault. She saw there were shelving compartments on the walls with smaller bricks of bullion. She went over to one of them, picked up a five-ounce brick of gold and put it in her pocket. She decided not to inventory the bullion until later.

As she was closing the vault door, she heard a doorbell. Looking up, she saw the desk was coming down. The entrance under the desk was closing. Panicking, she ran up the steps.

Carefully she looked around for the button to open it again. There was none. The button was on the outside of the stairs. She was trapped.

Remembering the other steps, she turned and went back down the stairs and across the room to the other stairway.

Instantly she went up the steps to a railed platform about six by six. There was a sliding door in front of her.

She slid the door to her right. It was a small room. There was a note taped to the wall in front of her.

She took the note down to read it:

> *'My dear sweet captive,*
>
>> *You are not as much of a captive as you might think. The doorbell sound is a warning that someone has entered the vault. That automatically closes the entrance under*

the desk. I hope you haven't left the safe door upstairs open. Now this is only an exit. You cannot enter the vault from here. Come in, close the door, push the button.'

She closed the door and pushed the button. Silently, the small room suddenly started to rise.

When it stopped, she opened the door and stepped out. When she closed the door, the room silently started sliding into the floor, leaving a wall in its place.

When it stopped, she opened the door in front of her and stepped into the library.

Looking back, she found that she had been in a broom closet.

Looking around she saw Douglas Kahn coming out of the office. He looked at her and said, "You're just as bad as Robb Michael.

"You leave the vault open when you leave the office.

"I used to catch Robb Michael here in the library all the time with the vault door standing wide open."

Embarrassed, Joanna laughed a giddy laugh, smiled at him, and said, "I was going to go right back in there."

Douglas Kahn smiled at her. "Sorry, I closed the vault."

Once again Joanna laughed a little. "That's okay. I can go back in later."

They talked for a while, then Joanna went back to the compound. She laughed a little giddy laugh at the way things turned out.

She checked on the boys and nursed them, then she went into her room and began pumping herself.

While pumping herself, she began to read the journal as the pistons of the pump silently slid back and forth in the glass case that held the working mechanism.

THE JOURNAL
AUGUST TWENTY-FOUR

Joanna, by the time you are reading this, Mr. Kahn will have given you the combination to the vault.

When you see the door of this vault, you will know the vault is large enough to walk around in.

There is another, rather large safe inside the vault. That's where I keep my private papers and this journal, plus a few bucks.

There are several journals, including this one, for each of the companies that I own in this vault.

Each of these journals is an accurate record for everything that has been done with that company.

Every transaction, every decision, and a complete record of everything that was said and done at every board meeting, one for every year, since each company began.

You must be certain to upgrade these journals as you go.

With this information, I'm confident you will do well at directing these companies. Even at this point, you are informed well enough to deal with these companies. This is a library in this vault.

Whatever you do, don't let Mr. Kahn scare you when he starts throwing big money numbers at you.

Now you know why I told you, if you knew what this was all about you, you would run like hell.

It's too late for you to run, my sweet captive. My God! If only I could tell you how much I love you. And how proud of you I am.

I sincerely hope you have figured it out before you read this.

The morrow is promised to no one but you, at least until the day I'm no longer here. On the morrow I'm going to take you to France.

AUGUST TWENTY-FIVE

This day I was going to take you to France. Sorry, it can't be done. You don't have a passport. So, after we get you a passport, I will take you to France.

Last night we had another picnic on the bedroom floor. The tuna fish sandwiches you made were great.

I want you to know that I really like these picnics. I want to have them more often.

JOANNA

Joanna stopped reading and started crying.

She remembered him telling her how to tell if the peppers are too hot to eat. She laughed through her tears as she pulled the suction cups off her nipples.

She laid down and cried again until she fell asleep. Two hours later, she awoke. Once again she pumped herself.

Again she started reading the journal as the breast pump, with its pistons sliding back and forth, silently did its work.

THE JOURNAL
OCTOBER TWENTY-SEVEN

We got back from our honeymoon this day.

Talk about a joyous trip. Oh, so much fun! When we first got there, you wanted to make love under one of the bridges, soon after dark.

You were wearing one of those evening gowns that wrap around, the kind that women don't like to wear underthings with.

It was dark under the bridge we chose. I remember it was very dark. I had opened the front of your gown and was making love to you.

Just as you were having an orgasm, a passing restaurant barge turned their spotlight on us, which was alright except they didn't turn it off!

They not only left the light on us, they stopped the barge.

They couldn't see my face because I had my face buried between your legs.

When I looked up, all I could see was that magnificent pair of tits, brightly lit up for all the world to see, with their crimson tips pointed straight outward.

It seemed everyone one on the barge was applauding.

When they started singing, "La Marseillaise," the French national anthem, you were suddenly hysterical.

You started laughing and couldn't stop. I was really concerned. I was afraid you might miscarry. Hysteria has been known to cause a miscarriage.

As concerned as I was, I was still a coward, Joanna. I kept my face buried between your legs. I knew as soon as I looked around, somebody would recognize me. I can't think of a better place to hide my face anyway.

When we were in England, that idiot made that crack about Americans having a fetish with big bosoms.

I wanted to punch him right in the kisser. I once told you I would never lie to you, Joanna. I haven't and I won't.

I'm a man. I admire that magnificent pair of tits of yours as much as any man. That's not the reason I chose you to be the mother of my children.

I needed someone whom would use your kind of thinking when raising children. I know you won't disappoint me.

I will also need that kind of logic for the other position you have been chosen for. By the time you read this, you will know what that position is.

That's also the reason I wanted you to learn how to fly.

You will be wanting to go halfway around the world on a moment's notice. You won't have time to wait for a commercial flight.

Congratulations, boss. I'm certain you will do well. So, go get 'em, Tiger.

I have a corporate bank account, separate from the Med Keandra Group. This is a registered corporation, RMK Corporation.

This corporation is not connected to the Med Keandra Group in any way.

All there is to this corporation is a bank account. You can now write a check for up to three hundred billion dollars.

I use this account as little as possible. Your signature is on this account. If you stumble, and find the checkbook right now as I write this, you could write the check right now.

You can sign Joanna Kimble, or Joanna Keandra, or Mrs. Robb Michael Keandra. All those signatures are on file at the bank.

In the case you found this journal, there are some credit cards and ATM debit cards for use on this account.

Use the money as you feel you must. I think you'll be able to buy the groceries. I also have a few trillion in the Keandra Foundation.

After I'm gone, the Foundation will be separate from my estate. Mr. Kahn is the executer.

My God! You wouldn't believe how much I love you. You are the brightest star in my universe.

Well, you are waiting for me downstairs. I want to examine you so I will have some idea how far along you really are.

Any luck at all, we'll have a healthy baby in a few months.

OCTOBER TWENTY-EIGHT

This day I discovered you are pregnant with two heartbeats. What a wonderful surprise.

Near as I can figure, you are about twelve weeks along.

You asked me how many children I would like to have. I told you I wanted six. I'm still going to work on it.

The way things happen in this world, I want to make sure there's someone there to inherit when you are gone.

But I wonder if I will be that fortunate.

Good God, my little captive. I'm lucky to have two on the way. If I've got my calculations right, your due date is about May seventh.

The numbers seem to be wrong for a third child. I would really like to have a Michael Jo. Oh, well, I plan on trying again, again, and again.

Well, you already know about that and how it's turning out.

JOANNA

Joanna stopped reading.

Then she thought, *Robb Michael, if you're right about us having a girl, then we are indeed lucky. I will name her Michael Jo.*

She will never understand how lucky she is because she was loved before she was even conceived.

I'm happy to have this girl for you. I only wish I was having twins again.

It was getting late. Joanna thought about the way things turned out. Mr. Kahn didn't have a clue about the vault having another room.

And it's obvious that he had caught Robb Michael the same way he caught her. Again, she laughed a silly kind of laugh just thinking about it.

She decided she would close the sliding wall to the vault room whenever she opened the vault.

She closed the journal and turned off the reading light. Laying there in the dark, she quickly fell asleep.

THE FOLLOWING MORNING

Joanna awoke to the sound of her sons wailing.

She got up and went in, undressed them, took them straight into the shower, soaped them up, and started nursing them as they were rinsing off.

Toweling them off, she started wondering what to fix them for breakfast.

As she was feeding them, Janice came down and watched her as she was teaching the boys how to drink out of a glass.

Watching her, Janice asked, "Are you going to stop breast feeding them?"

As Joanna held a glass for one of them, she said, "No. Robb Michael said not to stop breast feeding them until they push me away.

"He said the longer they breast feed, the higher their IQ will be.

"Robb Michael said there's something in breast milk that helps them learn faster and keeps them more reserved, more easy going.

"I've got enough milk to float a battle ship. I'm prepared to breast feed them forever. So, I'm going to breast feed them until they push me away.

"I was talking to another woman about it, and she told me she stopped breast feeding the first time her baby bit her.

"But Robb Michael said, if a baby bites, you bite them back.

"He said, they learn fast that way." Then, Joanna said, "They have to learn how to drink out of a glass, too."

After Joanna got dressed, she told Janice to watch the boys.

She had to go to work. She went into the house and then to the office. She opened the vault and then into the basement.

She opened the vault down there. She looked in the ledger. In the ledger, there were transactions listed with bullion sales.

Looking through the ledger, she saw that there were several well-known jewelry stores listed.

She decided to visit one of them. She picked up a thirty-two-ounce bar and took it with her. Joanna drove downtown to a well-known jewelry store.

After parking her car, she went inside and asked to see the proprietor. An elderly man came to the counter and asked, "May I help you?"

Joanna reached in her pocket and took out the five-ounce brick of gold and said, "Yes, I would like you to make a pendant out of this.

"I want it to lay flat against my chest.

"Can you do that?"

The man looked at her and said, "An unusual request, but yes, it can be done."

The man started to make out an order form, and asked, "Your name, please."

Joanna responded, "Mrs. Robb Michael Keandra."

The man stopped writing, looked at her, and said, "I have done business with your husband.

"Can I do business with you?"

Joanna looked him in the eyes.

"Yes, that's why I'm here. I have a bar with me, if you're interested."

"How big?" he asked.

Joanna smiled, and said, "Thirty-two troy ounces."

With that, she took the bar out of her purse and handed the wrapped bar to him.

He looked at the bar wrapped in brown wax paper. Then he carried it into a back room.

A minute later, he came out and handed her a check for $59,370.

Then he said, "Wait here and I'll have your pendant ready in a moment."

A couple a minutes later, he came out and handed her the pendant hanging on a gold rope and a small, plastic bag and said, "My condolences.

"I was sorry to hear about your husband.

"I wondered then if my supply had come to an end. I'm grateful to you that it did not." Joanna asked, "What's in this little plastic bag?"

"That's the gold dust from the hole we drilled in your little brick."

She handed it back to him. "You keep this.

"How much do I owe you for the pendant?"

The man looked at her and smiled a gentle smile. "Nothing. This is a gift to you." Joanna thanked him and extended her hand.

Taking her hand in his, he said, "I'm looking forward to doing business with you again."

BACK HOME

Joanna sat at the steel desk in the vault, thinking about the events of the day.

Then she thought of something that Robb Michael had said when she first started playing CEO.

"Joanna, it's fun doing business. It's great fun!"

Then she thought, *As usual, you're right, Robb Michael! Today I had the time of my life!*

Then she got out the ledger and began to write down the names of the jewelry stores listed there.

Then she thought, *Now I know some of what Robb Michael was doing while I was playing CEO.*

When she had written down all the names listed in the ledger, she opened the stairway to the basement.

After opening the vault down there, she carried a dozen bars of gold, six bars of silver, and ten bars of platinum, one at a time to the upper level.

She put them on a shelf there.

After she rested awhile, she went down and brought up several small bricks of various sizes.

She went out to the garage and started the Chrysler limousine and brought it around to the front door of the house.

When she opened the trunk of the car, she saw a safe in there. Without thinking she knew what Robb Michael had used the safe for. She spun the dial the three times and then eight-two-two. The safe opened. After she wrapped every bar and brick, she loaded them in the safe. After she closed the trunk of the car, she drove the car back into the garage.

She had worked up a good sweat.

She went into the compound and took another shower, then she lay down on her bed and started to read the journal.

THE JOURNAL
NOVEMBER TEN

I've been thinking about you a lot lately.

I've decided I'm not being fair to you.

You are my wife.

Therefore, you are entitled to know as much as humanly possible about me and my affairs.

First thing I'm going to show you is my house.

You know, the one that you want me to buy for you?

However, I'm not yet prepared to tell you that I'm dying.

I'm sorry, but the only way I'm going to let you watch me die is with you not knowing. Dying is a private thing, something I must do by myself.

When I chose you to be my replacement, I had no intention of falling in love with you, or anyone else.

You know what they say: Best made plans and all that. I fell in love with you before I knew it.

The one thing I don't want is for you to watch me fade away, knowing that I'm dying, and pitying me all the while.

Of course, by now you know one of the programs you were chosen for was to extend my bloodline.

However, I do want you to see me as I am.

For you to do that, I must keep you better informed than you are.

Also, I must keep some things secret, like the fact that I'm dying.

I know it's not fair.

However, you and I know life isn't fair. That's the way it is.

Recently you made the statement that I reach for you in my sleep.

I didn't know I was doing it. I'm glad you like it because I don't believe I can stop.

When you told me you would be my sex slave forever, I must say, I wasn't prepared for you to be as committed as you are.

To let me sexually molest you, while you sleep, unbelievable.

To start with, I didn't know I am. Now I know you will let me, I will still be doing it. Believe this? I'm rambling on paper.

I have never wanted to be near someone as much as I want to be near you.

JOANNA

Joanna stopped reading and thought about what she had just read.

It must have been horrifying for him, she thought. *Here he was, teaching me how to take his place, and trying to extend his bloodline, and all the while, the fact that he was dying was embedded in the back of his mind.*

I wish I could have sucked him more, fucked him more, fed him from my breasts more, anything that would have kept his mind off his fate.

I miss the taste of him, the feel of him.

How could I have done more? Joanna started to cry.

She cried out as if in pain. "My God! He was dying! I didn't know!"

Then the sobs poured out of her in a rush as she cried herself to sleep.

THE FOLLOWING MORNING

Joanna had no sooner showered and nursed her sons when the phone rang.

It was David Kahn. "Joanna, I'm with you today.

"We have to go to the plant in Reno."

Joanna rang Janice in her room and told her to get ready to travel. "We've got business in Reno."

Then she rang Mr. Numura and told him that she needed a ride to the airport.

On the way to the airport, she got to thinking: *This is what he wanted from me.*

I must not fail him.

I worked hard to get here.

I must not fail him. Then she thought, *I will not fail you, Robb Michael!*

TWO DAYS LATER

Joanna was sitting at her kitchen table, drinking a cup of coffee. She was thinking of the first frustrating day in Reno.

It seemed like the problems were beyond help until late afternoon.

Robb Michael once told her sometimes, when there is no solution in sight, just make a decision.

It doesn't matter if it's right or wrong.

The important thing is to make your decision flexible and get things moving again, so that's what she did.

Everyone got panicky and started yelling and shouting about how this kind of solution would solve no problems.

One of the lead people threatened to resign. She told him that quitting solves no problems. His resignation was accepted. After that everyone quieted down.

She told the superintendent to work within the framework of the decision and modify it, as needed.

That night she, Janice, and the boys stayed in a hotel.

Late the following afternoon, she went out in the plant to talk to the workers.

A few of them were, at one time or another, crowding around her to talk to her. She found she liked that part of the job best.

As she was drinking her coffee, she thought, *you were right, Robb Michael. All you have to do is make a decision, and make that decision flexible.*

She finished her coffee and decided to lay down for awhile.

She started to read some more of the journal when she heard the door bell.

When she opened the door, Mr. Numura the chauffeur was standing there.

"Can I help you with something?" she asked.

The man bowed a little. "Yes, I need to have a discussion with you."

"Certainly. come on in. Would you like a cup of coffee?"

The man looked at her cautiously. "I prefer tea, if you have it."

Joanna put a teapot on the stove.

After turning it on high, she said, "Sit down and tell me what you would like to discuss."

The man sat down and said, "This morning I was putting a small tool kit in all of the vehicles.

"When I went to put one in the Chrysler, I discovered why Mr. Keandra has eight ply light truck radial tires on that car.

"There's a rather heavy safe in the trunk.

"That's okay, but if you have a flat tire, you won't be able to get the spare out. The safe is sitting on the compartment that holds the spare tire. I would like to make some modifications on the car."

The tea pot started to whistle.

Joanna got up and poured hot water for his tea in a cup and set it in front of him.

Then she set a tray of tea bags on the table in front of him and said, "What kind of modifications?"

As he was putting a tea bag in his cup he said, "I would like to build a bracket that would elevate the safe so you can get the spare tire out without having to lift the safe out first.

"The way things are now, we would have to call a tow truck to lift the safe out before we could change the tire."

Joanna studied him for a moment, "Are you qualified to make these modifications?"

He suddenly smiled a confident smile. "Yes, I am. I can build a race car that will go 250 miles per hour.

"If I can do that, I can do any modification necessary. If we have an accident where we hit something head on, the way that safe is sitting in there now, it will come right through the back seat and crush anyone sitting in its path.

"I can build a bracket, out of metal tube, that will hold that safe where it's at, no matter what."

She looked at him thoughtfully. "Even in a high-speed accident? What will that safe do if we hit something at high speed?"

Once again he smiled confidently. "The bracket will collapse. It will bend forward and crush into the body of the car.

"But that safe will stay right where it's at."

"You seem certain, Mr. Numura."

"Yes. I've had some experiences with high-speed impacts."

That's right, you have, she thought. Then she said, "Mr. Numura, you make any modifications that you deem necessary.

"From now on, you don't even need to ask. Just keep me informed when you make these changes."

"You can count on it. Is there anything else you would like to know?"

She studied him once more then said, "Yes.

"Robb Michael told me that he decided to pay you a higher than normal pay scale in hopes of you staying on as our chauffeur.

"Are you going to stay? Or are you wanting to get back into racing?"

He looked at her and smiled. "I love racing, but it's time for me to quit the racing game. I was starting to take too many chances and it damn near brought me down.

"No. I'm not going to be racing again. I'll stay until you ask me to go."

With that he got up and started for the door.

She said, "Thank you, Mr. Numura."

He turned back and bowed, then turned, and walked out the door.

THREE DAYS LATER

Joanna had finished feeding the babies and was about to go into the house, to the office, when she heard a noise outside.

She went up the steps to the driveway.

Once outside, she saw her driver talking to some people that were measuring the property across from the garage.

Looking around, she saw Mr. Kahn and Mr. Numura talking with the people that were measuring the property.

When Douglas Kahn saw her, he came over to her. "You are wondering what we are doing?"

"Yes, as a matter of fact I am."

He smiled at her and said, "Mr. Numura came up with an idea.

"He wants to build a shop across from the garage to service the vehicles in. Security thinks that this is a good idea.

"They say, if we're doing all of our own service work, someone trying to sabotage our vehicles has less chance of succeeding."

Joanna looked around and said, "Who are all these people?"

"They are security. They are laying out an idea of how it might be.

"Then we will get James Reader Construction Company over here to come up with an actual plan on what, and how, to build.

"This is pretty much the same thing we did when we built the compound.

"You did authorize this, didn't you?"

She looked at Douglas Kahn and smiled. "As a matter of fact, I did.

"Thank Mr. Numura for expediting this project."

Joanna turned and went back into the house.

TWO WEEKS LATER

Joanna was pleasantly surprised.

The building for the new shop was completely done.

All that needed to be completed was to put the furnishings in.

She was told the furnishings would have to wait until the concrete floor had cured.

The building had the same exterior design as the house, but had big garage doors on the side facing the driveway.

She had been so busy that she didn't even get to read in the journal.

Later in the day, she had Mr. Numura drive her downtown to a jewelry store. Once the car was parked, she had Mr. Numura open the trunk.

When she looked in there, she got the shock of her life. All she could see was the spare tire standing up in the trunk.

She turned to Mr. Numura and asked, "Where did the safe go?"

The man smiled, reached in behind the spare, pulled a lever, and pulled the spare tire toward the rear of the car. There was the safe, behind the spare tire.

The spare tire was mounted on a bracket that was hinged to the floor, hiding the safe.

Looking at the safe, she saw the safe was sitting in a cage made of steel tube. She opened the safe and took out a thirty-two-ounce bar of gold, and then closed the safe.

She pushed the spare tire back in the locking position, hiding the safe. The safe couldn't be seen behind the spare tire.

Turning to her driver, she said, "Very good, Mr. Numura. Very good, indeed."

With that she closed the trunk deck.

Mr. Numura escorted her into the jewelry store. After she returned home, she felt tired, so she decided to lay down for awhile and read the journal.

THE JOURNAL
NOVEMBER ELEVEN
This day I took you on a tour of the house.

I think you were more impressed than I expected you to be. I knew you liked the exterior, that chalet architectural design. It's all yours, my little captive.

Use it anyway you like. I know I certainly have. I've made deals in the office and library that turned out better than anyone would believe, so you use this house anyway you think you need to.

I've found that sometimes it's better to work out a deal in the library, or even the living room, rather than the office.

People are more comfortable there. I believe whoever I'm dealing with is more comfortable there.

That's important.

Believe it or not, I've never brought a woman to this house to party with. I always take them to the townhouse.

The only time I had a party here was with a group of clients and their wives.

After showing you the house, we had to go to the hospital, where it seems, you met Dr. 'Frankenstein' Keandra.

I hope you liked him.

Of course, Douglas Kahn not only gave you the grand tour, he also gave you a rather detailed history.

Douglas Kahn is the most loyal man I have had the pleasure to meet. Oh, well, enough has been explained.

Now, I want you to know I'm looking forward to the next minute I'll be with you. And from there, to the rest of my life.

I told you to invite your family over for Thanksgiving. I'm hoping you will. You can't know how much I'm looking forward to it.

Now, I'm going to go down and snuggle up to you.

NOVEMBER TWELVE

This day I noticed you were exploring the house.

I knew you would be. Your curiosity has a way of getting the best of you.

You were shocked to see that the car garage is on the roof of the compound.

Believe it or not, the garage was where it is now before there was a compound. I had the garage torn down, and then the basement extended to build the compound.

The garage is more than twice as big as it used to be, not to mention the tennis court behind it.

Now we can park more than a dozen cars in there.

When you were worried about where your car was, it was right over your head.

The reason that I'm writing about this is to let you know how much I enjoy watching you figure things out.

NOVEMBER FIFTEEN

It dawned on me today the quality of my life is better than it has ever been before.

Watching you grow has become my favorite pastime. You're starting to grow a small bump in the front of your body.

On Thanksgiving, I wondered if anyone will notice you're carrying someone extra around with you.

Just so you know, I'm waiting impatiently for those little people to enter our world. Wondering what they'll be like as they grow up, knowing I'll never know.

I'm certain that you will give them guidance along the way.

What pleases me most about you is that you have kept doing your research, along with everything else you do.

Now you know the importance of research.

I love you, Joanna. I love what you are.

NOVEMBER TWENTY-FOUR

It's near midnight. After making love, you fell asleep.

Not being sleepy, I decided to come up and work on my journal.

Today was wonderful. A complete success. I was so proud of you. You kept everyone entertained.

I could only keep the chef until everything was prepared. Then he had to go home to his own family. That worked out okay, that's why I was serving up the turkey.

I enjoyed every minute of it, and I'm looking forward to the morrow.

When you told your father that I kidnapped you, I swear to God, I thought he was getting angrier by the second.

When you told him you were flying jets, I think you scared him a little.

By the time you told him you would rather live in the compound, I believe he finally had come to understand you.

As everyone was leaving, Kathy came up and hugged me.

While kissing me on the cheek, she told me to take good care of you because you're very much in love with me.

I hope that's not true. For when I die, it will be all the worse for you.

I've got to say it. This day I lived! I really lived! Now I'm going to go down and get in bed with you. I like the way you snuggle up to me in your sleep.

I fully expect to touch you wherever I can while you sleep. If you don't wake up, I'll know I was working on it.

JOANNA

Joanna stopped reading, and thought, *I wish you were still here.*

I long for your touch every night when I go to bed.

I miss the picnics we had at the foot of the bed.

The way you touched me and licked me.

The way I would lay my head on your belly and suck on you.

Sometimes reading this journal makes me realize just how much I miss you.

Joanna started to cry. Once again she cried herself to sleep.

When Joanna woke up, she heard the boys fussing.

She looked at the clock. 6:05 PM

She got up and started preparing dinner for them.

THE JOURNAL
DECEMBER FIVE

This day you informed me we are spending Christmas with your parents.

I forgot to tell you I invited Papa Eli over on Christmas night after late mass. I must remember to tell you.

This is going to be great fun. I love having him around. He can be a riot. However, he is going to have to behave himself while he is here.

There isn't anyone here to pick a fight with.

You don't know it yet, but he will take off the collar and pick a fight with someone. He likes to let it be known that they got their ass whipped by a priest.

There have been several times I've had to watch his back.

When I'm gone, I have provided for him in my will.

I'm very much looking forward to Christmas.

P.S: I still have to get you a Christmas present. I don't even know what you want.

Trust me, I won't let you go without.

I'm going to close for now.

I want to go down and play with (molest) your little body.

DECEMBER SEVEN

This day I bought a new Ford pickup truck.

I took you out to the tree farms near Damascus. I let you pick out a Christmas tree.

You were really excited as you watched them cut down the tree.

I loved watching you.

They loaded the tree into the back of the truck for us. On the way to the compound, we stopped at several stores and bought Christmas decorations.

After we had the tree decorated, we had so many decorations left over that you wanted to get another tree for the house, so on the morrow, I plan to take you to get us another tree.

Putting the tree in the living room in the compound worked fine. I will be interested to see where you want to put the tree in the house.

I've never had a tree where I live before.

Over the years, I've bought several trees for the companies and had the employees decorate them, but this is the first time that I've had a Christmas tree in the house where I live.

DECEMBER EIGHT

This day we took the truck out and picked out another tree. I believe this one is bigger.

After we got it in the house, we had to buy another tree stand.

The store was crowded with people, and it was great fun squeezing between the bodies in that store.

When we got home, we decorated the tree and placed it in front of the big window to the left of the door.

We hung a wreath on the front door.

Later in the day, Mr. Kahn came over for a meeting with me. He told me that he could tell by looking at the house that you haven't run off and left me yet.

I've got to say it, Joanna, you did a terrific job on the house.

DECEMBER TWENTY

This morning I served you breakfast by the pool.

I loved it! Maybe I liked it too much. You know, I may very well be going into a second childhood.

Oh well, too bad!

I went shopping and bought you another diamond pendant for Christmas. I'll be getting you more, but I'm not sure what to get you yet.

I have yet to figure out what you really like. I don't want to ask you. If I do, you might think that's what I'm going to get you. I want to surprise you, so I'm not going to ask you what you would like.

DECEMBER TWENTY-SIX

Well, we sent Christmas on its way. Boy! What a blast. Everything was going great.

I baptized both you and Emily. It scared the hell out of Emily. I covered it up for her.

In fact, I may have covered it up too well. Eli didn't know Emily is afraid of water.

He picked her up and threw her in the pool.

Believe that!

Oh, well, sometimes we need a little excitement in our lives.

After they left, I poured you a drink. Then we went to bed and made love. For some reason, I wasn't sleepy.

So, I'm up here in my office, writing about the events of the day.

You asked me if I would fuck Emily if she wasn't a nun. I think you knew the answer before you even asked.

I am not much on religion.

I believe the church over does it. I do believe in God. However, I can live without the church.

Don't misunderstand me. I respect Eli and Emily for choosing their lifestyle. But it's too limited for me.

Which reminds me, you asked me about the way I pray.

The one thing I didn't tell you is that I get a sick feeling in my gut every time. I even got a sick feeling in my gut when I was talking about it with you.

So, my little captive, now you know more than you probably would like to know.

I would drag Emily to my bed in a heartbeat. Being a nun has nothing to do with it. She's a woman, and that's the whole of it, that's what she was made for.

She's totally different than you, but she has some of the same qualities that you have.

She would be a perfect mother for my children. She would make certain that they would get the early childhood training that they need. She would make certain they are educated in the proper manner.

I don't even need to tell you this. You already know it. That's probably why you like her.

She isn't someone looking for a free ride.

I hope, by the time you read this, that you and Emily are friends.

Last night, when Eli and Emily were leaving, Emily said something to me.

You asked me what she said, and for some reason, I can't think of a reason I shouldn't tell you.

I wanted to tell you, but I feel I would be violating a trust if I tell you. I can tell you on these pages, because, by the time that you read this, I'll be gone. By then it might be important for you to know.

What she said was, 'Thank you for saving my life. At the time you saved my life, I realized how much I wanted to live. Thank you for making me realize how much I want to live.

I will do anything you want or ask me to. I mean anything. It is very important that you ask me to do something for you. I need to feel that I have repaid you.'

The whole time she was speaking, she was crushing her breasts into my chest. That was pretty much what she said.

At this time, I believe she is just being grateful.

When you're under water, breathing water, you know you are dying. It can be very traumatic when you think you're going to die.

It can be very discomforting thinking about it after the experience is over.

I know, that's the reason I chose you to carry on for me after I'm gone.

You can't possibly know how hard it was to write those last lines. I knew you were the one to be my CEO before I even met you.

On the second deal I made with you, I knew you would understand the importance of my psychological need of a bloodline.

If I have the two you are carrying, that will be great. I told you I would like six. But, knowing that I'm not going to be here, I know I may to have to be satisfied with two. And damned lucky to have those two, unless I can find a way to have more.

By the time you read this, I'm certain Mr. Kahn will have told you I've set up enough money in the Keandra Foundation to educate eight children of my bloodline.

That's more than enough to educate two.

The Foundation does very good work, so it's better they have a surplus of funds.

It's getting daylight now, and I'm getting tired. I'm going to close for now and go down and snuggle up next to you, then I'll take advantage of your little body.

JOANNA

Joanna stopped reading.

She had a vivid memory of that Christmas night.

She knew the minute she saw Robb Michael running toward the pool that something was wrong, but full comprehension hadn't set in yet. After he pulled Emily out of the water, she knew there was something very wrong just by the way Robb Michael was treating her when he reached between her legs to raise her bottom up and start pushing water out of her.

Robb Michael managed to bring her around.

It was then everyone realized the seriousness of the situation.

Of course, there was the way Emily looked at Robb Michael after he got her breathing again.

Emily's eyes followed Robb Michael everywhere he went.

Joanna knew then Emily wanted something from him, that's why she asked Robb Michael if he would fuck Emily if she wasn't a nun.

Thinking about it now, she hoped that he did.

My God! He was dying! She hoped he did everything that he wanted to do.

Then she thought, *I bet he did want her. I wonder if she would let him? I sure hope so.*

As Joanna was thinking about it, she turned another page in the journal.

THE JOURNAL
DECEMBER TWENTY-SEVEN

Last night I was thinking of Emily and her near-death experience.

While thinking of her, I believe I thought of a way to make a new type of life preserver. I'm going to run it by the engineers at one of the companies and see if it's feasible.

I can't help but think about what Emily said when she left yesterday. It might be an opportunity to reach my goals.

If I ever see her again, I will approach her to see if she is interested. I'm gambling it won't affect my relationship with you.

Something within me tells me I must keep going no matter what. I must do this!

I must keep going!

JOANNA

Joanna stopped reading once again and thought, *He was doing something.*

I wonder what? Is that why Emily left the church? Did she leave the church because she was ashamed? Was she pregnant? I wonder if I'll ever know.

Joanna got up and nursed her sons.

Then she started making out her schedule for the next week.

She also had to get in touch with the jewelry stores. The work was exciting.

During it all, she was thinking about what she had read in the journal.

The next morning after she had fed the boys, she went up to the office.

She was about to open the vault when Douglas Kahn came in.

After she greeted him, she asked, "Mr. Kahn, do you know if Robb Michael had a relationship with an Emily Van Hatten?"

Douglas Kahn was silent for a moment, then said, "Joanna, I was his lawyer.

"There is a such a thing as lawyer-client privilege. As close to you as I have become, I would normally tell you more. However, I wish you wouldn't ask me about Robb Michael's private life.

"He specifically asked me not to tell you, or anyone else, about his private life after his death. I loved Robb Michael. I loved what he was.

"The only thing I can tell you about him is he wanted me to gather his children together in thirteen years.

"He left another small journal that he wants me to read to them. I have read that journal.

"Personally, I think it's inappropriate for children that age, but as I said, I loved him and respected him. Therefore, I'll do as he asked."

She studied him for a moment, then softly said, "Okay."

She had Mr. Numura bring around the limo.

After she was in the car, and on her way downtown, she got to thinking about the journal and what Douglas Kahn had said.

Then she thought, *I can wait.*

NEXT DAY

The following morning, she was showering with the boys when one of them kicked her in the side.

She started to say something to the baby when she felt the kick again. It wasn't her son that kicked her. The kick was on the inside.

After the next kick, she said, "Boys, I've got a feeling that you're going to have another brother. I don't think a Michael Jo would kick this hard."

After she bathed the boys, she went to the phone and called the Holly Clinic and made an appointment for an ultrasound.

Her curiosity was getting the best of her. Later that day, she went into the Holly Clinic.

She told the technician she had a baby kicking the hell out of her, and she wanted to see if it was a boy or girl.

As she was getting the ultrasound, the technician explained how she couldn't get the baby to move in such a way that she could tell the sex.

The whole time, the baby was extremely active.

Finally, after two hours, the technician said, "You know, this little girl is going to be a handful. She darn sure isn't going to be still for a minute. I've got a feeling that this one is going to be a live wire.

"Have you got a name picked out for her?"

Joanna looked at her for a moment then said, "Yeah, Michael Jo."

The technician looked thoughtful for a moment then said, "Oh, yeah! That name is appropriate. Good luck, lady."

LATER THAT SAME DAY

Joanna sat at her kitchen table, feeding her sons.

Tears welled up in her eyes as she thought, *I wish you were here, Robb Michael.*

Later, Joanna went into her bedroom and laid down, then she picked up the journal.

THE JOURNAL
DECEMBER THIRTY

Today I got the life preserver that I had made.

While writing this, it dawned on me I should have tried it on. Because a woman's breasts will give her some flotation, therefore, the life preserver may not work on a man.

I just went down to the pool and tested the life preserver.

I tried it on you. While wearing it in the pool, the water came almost up to your lower lip. Just damn near perfect.

It held me up, but I wasn't comfortable wearing it. The adjustment straps aren't right. I'll redesign and then try it again.

JANUARY TWO

You and I stayed home to bring in the New Year.

We turned the lights down low in the party room, then turned up the music. We danced to most of the music on the jukebox.

At midnight, I poured us both a drink to which we toasted the old year and all it brought us.

I loved it. It brought us more riches than money. More wealth than what's in my vaults. In my mind, we were making love while we danced. We were making love as we talked. And we were making love as we wrapped our minds around each other's thoughts. Making love to you is wonderful, even if it's only in my mind.

JANUARY TWELVE

Suddenly, I find myself traveling again, taking care of business.

I told you that it might be a good idea to go places and socialize a little while I'm gone on these business trips.

It's not good to be alone too much.

I'm trying to think of a way to get you interested in doing some of the company work, but being pregnant isn't helping much.

When I had my team of engineers design the compound, I had them design it so you could run the companies and raise the children from there.

I never thought about you being pregnant and trying to do both projects, too.

JANUARY SIXTEEN

This day you told me you gave Emily a key to the compound. I started to tell you never to give a key to anyone, but then I decided not to say anything.

After all, you own as much of the place as I do. I have to learn to trust your judgment. I'm glad you like Emily.

I can't think of anyone better for you to make friends with.

JANUARY TWENTY

This day I let you play CEO.

Of course, you know now this is what I've been training you for ever since I brought you here.

I know you will do well. You're a natural. I told you I was going to go back to bed.

Didn't happen. Instead, I came up to my office to write in my journal.

Sometimes I come up here to write in my journal, and then fall asleep in my office chair instead.

I saw you off at eight-thirty. I finished my coffee at nine and came up here, poked around the house, made another pot of coffee down in the bar.

I did a little cleaning up around the party room, poured myself another cup of coffee.

By the time I got up to my office, it was quarter to eleven.

You'll be back about seven-thirty or eight this evening. I'll be waiting for you so you can tell me about your day.

That's all I'm going to write for now.

JANUARY TWENTY- LATE NIGHT

My God, what an exciting day.

First, while I was exercising in the workout gym, I got more of a workout than I expected.

Then I had to go downtown and put another deal together. It was snowing like a son of a gun! It was snowing so hard that you couldn't see a hundred feet.

Meeting a car without their lights on was a little more exciting than I liked. I'm grateful my car has all-wheel drive.

Somehow the snow seemed to add to the events of the day. Putting this deal together completely wore me out.

I got home late in the afternoon and took a shower and a nap.

I awoke a little before six. I felt elation like I've never felt before.

You got back a little after seven. Thank God you got home before they shut the airport down.

You were so hyped up about your day, I didn't get to tell you about mine.

I'll get around to telling you someday.

JOANNA

Joanna thought about the last paragraph and wondered about it. *There were things happening around that time that never got explained.*

That was about the time Emily disappeared, she thought. *Also, we were having more picnics in the house all of a sudden.*

That was so good. I loved dancing in the party room.

That's where Robb Michael taught me how to peel a ring sausage.

Then she laughed out loud as she started to read the journal.

THE JOURNAL
FEBRUARY FIFTEEN

This day promises to be a good day. The last few days I've been taking care of personal matters, but I managed to be with you on Valentine's Day. I took you to Chez Henri's for dinner, then we came back to the house. That party room works very well for you and me.

Maybe we can make a Michael Jo yet. It's fun to keep trying, even when there are no results.

This morning we tried again. I don't want to stop.

I think I'll go back down to the compound and keep you in bed all day.

FEBRUARY TWENTY-EIGHT

This day you are on your way to Sacramento.

The sun is shining, and for a winter day, it's a pretty pleasant day all around. The sun reflecting off the snow is dazzling.

It's going to be a big day for me. I've got a lot planned for today.

After Sacramento, there's Boise and then Reno.

As long as you're able, I'm going to let you carry the ball.

I want to be sure you can handle it. So far, you're doing great.

Having everyone call you Mrs. Robb Michael was a stroke of genius.

I've got something else in the works.

I may get to fulfill all my dreams yet.

When you find out what I'm doing, I believe that you will understand the why of it.

JOANNA

Joanna stopped reading. *There it is again*, she thought. *He's involved with something.*

Something that makes him feel really good about himself, or, as Mr. Kahn says, 'That confidence that he is.'

Joanna put the journal down and thought about it.

She knew he was heavily involved in something. But what?

Whatever it was, it made him happy, gave him something to look forward to.

She got up and went out in the kitchen and made a pot of coffee.

While the coffee maker was gurgling, she went in the bedroom, retrieved the journal, and thought, *whatever it was that he was working on, I think it pleased him. At least I hope so.*

When she got back, she poured herself a cup of coffee then started reading the journal.

THE JOURNAL
MARCH SIXTEEN

I've completed another deal, Joanna.

You'll hear about it, but Mr. Kahn and the Keandra Foundation will be in control of it.

I find myself struggling again, trying to keep up.

When I look at you and see you carrying your oversized bump around, I can't help but feel for you.

I'll be so happy when you deliver.

It's hard for me to keep up while you are playing CEO, and pregnant, too.

Yet, it's probably the best way for me to get done what I want.

I'm doing double time. But I love it.

You know how I am.

Or, if you don't, you should by the time you read this.

JOANNA

Joanna stopped reading and thought, *there it is again.*

He was doing something.

He was putting something together that really made him feel good.

I wonder if I'll ever know what it was.

I think Mr. Kahn is in the know because David Kahn was with me at that time.

She poured herself another cup of coffee and thought, *for that matter, David Kahn is with me now.*

Mr. Kahn, it seems, is always busy at the Keandra Foundation.

The only time I see Douglas anymore, is when he comes to the office to take care of business matters here.

The only time that I see Mr. Kahn and his sons, at the same time, is when he's chairing a meeting at the Foundation."

She thought for a minute, and then, *Richard Kahn was with Robb Michael at about that time.*

Now, I wonder what he had Richard doing.

Joanna turned the page and started reading.

THE JOURNAL
APRIL TEN

This morning I looked at you and I find it hard to believe that you are actually that big.

I swear, Joanna, it looks like you have a record-size watermelon in your belly.

You told me Eli was here this morning while I was gone.

You told me Emily has broken her vows and left the church.

I already knew. I see her once in awhile.

You need not worry about her. She is doing well.

JOANNA

Joanna stopped reading and smiled. *There it is!*

She thought, *He did it!*

He got together with her and had an affair, of sorts, with her.

I hope he got what he wanted from her.

I wonder if he let her know he was dying. No, he wouldn't do that.

If he wouldn't tell me, then he wouldn't tell her.

I hope on top of hope she doesn't feel guilty.

If he had something going with her, he needed her. I wonder how to let her know.

Joanna felt relieved and thought, *Knowing he was dying, he may have felt he needed something from her.*

I'll be thinking about this a lot.

She felt tired. She laid back on the couch and dozed for a while.

She heard the boys fussing, so she got up and settled them down, then went back to reading.

THE JOURNAL
MAY EIGHT

This morning you delivered two beautiful boys to us.

I'm on my way to reaching my goals. I'm so pleased.

With the way I feel, I could just burst.

How wonderful you've made my life.

Now I'm hoping, somewhere, inside the two of us, there's a Michael Jo lurking around.

This is something I want to work on as soon as you feel up to it.

I feel so full of anticipation I could explode. I can actually see where things can possibly come together.

I'm looking forward to meeting the challenge. Meeting the challenge is something I always look forward to.

This is something you already know about.

MAY SIXTEEN

This morning you asked me why I suck the nectar from your breasts.

I don't know if I can answer you satisfactorily, but now I will attempt to explain.

Years ago, I met a man that had a bad case of psoriasis, a skin disease that causes the skin to harden, break and flake off. Often times, it's painful.

At the time, there was no known remedy for psoriasis.

One day I saw him pull a leaf off a tree and rub it on his flaking skin. He saw me watching him.

He explained how he knew there was no cure, but once in awhile he would rub a leaf, a weed or some other plant on his skin in the hopes it would help or cure him.

He knew it wouldn't, but he kept trying.

Well, my sweet captive, he is me.

I know there is no hope for me, but I keep trying.

That's why I drink from you. I find myself obsessed with sucking on your breasts.

I suck from you as much nourishment as I can, hoping on top of hope, that somehow the antibodies in this life-giving nectar will bring me back to life.

Deep down inside, I have a feeling it will not.

Still, I find myself grasping for that leaf as I'm drinking this life-giving nectar from your breasts. I most likely will be drinking from you as long as your body supplies it, or until I'm not here anymore.

I'm hoping, and hoping on top of hope, the antibodies and other life-giving stuffs within will extend my life.

I find it interesting that my white cell count goes through the roof after I drink milk.

I'm doing research on this. My findings are most interesting.

I need more time to reach my goals.

I find myself running once again to keep up.

MAY EIGHTEEN

This day I asked Mrs. Numura if she would watch our babies for a while.

Then I took you out to the airport and had you fly the U2. You did very well.

You're a good pilot.

You flew north along the Cascade Range and then down into Nevada.

The first time you flew in this bird was one year ago today.

Remember the night that I took you up to the stars?

Well, I want you to know, I'm an equal opportunity employer. So, I let you take me up into the stars.

We couldn't stay as long as we would like. We have babies to care for.

I want you to remember something you said tonight.

On our way home, you stopped the car and told me that before long you would be able to do anything, maybe even save my life. Well, I hope you're right, but I have my doubts.

I'm using your body anyway I can toward that goal.

Sometimes I can't help but wonder if you think I'm a complete idiot. I know I sometimes feel like one.

This day I put an additional $700,000 into your account, at your bank, as per our agreement of this day one year ago.

You can't possibly know how pleased I am that you kept your part of the agreement. After we were married, I wondered if you would. You did.

I'm so proud of you.

JUNE TEN

This day we hired a nanny, Janice Lyman.

Janice seems to be able to handle things okay.

The boys are getting to be too much for me to handle, especially when you're playing CEO.

To take care of the boys, and take care of business at the same time, is a bit much, but somehow you seem to manage it.

At the same time, I purchased nine new Chryslers. I'm having them sent to the Coach Works to be modified.

If this works out the way I want it to, I'll be buying Lincolns, Cadillacs, and possibly Buicks.

Today, some of the new limousines are way too long for inner city business.

I'm interested in building a car that will work, something that will carry six or eight, and still maneuver well in city traffic.

I'm going to work on it.

Mr. Numura, the man that takes care of the grounds, has a brother in the hospital.

His brother is a race car driver.

When he gets out of the hospital, I may hire him as your chauffeur, if he'll take the job as your personal driver.

It's important to me that you have a driver that can get you away from dangerous situations. I would like you to have a professional driver, someone who can handle a car at high speed.

I don't like you coming and going to the airport, driving alone or in a cab all the time.

Mr. Numura told me his brother's car was going over a 160 when it crashed. After an ordeal like that, he may not want the job.

However, I'm interested in him. He may be what I need to protect you when I'm no longer here.

JUNE EIGHTEEN

This morning Mr. Numura's brother arrived from Europe.

I met with him and asked him if he would give me a driving demonstration. We talked for awhile, then got out the Chrysler and took it for a drive. First, we drove to Vernonia to a coffee shop and had a cup of espresso. Then we took the long way back on Highway 47, north to Rainier, then to the coast and back.

This man is a driver. The way he handles a car is unbelievable.

The way he drove that car you would have thought that he had been driving those roads for years.

Pay attention to him when you are riding with him. He will surprise you with his driving ability.

After we got back, we took you for a ride.

Then I hired him at double the pay rate.

Sometime you may need someone that can drive like he can, so don't let him go.

People with his talent are a must keep. I really enjoy riding with him.

JUNE TWENTY

I like the way you always take the babies with you.

Taking Janice along to assist you is a good idea.

I want you to know I never leave the babies alone with Janice when I keep them here.

They are our children. It's our responsibility to take care of our own, not the nanny's.

I have to admit that having her here is really helpful.

Even so, I don't think the nanny trusts me.

When I'm taking care of the boys, she watches me like a big bird with a curved beak.

This afternoon she was watching me while I was feeding one of the boys a bottle of milk.

I tried to tell her that the baby is safe when I'm feeding him when you're not home.

I told her, "When Joanna's home, the boys and I fight over who gets the tit first.

"The boys usually win the battle because they can scream louder, longer.

"Sometimes Joanna feeds them both at the same time.

"I can't cry as loud as they can, so I have to wait until the babies are done eating before I get to eat."

You should have seen the wide-eyed look that woman gave me.

AUGUST TWENTY-TWO

This day is our first anniversary.

With the activities in my life, it's hard to keep up.

I took Joanna to the Chauncey's Pub for breakfast.

For lunch, I'll take her to Samuel's.

They have made the best burgers in the northwest for over eighty years. They're still in the original building.

I love watching her eat one of those Big Burgers.

When she takes a bite, the juices run down her face, and drip off her chin.

Tonight, I'll take her to Chez Henri's.

She loves that place.

I'm managing somehow.

I have a patient at the hospital I must watch, after which I'll have a clear schedule.

OCTOBER TEN

This day you informed me you want to have Thanksgiving dinner in the compound instead of the house. It's okay with me.

I'm going to have to take care to make sure it all comes around right. There are other things in the works for that day.

I'll have to plan carefully.

With all the excitement in my life, I don't want to miss any of it.

NOVEMBER TEN

This day turned out to be an exciting day.

Things are coming together better than I could have imagined.

I'm celebrating this day. I really feel good.

Plus, I had another surgery to do.

Nothing could have turned out better for me.

NOVEMBER TWENTY-FOUR

This day I'm just sitting here reading through what I've already written, remembering the holiday.

Once again, we managed to create a party atmosphere.

That turkey-shaped cake, with the light and dark meat in all of the right places, was a sensation.

What a wonderful idea you had when you baked that cake.

I ate some of the white and the chocolate with vanilla and chocolate ice cream. I have to say it, it was great.

DECEMBER TWENTY- SEVEN

This day you are in Reno, playing CEO.

At this time, I'm letting you do all of the work.

I must not interfere. Before too long, you will be the only one doing it. Once again, I'm busy playing catch up.

I've got things to do right here in Portland. This is such an exciting city. I love it. Going places to eat, and being entertained, really makes my life.

I'm glad you take the babies with you.

I'm finding that I need more rest.

I find myself taking a nap, sometimes twice a day.

When I tell you what I've been doing, you're not going to want to believe it.

I believe you will understand the reasoning behind what I'm doing. More and more you are discovering what I am.

You'll sort it out. When you do, I hope you're not disappointed.

If I'm still alive at this time next year, I'll be surprised, because I'm starting to slow down and I know it.

I'm doing everything I know to slow it down.

Surprisingly enough, I believe the antibodies from your body are working. The growth of this tumor has slowed down.

JANUARY FIFTEEN

I went to the Holly Clinic and ran some tests.

The growth has definitely slowed down. It's not growing at the same rate as last month.

It hasn't gone into remission, but has slowed dramatically.

I don't know if it's the nectar from your breasts, or if it's just a normal thing that's happening.

I wish I knew more than I do. All I can do is watch it slowly drain my life away.

Sometimes I think I should feel ridiculous sucking on your breasts, like a baby, but I don't. I love it.

However ridiculous it might seem, I'm finding there are properties in breast milk that are beneficial.

My white cell count is up dramatically.

This is a good thing.

I'm certain that it's from drinking your breast milk.

I honestly believe that my immune system is stronger.

I'm starting to believe that it would benefit a whole family to breastfeed when the mother of the house has a baby.

Any doctor who would make this statement publicly would be ostracized clear out of the country.

The facts are there.

The antibodies not only boost the immune system of a baby, I believe they boost the immune system of anybody.

The antibodies are only in the milk for six or seven months.

After that, the fluid changes, but the properties within it are still very good.

I don't know if everything beneficial in mother's milk is known.

This is the reason I drink from you. I want to go on with you forever.

I want that promise of happily ever after. But happily ever after, it seems, is a derelict promise.

I need the thought that we can go on forever.

I know it's a derelict promise. A promise that is empty, hollow, and can never be.

Good God! I'm starting to ramble on paper.

I'm so tired today.

I must take a little nap before you come home. I don't want you to see me like this.

I may not be doing as well as I would like, but I'm not ready to quit my practice yet.

FEBRUARY ONE

This day I'm driving home instead of flying.

I've had some limousines made, and I'm driving one home.

As I'm writing this, I'm in a motel room.

The snow is so deep here in the Siskiyou Pass that travelers can't get through, but I'm comfortable and warm.

I really can't say anymore. Hopefully on the morrow I'll be on my way.

FEBRUARY TWO

The powers that be never got the highway open for traffic until late afternoon.

Not being able to go until late, I didn't get far.

This night I'm staying in Grants Pass.

Hopefully I'll be home on the morrow around noon.

FEBRUARY THREE

This day I had you drive the new limousine I had made.

You told me you liked it.

I was so tired, I fell asleep.

I seem to tire more easily now, but there is so much more happening in my life.

It's like I don't want the day to end. At the same time, I can't wait till the morrow.

I love it. I wish for it to never end.

I try not to make plans for the morrow. I just let everything happen as it will.

I love you, Joanna.

FEBRUARY SEVENTEEN

I seem to be spending a lot of time at the Holly Clinic.

It's really a small hospital. It has all the facilities of a hospital.

Somehow, I find myself there more and more.

This was the first medical facility I had built. I have always made sure to update this facility as technology advanced.

I always will.

The Holly Clinic is just as advanced as the Keandra Surgical Hospitals around the nation.

About a third of the surgeries I have performed were at the Holly Clinic.

FEBRUARY FOURTEEN

Today we went to Chez Henri's to celebrate Valentine's Day.

I really enjoyed the way this night turned out. After Chez Henri's, we went to Nick's Comedy Club for a while. It was great fun.

Then home to the party room.

You had a few drinks, and I became intoxicated with the mood of the evening.

We went to bed in the compound, trying to see if we could coax Michael Jo to be conceived.

She's late getting here, makes me wonder if she will be late getting home after a night out with friends.

Now that I've thought of it, I'll be thinking about it more than I should.

I think the reason you're not conceiving is because you are still nursing the babies.

Your uterus hasn't opened up yet, but I don't want you to stop nursing the boys.

It's more important to have them turn out to be what they are supposed to be than to have you pregnant again.

MARCH ONE

This day I wrote myself a prescription for Viagra.

I'm starting to feel frustrated.

No matter how often I fuck Joanna, I can't seem to get her pregnant.

It's getting harder to keep it up. But keep it up, I must.

I'm going to stop writing in this journal. There is too much happening to keep it going.

Quite a lot of stuff is going on to keep going on this.

There's another journal I'm writing in.

That journal has sensitive things in it.

I don't want it read for at least ten years after my death, maybe more.

I must consult with Douglas Kahn about this before I go on. So, we wait and see.

Robb Michael

JOANNA

Joanna put the journal down, and thought for a moment. *It must have been exhausting living the way he had to live.* She thought, *I need to think about this more.*

She had read the journal several times.

Somewhere in the back of her mind, she had questions. But she didn't feel like sorting them out.

She knew she would read the journal over, and over again.

At the same time, she had less and less time to herself.

It seemed that business was encroaching on her private life.

She thought about it for a moment, *Damn you, Robb Michael. There's so much I have to do that it doesn't leave time for anything else.*

Joanna looked down at herself. She was getting big.

"It won't be long before you're here, Michael Jo," she said aloud. "I wish your father was going to be here to see you as you're born."

She felt like she wanted to cry, but knew she didn't have time. She had so much to do.

JULY FOURTH

Joanna fixed herself breakfast and was eating when her water broke.

She knew she had to get to the hospital soon.

She called Mr. Numura and asked him to bring the Chrysler around.

Then called Janice in and told her that her water broke and to watch the boys while she went to the hospital.

When her driver got there, he knew instinctively there was a problem. Joanna could hardly stand up.

He picked her up and carried her to the car, then he fastened her seatbelt.

As he started the car rolling, she told him she wanted to go to the Holly Clinic. When they got there, they wheeled her inside.

She was prepped and taken to a room.

In between her labor pains, she couldn't help but think they had outrun a police car along the way to the clinic.

Two hours later, she had the baby and they were cleaning her up.

After they had taken her to her room, they told her a Mr. Numura wanted to see her. She told them to show him in.

As he came into the room, he said, "You don't need to scare me like that, you know."

She couldn't help herself. She started laughing, and asked, "Did we outrun a police car on the way here?"

The man bowed slightly and said, "I believe we got quite some distance ahead of him.

"I was in a bigger hurry than he was. But I don't know that we outrun him. I'll tell you in a few days."

As she listened to him, she thought, *That poor cop. As well-trained as he was, he never had a chance against someone like Mr. Numura.*

Then she asked, "How fast will that car go?"

He paused a moment and then said, "I've made some modifications on two of the limousines, the Chrysler and the Lincoln. Both cars will top two hundred. However, other than the test drives, I never thought I would have to drive that fast."

"If you didn't think you would have to go that fast, why did you modify the cars to go that fast?"

He smiled and then said, "Just in case." He paused, then softer, said again, "Just in case."

"What if we would have had an accident?" she asked.

Smiling, he said, "I wouldn't have stopped.

"Both cars have been reinforced with light tubing inside the front for just that reason.

"With the wealth that seems to surround you, it's important to be prepared for such an occasion.

"It was more important for me to get you here than it was to stop."

After Mr. Numura left, they brought her baby into her.

The baby was crying, so she turned on her side and started nursing her.

As the baby was nursing, Joanna started crying.

The nurse, concerned, asked, "Is something wrong?"

Joanna couldn't stop crying.

Between her sobs, she said, "Michael Jo's father wasn't here to greet her when she arrived. Robb Michael loved this baby before she was even conceived."

The sobs poured out of her in a torrent.

THE FOLLOWING DAY

Joanna lay in bed, thinking, *If Robb Michael isn't here, I don't want to have another baby.* She called the doctor in.

When the doctor came in, she said, "I want to have a tubal ligation.
"How soon can I have it?"

"Right now, if you wish," he replied.

She thought a bit and then said, "Yes, I want to do it, as soon as possible."

TEN MONTHS LATER

Joanna drove up to the National Guard gate at Portland International Airport at nine-thirty in the evening.

It was May eighteenth.

She had secured clearance earlier in the day.

The guard at the gate was new. He was younger, and she had never seen him before.

"Can I help you ma'am?" He asked.

She looked at him and smiled. "Yes.

"I'm Mrs. Robb Michael Keandra. I'm taking the U2 up tonight. Have they got the bird ready?"

"Yes, ma'am, the aircraft is ready, but I didn't know a woman was going to take it up. I'll have to check before I let you enter."

About that time, a military vehicle drove up.

The man driving was the man that helped her into the U2 the first time she flew in it. "Mrs. Robb Michael, how good to see you.

"When you get suited up, I'll give you a hand. See you out at the bird." The guard motioned her through the gate.

As she got out of her car, she stopped.

She looked down and smiled. *Isn't that strange.*

She thought, *just because I'm going to fly the U2, I can feel Robb Michael's presence.*

After she suited up, a military vehicle took her out to the U2.

The man helped her into the front cockpit. She closed the cockpit and started the engine.

She had no sooner than got to the end of the runway when she got clearance to lift off.

She gently pushed the throttle forward.

The U2 moved down the runway, and into the clear sky, as though in one movement.

Quickly she took the U2 up into the stars.

As the plane got up to sixty thousand feet, the engine sounded different.

Looking at the dash, she wondered what was wrong. Suddenly, she started fumbling with the throttle.

In her mind, she heard, *'Don't manhandle the throttle. Move the throttle touchy-feely till you hear the engine sound the way it's supposed to.*

'You remember what it's supposed sound like. Do it.'

Quickly she moved the throttle gently till the engine sounded the way she remembered it.

Then it hit her. It was like she heard Robb Michael's voice. She sat quiet for a long moment, thinking.

Then she said, "Robb Michael, is that you?"

No answer.

Then she just cruised along, looking at the stars.

I'm certain I heard it, she thought. *I'm certain I heard you, Robb Michael.*

Then aloud she said, "Where do I go from here?"

Once again in her mind, she heard his voice again. *'How do I know? You've got the stick.'*

Joanna started to cry as she turned the plane west.

"You are here, aren't you?" she said aloud. Then quiet.

She flew west for about an hour, hoping to hear him again.

Then, in her helmet, she heard, "Hello, U2. Please identify yourself."

She looked around. As clear as the radio signal was, he had to be close to her.

She didn't see anyone, but she said, "Who am I talking to?"

"Lieutenant Commander David Walker, United States Navy.

"How wonderful to hear a lady's voice come out of a U2. I'm in an F16, about ten thousand feet below you. Who am I talking to?"

Joanna thought for a moment. Then she said, "I'm Mrs. Robb Michael Keandra. The Med Keandra Group has this U2 leased from the government."

"Do you know where you're going? What's your destination, Mrs. Robb Michael Keandra?"

"In a minute or two, I'm going to make a turn and return to PDX. Where are you going from here?"

"Back to the carrier, ma'am. I just came up to see who was joyriding.

"What a pleasant surprise to find a lady out over the Pacific on a nice, starry night.

"Have a nice flight."

"Thank you, I will."

She flew along for another twenty minutes before making her turn. Two hours later, she was back on the ground.

They put the little wheels under the wings, then she started on her way back to the hanger.

When she stopped the engine, she sat in the cockpit and started to cry.

She was certain she had heard Robb Michael's voice.

After a minute, she climbed out of the cockpit and started walking toward the building.

As she walked, she said, "Robb Michael, if you are really there, say something once more.

"Anything, please!"

As she entered the building, she started to take off her helmet, when in her mind she heard, '*I shall always love you, Joanna.*'

Once more she started to cry, thinking, *I did hear it!*

I did!

When she got home, she went straight to bed.

Lying there she wondered if she was really hearing him, or if it was all in her mind.

Then she thought, *I think it's just wishful thinking. But he told me what to do!*

While lying there thinking about him, Joanna felt that he was near.

She felt she was going to be alright.

Then wondering if he was always there, she fell asleep.

FOURTEEN YEARS LATER

Joanna got a note from Douglas Kahn, telling her to gather all the children together and meet him at Robb Michael's grave.

She knew this was coming.

In accordance with Robb Michael's will, they were supposed to gather together thirteen years after his death and read the journals and other communications to his offspring.

A year ago, she asked Douglas Kahn when he was going to follow through with Robb Michael's wishes.

He told her he was going to wait one more year because he didn't feel the journal was appropriate for young people of their age group.

Joanna couldn't help but wonder if a one-year difference would really make a difference in maturity at their age.

Joanna called her boys together, along with Michael Jo, and told them they were all supposed to go and hear all their father had written after he discovered he was dying.

Robert and Roger were curious about it and had been anxiously waiting for the last year to hear what it was all about.

Michael Jo, on the other hand, seemed to have a more mature outlook on it.

They were a little upset because Mr. Kahn thought them too young to hear what was in the journals.

Mr. Kahn wanted to read the journals at Robb Michael's gravesite.

Joanna felt Michael Jo was in some ways older mentally than Robert and Roger were. It was obvious Michael Jo had a stronger will than her older brothers.

Even as a toddler, she let it be known she wasn't going to be pushed around by her brothers.

When she started school, she was a leader. Other kids followed her lead whenever they would be playing games. They seemed to look to her to show them the way.

But it was just as obvious, Michael Jo didn't want to be a leader. There were times Joanna worried about Michael Jo.

Because, even though Michael Jo was a team player, Joanna, watching her grow up, could see what was obvious, she was a loner.

Despite that fact, Michael Jo proved to be a good kid.

Like her father, she seemed to have a sense for business. She let it be known she was going to go her own way in her own time and pace.

Joanna let her start her own stock portfolio when she was eleven.

Michael Jo proved to be an aggressive stock trader. In that way, Michael Jo was ahead of her brothers.

However, Roger and Robert were always looking out for Michael Jo.

On the other hand, they seemed to always be there for Joanna. They clung to her in a way that was reassuring.

All of Joanna's children were studious and ambitious.

She was certain Robb Michael would have been proud of all of them when she felt he was near.

She called Mr. Numura and told him to bring the old Chrysler limousine around to the front of the house.

She told Michael Jo to tell the boys it was time to go.

She had moved her family to the main house when the boys were six years old and started school.

Since Robb Michael had died, Douglas Kahn rarely came into the house anymore. His position at the Foundation had kept him busy.

When he did come to the house, he rang the door bell before he entered. If nobody answered the door, he would let himself in.

She worked almost exclusively with David Kahn, once in a while with Richard Kahn. Almost never with Douglas Kahn.

Richard Kahn was also doing Foundation work.

The last time she saw Douglas Kahn, she noticed that he was getting up in years.

His age was showing dramatically.

Mr. Numura brought the car around to the front of the house.

The sun was shining on this January day, but it was a cold thirty degrees.

They were all dressed for the weather.

After they all got in, and were under way, she said, "I don't know what to expect when we get there.

"I hope you all are attentive. Mr. Kahn is going to read something to all of us.

"He told me that it's something that your father wrote, and that the language is of adult content.

"Don't be afraid to interrupt and ask about something if you don't understand what is being read to you."

As they approached the gravesite, Joanna saw a large motor home sitting nearby.

As they were getting out of the car, they all noticed a pretty, young blonde girl sitting on Robb Michael's headstone.

Joanna followed her children to the tombstone.

She heard Michael Jo ask, "Why are you sitting on my father's tombstone?"

The girl sat and looked at Michael Jo, and then the rest of them.

She was wearing a tan suede coat with a fur collar and cuffs and long, red and white, stockings that disappeared under the coat.

Comprehension on her face, she paused and smiled for a moment, and then said, "You are Michael Jo.

"And those guys standing behind you are Robert and Roger. You know, I've wanted to meet you guys for years.

"I've heard about you guys ever since I can remember. Do you know who I am?"

Joanna stood looking at the girl.

The girl was slender, had blue eyes and reddish blonde hair; like Michael Jo, she had started to blossom early.

It was obvious, even through the suede coat, her bust line was large for her age.

Michael Jo kept looking at the girl. "No, who are you?"

"I'm your sister," she said softly.

Michael Jo and her brothers all turned and looked at their mother.

Joanna looked at the girl and asked, "How is your mother, Emily?"

Comprehension, once again, on the girl's face. "You just told me why you're the woman my father loved most."

Joanna was astonished. "Did I?"

"Yes. You have an analytic mind. To him, that would be a turn on. Wow! I bet he was enthralled with you!"

Joanna looked at her once more, and thought, *I know now why Emily left the church.* Then she asked, "What's your name?"

"Robbin Michael. Everyone calls me Robbin Michael, with two B's"

Tears welled up in Joanna's eyes as she remembered when Robb Michael introduced himself.

She thought, *Oh, God! Here we go again!* Then she asked, "Where is your mother?"

"In the motor home, with Mr. Kahn and my brothers."

"Two brothers, right?"

The girl looked her right in the eye. "Right, that makes six!"

"Mom tells me, he wanted six, and he always got what he wanted."

"Yes, he did," said Joanna. "He always got what he wanted. He knew how to make it so."

Michael Jo asked, "You have two brothers?"

"Yes."

"Tell me, do they always follow you around? Always interfering with what you're trying to do?"

Robbin Michael looked at her half-sister seriously. "How did you know?"

The two girls looked at each other.

Michael Jo, slowly, said, "I think I'm going to like you."

Joanna said, "I think we better go inside. Mr. Kahn doesn't know we're here."

As they walked back to the road, Joanna noticed the custom dark red Chrysler minivan. "Is that your mother's little truck?"

Robbin Michael looked at her. "Yes. That's her favorite car.

"My father gave it to her a few months before he died.

"She only drives it on special occasions. To her, this is a special occasion."

The girl thought for a moment, "She's right. Today is special.

"We're going to learn about our father."

Together they entered the motor home. It was toasty warm and well-lit.

There was a generator running somewhere under the motor home.

Joanna saw that her niece, Dani, was also there.

Mr. Kahn was pouring cocoa into a cup being held by a young boy about the same age as the twins.

Douglas Kahn looked up.

Seeing Joanna, he said, "Joanna, this young man is Eli Jacob Keandra."

Motioning toward a young boy sitting with Emily, he said, "This young lad, sitting with Emily Van Hatten, is Edward Andrew Keandra.

Joanna looked at each one, and said, "I'm glad we finally get to meet."

Turning to Emily, she said, "Hello, Emily. I've wondered about you for some time. I'm really happy to see you."

Emily looked back at Joanna and said, "My, you don't seem to age like the rest of us. You look really good."

Joanna went over and sat next to Emily. "I would very much like to hear about your life and how it all came about."

As Emily was about to answer, Douglas Kahn interrupted. "That's why Robb Michael wanted everyone to meet here today. I'm supposed to read to you all his journals.

"They will explain his reasons and motives for behaving the way he did, and why. However, we will not begin until everyone is here."

Joanna looked around, then asked, "Why is Dani here?"

Douglas Kahn looked at her and said, "She's my assistant. She's been working with me at the Foundation for the last three years.

"She was also special in Robb Michael's life."

Joanna then asked, "Who else is supposed to be here?"

Douglas Kahn held up two fingers. "Two more. Joanna, would you like something hot? I have hot cider, cocoa, coffee?"

As he handed her a cup of hot cider, he said, "I want you all to know I met Robb Michael Keandra when I was in the hospital, dying.

"He saved my life, the same as he saved the life of countless others."

As Douglas Kahn was speaking, the four boys got up and gathered together, curious to learn about each other.

It was then the door of the motor home opened and a woman and a young girl entered.

Robbin Michael jumped up and went over and hugged the girl. "Natalie? What are you doing here?"

Douglas Kahn interrupted. "She is your sister. How is it that you know her?"

Robbin Michael looked at Douglas Kahn as though she was looking at a crazy man. Then she said, "She and I go to the same school. She's my best friend.

"What do you mean she's my sister?"

Douglas Kahn studied the girl for a moment and then said, "When your father died, he left a rather extensive will.

"In his will, he instructed me to deliver several, large envelopes to various individuals, including Natalie Lane's mother.

"When I saw that her mother was pregnant, I instructed her to have a DNA test on her baby when it was born.

"As a result of the test, your best friend's name became Natalie Keandra.

"Her mother, Julie Lane, didn't choose to use the name Keandra until Natalie was old enough to inherit.

"Your father was absolute in his convictions. He wanted all his offspring to inherit equally.

"That's why he left his DNA on file at the Holly Clinic. It's also on file at the Keandra Foundation."

Douglas Kahn paused for a moment and then said, "Natalie is the oldest of the three girls, by twenty-nine days.

"Michael Jo is thirteen days older than Robbin Michael."

The two girls hugged each other once more as Robbin Michael said, "Natalie, this is great. It couldn't be better."

The two girls looked at each other with wonder.

Robbin Michael continued speaking. "We have a sister. You'll like her. Her name is Michael Jo."

Michael Jo looked at the two girls with a look of wonder and said, "This is getting crazy.

What was our father doing? Why was he having sex with so many women? Was he deliberately trying to create chaos?

"He must have been nuts. I mean how many more are there?"

Douglas Kahn, smiling, said, "That's why we are all here.

"To learn why Robb Michael deliberately chose to do what he did.

"Your father," Douglas Kahn paused for a moment, and then said, "was my close friend.

"Your father was the most gifted man I knew. He knew how to get people to work with him.

"On everything he did, he succeeded, because he knew how to get people to accomplish what he wanted from them.

"He saved my life, my sons' lives, and the lives of several others.

"I will never let him down.

"As I read his will, and his instructions to me, it's as though he is still alive and leaving notes here and there, like he always did.

"It's been fourteen years since his passing, and he is still letting us know what he wants from us.

"I still struggle to please him. I believe I always will.

"Your father knew that under the direction of Joanna Keandra, the corporations would continue to flourish and expand.

"And they have.

"Therefore, he wanted all of his offspring to be a CEO committee.

"To rule by majority. With the entrance of Natalie, we have a tie breaker.

"You all will begin working with Joanna on the side lines, watching her to learn how to influence people.

"How to trust them. how to get them to lead the way.

"Robb Michael Keandra believed that the people working for him were the best.

"He believed those people, working at a job for a period of time, would become expert at what they were doing.

"Therefore, their judgment could be trusted. He not only believed that, he proved it on several occasions.

"We must never have doubts about people once they have established themselves. They have to be trusted.

"He used to stop and talk to everyone that worked for him, because he trusted them and their opinions.

"If they ever break that trust, they will no longer be of use to us.

"Now, first we will go through the journal Robb Michael started when he first discovered he was dying.

"There will be times that you will become emotional. I become emotional every time I read it."

They all remained silent as Douglas Kahn began to read the journal aloud.

TWO HOURS LATER
They all sat deep in thought when Douglas Kahn had finished reading the journal.

Joanna thought about some of the things Robb Michael had told her as she had been listening to Douglas Kahn reading the journal.

He had told her to be careful when choosing someone to get sexually involved with.

As she thought about this, she remembered some of the most disastrous events of her life.

Few were worthwhile. *Thank God for the townhouse.*

If I had ever taken any of those guys' home, it could have been even more disastrous.

Oh, well, she thought, *it's history now.*

And history can't be changed.

Then she spoke, "After I started living with Robb Michael, I got to where I could sense when he was near.

"One night, about thirteen years ago, I took the U2 up. I sensed he was near before I even left the ground.

"While flying it at altitude, I started having trouble with the engine.

"I swear, I heard him tell me how to make corrections in engine performance."

Almost imperceptibly Douglas Kahn shook his head in disbelief.

Joanna continued speaking. "There have been several times since, I have sensed his presence.

"I say this, because when we were entering the motor home, I sensed his presence again."

Emily asked, "Do you feel it now?"

Joanna paused and thoughtfully looked down at the floor as though in a daze.

Then she said, "No"

They all focused on Douglas Kahn as he laid the journal down and picked up another one.

He held the journal for a moment, then he opened the front cover and sat looking at the first page.

Then he spoke. "I have read this journal several times.

"When I first read this thing, I didn't see much, if any, value in it, but he let it be known that he wants you all to know the contents of this journal.

"Sometimes I have difficulty reading this, but it was his will for you all to hear it.

"I warn you, some parts of this journal are pretty graphic.

"About the third time I read this, I realized what I read was exactly what he was.

"He would do anything he thought necessary to get what he wanted done!

"After I've read this, anyone that wants to read it for themselves may do so.

"I have had copies made for each of you.

"I will pass them out to you before you go home."

With that Douglas Kahn began to read aloud:

I want my children to read my journals so they will know what I am.

I want them to read even the company journals that I have written in.

I want them to know what is in their blood.

My best man, Douglas Kahn, may not understand the reasoning for this, but after a while, my children will.

When they discover what's in their blood, they will know what possibilities are available to them.

I want them to know that they are an extension of me.

Don't get me wrong, I don't want my children to carry on for me.

I want my children to carry on for themselves.

Their dreams! Their ideas! Their goals!

They are an extension of me!

To my children:

You may not like what you read here. You may not like me.

After you read the contents of this journal, you will think about your mother and wonder why she is what she is.

I want you to know that she is what she is, and entitled to be what she is.

The same as you are what you are.

If you don't like what you are, only you can change it.

I like what your mothers are, and I would never ask them to change.

By now you may think you know what I am.

You may or may not like what I am.

I am what my God made me.

I am your father!

I will not apologize for being what I am.

You are now wondering why I have been having sex with so many women.

You may have a tough time figuring it out.

But remember, you wouldn't be here if I hadn't.

You are here because I want you here!

I want you to live. I want you to be happy to be alive.

I want you to know that I liked my life. I want you to know I liked what I've done with my life.

As you hear this, then read this, I want you to know what can be done as long as you are responsible and remain in control of what you do.

The following is the only thing I will ever tell you what to do!

Read on!

EMILY

LATE CHIRSTMAS NIGHT

I'm not certain how to begin this journal, but I feel I must record this night's happenings.

It all began when I baptized Emily.

The very minute I carried her into the water, she grabbed me by the cock.

Her fear of the water was so great, I had difficulty acting out the roll play of baptizing.

She had a death grip on my cock you wouldn't believe.

With the grip she had on me, I believed she might very well pull it out of me.

She was so scared of being in the water that she was on the verge of panic.

When I finished the baptizing thing, while still in the pool, I carried her over and set her on the deck.

Still she wouldn't let go of me. Nobody noticed she had me by the cock because her hand was below the water line.

It wasn't until I told her, "You can let go of me now" that she let go. When Emily grabbed me, it gave me an erection.

I'm surprised that Joanna never noticed as I carried her into the pool, or maybe she did and didn't say anything.

A while later, Eli threw Emily into the pool.

I knew she couldn't swim, so without thinking, I dove in after her.

When I dove into the pool, I saw her looking at me as she was lying near the bottom of the pool.

The way she looked at me was like she didn't believe anyone would come for her. Suddenly, she reached up to me as I was on my way down.

As I got a hold of her, once again she had a hold of my cock as I pulled her to the surface. She let go of me as I placed her on the deck and started pushing water out of her.

Later, when Eli and Emily were leaving, we all discovered that it was snowing, huge flakes.

Standing in the doorway, we were hugging each other goodbye.

She pushed her breasts against me.

Emily quietly said, "I want to live!

"Thank you for making me want to live. I shall always be grateful to you.

"For making me want to live, I will do anything you ask.

"Please ask. I'll be waiting for you."

I didn't know what to say, so I said nothing.

I saw snowflakes sticking to their clothes as they walked toward Eli's car.

As we watched them get in Eli's Buick and drive away, it was snowing pretty hard.

Even so, I saw Emily looking back at me through the falling snow.

The way she looked at me, I knew she really wanted something from me. This may be all I write about Emily.

The way this all came about, I felt I should record it. It was very dramatic. I can't help but feel there is going to be more.

If not, this journal may never be read which might well be best and good.

She certainly got my attention.

If never I see Emily again, I shall always remember this night.

I doubt that anything will come of this.

However, I can't help thinking there's going to be more written in this journal.

If not, I'll probably toss this page in the trash.

FEBRUARY TWENTY

This day I find myself once again writing in this journal, something I was beginning to think I would never do.

It's been nearly two months since I had anything to write in this journal, but this day I got a surprise.

This day Joanna is in Seattle, playing CEO.

Something I have been wanting her to do since before I hooked up with her. After she left, I went back to bed and slept till eleven.

When I awoke, I made another pot of coffee, then went in the gym for a fifteen-minute workout.

I took a shower, then sat on an exercycle for a minute to bring my thoughts together.

Suddenly I saw Emily climbing the steps of the pool. I didn't even know she was in the compound, but there she was, climbing out of the pool, wearing nothing but that little life preserver I had made.

As she was walking toward me, her wet hair was dripping down her front.

Her breasts were jiggling and swaying as she walked, water dripping off, splashing every direction imaginable as she moved toward me.

As she moved toward me, she was removing the life preserver.

She never made any attempt to conceal herself. I told her there was a robe in the towel closet.

She said, "I don't want to wear anything just now."

She's incredibly beautiful. I like looking at her, as I like looking at any beautiful woman.

I didn't say anything. I just sat there and looked at her. I remembered I was only wearing a robe.

I watched her as she picked up my towel.

She turned around and placed the towel on the bench to sit on.

I saw that her wet hair was also dripping down her back. I had a feeling I knew what she wanted.

I was mistaken. She took me by surprise.

She said, "I want to make confession to you."

I told her, "I'm not a priest."

She said, "The confession I want to make I've never made to a priest, and I never will." I looked her square in the face and told her to give it her best shot.

I've always wondered what a priest felt like when someone was revealing their inner most secrets.

Well, I found out!

She sat quiet for a while.

Then she told me that when she was growing up, there were two men molesting her.

One was an uncle, the other was an older cousin.

She told me she would like to kill her uncle to this day because he made her like something that she wasn't prepared to like.

She told me he held her down and pawed her like an animal.

She said that he would stare her in the face and gently stroke the sensitive places on her body with no sense of feeling or passion at all.

He would slide his hand between her legs and gently stroke her.

When he had her feeling the passion of the moment, he would force her to suck his cock.

He did this to her from the time she was twelve.

When she was seventeen, her older cousin got drunk one night and raped her.

She told me when he was done, she was a bloody mess.

He laughed at her and told her to go clean herself up, then went out, got in his car and drove away.

She told me after that she didn't want to live anymore.

She no longer wanted to be in society, so she decided to become a nun.

She said she didn't want to be a part of, or participate in, any kind of normal society, just work. She said all she wanted to do was work.

She did everything they told her to do, and everything she could see that needed to be done.

It was easy to do all she did because she wasn't living anymore.

She looked me square in the face and said, "Then I met you."

One of the first things she heard me say was, "It's alright to be decadent."

When she heard me say that, she was taken back a little bit, because of the life she had chosen, decadence could never be a part of it.

Then I baptized her and let her know it's alright to be stupid. Eli proved it by throwing her into the pool.

She said, when she was on the bottom of the pool, sucking in water, she saw me coming down for her.

She told me if she ever got in a situation like that she never believed anyone would even bother to come for her.

When she saw me coming, she knew then she wanted to live again.

I remembered her reaching for me as I swam down to get her.

She told me she wanted everything I told her that it's alright to be.

It was then she said, "I want you to take me down and fuck me every way you can think of. I mean it. Make me suck your cock and swallow everything that comes out of it, until I beg you to stop."

As I listened to her, she was scaring the hell out of me. I don't care who you are. You're not prepared to hear something like that when a woman says it to you point blank.

Strange as what she was saying, I realized she was suffering from a lack of sex. Also, I realized she was what I needed to reach my goals.

This was a way for me to extend my bloodline.

I told her to get dressed. I was going to take her out of there.

I went up to my bedroom and quickly dressed, then I returned to fetch her.

After she dressed, her hair was still wet and matted in places.

When we went outside, it was cold and snowing.

The snow was coming down hard. Big flakes. You couldn't see but about a hundred feet.

She stood by my car, looking at me.

In spite of her damp hair, the snow was sticking to it and her clothes.

I told her to get in my car, out of the weather, then I got in and started the engine to get it warm.

I asked her where she was parked.

She told me she didn't have a car. She rode the bus to get here.

I put the car in gear and drove out of the driveway.

I had no sooner turned toward town when she said, "You're going the wrong way. I live in the other direction."

I told her, "I'm not taking you where you live.

"I'm not ever going to take you to where you live.

"If you want me to make you suck my cock and swallow everything that comes out of it, we're going the right way.

"If you have changed your mind about that, say so now."

It still bothered me that she would say something like that.

She looked at me and asked, "Are you taking me to a hotel?"

I told her, "No, I'm taking you to a townhouse I own, up in the west hills, overlooking the city."

She looked out the windshield and asked, "Are we going to be able to get there?"

The snow was coming down so hard you couldn't see a hundred feet in front of the car.

I told her, "If you still want to get there, yes, we will get there, even if I have to get out and push.

"Do you still want to get there?"

She looked me in the eye and said, "Yes, I still want to get there."

Then I told her, "This car is all-wheel drive. It'll get there."

I drove into the west hills from the backside so I wouldn't have to go into the core area of the city, then up the hill to the townhouse.

The snow was stacking up fast.

Quite often when we met a car, it was in my lane.

It was a slow ride, sometimes more exciting than I like.

Along the way, Neal Diamond sang "yesterday's gone" through the speakers of the radio.

Throughout the music, the truth of his song slammed the hell out of me. Suddenly, I had tears in my eyes.

When we arrived, it was coming down so hard it was practically a whiteout, and it felt colder. The temperature was dropping.

The snow was sticking to our clothes again as we approached the front of the house.

Once inside I turned up the heat.

She asked, "What are you going to do?"

I told her, "I'm going to make you my sex slave.

"I'm going to give you everything you said you wanted, and more.

"You want me to make you suck my cock, and make you swallow everything that comes out of it? Well, that's exactly what I'm going to do!

"I'm going to feed you my cock, and you better swallow everything that comes out of it, or you'll be doing it over again.

"When I'm done, I'll tell you what I want from you in return! Now, go up the stairs!"

As I watched her climb the stairs, I thought, *If I don't do this right, I'm going to lose it all.*

When she reached the top of the stairs, she stopped. She turned and looked down at me with her palms up.

As I took off my coat, I told her to take her clothes off.

By the time I reached the top of the stairs, we were both naked.

I told her to get on her knees.

I fed her my cock.

When I came, she sucked it out of me as fast as it came.

The sensations were so great, she damn near drove me to my knees.

Then she sucked my cock till it came up again.

I honestly didn't think I could continue, but I did.

I had to make it work.

She never did beg me to stop.

We never made it to a bedroom.

We were fucking on the floor in the hall.

She was wild.

I've never been with a woman as aggressive as this before.

I fed her my cock twice this day.

Both times, I actually wondered who was fucking who.

I did what she said she wanted me to do, because I know why she wanted me to do it to her.

Like a football player once told me, he said he needed to feel the pain so he would know he was alive.

She needed to know she was alive.

I made her feel that she was living because I need something from her.

When we were done, she asked me what I wanted from her.

I told her I wanted her to have three babies in two years.

She asked, "Are you serious?"

I told her, dead serious.

She said, "I've broken my vows. I have to leave the church, but I'll manage to find something."

I told her I didn't want her to find anything for the next two years.

I told her I would be in control of her life for the next two to three years.

I told her she's going to stay here in this townhouse until I find a more suitable place for her to live.

It was then I left her to return to my house. I knew If I didn't leave, all could be lost.

I had to get away from her, so she could do some thinking about what she wanted, what she did, and how to pull her life together.

As I left the house, I looked down over the hills at the lights of the city. You couldn't really see the lights.

It was like looking at a glow through a fog.

If I live a thousand years, I will never forget this cold day the lush snowflakes fell.

Those snowflakes created a winter wonderland, an enhancement.

A whole new adventure for me began this day, a time and opportunity for me to be there for someone that's willing to be there for me.

I am grateful.

MARCH TWO

Since I brought Emily to the townhouse, I've been with her most of the day every day.

As she wanted, I've fed her my cock, sometimes twice a day. Sometimes I would only fuck her once a day.

This day, as I was feeding her my cock, I thought about the time Joanna asked me if I would fuck Emily.

I had told her I would.

I'm now doing it possibly more often than I should.

After my experiences with Joanna, I believe it's takes longer to get someone pregnant if you fuck too often.

But still, I'm going to fuck her as often as I can.

It's absolutely imperative to get her pregnant as soon as possible.

My hopes are high. I must try to make something more out of this relationship.

For her to have peace in her own mind, this has to work out the way she wants, too.

MARCH NINETEEN

I spent all yesterday sexually involved with Emily.

This day I came to the townhouse at about nine in the morning and fixed Emily breakfast.

After breakfast, I fed her my cock for the most part of an hour.

It was about all I could take. She devoured me like a starving animal.

We stopped and had coffee, then I fed it to her again.

At two she told me she was hungry, so I took her out to Sylvia's, a fine Italian restaurant, and told her to order whatever she wanted.

It started snowing again.

While she was eating, I saw that she kept looking at me the way she looked at me the night when I pulled her out of the pool.

She ate slowly and had eaten everything they served her.

The snow had been stacking up while we ate. We started on our way back to the townhouse. It took over an hour.

When I got her there, I fed her my cock again. Once again, she devoured me like a starving animal.

I had it in mind to fuck her. But I didn't have anything left in me.

I had to be back at the compound, so I kissed her an open mouth kiss, then left her there, looking like she wanted more. On my way to the compound, I met with Richard Kahn.

I told him I wanted him to find me several houses to look at. I needed him to find at least ten, maybe fifteen places.

I wanted these places to be five to twenty acres, or more, with some timber, maybe water on the property.

Later this day, I got with Emily again.

We started fucking each other like the morrow is never going to be.

The truth of that statement haunts me, yet, I make plans for the morrow, every day of my life.

MARCH TWENTY-SEVEN

This day Emily and I went looking at the houses Richard Kahn had found.

Emily thought most all of them were too big. She told me all she needed was a small three- or four-bedroom house.

I told her I wanted my children to grow up in a larger house with some property for them to run wild.

I was lucky. When I was growing up, I had the whole county to run wild. Most young people don't have that opportunity this day.

Late in the afternoon, we still had four houses to look at when we found the one she wanted.

It's in the hills of Clackamas County, south of Damascus.

It's an older house that looks like a Swiss chalet, with four thousand square feet of living space.

It was obvious that Emily fell in love with the place the moment she saw it.

The place sits on thirty-one acres. Over half of the place is in timber, with a good-sized creek running through it.

That creek is a small river. It's four to five feet deep and twelve to fourteen feet wide.

It flows into the Clackamas River.

I swear to God, the Clackamas River runs colder than the North Fork Santiam.

The North Fork Santiam is goddamn cold. That's why I swim in the Little North Fork Santiam.

It flows slower, so it's a little warmer.

I told Richard Kahn to buy the place outright and to put it in the name of Emily Van Hatten.

MARCH THIRTY-ONE

This morning Emily informed me she's late. She believes she's pregnant.

I find it hard to believe she's pregnant, but I'm hoping she's right.

At her age, she must be close to menopause.

As soon as I can get to her, I'll examine her, but first we have to furnish the house we bought.

I don't want to keep her in the townhouse any longer than necessary.

The townhouse is a good place to practice sex techniques, but really too small to live in.

MARCH THIRTY-ONE, LATE NIGHT

This day I bought a couple of truckloads of furnishings for the house.

Later in the afternoon, I gave Emily an examination.

Surprise, surprise! Emily is pregnant! I'm so happy, I could walk on air.

Joanna called earlier and said she is staying overnight in Reno.

She has more problems that need to be addressed before she comes home.

Joanna is doing very well at taking care of business.

That's just what she was chosen for.

Her performance makes me so happy, I feel I can walk on the ceiling.

I can't believe how good things are coming around.

It's nearing midnight.

Joanna's nearing her due date. It's hard to believe how big she's getting.

On the morrow, I'm going to stop her from going on business trips.

It's too dangerous for her to be doing these things.

I'll take over for a while.

When I'm not here, I'll have Mrs. Numura stay with Joanna.

APRIL THIRTEEN

I find it interesting.

Since I've been back taking care of business, I can't help but feel that the board members of every company I go to would rather have Joanna presiding over the meetings.

This is a good thing, more than I could hope for.

I hope that soon she will be able to get back into the business end of things.

I can't spend as much time with Emily as I'd like, for obvious reasons.

When I do spend a little time with her, she practically rapes me.

She likes to straddle me, sitting on my lap with me inside her, while facing me,

Her breasts are filling with colostrum.

Colostrum is full of antibodies and God knows what else, another source for me.

I haven't told her I need what's in those beautiful breasts.

I don't think she even cares.

She commands me, "Suck on them till they hurt!"

It's a good thing she's there.

Right now, Joanna can't do anything sexually.

The last time I tried with Joanna, she said it was too much for her.

APRIL TWENTY

I don't leave Joanna alone anymore.

She can deliver at any time.

It's such a joy to be with her and help her. You can tell she feels awkward. Sometimes I have to help her to stand up.

Through it all, I discovered she plays a mean game of chess.

I had Douglas Kahn stay with her while I went to check on Emily.

Emily isn't even showing yet, while Joanna looks like she's about to explode.

I only stayed with Emily for a short period of time, then I came back to the compound to be with Joanna.

I must not leave Joanna alone now till she delivers.

It's too risky.

MAY EIGHT

This morning I became a father for the first time, that I know of.

This day is truly a day for celebration.

I now have two healthy baby boys.

In another six months, I hope to have one more.

Another set of twins would be great, but doubtful.

Yes! This day is a great day for me.

Joanna named them Robert Michael Keandra and Roger Scott Keandra, after my father and her father.

Michael was my mother's name, but I don't care what she names them.

I'm just glad to have them here.

I plan to have more, and yet I don't even know the how of it.

I'll make some kind of plan for my bloodline.

How I'll carry out this plan, I haven't a clue.

It has become an obsession with me.

MAY THIRTEEN

Since I brought Joanna home, I've been busy.

Taking care of babies can be different.

I've been changing diapers, giving them a bath, cleaning them up after they puke, or puke on me.

You name it, I've been doing it.

Mr. Kahn informs me that this is usually done by a woman.

I told him I don't care. No one's going to stop me.

I've been waiting for this moment ever since I brought Joanna to the compound.

Nothing is going to stop me now. I'm having the time of my life.

Everyday I look forward to the morrow.

I swear to God, what's left of my life is working out better than I ever could have hoped.

MAY SEVENTEENTH

This day is the anniversary of the day I brought Joanna to the compound.

She seems to be very happy.

She goes downtown a lot.

It's like she's making up for lost time.

She's doing everything I want her to do.

Strange thing, I've never told her to do anything.

I must make room in my schedule for her.

This is a must.

I'll take her to Chez Henri's for dinner, if she wants to go.

MAY EIGHTEEN

Last night after dinner, I took Joanna out to the airport and made her fly the U2.

I could tell she loved it.

She flew the length of the Cascade Range, then anxiously flew back so she could be with our children.

When we were driving up the back driveway, she stopped the car and told me, before long, she will be able to do anything, maybe even save my life.

She doesn't know I've already got her working on it, with the antibodies from her body. It's been a year now since I brought her to the compound.

This last year has been full of sex, adventure, laughter, pleasure, and joy, with a little mystery thrown in.

We are now going into our second year.

I hope it will be as successful as the first year has been.

I still don't know if she knows I'm in love with her.

If anyone reading this drivel doesn't understand all of this, that's alright. I don't know that I understand it myself.

Once again I put $700,000 in Joanna's bank account, as per my agreement with her.

I'm so proud of her.

I shall love her forever.

MAY TWENTY-ONE

Yesterday I had to go to Reno, on business.

When I returned, it was early in the evening.

I stopped at Emily's before going to the compound.

She told me that it's lonely in the house by herself.

She asked me how long I could stay.

I smiled and told her I would stay for as long as she could suck my cock.

I was only joking.

She wasn't. She must be very lonely.

She started sucking.

As daylight was coming through the windows, she stopped.

I swear, I believe she was dozing while she was sucking.

She doesn't know I was about to beg her to stop.

I felt for her. Nobody should be that lonely.

I feel that in some way I failed her.

I have to do something about that.

When it comes to sex, she can be a ferocious animal, but I'm willing to play her games because I need her to fulfill a part of my life.

I hope she will have one child and be pregnant with another before I'm gone.

When she was done, my cock was sore. But I'll never complain to her about it.

On this day, I slept until three in the afternoon.

It was then that we made love to each other, gently and lovingly.

I felt good about it.

My cell phone, vibrating in my pocket, let me know someone had found me.

When I answered, I was informed that I had to be in Seattle ASAP.

As I was leaving, Emily said, "Look, no matter what we do, I don't want to come between you and Joanna."

It was then I told her, I have a couple deals with Joanna, and she is making good on her end.

I told Emily I expected her to keep her end of our deal.

Keeping up on our deal is more important than anything else she could do right now.

We had discussions on how we should raise our children.

We also discussed how they should be educated.

With what they are going to inherit, they will need special training.

She wants to know why it's so important for me to have two families.

I told her I wasn't going to tell her at this time.

She asked at what time I would tell her.

I said, "Believe it or not, you will figure it out without being told.

"Joanna is only going to have three children.

"I want six, so you are going to have the other three.

"I am not even going to tell you what to name them, as long as their last name is Keandra.

"I just want you to have them. For doing this, you will receive $15,000 a month for the rest of your life.

"You will be careful with your life. I want you to still be alive when it's time for the children to inherit.

"I have a corporate will. In that will, any child who can check their DNA, and prove they are of my bloodline, will inherit an equal share of my estate. Hopefully, one or more of them will be able to hold together what I and Joanna have put together."

I got in my car and drove to the airport.

As I drove, I realized that my relationship with Emily had finally become something more. To this I say, "Thank God!

"Now, it can mature normally."

MAY TWENTY-FIVE

Yesterday Joanna hired a nanny. Her name is Janice Lyman. She seems to be capable.

I will be able to spend more quality time with Emily.

I've noticed every time I go see Emily, the house is rearranged. She not only moves things around the room, she moves things from room to room.

She's very energetic.

I warned her about the possibility of a miscarriage when overexerting herself. I don't want Joanna or Emily to lose a baby.

I need those babies to reach my goals.

This day she informed me that she received a notice from the Keandra Foundation, telling her that she has been given a grant of $15,000 a month until the day she dies.

She told me it makes her the highest paid whore in the world.

I told her she's not a whore.

A whore is a woman, or a man, that will have sex with anyone that will pay their price.

She's not having sex with anyone that will pay her price, just me.

That makes her a kept woman, not a whore. A married woman is also a kept woman.

I also told her that a woman that has sex with anyone that wants her is also not a whore.

She is called a chippy, or a loose woman, because she is not asking for pay for her services.

And I write in these pages, I've been sexually involved with several women in my life.

I have never considered any of them a whore.

I thought so highly of some of them that I made provisions for them in my will.

I told Emily that she is not my whore!

I chose her and Joanna to be the mother of my children.

That's what I want from both of them.

If that makes them a whore, then all mothers are whores.

Personally, I refuse to believe it, I don't understand why anyone does!

MAY THIRTY

I've been with Emily most of this day. Emily has calmed down. When we're making love, it's slow and gentle.

Something has changed. She is no longer a raging animal.

It was like she was trying to show me that she wants something more than just sex.

I didn't tell her I also want something more than just sex.

I just kept quiet and accepted the change.

When I caress her, she clings to me. It's a gentle thing.

The way she clung to me, it was like she didn't want me to let go. I knew at that moment I will never leave her.

She's mine to keep till the day I die.

That's not long enough, and can never be long enough.

There's no way to make sense of it.

I shall keep her, along with Joanna, until the day I die.

I told Emily I'm thinking of retiring from my medical practice.

When she asked me why, I smiled and told her I only want to practice medicine with her.

I told her I would give her an injection once in a while, and then examine her occasionally to see if the injection was productive.

JUNE TWENTY-FIVE

This last month has gone very well. Emily has the house arranged the way she likes it. I'm starting to feel comfortable in the place.

Looking at Emily, I can see a bump starting to show.

I feel comfortable with the way our relationship is maturing.

JULY FOUR

On this day, I had a picnic on the front yard of my house with Joanna and my sons. It was wonderful.

As we were eating, the boys and I ganged up on Joanna and sucked on her tits. She laughed hysterically as we were doing it.

I knew she felt silly through it all, but it was wonderful.

This day was a great day.

After the picnic, we all went in the house.

We put the boys down for a nap, then Joanna and I worked at bringing Michael Jo into being.

From there, I went to Emily's place to check on her.

I need to make sure that nothing happens to her, or the baby she's carrying.

AUGUST NINETEEN

This is my birth date. Yet it was just another day.

Joanna is in Boise.

I had to go to the hospital to do a surgery. It took most of the day.

From there, I went to spend the rest of this day with Emily.

As usual, I was hyped up after the surgery. Emily helped me come down.

Her baby bump is in the way, but that's alright.

I'm waiting anxiously for the baby within to come out.

These things never seem to come along fast enough.

Near the end of the day, I realized I was tired.

I barely made it back to the compound.

I fell asleep while sitting in the car. When I awoke, it was dark. As I got out of the car, I realized I was sleeping more.

When I went into the compound, I found that Joanna left a message on the answering machine. She's staying in Boise another day and then off to Los Angeles. I'm going to bed.

AUGUST TWENTY

This day I went to the hospital to check on my patient.

Julie Lane was there.

She has always been a great help. She asked me if I would have coffee with her.

When we got to the cafeteria, we sat and talked for awhile.

It was then she told me she pulled a couple shifts over at the Holly Clinic.

While she was there, she saw my file.

She told me she knew I was in trouble.

She said if there's anything she could do, all I had to do was ask. She would be there for me anytime I needed her.

She's a professional and knew how to discuss my condition with me. I told her everything is taken care of.

I told her Joanna was chosen to take over the Med Group, and I made an agreement with her to have my offspring.

She was surprised to hear I had planned ahead.

I told her everything is going well.

After coffee, we went up to ICU to check on my patient.

She was getting off shift and told me she had to hurry or she would miss her bus.

I offered to take her home.

When we arrived at her place, she invited me in to unwind.

I wasn't there any time at all when I found myself in her bed.

Making love to her brought back memories.

Her body is slender with large C cups, or small D cups.

As much as I know about the human anatomy, I still don't know how to tell the difference.

Hell, I doubt if I'll ever know.

I can't help but want more with her but my life is complicated now.

As I was leaving, she told me she was there for me.

I could rely on her for anything I might want or need.

Talk about food for thought.

AUGUST TWENTY-ONE

This day I went to the hospital to check on my patient.

Once again, I had Julie Lane on duty at ICU.

After I checked on the patient, I told Julie Lane I was going to lay down for awhile. I was tired. I went into my office.

There's a standard double bed in there for me to nap on while I'm waiting to see what my patient's vital signs are after the patient awakens.

I took my clothes off and lay down.

Just as I was about to fall asleep, I felt someone get on the bed.

I heard Julie Lane's voice before I opened my eyes.

As I felt her slide under the covers she asked, "Would you like some company?"

As she laid her naked body against mine, I told her that she was always welcome in my bed.

It was then she told me that when we made love the night before, she was no longer taking a contraceptive.

She hadn't been sexually active for some time, so she quit taking contraceptives.

She told me she wanted me to know in case she got pregnant.

She said if she was pregnant, she could have an abortion if that would please me.

I told her, and I write it down here on these pages:

"I don't want you or anyone else to have an abortion.

"If you get pregnant, you get in touch with my best man.

"He will make sure what I want gets done.

"You promise me that! Right now!"

She promised, but I wonder if she will.

She is a very proud woman, and she, like Joanna and Emily, is very self-sufficient.

I didn't tell her, but I want her to have my baby and maybe more than one.

I know the logic of this makes no sense, but I'm formulating a plan for these children.

I want them to know what I've been doing since I discovered I'm coming to an end.

I want them to know at a very young age what I've done, and what they can do.

Hopefully, something positive will come of it.

I fully expect this plan to be carried out.

I know that Douglas Kahn will do my bidding, no matter what.

So, those of you that read all of this drivel, learn how to live with it.

More than anything, I want everyone connected to be happy.

By that I mean, happy to be alive and productive!

In between times, I got dressed to check on the patient.

I was sexually involved with Julie a few times this day.

In between times, we talked.

She told me she didn't know what Joanna and I had was a business deal.

I told her it started out that way, but I have come to love Joanna very much. Then I told her there's another woman helping me bring my plan together.

Julie looked at me like I might be mentally deficient and asked me if I was certain this is what I want.

I smiled at her and said, "Have you ever seen me when I wasn't certain of what I was doing?"

She made me laugh when she said, "There were a few times when we were in surgery that you would stop and stare at nothing, then begin cutting like it no longer mattered."

I laughed because she was right.

Whenever I stopped like that, I already had it in mind that I have just killed the patient.

I have often wondered, why didn't the patient die?

I always remembered the cuts I made.

Sometimes, at a later date, I made the same cut to save another patient's life.

I'm still not sure why those cuts I made worked!

I even went down and did autopsies on patients who had died of natural causes, to see and study what those cuts were affecting.

I'm so glad I didn't have to come down here to see the body of someone who died under my knife.

I still wonder why I never lost a patient.

Was something bigger than me guiding my hand? I'll never know.

To experiment with someone's life is very stressful, but I know of no other way to help them.

Sometimes, when someone was on the table, I was afraid to make a cut. Somehow I found myself doing it, then I wondered why I made the cuts I did. I still wonder.

There were some patients that were so badly deteriorated, I knew I couldn't save them, so I never tried.

Now I wonder if I should have tried anyway, but I wonder what I could have done.

AUGUST TWENTY-FIVE

This day I told Douglas Kahn to keep an eye on Julie Lane.

If she's pregnant, her baby's an equal heir to my estate and must be taken care of.

Julie Lane is to be given the same arrangement as Emily.

As I write this drivel, I can't help but wonder what my children are going to think when they all meet each other.

I hope they will just be happy to be here and alive.

Most of all, I want them to know what I am. I want them to know what's in their blood.

I want them to explore the world they live in.

Every generation has something new and fascinating to get involved with.

That's exactly what I want them to do. I don't want them to all be alike. I want them to explore the differences between themselves, get involved before anyone else does.

With the resources they've got available to them, they'll figure it out.

OCTOBER TEN

Emily informed me she's planning a Thanksgiving Day dinner.

She wants to know if I'm going to be there. I told her I'll have to do some planning.

Joanna wants to have Thanksgiving in the compound this year.

It's going to be interesting to see how this all comes together.

I'll find a way, I always do.

Every time I write something in one of these journals, I feel I should write more.

I can't write more.

I don't have enough time to spend with the mothers of my children, or the children.

NOVEMBER TEN
This day Emily delivered a baby boy, at 3:30 AM, Eli Jacob Keandra.

It can't get any better than this.

I feel I can walk on the ceiling.

I now have three. I have only three to go in about a year.

If I only have these three, I'll be most fortunate.

NOVEMBER SIXTEEN
Emily decided to have her Thanksgiving dinner prepared on the day before Thanksgiving.

She wants me to spend the day with her. I could very well do that for her. I look forward to seeing her.

Somehow she has made me feel comfortable when I'm around her.

NOVEMBER TWENTY-TWO
Yesterday I spent the last half of the day with Emily.

She baked a turkey and a small picnic ham.

This morning she served me ham and eggs for breakfast, with turkey gravy on turkey dressing.

Wow! It was so good. I can eat like that anytime.

I spent the night with her.

I held my son by Emily for over an hour before having to return to the compound.

I then returned to the compound just in time to serve dinner to Joanna's family.

This day was sweet. It came together better than I could ever imagine.

Then, as I was serving the turkey, Dani asked me if I would teach her how to do business.

There was a bit of a struggle with her mother, but I let her know I would help her get started with business.

I told Dani I would meet with her in private to teach her how to do research, and then teach her how to invest with what she learned.

What a joyous day.

DECEMBER ONE

I had Mr. Kahn check and see where Dani was going to school.

It turns out she is in middle school, so it won't be a problem getting together with her.

I went to the school and waited for her to get on a school bus, then I followed the bus to where she got off. I tooted the horn at her.

Cautiously, she came over to my car and looked in.

When she saw it was me, she got in.

She wanted to know what I was doing there.

I asked her if she really wanted to learn business. She gave me a definite yes.

I told her I would front her a thousand dollars' worth of stock, and I would introduce her to a stock broker. He and I will help her get her start.

I told her one day she would have to pay back the money I fronted her.

I told her we will have to meet secretly, but she can learn business.

I made her promise never tell anyone about this deal I made with her.

The reason I wanted to meet with her privately was because I don't want any outside interference.

I told her I wasn't much older than she was when I got started, and I had to do it secretly, too.

If someone suspects she's doing something covert, they will question her long and loud.

It's very important she keeps this deal secret, no matter what.

She agreed, and then she asked me if I thought she was smart enough to learn business.

I told her, "You don't have to be smart. All you have to do is know how to add and subtract. If you sell something for less than you paid for it, that's not good business."

This girl is smart. She picked up on it as fast as I said it.

I plan on meeting with Dani for a few minutes every day until she learns how to research the stock I give her.

CHRISTMAS

This day Emily surprised me.

She told me she's pregnant again.

I've never heard of a woman getting pregnant again this soon after giving birth.

I gave her an examination to check and see if she's right.

To my surprise, she's right. She's going to have another baby.

This is so rare.

When a woman is nursing, her uterus closes up.

This usually prevents pregnancy. Not this time.

This is a Christmas to remember.

Joanna and I are going to spend Christmas Day at her parents' place again this year.

She's probably wondering what's keeping me. I better close for now and go help her.

I bought a lot of stuff for everyone this year.

Now that I've gotten to know people, I feel more comfortable giving them something on these holidays.

JANUARY THREE

Last night I spent the night with Emily.

We had a couple of drinks, and I told her about spending New Year's Eve with Eli.

She laughed herself silly when I told her how Eli made a few people repent.

There are a few things in this world that Eli can't help himself with, but he does enjoy his calling, as he calls it.

I love Eli.

He has always stayed with his beliefs, and it's always been a great joy watching him.

This day I met with Dani after school.

I told her what websites to explore with the computer I gave her for Christmas.

She's really excited about what she has already done with this project.

I told her I can't help her with her decision-making. She has to do it all on her own.

I told her she could ask me what I know about a stock, but I'm not going to advise her on whether or not to buy or sell.

She must learn how to make these decisions for herself.

JANUARY TWENTY

This day was different.

Emily told me that this is the anniversary of the day she started a new life.

Then she told me that she wanted to live that day over.

I asked what she meant.

It was then that she said, "I want you to take me down and fuck me any way that you can think of.

"Make me suck your cock and make me swallow anything that comes out of it. And don't stop until I beg you to stop!"

I smiled and asked her if she was serious.

She never answered.

She called her nun friend and had her watch our son, then had me take her to the townhouse.

We had no sooner than got there when she went up the stairs and took off her clothes.

I took off my clothes, went up the stairs, told her to get on her knees, and then fed her my cock.

We spent the day fucking wildly.

I wouldn't call it making love.

She definitely let it be known that there was still a wild animal within her being.

As before, she never did beg me to stop.

We were practically tearing up the hallway.

The words "please stop" were bouncing around inside my head, when suddenly she calmed down and crawled up and laid her head on my chest and went to sleep.

It was a good thing she did.

Literally, I was on the verge of begging her to stop.

Later that night she told me, "Today was the perfect anniversary gift."

JANUARY TWENTY-FIVE

Three days ago, I took Emily down to the Coach Works to see some Chryslers I had stretched.

As Emily was walking around one of the cars, she said, "It's very pretty, but too big. Can't you get me something smaller with more room?"

I never thought about her having a car before, so I ordered her a new Chrysler minivan before we even left to come home.

We had flown down in a corporate jet, but we drove one of the limousines back.

We made a time of it and took a couple days coming back. Young Eli was on his best behavior. He's a good baby.

There was heavy snow up in the Siskiyou Mountain Pass, so we stayed in Yreka, California for a night.

The following day, we didn't travel far. They didn't get the snow cleared until late afternoon.

That night we stayed in Grants Pass.

We weren't in any hurry to get back to Portland.

FEBRUARY FIFTEEN, LATE NIGHT

This day was strange in a way.

I celebrated Valentine's Day again.

I took Emily out to Rockford's, one of the finer restaurants in town.

She loved the place, and we had a good time.

She had a nun that she knows take care of our son.

I had the feeling the nun is a longtime friend.

After we came back to her house, the nun left, and we made love. It was slow and gentle, so totally different than when we first got sexually involved.

I'm waiting anxiously for her to have our second child.

I have come to believe that we have something more than before, much more. I hope it never ends.

Time for me to get to bed.

I'm finding myself falling asleep.

APRIL THREE

This day I met with Dani.

She is doing very well with her investments.

She paid me back some stock for the money I fronted her.

For a fourteen-year-old, she is pretty quick. I have to admit, I'm proud of her.

She told me she realizes she's on her way to financial success.

She told me she's willing to do anything to repay me for giving her this opportunity.

I noticed she wasn't wearing a bra. I told her she's already repaying me by being successful.

I thanked her for the offer.

I also told her how important it is for her to stay in school. She may not believe it now, but later she will see how it helps her.

For one thing, school teaches you patience and shows the world you have staying power.

I don't want her to hurry while doing her school work, learn to take her time and do a better job with the school work.

APRIL THIRTY

This day I did something I should have done sooner.

I hired a professional driver.

He's my grounds keeper's brother. I always thought I was a good driver.

After riding with this man, I discovered I don't know near as much about driving as this man does.

There were times we were going over 130 miles per hour.

This man drove that car so fast through some of the curves, it felt like the car was bending in the middle going around them!

Man, what a ride!

I loved it. I plan on doing it again.

Anytime a man can take a car this big, make it perform like a sports car like this man did, has a job with me forever!

It's becoming more important to have Joanna ride with him, or someone like him, to the airport whenever she has to leave town.

MAY FIVE

I ordered two more limousines to keep around the house, a Buick and a Lincoln MKZ.

I had both cars made special.

Like the Chrysler, the Lincoln is all-wheel drive for when the weather is unforgiving.

I told Mr. Numura to find me another driver for the Buick.

His brother can fill in as a driver until we find someone, then have security check him or her out.

I don't know why I write this unimportant stuff down. I'm rambling on paper again.

MAY EIGHT

This day is the first anniversary of the birth of the twins. Joanna baked them a cake.

She put half a cake in front of each of them.

I enjoyed watching them make the damnedest mess I've ever seen.

I like taking them outside and watching them play on the grass.

I'm wishing I had done this ten or fifteen years ago.

Remembering what I was doing fifteen years ago, seems like it was a day before yesterday.

It went by so fast.

MAY NINE

Dani called in a panic.

She lost money on one of her investments.

I told her that's why I had her invest in several different places, because you never want to put all your eggs in one basket, so to speak.

She wanted to know if she should sell and take the loss. I told her it would be up to her.

If I told her to sell, and the price went up, she could blame me for poor judgment.

I told her it's time for her to learn patience, that's part of playing the game.

She's actually doing quite well.

I'm certain she thinks I'm abandoning her, I'm not.

She'll figure it out.

Mr. Kahn keeps warning me that I'm taking a big risk guiding this girl without parental consent.

I told him, "My whole life has been a risk. She wants to learn how to take risks. That's what it's all about.

"I'll risk it.

"I hope someday she will risk it."

MAY EIGHTEEN
Once again I took Joanna up in the U2.

We wasted a lot of time up high, but it was something I wanted to do. I don't believe I'll be here to do it again next year.

I put $700,000 into her bank again.

I wonder if she even knows I'm doing it.

She never says anything about it.

JUNE TEN
I stopped and saw Dani.

She's on summer vacation.

She told me she did sell and took the loss.

Good for her, now she's free of it and exploring something with more promise.

I really like this kid.

She's showing me real promise.

Win or lose, I'm with this kid a hundred percent.

I set it up in the Foundation for them to pay a bookkeeping firm to do bookkeeping and taxes for her.

She also has to learn to do her own bookkeeping.

The bookkeeping firm checks her figures and prepares her tax files for her. I helped her get a tax number.

She asked me if it's illegal for her to own stock and bonds. I told her it might be. Then I told her that the government doesn't care what you do, as long as you pay taxes on the profits.

It reminds me of when I first started investing.

I was almost fourteen.

I had to bribe a stock broker to buy stock for me.

I asked Dani if she has told anyone about our deal.

She said no. She asked what she should say, if asked.

I told her to just smile and say, "You made a deal. That's all anyone needs to know."

I also told her whatever she does, "Don't spend money." That will draw attention to her.

By keeping her money invested, it will be there when she needs it.

She wasn't wearing a bra again.

I wonder if she dresses that way all the time, or if she's doing it for me. Like all of the women on her side of the family, she's nice to look at.

JULY TEN

I met with Dani for a few minutes this day.

She's all hyped up.

One of her stocks hit it big time.

She told me she sold it off and put it all in bonds.

This day the kid was all smiles.

Once again, I noticed the kid wasn't wearing a bra.

I know she will do anything to please me.

She doesn't know she already has.

From there, I went to be with Emily.

Once again she's getting big.

She told me she had an ultrasound.

The baby's going to be a boy.

When it comes to girls, it seems I only get the big ones.

AUGUST NINETEEN

This day I turned fifty-eight.

Joanna threw a little party for me in the party room.

She invited her family, her friend Kathy and her husband, and Eli who, of course, had to haze me a good lot.

I jokingly told him that he might as well enjoy it because next year he wouldn't be able to harass me anymore.

He doesn't know I wasn't kidding.

I'm using pain killers now. Julie Lane is helping me, because I'm also on dialysis now. Eric and Phyllis brought their children to the party.

Dani came over and we talked for awhile.

Eli wanted to know what's going on between us. He's never seen a teenage girl want to talk about the stock market before.

I noticed Phyl was watching us, too.

I love it when people become suspicious. I've lived with it all my life.

When people see something they don't understand, they immediately suspect the worst. People have always suspected me of the worst.

From my medical practice to my private life, people have always suspected me of the worst ever since I can remember.

Sometimes when Dani and I meet, she doesn't wear a bra.

Like her mother and her Aunt Joanna, Dani's carrying more tit than most.

I've wanted to say something about it, but I've kept quiet. She's nice to look at.

Some lucky guy in her future is going to go nuts being with her.

She's a smart girl. She'll figure it out.

She is most probably my final glory, the last time I will taste the sweet glory of success.

SEPTEMBER ELEVEN

This day Emily delivered my fourth son.

She named him Edward Andrew Keandra.

I doubt if I will have any more.

I'm not feeling well. It seems I have to struggle to involve myself with sex.

I force myself with Joanna.

I don't want her to see that I'm deteriorating.

Sometimes I see Emily looking at me.

I believe she has figured it out.

She hasn't said anything, but I believe she knows I'm not going to be here much longer.

I'm just guessing, but sometimes I'm pretty good at guessing.

I do hope she gets pregnant again, but there is little hope.

I'm not feeling well.

I still intend to try.

THANKSGIVING

This day is anything but festive for me.

I'm high on morphine.

Things are harder to do. I have great pain. I try not to let it show.

The morphine helps a lot, but it doesn't solve everything.

I'm dying and, I know it.

It won't be long, and I will no longer be.

I'm struggling, trying to get things done.

I've discovered I'm no longer capable.

I'm certain Joanna is pregnant. Michael Jo, I wish you had decided to show up a little sooner.

I'm not going to be here to greet you.

The important thing is you're going to be here.

I wanted you here three years ago.

Coming late, like you are, means I'll never get to hold you.

I believe Julie Lane is pregnant. I hope it's a girl.

I'll never get to hold her, either, but I do want her. How do you tell someone that you love them and want them before they're born?

Nobody can possibly know how badly I want a baby girl from Julie Lane.

Reading back on this, I'm rambling on paper again. I'm tired. I'll be coming to an end soon.

I don't know if I can write anymore.

SUDDENLY REAL FEELINGS BEGIN TO SHOW

Douglas Kahn put down the journal and said, "That's all he had written.

"He wrote that last page just fifteen days before he passed away.

"I remember those last days he lived.

"Watching him come to an end was all I could bear.

"He had me drive him everywhere he wanted to go.

"I wanted to tell him that he has a chauffeur he could make use of.

"Somehow I had the feeling he didn't want anyone to know where he was going, or what he was doing, not even the chauffeur. He as much as said so.

"Except when he was with people, he lived his life as simply as a minimum wage worker.

"Most times he lived on junk foods and soda pop.

"In his way, he was a very private person.

"I took him to meet with Dani several times.

"Sometimes when he was with Dani, they would snack on cold Pork and Beans, still in the can. How they could eat like that, I'll never know.

"I took him out to Clackamas County, to Emily's place, several times, and to the hospital quite often.

"I saw him meet with Miss Lane, too. Quite often they would meet at the Holly Clinic.

"One time he had me drive him to meet with Dani.

"When we were getting ready to leave, he took hold of her and held her near, speaking quietly in her ear.

"That was the only time I saw him touch her. I remember he kissed her on the mouth. When we left her, she was crying.

"That was two days before he passed away.

"After we left Dani, he called Joanna and told her he was on his way home and wanted to go out to eat and to meet him in the limousine.

"As I pulled into the driveway, he told me that he had a fool for a patient. I no sooner than stopped when he got out of the car.

"He thanked me, when he stepped into the limousine."

Joanna, crying softly, was sitting on the couch listening when she heard her son Roger say, "Dani, was my father fucking you, too?"

Joanna started to say something but remained quiet.

Dani stood and walked to the middle of the room.

Tears were flowing down her face.

In a trembling voice, "I wish he had. I wanted him to.

"Quite often when we met, I would be wearing only a blouse and skirt, nothing on underneath.

"But no, he didn't.

"He always told me the only thing he wanted from me was for me to taste the sweet glory of success.

"I remember the day he made me cry.

"It was while he was holding me that he whispered in my ear he was never going to see me again.

"He kissed me on the mouth, then turned and got in the car with Mr. Kahn, and they drove away.

"He never told me he was dying.

"That was the only time he hugged me.

"I wasn't wearing anything underneath at that time, either. I was always his for the taking."

Douglas Kahn interrupted. "You all were. You all looked forward to it. You all loved him for it.

"Every woman he knew was his for the taking. They were there for the taking because he was always there for them."

Dani started crying.

Softly, she said, "I still miss him. I loved him so much. He was the only one that really understood me.

"After he died, he left me an envelope, a part of his will. There was a check for a large sum of money. He told me if I could double it in four years, I could keep it."

Douglas Kahn, fixing drinks, asked, "Did you double it?"

Dani quietly nodded, saying, "I didn't have to give it back."

Michael Jo stood up and walked over to where Douglas Kahn was fixing more hot drinks.

After getting a hot cider, she turned and faced them all and said, "My mother has often told me that I was loved before I was conceived.

"The full impact of that statement never hit home until I heard what's in his journals. "Dani, I love him, too. I wish he would have lived.

"But I wonder, if being his offspring, we would have seen that side of him if he had lived.

"I think all of us had an idea of what he was, but reading his journals, I'm certain all of us were wrong. He was more. Much more.

"We found out exactly what he was. He would do anything necessary to achieve what he wanted.

"The sex he had with Emily was a means to an end.

"I don't believe any of us were correct in what we believed he was.

"I hope one day to meet a man like him, but I don't believe I will. If I do, I'll have to trust him to be what he is."

With that being said, Michael Jo sat by her mother and was silent. Joanna, teary-eyed, suddenly looked at the floor and smiled.

She gently put her hand on Michael Jo's hand and whispered, "He's here. I can feel him."

Eli turned and looked at his mother. "Mother, how could you tell him to do those things to you?" Emily stood up and faced them all.

After a long pause, she said, "Pay attention girls, because what I'm going to say is for your benefit.

"You boys better also understand what I'm saying. Everything you heard in those journals is true. When I was as young as you, I was being molested. It's an ugly side of life, but it's still life.

"It takes something out of you, but as much as it takes something out of you, it makes you stronger, you're still living.

"I didn't want to live it anymore, so I became a nun.

"When you're a nun, you work, and work, and work!

"Then I met your father. He let it be known, it's okay to live, no matter what life is.

"It's okay to be decadent.

"It's okay to live anyway you want, as long as you do it responsibly.

"That same night, he saved my life.

"In the moment he was saving my life, I knew I wanted to live again, no matter what life is.

"When the opportunity came, I jumped on it.

"I told him I wanted him to make me suck his cock and make me swallow everything that comes out of it, not because I liked it, but because I wanted to live again. I needed him, and he knew it.

"What you heard from those journals is true.

"He was there for me."

Tears were streaming down her face. "He was always there for me. That's why I did it. I remember that first day.

"When he got up and left, I went down and looked out the window at the snow.

"It was like looking into a fog.

"Sometimes the snow came down so hard that you couldn't see the city, only the glow of the lights.

I hadn't dressed yet. As I stood in front of the window with nothing on, I felt happier than I have ever felt before.

"The house was warm, but looking out at the snow made me feel cold.

"After I sorted out my thoughts, I found myself wanting him to come back and do it again.

"He was special enough, I'm willing to do it again.

"There will always be some things that you don't like to do.

"But, like it or not, it's part of living, so you'll find yourself doing them. That makes you stronger, so don't be afraid to live.

"Just make sure the man you're doing it for is special enough.

"If you discover that he's not special enough, get away from him fast as you can. Don't stop and think about it, or you may not escape him.

"I'm going to say to all of you, if Robb Michael Keandra was to come through that door right now, I would get on my knees and let him feed me his cock, as he called it.

"I would do it just to welcome him back!

"Now, you young men hear what I'm saying.

"When you're involved with a female of the species, be responsible, and most important, be there for her.

"Learn how to be responsible as soon as you can.

"If you're not, you won't be very special to anyone.

"That's what made him special to everyone.

"He was always there for them. He always found a way to be there."

Emily sat down. All of Robb Michael's offspring sat looking wide-eyed at each other.

As Emily was sitting, she continued speaking. "Robb Michael came to see me the night before he died.

"When I heard the cackling in his throat, I knew he was dying.

"I've done enough work in hospitals to know a death rattle when I hear one.

"I knew then what he wanted me for.

"I was glad I was there for him.

"I knew he was seeing Dani.

"I didn't want to know about it. Not knowing is sometimes a better part of life, too!

"He had told me he was doing something with her.

Then for some reason, the girls all looked at Dani.

Dani looked back nodding her head affirmative said, "Yes, for him, I would get on my knees and not even think about it.

"He was always there for me.

"There was one time I thought he wasn't, but he was there.

"He just wouldn't make any decisions for me. He wanted me to think for myself.

"If it wasn't for him and his patience, I wouldn't have what I have today.

"So, yes! I would get on my knees for him. I would do anything he asked because of the kind of man he was."

Emily interrupted, "Robb Michael wouldn't let you do that unless you told him to make you.

"Then he would tell you what he wanted from you in return.

"I believe he wanted to capitalize on everything he did.

"Whatever it was he wanted, you would find yourself wanting to do it.

"I believe he got what he wanted from you."

They were all listening with their heads bowed.

With tears streaming down her face, Julie Lane stood up and said, "Look, I knew he was dying before anyone else did.

"I was helping him with medication and dialysis.

"Quite often we would be in hospital five to six hours a day. I knew there was no hope for him.

"I also knew I was pregnant before he died. I didn't tell him I was in love with him.

"I wasn't planning to tell him, or anyone, about my pregnancy. I loved the idea of having his baby and never letting anyone in the world know.

"Mr. Kahn changed my mind. He made me realize it was important to Robb Michael for this baby to have his name. Now I wish I had told him."

Turning to Natalie, she saw that the girl was silently crying, "Natalie, are you alright?"

The girl looked at her mother, "My father wanted me!" she said softly.

"I always thought he was just a playboy. That he didn't care about us!

"He wanted me! He really wanted me! My name isn't Natalie Ann Lane.

"My name is Natalie Ann Keandra, and I'm going to tell everyone."

She paused and then said, "My father wanted me!"

Julie Lane, eyes moist, looked at her daughter. "Yes, he did. I agree it's time for you to let the world know who you are."

She turned and looked toward them all. "We will all discuss what we heard today.

"Every time we meet, we will find ourselves talking about what we learned today.

"I believe all of us will read these journals, again and again.

"Right now I think it's time for all of us to change the subject.

"We all know now what he was. We all love what he was!

"What I liked about him most was his confidence.

"Whatever he wanted to do, he did. He would do some things that nobody else could, just because he knew he could. He was the most confident man I have ever met."

Looking at nothing in particular, Douglas Kahn, with moist eyes, interrupted and softly said, "Genius that he was, in the whole of his medical career, he only lost one patient, himself."

"It's forever gone, you know. That confidence that he was."

FIN